**"You never answered my question,"
Tyler said.**

Skye tipped her chin up. "What question is that?" she asked, knowing full well what he was referring to.

"The one about why we never got along."

She gave a careless shrug. "I don't know... Spiders. Snakes. The incessant teasing?" His knack for finding little weaknesses and insecurities and exploiting them. "You were merciless toward me."

"You mean I was acting like a preadolescent boy who liked a girl?"

She stared at him, stunned, as heat flooded her cheeks, which was ridiculous.

Tyler gave a little laugh. "You didn't know?"

"How could I know?"

"I thought I was telegraphing my feelings pretty well back then."

Skye rolled her eyes, thankful to have something to distract her from the other questions crowding into her head—such as why had he asked her out in high school?

He hooked his thumb into his belt loop. "This isn't going to be easy, is it?"

"I see no way that it can be," Skye spoke truthfully, thankful that he hadn't glued in to the direction of her thoughts.

A BULL RIDER
TO DEPEND ON

BY
JEANNIE WATT

First Published in Great Britain 2017
By Mills & Boon, an imprint of HarperCollins*Publishers*
1 London Bridge Street, London, SE1 9GF

© 2017 Jeannie Steinman

ISBN: 978-0-263-92294-3

23-0417

Our policy is to use papers that are natural, renewable and recyclable products and made from wood grown in sustainable forests. The logging and manufacturing processes conform to the legal environmental regulations of the country of origin.

Printed and bound in Spain
by CPI, Barcelona

Jeannie Watt makes her home in Montana's beautiful Madison valley, where she and her husband raise heritage beef. When she's not writing, Jeannie enjoys collecting patterns and sewing vintage clothing, riding in the mountains and hiking with her husband. Sometimes she goes fishing, too, but she usually daydreams more than she fishes.

To Gary—the man with whom
I've somehow managed to spend
every major holiday without electricity.

Chapter One

Skye Larkin hated thinking ill of the dead, but as she pushed through the bank doors for the fourth time in two weeks, she was very, very angry with her late husband. And beyond being angry, she was, for the first time since learning the true state of her finances, afraid.

It'd been a shock, yes, to discover that the money she thought she had socked away to see the ranch through lean times was no longer there—that her husband had drained the accounts during his road trips, despite his assurances that he'd given up gambling—but for the first six months after Mason has passed away, she'd told herself it would be all right. She'd squeak through somehow. Make the payments, start to pull ahead.

At the six-month mark she had to face the reality that she wasn't pulling ahead. In fact, after a couple of disasters, she was falling further behind, and the money she'd counted on to see her through these rough spells was now in the coffers of some high-rise Vegas casino.

Damn Mason's gambling.

And not to mention all of his buddies who encouraged him to go out when he shouldn't have. If Mason had stayed in his hotel room as he wanted—as he'd promised—then he wouldn't have gambled. But no. His buddies would have none of that. One buddy in particular. And Mason had never been one to say no to a friend—even if that friend was nudging him along on the path to self-destruction.

Skye's mouth tightened as she jerked open the truck door. She was behind one payment on the ranch and two payments on the truck. The first of the month—payment time—was inching closer, and she was rapidly running out of options. She climbed inside and rested her forehead on the steering.

She couldn't operate the ranch without the yearly cow loan—the money that saw her through until she sold cattle. Having very few paydays during the year was the reason for the ranch account. Mason had no doubt planned to pay the account back with his next big win, either in the bull-riding arena or at the tables.

Mason always had big plans and every intention of carrying them out. He was young and no doubt thought he'd have lots of time to accomplish what he wanted, to rebuild Skye's small family ranch, to start breeding bulls. An inattentive driver on the Vegas strip had put an end to all of that. And an end to Skye's inherent belief that everything would work out if she was patient enough.

Things were nowhere close to working out.

Skye pressed her lips together and put the truck in gear. The now-familiar grinding sound came from the rear as she backed up, but, as usual, it disappeared when she put the truck in a forward gear. She ignored it. Worrying wouldn't help anything. If it did, then the ranch would be solvent.

And now, plan B. The one she'd hoped to avoid. But after Mason's funeral, her friend Jess Hayward had told her to call if she needed help. Made her promise to call. And she was going to make that call, regardless of whom he was related to. Now. Before she talked herself out of it.

Pulling over to the side of the road, Skye searched through her contacts and found Jess's number. As luck would have it, he was in town. That was a good sign. Right?

"Sure," he said when she asked if he had a few minutes to meet. "I'll buy you a meal."

"No, thank you." She wouldn't be able to eat while she was all worked up. "But I'll have a Coke while you eat."

"Maybe we can both have a Coke at the Shamrock and you can tell me what's up."

"Yes. That sounds good." Ten minutes later she walked in the door of Gavin, Montana's favorite drinking establishment and crossed the room to where Jess was already waiting at a table with two large Cokes in front of him.

Skye sat down and attempted a casual smile, which was harder than it should have been, due to the butterflies battling it out in her midsection. "It's been a while."

"Yeah. It has." There was a touch of irony in his voice. Well deserved, since it had been over six months since she'd seen him.

"I'm sorry about that. Work and the ranch." She made a small gesture. "You know."

The expression in his eyes told her he understood

what she was trying to say. She'd holed up physically as well as emotionally.

"This is really hard, Jess, so I'm just going to spit it out. Would you be able to float me a loan? Short term?"

"How much?" He made a move for his wallet, and Skye put up a hand, stopping him.

"A lot." She took a steadying breath. "I'm behind on the truck payments. It's close to paid off, and I don't want it to go back to the bank."

Jess's expression clouded, and Skye continued before she lost her nerve. "I'm a little behind on the ranch, too."

"Wow, Skye." He spoke softly.

"Not a lot there. One payment, and I'm going to make a double payment this month and catch up. But those two things together have made it so that I can't get a cow loan. And if I can't get a cow loan, then I can't operate, and what I make at the day job is a pittance compared to what I need." She leaned back, feeling drained after the blurted confession. "I should have never agreed to mortgage the place, but obviously, I hadn't expected Mason to die."

Jess shifted in his chair. "I'm not in a good place right now."

"Oh. I thought…" Skye's voice trailed off. Rumor had it that when Jess's parents sold the family ranch, they'd given each of their twin sons a healthy portion of the profits. If it hadn't been for that much-repeated story, she would never have asked. "I apologize."

"No." He looked affronted. "I know why you asked, but Ty and I pretty much insisted that the folks invest the profit from the ranch into their own futures." One corner of his mouth tightened a little. "They didn't make a lot of money on the sale. Just enough to get out from under the debt and get started again in Texas."

"That's what I get for listening to rumors," Skye said, still feeling embarrassed. "According to some of the old boys, you and Ty are rolling in dough."

"That's why I'm living in a crappy camp trailer."

Skye started to smile in spite of herself. "I guess I should tell you that rumor has it you're just biding your time until you start building your 'big house.' You're in the process of looking for the right piece of property."

Jess laughed and then reached for his untouched drink. Skye did the same. She still had the problems she had when she walked in, but somehow, talking to Jess made her feel better. As if she weren't all alone.

"You know, Skye…" She looked up from her glass in time to see an uncertain expression play across his features. "Tyler's doing well. He's had a couple big paydays. The last one was huge."

It felt as if a barrier had slammed into place at the sound of his twin's name. "And I'm certain he wants to share his money with me. If I talked to him, he'd probably loan you the money."

"Can't do it," Skye said. Because Tyler Hayward had been a big part of Mason's problem and she didn't see how she could live with herself if she tried to make him part of the solution.

Jess didn't try to argue with her. He knew better. When they'd been kids growing up within a few miles of one another, she and Jess had become good friends. His twin, not so much. Tyler had been brash and loud and kind of mean. To her anyway. Snakes, spiders, smart-aleck remarks. He'd never shown any mercy.

Childhood issues she could have forgiven, but he'd

also been instrumental in causing her current situation—*that* she couldn't forgive. Tyler and Mason had been good friends. Great friends—the kind who gambled and drank together. Mason had tried so hard to give up the gambling, but, as he'd told her so often, the only way he could do that was to not go out. Tyler Hayward was all about the party, and he wanted his good buddy with him. The thing that really got to her was that she'd specifically asked Tyler to stop encouraging Mason to go out, and he'd blatantly ignored that request, which was why she wasn't about to humble herself before him now and ask for money. She'd find a way.

"I assume you've had no luck with the banks."

Skye shook her head. "Not for lack of trying. I owe too much on the mortgage to use the place as collateral. If I can get the cow loan, catch up on the truck… I think I'll be okay. I'll have to live really tightly for a year or two…" Her voice trailed off as she watched the expression shifting on Jess's face. This was killing him almost as much as it was killing her. "But hey," she said, forcing a smile that didn't fool either of them. "I've been through worse. You know I have."

Jess let out a breath. "If it's okay, I'll make some inquiries—no names—just to see if anyone can float a cow loan."

"I'd appreciate it," Skye said softly.

"I know how hard it is for you to ask."

Indeed, Skye was not a good asker—not after having self-sufficiency hammered into her for her entire life.

"That's why I came to you," Skye said. "You get it." Unlike his brother. Why couldn't he have understood Mason's problem? Played ball? If he had…well, she couldn't say Mason would be alive today, because he'd been on his way to the casino resort to check into a room when he got hit, but she'd be a lot better off.

"And now that I know how Ty's doing with his bull riding, how are you doing with yours?"

"Stalled out at the moment. I'm living lean, still doing contract construction and trying to save enough money to follow Ty onto the circuit. You know, while I'm still young enough to get beat into the ground and bounce back."

"You're good, Jess. You should give it a shot."

He lowered his gaze to study the table, as if this wasn't a topic he was comfortable with. When he looked up at her, his expression was serious. "If I had the money, you know I'd give it to you."

"Loan it to me."

"That's what I meant. Right now, living in the camp trailer, sharing it with Ty when he's back in town…the prospect of hitting the road next year is one of the only things keeping me sane."

Skye drove home telling herself not to worry. She still had options, and she'd worked extra shifts to catch up on the ranch loan. She just needed to do the same with the truck. And the cow loan…she'd figure something out.

The porch squeaked under her feet as she mounted the stairs—a noise she'd long equated with her husband coming home from a bull-riding event, or back from the barn after chores. A good noise still, even though it made her feel lonely. She and Mason had had good times.

She pulled out her keys and unlocked the door, holding it open so that Jinx could shoot out as usual. The big gray cat disappeared into the lilac bushes without so much as a backward glance, but come morning, after he'd done his best to decimate the mouse population in the sheds and barns, he'd be back, wanting attention and lots of it.

Skye walked inside and hung her purse on the coat rack near the door. Her house was spotless. When she couldn't sleep, she cleaned. And cleaned and cleaned. It cost very little money to clean a house, and it wore her out and thus made it possible to get at least a few hours of rest before heading to work in the morning.

But tonight she hoped she could simply fall asleep the way she used to be able to. Mason had once teased her that when ten o'clock came around, her eyes automatically shut regardless of where she was. It was for the most part true. Skye was a morning person, which was why the morning shift at the café had seemed so perfect—right up until sleep started to escape her, around the same time that the bills started stacking up.

Partial payment was now the name of the game. She hadn't been turned over to collection, but if she missed one more truck payment...

Her stomach tightened, and she hugged her arms around herself. Looked like another night of heavy cleaning and organizing.

Chapter Two

"Good thing I'm a minimalist," Tyler Hayward muttered as he edged past his brother as he made his way down the hall of the camp trailer.

"You're welcome for the roof over your head," Jess muttered back as he headed into the cramped living room.

"I appreciate it," Ty said. Cramped or not, he did.

Not that long ago, when he came home, Tyler crashed in his own room in the house he grew up in, but after his parents had sold the ranch and moved to Texas to be closer to his grandparents, he started staying with his twin. Practically on top of him, actually since his "room" was a built-in bunk in a niche in the hallway leading to Jess's small bedroom at the rear of the trailer. His gear was stacked in a pile in the living room. He had to admit that Jess was being a good sport about him invading his space. At this point in his life, he had no idea where he would eventually land, or even what state he would call home. Texas, to be close to the folks? Or Montana to be close to his twin and the people he'd grown up with? Since his parents seemed to visit Gavin every couple of months, he was leaning toward Montana, which meant getting his own place.

And for the first time ever, he was in a position to do it. His previous season had been good. No. Make that great, and he wanted to get something nailed down, pay cash and then only have to worry about maintenance and upkeep. A small place with ten acres or so. Enough to keep a few horses, a few cows. Nothing fancy.

After stowing his duffel under the bunk—at least there was room for that—he came back out into the living room/kitchen, where his brother was now settled in the living room, beer in one hand, remote in the other.

"You know…if you wanted to invest in a bigger trailer, I'd go halves with you." He'd offer more, but his brother was proud. A little too proud sometimes.

"This'll do for now."

Jess had always been the careful twin—except in the arena. Once atop a bull, he rode with the best of them. The only problem was that he was never able to commit himself to a season. To take that risk.

"One of us has to have a job," he'd say whenever Tyler badgered him to go pro. Ironically, Tyler was now the one with the money. No house, but money. Thankfully one was rather easily parlayed into the other.

"How long are you going to save?" Tyler asked as he got a beer out of the tiny fridge and joined his brother on the beat-up sofa their mom had left behind during the big move. He propped his foot up on the wooden chest that served as a coffee table.

"Before…?"

"You make some kind of a move?"

Jess changed the channel. A couple of times. "Until I feel ready. Okay?"

Tyler put up a hand. "Just checking." Again.

Jess changed channels Again. Ty figured it would be

another night of watching five minutes of a show then moving on as his brother became restless, but instead he muted the television and put the remote on his lap. "Skye came to see me today."

Ty had years of practice not reacting to Skye's name when it came up. He'd had a raging crush on her for as long as he could remember. She'd hated him for as long as he could remember. No matter what he did to impress her, it didn't work, and eventually he'd given up and decided he really didn't like her all that much anyway.

But he did. When they'd gone to high school, he'd even asked her out once. She'd thought he was poking fun at her and never gave him a chance to explain. Off to college she went, and when she came back, she was engaged to Mason. Ty's friend. A guy he liked just fine, but sometimes had a hard time respecting. Being around the newly engaged couple had been Ty's own private hell.

He knew for a fact that Mason never would have asked Skye out in the first place if he hadn't known that Tyler had a thing for her. Mason and Tyler had competed in all venues of life, and in this case, Mason had won. Skye had refused to give Tyler a chance, and that had always stung a little.

Tyler put his feet up on the trunk in front of him. "Why did Skye come to see you?"

"She needed a loan. She's behind on some payments and can't nail down a cow loan."

"How much behind?"

"I didn't get a dollar amount. She needs the cow loan." Jess raised his eyes to meet his brother's.

"I can lend her the money." He spoke flatly, as if he had no emotional stake in the matter.

"Yeah," Jess said. "I mentioned the possibility and…" He gave his head a small shake. "She wasn't in favor."

"But you're telling me anyway." He knew his brother wasn't twisting the knife, so…

"I thought you'd want to know."

"Why?"

Jess lifted an eyebrow, and Tyler let out a breath as he dropped his gaze to study the toes of his dusty boots. The thing about being a twin was that it was pretty hard to keep the guy who looked like you from reading you. He'd denied having any kind of lingering feelings for Skye after she'd married Mason—had said that he'd moved on from that hopeless affair—but Jess wasn't fooled. Ty knew because he could read his twin as easily as his twin read him.

"Right," he muttered. The situation between him and Skye was complicated—or at least it was on his end, where feelings of guilt, frustration and resentment were coupled with an attraction that refused to die. On her end, it was simple—he was the bad guy who'd encouraged her husband onto the path of self-destruction, and she'd made no secret of her beliefs.

He was guilty to a degree. Despite Skye asking him to stay far away from Mason while on tour, he hadn't seen where a few wild nights would hurt anyone—but he also hadn't known how far Mason would take the whole partying thing. By the time Tyler realized what was happening, it was too late to do anything about it. The most unfortunate part was that there wasn't a good way for Tyler to defend himself. How did you tell a woman that she didn't know everything about her husband and his code of ethics?

You didn't. Not after that guy was dead.

Jess cleared his throat. "Skye won't be happy about me telling you, but I thought...you know."

Tyler shot his brother a quick look, read the concern on his face and wondered if it was for him or Skye. He couldn't help but smirk as he said, "That she might be desperate enough to accept help from the bad twin?"

"Something like that." Jess picked up the remote and changed the channel again. "It might give you a chance to smooth things with her."

Tyler gave a *yeah, right* snort as the pitcher on the screen threw a perfect strike. "She doesn't want them smoothed."

"She doesn't know the facts."

Nor would she...although he had to admit that this might be an opportunity to show Skye that he wasn't the jerk she thought he was. He might have had difficulties controlling his wilder impulses back in the day, but beneath it all, he was a decent guy. Just like his twin.

And as far as Mason was concerned—Mason was always his own boss and Skye needed to accept that.

WHEN SKYE GOT off shift at one thirty, Jess Hayward was waiting for her by her car.

Only it wasn't Jess.

The warm smile on her face cooled as she realized that the guy loitering at the edge of the parking lot was Tyler Hayward. With the exception of the small scar on Tyler's chin, the brothers were nearly identical, right down to their haircuts—but there was something different about the way they stood. And moved. Skye had learned long ago to tell them apart at a distance. If Jess was walking toward her, she went to meet him. If it had been Tyler…she'd changed direction to avoid whatever irritating thing he was about to do to her. When they were younger, he'd threatened her with various amphibians. As they'd grown older, frogs and salamanders had changed into smart-ass comments.

"Good morning," he said as she stopped several feet away from him.

"Good morning," she echoed coolly, knowing instantly that Jess had ratted her out. With the best of intentions, no doubt, but now she had to deal with Tyler.

"You're looking good, Skye."

A compliment. That was different.

"You, too." She spoke with polite indifference, but, infuriatingly, the fact of the matter was that he really did look good.

He shifted his weight and folded his arms over his chest, as if debating how to launch into what he'd come to say. "We haven't talked in a while, Skye."

That was true. With the exception of him offering stiff condolences at Mason's funeral, they hadn't spoken since they'd faced off in the parking lot behind the Shamrock Bar almost two years ago, shortly after she'd discovered that Mason had been gambling again. She'd asked Tyler to stop encouraging her husband to go out. He'd told her he would. He'd lied.

Skye got her keys out of her pocket. No longer smiling, she tilted her head. Waited.

Tyler took the plunge. "Jess told me that you are in need of a loan."

She shook her head. "Not any longer."

"Ah." He looked as if he wanted to ask why, but her stony expression must have made him think twice.

"Thank you for asking." She hoped that would cause him to move along, and indeed he did take a couple of steps, but toward her rather than toward his truck.

"You know…" he said, his expression becoming serious. Too serious, really. "…we've had our differences, but I was Mason's friend—"

"That was the problem, wasn't it?" The angry reply burst out of nowhere, and Skye instantly clamped her mouth shut to keep from saying more. She needed to get out of there, away from this guy who so easily triggered her. She moved around him to her car, but before she could open the door, he put his hand on it. Her gaze jerked up, and he dropped his hand.

"Mason was a grown man, Skye. He made his own choices." His voice was so low and intense that it was little more than a growl.

And you didn't help matters. The words teetered on her lips, but she bit them back. She wasn't getting into this. Not here. Not now. She forced her expression to go blank and uttered a lie. "I'm sorry, Tyler. That was uncalled for." His gaze narrowed, telling her he wasn't buying the false apology. "It was a busy shift, and I'm a little tired. I didn't sleep well." Total truth, there. "I appreciate your trying to help."

"The offer stands." The way he spoke made her wonder why.

"I'll keep it in mind."

And she'd file it under Fat Chance. She was not asking for help from the man who was in a large way responsible for the situation she was now in. The very fact that he offered…

"I need to go, Ty." *Before I tell you what I'm really thinking.*

He studied her, as if debating whether or not to prolong the conversation, and she in return studied him, her gaze unwavering. He was handsome. Dark and lean and dangerous looking. Ty had always kind of intimidated her. He was so different from his easygoing twin, who'd been one of her best buddies growing up. Funny how those things went.

His mouth tightened a little as they silently regarded one another, the atmosphere growing more charged by the second, and for some reason the movement of his lips caused a tiny ripple in her midsection.

Yes. Dangerous.

Skye tore her gaze away and opened the car door. When she closed it, a wave of relief washed over her.

Safe.

OH YEAH. That had gone well.

Ty forced his tight jaw muscles to relax as he walked back to his truck while Skye all but laid rubber in her hurry to get away from him. It was obviously easier for her to blame him rather than Mason for the trouble she was in. He understood, but that didn't mean he had to like it.

Nope. He pretty much hated it. But what could he do? Chase her down and tell her the truth about her husband? He might be angry, but he wasn't that angry. He needed to let this go, focus on the here and now, on the things he could control, like where he lived.

Instead of getting into his truck, he reversed course and walked into the café.

"Hey, Ty."

Angie Salinas greeted him with a wide smile. *See, Skye... Angie likes me.* And Angie probably had more of a reason to dislike him, because they'd dated in junior high for almost a week, before he broke up with her on Valentine's Day. He was a smooth operator back then.

"Angie." He smiled up at her as she waved him to a booth. "I don't need a menu."

"Know what you want, eh?"

"Grilled chicken."

"Sandwich?"

"Just the chicken, but go ahead and charge me for a sandwich." He ate all the protein he could to keep his muscles in shape, stayed away from useless carbs. As he'd gotten older, he'd started paying more attention to things like diet and exercise. Funny how a body could get beat around for only so long before it started requiring extra attention.

"Salad or something?"

"A salad would be good. Dressing on the side."

"You got it." She jotted a few words on her pad and headed off to the counter.

Ty drank some water, did his best to tamp down the irritation still lingering after his encounter with Skye, then pulled out his phone and went to the real estate listings. He and Jess might have been wombmates who could practically read each other's minds, but if they had to share that tiny trailer space for much longer...well...he saw no good coming of that. It was time to move out.

A house would be nice, but he had nothing against buying a used trailer, as Jess had done. In the beginning anyway. The important thing was that he wanted to buy whatever he decided on and own it free and clear while he had the bucks to do so. Traveling the circuit was expensive. Keeping his bare-bones insurance policy was expensive.

When Angie brought his food, he put his phone aside. "I'm looking to buy some land," he said. "Know of anything?"

Because if anyone was going to know anything, it was Angie. She had six siblings and she worked in a café.

She cocked a hip, frowning a little as she thought. "Nothing springs to mind, but if I hear of anything I'll let you know. If you're around." One corner of her mouth quirked up. "Will you be around?"

"I'm not retiring, if that's what you mean. I'm just planning for the future."

"That is so out of character, Ty."

He grinned at her and she smiled back before heading to another table. It really wasn't out of character, but Jess was so responsible that by contrast he appeared to be reckless. He had his moments, but deep down, he wasn't all that different from his brother.

Try telling Skye that.

He wasn't going to tell Skye anything. Why beat his head on a wall?

Chapter Three

As soon as she got home, Skye took off her uniform and put it directly into the washer before pulling on worn jeans and a crewneck sweatshirt, dressing in quick jerky movements. She wanted to stop thinking—to turn off her brain and just…be.

As if.

It was going to be another sleepless night. She was certain of that, just as she was certain that Tyler was to blame…although it wasn't in the way that she usually blamed him. He'd simply uttered a truth that she hadn't wanted to hear. A truth that had echoed through her brain for the entire trip home.

Mason was a grown man. Mason had made his own choices.

She knew that. But he'd also had an addiction that his friends could have helped him manage. They didn't. End of story.

She gathered her hair into a ponytail, slapped on a ball cap and headed out the door to take care of her menagerie.

Skye loved animals, as had Mason, which was why she now had so many mouths to feed in addition to the cattle. Cattle she wouldn't have for much longer if she couldn't secure a loan to buy the hay she needed to feed them. If she had to sell the cattle at a loss, see all of her hard work go by the wayside, it was going to kill her. She could catch up on the truck payment if she sold, but without that cow money being there when she needed it, she couldn't afford the ranch. And if she couldn't afford the ranch, then she was going to have to give up her livestock.

Her animals had been the one thing that had seen her through after Mason had died. How could she even think about giving them up?

Simple. She couldn't. And she wouldn't.

Her mini-donkey, Chester, came trotting across the pasture with the old mule, Babe, not too far behind as Skye walked the short distance down the driveway to the barn. Chester ducked under the bottom wire of the fence as if it wasn't there and continued on to Skye, stopping directly in front of her. Skye reached out to rub his wiry forelock, shaking her head as Babe gave a loud protest from the pasture.

"You know it upsets him when you do this," Skye chided the little donkey, who rubbed his head on her hip, almost knocking her over. Babe called to his buddy again in his rusty voice, and Skye gave the little donkey a push. "Back to the pasture."

The donkey showed no signs of minding, so Skye went to the dwindling haystack and tossed several flakes of alfalfa over the fence into the low feeders. Chester shoved his way back under the wire and joined his friend, who was already tossing hay in the air, looking for the good stuff. Vanessa, the Canada goose she'd rescued from the creek when she'd been a hatchling, waddled out of the barn and into the pasture where Skye's mare, Pepper, and Mason's gelding, Buzz, grazed near Mr. Joe, the horse who'd raised her. The grass was tall and would feed the three for several weeks. The cows had decent pasture, too, on the remnants of the newly cut alfalfa field. Her closest neighbor, Cliff, had cut her hay twice this year... Thank goodness for good neighbors. But the fields hadn't produced nearly enough to see her through the winter.

Hay. Money. Problems.

She had one more bank appointment. A smaller bank that was friendly toward ranchers—probably the first place she should have gone, except that it was in a small town thirty miles away from Gavin, and she felt a loyalty to the bank that had given her the mortgage. The bank that was not one bit interested in working with her now that she'd hit a bump in the road.

She understood the concern, but it wasn't like she wanted the money for a vacation or something. She wanted the money so that she could make money to pay back the bank and thus save them both a lot of headaches and hassle. The bank guy didn't see it that way.

She felt hopeful about the new bank, though. She'd gone to school with the loan officer and felt certain she could talk to him as a person, explain the run of bad luck and exactly how she planned to work her way through it. One loan. That was all she needed to prove herself.

Jinx the cat came trotting toward her from the direction of the barn and threw his heavy body against her legs. Now that he'd had his night out, he was ready for some TLC, so Skye leaned down and scooped him up.

"Well, Jinxy old boy, I struck out again."

The cat butted his head against the underside of her chin as if telling her he had total faith in her. She set the cat on the lodge pole fence, and he trotted easily along the top rail to the next post, where he stopped to groom himself.

Ah, to be carefree.

Although, honestly, Skye didn't need to be carefree. Being a widow had knocked most of the carefree out of her, and she truly doubted that she'd ever get it back. What she wanted was to be secure. Secure enough to not worry about losing her place. Secure enough to provide for her pets and livestock.

Secure enough to not lie awake worrying at night.

Was that too much to ask for?

SOMETHING WAS UP with Tyler's cousin, Blaine Hayward. Whenever he shifted his jaw sideways and did the thousand-mile stare instead of making eye contact—or in this case, watching the high school kids practice bull riding in Hennessey's practice pen—he was dealing with something. And Tyler had a strong suspicion that whatever his cousin was working over in his head involved him. Blaine was dating Angie Salinas from the café, and Skye worked with Angie. Blaine had barely met Tyler's gaze once that day, which meant that Tyler was probably at the center of whatever.

"Something on your mind?" he finally asked after they'd watched the last practice ride.

Blaine shot him a sideways glance, looking relieved at the question. "I heard you offered Skye a loan."

"Where'd you hear that?" Because Tyler couldn't see Skye spreading the word. She had her pride.

"Angie saw the two of you talking yesterday, and asked Skye about it, because…well, you know how things are between you two."

Yeah. He did.

"And Skye told her about the loan?"

Blaine met his gaze then, dead on. "Skye told Angie that you were trying to buy a clear conscience."

It took Tyler a couple of seconds to say, "No kidding." He even managed a fairly reasonable tone, given the circumstances, but he didn't know how much longer he'd be able to do that. Not with his jaw muscles going tighter every second. *Buy a clear conscience? Really, Skye?*

Blaine shrugged his big shoulders. "You know she blames you for Mason's issues."

"Because Mason was such a saint."

"She needs to think so."

Tyler understood that, but still…to accuse him publicly—because anything said to Angie would soon become public—of trying to *buy* a clear conscience when all he'd wanted to do was to help her?

That grated.

Really grated.

"Don't do anything to make me regret telling you this," Blaine muttered. Ty frowned. "I'm serious, man. Angie will kill me."

Ty gave a nod, somehow keeping himself from pointing out that Angie had probably already filled in half the town, which totally ticked him off. He could deal with being the scapegoat for Skye's dead husband's behavior, but he was not going to put up with her spreading blatant rumors about him.

He was going to have a word with Skye. Set the record straight. Most of it, anyway. And he was going to have Skye issue a retraction—via Angie or any other method she chose.

ANY HOPE SKYE had of negotiating a loan with Marshal Valley Bank was squelched the instant she took a seat at the loan officer's desk. Dan Peterson wore "the look"—the one that clearly indicated that he'd investigated matters and, even though his bank was smaller and more lenient in their lending practices than most, and even though they'd known each other since high school, Skye didn't qualify for a second-chance loan. She gave it a shot anyway after they'd exchanged stiff opening pleasantries. She explained the reason for the mortgage, how she and her husband had accidentally overextended, and because of his gambling addiction had lost the fund that was supposed to see them through rough times. She handed over her figures and explained that there would be no more gambling, that her husband was dead and she was trying desperately to hold on to her ranch.

It was obvious that the guy felt for her, and equally obvious that his answer had to be no.

"For now," he'd told her when she'd gotten to her feet. She was used to the rubbery-knee, rock-in-her-stomach feelings by now, so she simply smiled when he said, "Come back in six months, when your payments are current, and we'll talk."

Six months. Dead of winter. When her cows needed the hay. Right.

"I wish I could do more, Skye, but my bosses—"

"I understand, Dan. Thanks."

She drove home, racking her brain as to her next move. She could maybe eke out six months. If nothing happened. If the strange sound in the truck's reverse gear didn't get more persistent. If the animals all stayed healthy. If she could nail down another part-time job, work eighteen-hour days. It wouldn't have to be forever. Just long enough to catch up. But it also wouldn't buy hay for her cattle.

Skye felt tears start to well up, but she blinked them back, suddenly sitting taller in her seat when she saw the truck parked next to her house.

Ty Hayward's truck.

Unless Jess had borrowed it.

Yeah. That had to be it. But when the man got out of the driver's seat as she pulled in, she instantly knew it wasn't Jess. They might be twins, but Ty's movements were different, smoother, more catlike than Jess's. More…predatory.

Ty Hayward had come to call, and she hated to think of what that could mean. She was very certain, however, judging from the grim expression he wore, that he wasn't there to offer her money again.

SKYE STARTED WALKING toward where Ty stood beside his truck, stony expression firmly in place. Her hair was pulled into a sophisticated-looking bun thing instead of tumbling around her shoulders in dark waves as usual, and she wore a light blue dress with sensible heels.

He instantly surmised that she'd been to another bank and that things had not gone well. Ty told himself he didn't care.

"Hello, Tyler." She came to a stop a few feet away from him, just as she had the day before, and adjusted the position of the purse strap on her shoulder, keeping her fingers lightly curled around the black leather.

"Skye."

"What brings you here today?"

Coolly spoken words, but Ty read uncertainty in her expression. Guilt, perhaps…?

"I'm for sure not here to offer you money." He took a lazy step forward. "I want you to set the record straight."

"What record?"

His voice grew hard as he said, "Where do you come off telling people that I'm trying to *buy* a clear conscience?"

Skye gaped at him. "What?"

He cocked his head. "What part needs repeating?"

"I never told anyone you were trying to buy a clear conscience."

"Well, that's the story going around, Skye. I wonder how it started." He didn't need any hints as to how it spread. Angie was something. He took another step forward, doing his best to ignore the fact that she looked utterly confused. "I tried to help you, Skye. I wanted to help you. It had nothing—not *one* thing—to do with my conscience."

Her chin went up at that. "Nothing?"

He shook his head, realizing then just how deeply ingrained her dislike of him was. She was never going to believe anything but the worst of him, and he wasn't going to try to convince her otherwise. "I'm wasting my time here." He turned and started back across the drive toward his truck, cursing his stupidity in driving to her ranch. The damage was done. And realistically, he'd never expected her to be able to make the situation better, but he wanted her to know what she'd done so that she didn't do it again. Mission accomplished.

He jerked the truck door open, and then, because

this could well be the last time they ever spoke, he said, "For the record, I never gambled with your husband."

An expression of patent disbelief crossed Skye's face, but before she could speak, he said, "I know it's really handy to blame me, since you've never cared for me. I'm a nice, easy target to make you feel better about things, but here's the deal—I don't gamble."

"Ever?"

"More like never as in…never."

"You're saying my husband lied to me."

Sorry, Mason, but the roosters have come home to roost. "I'm saying he used me as an excuse."

"You never partied with him."

"Of course I partied with him. We drank together. A lot. But we never went gambling."

She looked at him as if he was missing the point. "If Mason had stayed in at night, if he hadn't drunk too much, then he wouldn't have gambled. But would you leave him alone? No."

"He never once said anything about wanting to stay in." That was the honest truth. "He never acted like he wanted to stay in." And Tyler hadn't seen the danger of encouraging him to go out until it was too late. But Mason would have gone out no matter what. Tyler was convinced of that.

"Or you're not presenting things the way they really were."

Ty's eyes narrowed. "Why would I present things any other way?" In other words, why would he lie?

"I don't know. Guilt, maybe? Public image?"

"I'm not lying, Skye. I know you believe that I'm the reason you're broke. I'm the reason Mason had hangovers. Yes, you asked me to leave him alone. No,

I didn't do it. But I didn't encourage him to gamble and lose all of his money—or to gamble some more to try to make it all back. That was fully his thing."

Tyler's jaw tightened as he fought the urge to tell Skye the whole truth. To tell her what her husband was like on the road. To tell her that gambling wasn't the only vice Mason indulged in.

But angry as he was, he couldn't do that to her.

He also couldn't handle being in her presence any longer. "You want to hide behind a lie? Fine. Have a good life, Skye." The words came out bitterly, as if he cared in some way about what she thought, but he didn't.

"You, too," Skye said in a stony voice, before walking past him, her heels tilting in the gravel as she made her way around his truck. She was almost directly in front of the vehicle when she stopped dead in her tracks.

Ty followed her line of vision and instantly saw the problem. One of her horses was down, next to the water trough, and from the way it was lying with its neck stretched out and its head at an odd angle, he didn't think it was napping. He got back out of his truck at the same moment that Skye started running toward the pasture in her heels.

He might be angry. He might have been happy to never see Skye again. But no way was he going to drive away when she had a horse down.

The horse needed help even if Skye didn't.

Chapter Four

Mr. Joe lay stretched out on the ground next to the water tank, and even as Skye raced toward him, she knew it was too late. She slid to a stop close to his head, dropping to her knees in the dirt and reaching out to stroke his face. His eye came open and rolled up at her. He blinked once and shut his eyes again as he gave a rattling breath.

"No, no, no." Skye barely registered what she was saying as she stroked his ears and then wrapped her arms around his neck, burying her face against him, pulling in his scent. This day had been coming. Mr. Joe hadn't been able to hold weight for the past year, despite her best efforts and bags and bags of senior horse chow, but, dignified gentleman that he was, he'd never shown any sign of weakness or pain. He'd eaten what he could and spent his days ambling around the pasture, hanging with his best buddy, Pepper, or just sleeping in the sun.

Tyler dropped down beside her, checking the horse's pulse at his throat and then running a gentle hand over the animal's jowl as his gaze traveled over the horse's bony frame.

"How old?"

"Twenty-eight." The words stuck in Skye's throat. She swallowed and said, "I knew it was coming, but I'm not ready yet." As if she'd ever be ready.

She jerked her gaze away from Tyler's before tears could form. Why did he have to be here for this? But he was here and her horse was dying and she had to deal. Again she rested her cheek against her old gentleman's neck and squeezed her eyes shut, blocking out. Denying. She felt the last breath. Felt him go still, but she did not move. Could not move. Mr. Joe had been with her since she was ten. He'd been her 4-H horse, her very slow rodeo horse, her friend, confidant. Companion. After Mason had died, she'd spent hours grooming the old gelding, talking to him, mourning his weight loss and the inevitable, but loving him while he was there to love.

Now the inevitable had happened, and another big hole opened up in her heart.

Tears now soaked the old horse's mane, and her cheek felt grimy from the pasture dust sticking to it. She blinked hard again, then pushed back onto her knees, small rocks biting into her flesh as she ran her hand over the gelding's soft coat one more time.

She knew Tyler stood a few feet away now, but she kept her eyes on the horse. He'd best not try to touch her, comfort her. She didn't need other people to help her deal with her loss. She was a master.

And there was always the fear that she would break down if she had the luxury of human contact as she mourned. When she'd lost Mason, people had gathered near, helping in any way they could, while she was still numb, still going through the motions. It wasn't until she was once again alone that the pain had ripped through her, burning in its intensity as she faced an empty ranch, empty house, empty bed.

Tyler moved a few steps toward her, then stopped as she shot him a look.

He let out a breath, pressed his lips together. There were lines of strain on his face, as if he wasn't certain what to say or do. There was nothing he could say or do. Her horse was gone, and he was there when she didn't want him to be.

"Do you want me to call Jess?"

"Why?"

"He's better with the backhoe than I am."

The backhoe. He was going to help her bury Mr. Joe. "I...uh..." She wiped the back of her hand across her damp, sticky cheeks, then lifted her chin as new tears threatened. "I'll call Cliff." Her five-mile-down-the-road neighbor.

Tyler's expression hardened. "Or Jess and I could bury your gelding."

"I'm not trying to be ungrateful." But it was her right at the moment as grief once again wrapped around her.

"You just want me off the property. I get it. Wish granted." He turned and headed toward his truck.

TYLER SMACKED THE steering wheel with the heel of his hand as he waited at the crossroad for a slow-moving cattle truck. Always the bad guy. He was getting pretty sick of being the bad guy—especially when he hadn't done anything. Okay, he'd purposely defied Skye, but not in a way meant to do her harm. Everybody partied while on the road, and Mason would have been as likely to stay in his hotel room when everyone else was having a grand old time as he would have been likely to quit bull riding to become an accountant.

Tyler pulled out onto the gravel road, debating about whether to call Jess and tell him to go bury the old horse, or whether to let Skye handle it on her own. He'd hated leaving her alone, but it seemed as if staying would have made her even more unhappy.

He'd tried to be nice. Twice. He was done.

Jess wasn't there when he got home after a quick stop at the grocery store.

He let himself into the unlocked trailer, set down the bags and opened the tiny cupboard next to the stove. There was a reason he was eating out more than he should. It was hard to cook in the camp trailer, and even harder to keep enough food on hand. He had to step over his gear as he made his way to the kitchen, so he stopped and pushed it out of his way with his foot as best he could. He wasn't crazy neat, like his brother, but even he was getting tired of stepping over and around everything in order to move through their living space.

He had to get out of there while he and his brother were still on speaking terms—that was a given. His first event was in two weeks, but sometimes he had his doubts as to whether they would last that long. Jess was a peaceful guy, but even he had his limits, and living in close contact with his twin was pushing them. Tyler opened the cupboard, then closed it again and leaned his forehead against the fake wood.

When a guy was a winner, he shouldn't feel so much like a loser. What was he doing here in this tiny trailer, making his brother feel cramped and uncomfortable?

Ty shoved the full bag of perishables into the fridge

and then left the trailer. He needed to move, try to shake this thing that kept bothering him...whatever that thing was.

It took him only a few miles of road to pinpoint the thing.

Being wrongly accused. He hadn't tried to keep Mason on the straight and narrow, but he hadn't encouraged him to stray either. Not in gambling, nor in any other way. He'd just been a friend. Someone to party with. If it hadn't been him, then it would have been someone else. Mason rode hard and played hard. As far as he knew, he was a good husband to Skye— except for when he wasn't.

The parking lot at the Shamrock was full. Tyler parked close to his usual spot in the wide gravel parking lot behind the building but didn't get out of the truck immediately. Did he want to socialize?

The fact that he was questioning the matter told him no. He did not. Rare, but it happened, especially when something was eating at him.

He leaned his head back against the seat rest, half closed his eyes and watched as people came in and out of the back door of the establishment. When he saw Shelly Hensley go in, he made his decision. No socializing tonight. Shelly was banned from the place, and he wasn't up for the ruckus that would ensue when the owner, Thad Hawkins, or his nephew, Gus, escorted her from the premises.

Decision made, he reached for the ignition.

Was he getting old?

No way. He was just not in as much of a mood to socialize as he'd thought he was. He'd go back to the trailer, eat something, crawl into his bunk and read. In the morning he'd go for his run, then hit up some Real-tors and do his best to find a place to buy before he let his winnings trickle through his fingers...and before he and his brother came to blows. The last time he'd won big money, he'd made a healthy donation to the recovery of a fellow bull rider, a guy with a new baby and a toddler, and a broken back. He didn't expect to see that money back anytime soon—which was why he needed to invest his new winnings now. While he had the money in hand and before another of his friends got seriously injured. He wasn't a light touch, but a friend in need got whatever Ty could give.

He'd barely touched the key when someone knocked loudly on the back of his truck and then a familiar face pushed against the window, features distorted through the glass. Tyler lowered the window, forcing Cody Callahan to jerk back. The kid was eight years younger than him, and an up-and-comer on the bull-riding circuit.

"How many times do I got to tell you not to beat on my truck?" he asked.

"I needed to get your attention." Cody jerked his head in the direction of the back door of the Shamrock. "Going in or coming out?"

Tyler debated for a second. "Going in." Now that he had company, he may as well make a night of it.

"Then shake a leg, man." Cody stepped back so that Tyler could open the door. "I'm parched."

HUMBLE PIE NEVER tasted good. Today it was going to taste like ashes, but Skye was going to eat it and smile. As well as she could, anyway. She was working the second half of the morning shift that day, having traded shifts with her pregnant coworker, Chloe, but she'd called Angie at the café just before opening and asked the question that had weighed on her mind for a good part of the night. Well, yes, Angie confessed, maybe she had told Blaine that Tyler was trying to buy himself a clear conscience by offering the loan. And…yeah… it was possible she'd mentioned it to other people. No, she wouldn't say anything else about the matter…but it was probably too late.

No kidding.

Skye had hung up knowing that Tyler was right about one thing—she should have sidestepped Angie's question about why she and Tyler were talking near her car instead of telling her the truth and providing rumor fodder—but in all honesty, she'd hoped that Angie might know of someone who could help her obtain financing. After all, Angie knew everyone. How on earth was Skye to know that the woman would put her own spin on the matter? Usually she gossiped verbatim.

Things will blow over. Somebody will do something gossip-worthy. It'd been a while since Shelly Hensley had picked a fight in public. Maybe she'd do something spectacular and then everyone would forget about Skye and Tyler. Regardless, she felt as if she owed Ty an apology for the rumor. She may not have spread it, but there was no getting around the fact that—whether he did it out of guilt or generosity—he'd tried to help and she'd conveyed the wrong message to Angie, expressing amazement at his nerve when she'd discussed the situation, and Angie had eaten it up.

After finishing her morning chores, Skye let herself into the house and walked through her sparkling-clean kitchen to pour a cup of coffee. The coffeemaker gleamed and there wasn't one water spot on the carafe, but cleaning everything she could get her hands on last night hadn't done much to take the edge off the pain caused by losing her equine friend, or to still the whispers of doubt that had been growing louder as the hours passed.

Mason hadn't lied to her about Tyler…had he?

His only lies—and they had been major—had been by omission. He'd neglected to tell her about his growing gambling problem—he probably would have never told her if he hadn't won a huge check and brought home exactly nothing. All of his winnings had been lost on a casino table in one unlucky roll of the dice. He'd tried to defend himself; tried to explain that since he'd dislocated his shoulder during the ride, he probably wouldn't have gotten another big check that season. He'd needed to double their money.

Skye had simply stared at him as they sat together in their hotel room, wondering who this man was. How he could have made such a reckless move with their future. When asked that question, he'd broken down, explained that he had a growing problem. It wasn't the first time he'd gambled, but usually he either won or broke even. His record had given him confidence. What were the chances of losing everything when he'd played so carefully and consistently?

That was when they'd mortgaged the ranch, because the ranch fund had been too small to save them, and Mason had sworn he wouldn't gamble—that he wouldn't even go out in the evenings. He'd stay in his hotel room or in the camper. Watch TV, play video games.

When he had gone out, instead of staying in his room, he'd confessed, as if Skye had spies. She hadn't. He was her husband and she trusted him, so when he said that he went out only because of Tyler's relentless needling, she believed him. Since he brought home his checks when he won—the actual checks—and handed them over to Skye, she had no reason to believe he was gambling. No reason to suspect that he'd tapped into the ranch fund.

It had been a little after midnight and deep into the cleaning when she acknowledged to herself that, if Mason had secretly emptied the ranch fund because of his addiction, he might also have lied about Tyler. He might have needed an excuse in case he was seen at the tables. He was there watching Tyler gamble.

She may be totally off base. Tyler could be guilty, but they had to live together in this small community, and on the off chance that he was innocent, she was going to apologize for that, too. Make nice. End this thing between them once and for all.

Skye sipped her coffee, then pushed it aside. It tasted like acid.

Decision made, she picked up her purse and headed for the door, pausing on the porch to stare off across the field to where faithful Mr. Joe lay. Cliff had operated the backhoe for her—her skills there had never been beyond beginner basics—and helped her bury her horse in his favorite sunning place in the pasture.

Her throat started to close up again, but Skye swallowed the big lump and headed for her car. She didn't think she had any tears left to shed, but one never knew and she didn't need her eyes any more swollen than they already were—especially if she was going to confront Tyler Hayward.

Chapter Five

Tyler's head came up off the pillow as the beating sound intensified, but he was having trouble opening his eyes. When he finally pried one lid open, he realized that someone was knocking on the trailer door. Short intense raps that seemed to echo in his head.

"Get that, would you?" Jess called from the back of the trailer. He sounded the way Ty felt. Like crap.

"Yeah." The word croaked out of his throat. "Coming," he yelled as he shoved his legs into his jeans.

He heard the sound of retreating footsteps as he approached the door, stumbling over his boots on the way. Whoever had been at the door was leaving, but since he was now vertical and semidressed, he figured he may as well see who the visitor was. Pushing open the door, he stepped out onto the small landing his brother had built out of scrap lumber. Skye Larkin was walking toward her car, which was parked where his pickup would be if he hadn't left it at the Shamrock and caught a ride home with Blaine.

"Hey."

Skye stopped dead, her back going stiff, before she slowly turned. And even though he was sore at her, he couldn't help but think, as always, how ridiculously beautiful she was.

"Hi," she said, her voice almost as stiff as her back. She started back toward him, keeping her eyes firmly on his face. Apparently she didn't want to admire the wonder of his naked torso. Well, women who didn't want to see half-naked men shouldn't knock on their doors at unearthly hours.

"Can I help you with something?" His words were clipped, his voice cold. Couldn't help himself.

"You can accept my apology."

Unexpected, to say the least. Especially since she'd apparently made a special trip to do so. "You're apologizing?"

She came to a stop close to the bottom step, and since Tyler didn't feel right looking down at her, he started down the steps. Skye took a measured step back, and he stopped. "I am. I was rude yesterday."

"Your horse died."

Her eyes were red and puffy, as he imagined his were. He didn't drink that often anymore, because it interfered with his training, but last night he'd made up for lost time.

"Yes. Well, regardless, sorry. I shouldn't have told Angie about the loan...but you need to know that I'm not responsible for the buy-the-clear-conscience bit."

He narrowed his eyes at her. If she wasn't responsible for the part that had offended him, then he had only one question. "Why the apology, Skye?"

"Did some thinking last night."

"And realized you needed the loan."

The expression that crossed her face, the way she blinked as if she'd just been slapped, made *him* feel like apologizing, except that he'd done nothing wrong. He'd offered her a loan. He'd offered to help bury her horse. He was not the bad guy.

"This has nothing to do with the loan," she snapped. "Except for the part that Angie embellished." She glared at him briefly, then turned and stalked toward her car. Tyler fought with himself until she was almost there, then bounded down off the porch, making his head throb a little. She heard him coming and stopped with her hand on the car's door handle. She turned on him with another killer glare and said, "What?"

He regarded her for a moment. Her nose wrinkled a little, and he realized he probably smelled like a brewery. Tough. "I want to know something, Skye. What do you have against me?" She opened her mouth, then closed it again. Her jaw muscles went tight as if she was working very hard to keep words from spilling out.

"Too many things to articulate?" he asked with mock innocence. His voice hardened as he asked, "Do you need the money I offered you, Skye?"

"That's not why I came."

"And that's not an answer."

She closed her eyes as she let out a breath, her dark lashes fanning over her cheeks as she debated responses.

"The truth will do just fine, Skye."

Her eyes flashed open. Blue fire. "Yes. I need the money."

"What happens if you don't get it?"

"I'll probably lose the truck and…I don't know about the ranch. Depends if I can get another job."

"Two jobs?"

She nodded, her lips now clamped firmly shut. Tyler

raised his eyes to the horizon. The sun was well above the tree line. Maybe it wasn't such an unearthly hour after all. He breathed deeply, drawing in the scent of grass and pines and Skye. Something in him stirred, and he told it to stop.

When he looked back at Skye, she was eyeing him warily, as if she were teetering on the brink of something and he had the power to tip her one way or the other. She hated it. He could tell.

He forced the corners of his mouth up. They fought him, but he got the job done. "I won't give you the loan…but I'll buy into your operation."

Skye's chin jerked up. "Wh-what?"

"I owe it to Mason. He was my friend—whom I did not gamble with." He needed to make that last part clear. "Here's the deal. I'll become your partner. I will infuse cash into your cattle operation, help you catch up on your payments."

"What do you get out of it?" Skye asked.

"Half your profits."

"Then you won't get much."

"And I want a place to live."

Her eyes flashed, and then she held up her palms as if to ward him off. "You are not moving into my house."

"I'll move a trailer onto the place."

"With Jess?" There was a hopeful note in her voice that irritated him.

"No, Skye. The whole point of this is to not live with my brother." He rubbed the side of his face.

"I need more details. Like…how long will we be partners?"

"Until you buy me out again."

"For the original amount?"

"That wouldn't be very good business."

"Two percent interest?"

"Three." Which still wasn't that great of a return, but, in truth, he wasn't a very good businessman.

"I need time to think. And I need more concrete terms."

"Three days," Tyler said. "If you're still interested, we meet with C.J. and iron out the terms. I'll make the appointment today."

"And cancel if I say no?"

She wasn't going to do that. He was almost certain that she couldn't—not unless some white knight appeared on the horizon. "Sure. I'll cancel if you say no."

She gave her head a small shake, as if unable to believe she was in this situation. She was—and it was not a situation of his making, regardless of what she might think.

"Hey, Skye…"

She looked up at him, only this time her gaze skimmed over his bare chest, pausing at the scar on his left pectoral muscle, before moving up to his face.

"I'll be gone a lot of the time. Most of the time. Consider that while you make your decision."

"Yes." She lifted her chin, a faint frown pulling her delicate dark eyebrows together. "I will consider that."

SKYE'S HANDS WERE shaking on the steering wheel as she pulled out of the parking place. Anger? Gratitude? Lust?

Because while Mason had been a hard-body, Tyler was incredible. And she was using his incredible physique to distract herself from the issue at hand. He had just offered to buy into her operation. Tyler Hayward. Bad influence. Bane of her existence.

Savior?

It was too much to take in, so she blanked out her mind as best she could and drove to work, parking in the same spot where Tyler had accosted her a day ago—incredible how quickly time flew by—and offered her a loan.

She gave a small snort as she locked her car. She should have swallowed her pride and taken it. It would have put her in a better position than she was in now. How could she let him live on her property? What kind of life would that be, going about her business, caring for her animals, with Tyler there?

One that she may have to endure because unless some miracle came out of nowhere in the next three days, that was exactly what was going to happen.

Maybe Tyler's offer is the miracle.

Was this what her life had come to? A place where Tyler Hayward was her miracle?

She jerked open the back door of the café and stepped into the small room that led to the kitchen. She hung up her sweater, pulled her freshly laundered apron out of her tote bag and tied it on.

He might be her miracle, and she might be grateful to the soles of her shoes, but it was never going to sit well with her. He said he was doing this for Mason. Probably out of guilt.

Yes.

She yanked the bow at the back of her apron tight.

That was it. Guilt.

She could live with that motivation. It wouldn't make it any easier having him on the place, but she could save her money, maybe get that second job she'd talked about. Pay him back super fast.

Get her ranch back…get her life back, such as it was.

"Are you okay?" Chloe called from the register, frowning at Skye's puffy face. A night of cleaning and crying did no one any good.

"My horse died yesterday."

"Ooh." Chloe wrung her hands together then settled them on top of her pregnant belly. "I'm so sorry."

Skye nodded in acknowledgment rather than speak and risk tearing up. Chloe reached down and pulled Skye's notepad out from under the counter.

"Kind of empty today," Skye said as she slipped the book into her apron pocket. As in totally empty, which was a bummer. Tips wouldn't go far in helping her out of her present situation—but they would put some gas in her car.

"The breakfast rush was good. Thanks for letting me work that half of your shift. I'll split the tips with you."

"Not necessary. I'm sure lunch will be good, too." Skye traded Chloe shifts, or half shifts, if necessary, on the days Chloe had OB appointments, and today it had worked out because after her cleaning frenzy, Skye had fallen into bed around 3:00 a.m. and managed a couple hours' sleep, which she wouldn't have gotten had she opened at 5:00 a.m.—even though she'd been awake at that time and on the phone with Angie.

Speaking of which…

"Where's Angie?"

"She's running a quick errand. Something to do with her sister's wedding. She should be back any minute now."

Skye hoped it wouldn't be awkward, just the two of them and no customers, but knowing Angie, she'd already moved on from their early morning conversation.

"Angie said that Tyler offered you a loan." Skye waited, but instead of mentioning the clear-conscience aspect, Chloe shot her a curious look as she undid her apron and slipped it over her head. "Is everything okay?"

"Couldn't be better," Skye said. Then, figuring she may as well start her own rumors and have them be truthful, she added, "We're going into business together."

The heavy ceramic mug Chloe was holding slipped out of her hands, landing with a thud on the Formica countertop. "What kind of business?"

"Ranching." Skye looked past Chloe to an older couple that had just pushed through the door. "I'd better seat them."

Skye seated the couple, got them water and menus, then drifted back to the register. "Nothing firm yet, but we're in discussions."

"Why would you do that?" Chloe asked, sounding genuinely concerned.

Skye smiled at her. It felt like a weary smile, a smile one might find on a woman who'd lived for eighty decades instead of almost three. "Sometimes life backs you into a corner and all you can do is graciously say yes when someone offers you a way out."

"I don't see this ending well," Jess said to Tyler as they stood side by side, leaning against the rails of Hennessey's outdoor practice pen. Bull-riding practice would move to the indoor facility once the weather grew inclement, but Ty didn't think he'd be home all that often during that time, but if he was home it was going to be grand having a place to live where he wasn't practically on top of his brother. That was the only part of the plan that Jess did fully approve of.

"I'm not taking advantage of her. I'm helping her in the only way she can accept."

"Offer her the loan again."

"No."

"Why?" Jess tipped back his hat as he turned to eye his brother.

"Because this works for both of us. Skye gets out from under the debt and I get a place to put my money."

"And a place to live."

"The best part of all." He raised his chin as the chute across the pen opened and a young riderless bull charged out, twisting and bucking. "He has potential."

"That he does. I like the new lines Hennessey is breeding."

So did Tyler, although he'd be retired from riding before most of the young stock was ready to buck for real. Once the young bull had disappeared through the gate and the crew started loading another, Tyler shot his brother a look. "You know that I'm grateful that you gave me a roof. I'd do the same for you."

"If things don't start looking up, that may happen sooner than you think."

Jess's job wasn't all that stable, which was one reason he was living as cheaply as possible, and in Ty's way of thinking, that opened up opportunity. "Then you can try your luck on the circuit guilt free. You aren't shirking your duty. Your duty shirked you."

Jess was not impressed with his brother's argument.

"Look." He paused, and Tyler prepared himself for the lecture. "Look" followed by a silence meant something important was about to be imparted.

"Don't do anything to mess up Skye's life. She's had enough trouble."

Tyler waited for the rest. Nothing. He tilted his head, frowning a little. "Do you honestly think I want to mess up Skye's life?"

"I know you're irritated at her for thinking the worst of you."

"Totally guilty." He looked back across the arena as a bull came down the alleyway. "But I see this as an investment and a business proposition. If Skye's life gets screwed up, so does mine."

Chapter Six

Skye felt numb as she left the lawyer's office a little less than two weeks after Tyler had made his proposal to her. *This is the lesser of two evils.* It was either go into partnership with Tyler, hope for a miracle—which hadn't worked out all that well so far—or lose the ranch a little at a time.

"Cheer up," Tyler said, lightly tapping her on the arm with the rolled-up papers he carried as they walked together down the tiled hallway toward the exit. "I'm back on the circuit in a week. You'll barely see me."

"Except when you're here."

"That's no way to talk to your partner," he said mildly, but she sensed steel just under the surface of the comment.

Okay, so her tone wasn't the most gracious, but she was still coming to terms with the situation. "Sorry," she muttered.

Tyler put a hand on her shoulder, and she instantly stopped walking, but he didn't drop his hand immediately. The casual contact made her feel way too aware of him, which Skye didn't like one bit. She couldn't help it—Tyler made her jumpy.

"I don't want your sorry."

Too late. She swallowed the retort. "You're right. We need to work together. I appreciate your stepping in to help me out." She sounded sincere, and she was... except she couldn't help dwelling on the fact that her copies of the legal agreement were carefully filed in her dad's tooled leather briefcase, which she'd dug out for the occasion. Tyler's were rolled in a tube, which he carried loosely in one hand and would probably soon toss into the backseat of his pickup. They were so different—and, in many ways, he was so much like Mason—how on earth were they going to partner successfully?

Compromise.

Except that she didn't want to compromise on her own ranch.

It isn't your ranch anymore...not until you buy him out.

The truth hurt.

"How do you suggest we proceed?" she asked as he dropped his hand, making Skye feel as if she'd suddenly been set free.

"As carefully as possible." When she frowned at him, he said, "I worked up a plan. Maybe when I get done moving my trailer onto the property, we can go over said plan."

"Sure." Skye couldn't say that she liked the idea of Tyler making plans. In fact, knowing that he was formulating plans for her—their—ranch made her feel even more territorial. Sucking in a breath, she started for the door, which Tyler opened for her. "When do you think that will be?"

"Tomorrow. When you get off shift."

"Tomorrow is my day off."

"Great. You can help me skirt my trailer."

"Happy to." *Was this really happening?* She couldn't help a quick glance at him and saw that he wasn't fooled by her show of positivity.

They walked down the sidewalk to the parking lot. Tyler's truck was on the far west and hers was on the far east. She hadn't planned it that way, but it worked for her. Tyler stopped at the point where their paths diverged, hooking his thumbs in his belt loops. He hesitated for a moment, then said, "I know you hate this, but as I see it, it was me or the highway."

He understood her situation exactly—but it would have been hard not to. It wasn't as if she were dodging the facts or misrepresenting anything. Tyler and his newly hired accountant had gone over her tax and ranch records for the past several years. He knew her situation, and he knew what he was getting into.

"You're correct." This was the eating-humble-pie part that she hated so much.

"I want this ranch to work. If that means sorting out what needs to be done and assigning responsibilities, so that we don't get in each other's way, that's what we'll do." He stepped a little closer, and Skye's breath caught. She wasn't used to being this close to Tyler Hayward. For years she'd done her best to stay far away from him.

"Actually, the ranch runs pretty well."

"Meaning...?"

"I can run the ranch just fine on my own. I've done it for years. You can take your half of the profits. You'll have a place to stay."

He smiled. "You're essentially demoting me from partner to tenant?"

His tone told her it wasn't going to happen. He wouldn't let her run her ranch alone. She quirked one corner of her mouth up into a grim half smile. "If I thought you'd let me, I'd do it in a heartbeat."

"What makes you think I won't let you?"

"You want me to squirm."

His expression shifted ever so slightly. She'd struck a nerve.

"Your ideas of my motivations are off base."

"Maybe so," she allowed, even though she didn't believe it. Fighting with her "partner" wasn't conducive to peaceful coexistence until she could buy him out. "Habit. I'll work on it."

"I'm moving the trailer in tonight. I'll see you tomorrow to discuss our partnership. What time works for you?"

"Eight o'clock." She wanted to get it over with. Yes, it was going to mess with her day, but she needed to get used to Tyler messing with her days. "I'll see you then."

Determined to have the last word, she turned on her heel and almost twisted her ankle. Somehow she managed the first few steps in the direction of her car without limping, because she knew for a fact that Tyler was watching. Watching her and quite possibly smiling that…*smile* of his. The crooked one that made her feel off-kilter and self-conscious.

Yes. That smile.

Well, maybe working with her on the ranch would help wipe that smile off his face.

AT LEAST SHE hadn't fallen when her heel caught, because if she had, then Tyler would have had to fight instinct and let her pick herself back up. Skye Larkin wanted as little to do with him as possible, and because she was now beholden, she was all the more determined to keep him at arm's length.

He dug his keys out of his pocket and headed for his truck. *Too bad, babe.* He was her partner, and they were going to tune up the ranch so that it made money. Things wouldn't change that radically, but he had some ideas and there was a boatload of repairs to make around the place. He wouldn't have a lot of time to do those himself, but he could hire them done if he continued winning.

He saw no reason why he wouldn't. Winning was what he did.

The trailer he'd bought used was almost twice the size of the one his brother was living in. He'd offered to trade, because he was going to be home a heck of a lot less often than Jess, but Jess had said no. He'd earn his own bigger trailer. Tyler didn't fight him. He liked the new-to-him trailer and figured he'd be comfortable there when he wasn't on the road and his twin would have adequate space in his own home now that he wasn't sharing.

Less than two hours after signing the legal agreement, Tyler and Blaine parked the trailer on the far side of the dilapidated bunkhouse, where he had access to sewage, power and water lines. All the niceties of home—most of which he'd lacked in his early days on the road when he'd dry camped. Now he drove or flew to his events and stayed in motels and hotels more often than not. It was good to be in the money, to be comfortable on the road.

The trick was to stay in the money. The one given in a bull rider's career was that it could end at any time—

or, at the very least, be subject to an extended hiatus. He'd been blessed with a relatively injury-free season so far, which he attributed to luck and his more intense training and eating regime. Nothing like winning big to motivate a guy to do it again.

"I can't believe you're going to live here," Blaine said as he dusted his hands off, then lifted his chin as the little donkey they'd put back into the pasture twice came trotting toward them again. "That little guy needs to be in sheep wire."

The mule, who was apparently the little guy's bosom buddy, leaned over the fence and called for his friend.

"My turn," Tyler said as he headed toward the donkey.

"Should we leave him out? We can keep an eye on him."

"And listen to that?" Tyler called back, his voice nearly drowned out by plaintive mule cries.

"Good point."

Tyler easily caught the donkey and after a moment's thought led him toward the barn, where he put him into a small pen that opened out onto the pasture. The mule trotted toward the pen, and the two were soon bonding over the planks. Tyler wondered how long it would be before the little Houdini figured a way out of the pen. Apparently he stayed in the pasture on the honor system when Skye wasn't home—not a big surprise given how loose the wire was on most of the fences.

"We should have done that in the first place," Tyler said as he rejoined Blake by the trailer. They stood for a moment regarding the ranch, and Tyler was fairly certain that Blake saw exactly what he did—a ranch that had been something back in the day, and could once again be something, but not without an infusion of cash. Tyler's cash.

"Are you sure about this?" Blake finally asked.

"I had to invest in something. This seemed good."

"Because of what Mason did?"

This again. Tyler stopped adjusting a hose and gave his cousin a hard look. "Because Skye shouldn't lose her ranch due to his...indiscretions."

Blaine pushed his hat back. "You going all white knight?"

Tyler smirked up at him from where he knelt in the dirt. "I think the princess welcomes the arrival of the white knight." He went back to work on the clamp. "I'm investing my money."

Blaine looked around. "I've seen better investments."

"The place is a little run-down. A lot of places are." The droughts of recent years had been ruthless, but the weather seemed to have shifted last year, and for the first time in ages they had a normal snowpack, which meant normal water, which meant better production.

The ranch wasn't a bad investment. He wouldn't let it be. When he wasn't on the road, he'd help Skye work the place, and when he was, she was more than capable of handling things. Probably more capable than he was in some ways. She knew the place. She'd grown up there. It was going to take her a while to get used to having him around, but as he saw it, she'd better get used to it, because it was also going to take her a while to buy him out. Ty was very curious to see how things played out between them.

So was Blaine. "I hope you guys don't kill each other or something."

"We'll do fine…after the initial period of adjustment."

And that, he had a feeling, was going to be interesting.

SKYE DECIDED THE best place to meet with Tyler to go over his plan for the future of her ranch…which was actually now *their* ranch, as much as that pained her… was at the old picnic table in her yard. That way she wouldn't get that trapped-with-Tyler feeling. Being in a small space with the guy, like her kitchen, made her feel edgy and self-conscious, and that was the last thing she wanted. This first meeting would set the tone for their working relationship, and she wanted every advantage.

At eight o'clock she came out of the house with a carafe of coffee, two cups and a small pan of warm take-and-bake cinnamon rolls. As she unloaded the items from the tray she'd used to carry them, Tyler came up the walk.

"Wouldn't it have been easier to meet in your kitchen?"

"But it's so nice out here," she said lightly as she poured a cup of coffee. She raised her eyebrows at him politely as she gestured to the second cup.

"Please." He sat down on the bench on the opposite side of the table from where she stood. She poured the coffee and pushed the tin of rolls closer to him. He shook his head, and she gave him a curious look.

"I watch what I eat. No useless carbs."

Skye blinked at him. How was she supposed to enjoy eating her roll when someone with a nutritional conscience was sitting across the table from her?

"That gets you no points in my book," she murmured as she maneuvered her way onto the bench.

"Nutrition plays a big part in building muscle mass," he said as he took a drink of coffee. "Why don't you want me in your kitchen?"

She ignored the question, because there was no way she was giving a truthful answer to it, and defiantly pulled a cinnamon roll out of the pan and set it on the napkin in front of her. Tyler's stomach rumbled audibly, and she almost smiled.

"What did you have for breakfast?" she asked as she took a bite of the flaky roll.

"Four eggs. But that was almost three hours ago."

He had eaten at five?

He read the question in her face and gave a casual shrug. "I wanted to take a look at the place."

"Without me." As soon as she spoke, Skye wished she could take the words back. He had a half interest in the place. He could do whatever he wanted.

"I didn't know if you were awake."

"I work the early shift at the café, so I'm usually up at five."

"Good to know."

Skye didn't know why. It wasn't like they'd be doing anything together. As she understood it, the point of this meeting was to delineate responsibilities so that they could stay out of each other's way. "You said you have a plan."

"Nothing on paper, but I do have an idea or two."

Skye took another bite of the roll, but she barely tasted it, which was a shame, because she rarely indulged. Tyler set down his cup. "You've run this ranch for a long time essentially on your own."

"True."

"It's not in very good shape." She opened her mouth to defend herself, but Tyler raised his eyebrows and she closed it again, figuring it was better to let him finish insulting her and then mount a defense. "Which is no surprise given the circumstances."

She bit into the cinnamon roll, then slowly chewed, glad to have a reason not to speak.

"The outbuildings need to be reroofed. There are fencing issues. The corrals haven't been cleaned in a long time."

Skye swallowed and dabbed at her lips with the paper napkin. "Anything else?"

"I didn't have a lot of time to look at the equipment—"

"It's all fairly new. We invested after Mason won those big back-to-back checks three years ago."

"Good use of the money."

"Better than some of his other uses," she said, her mild tone belying the tightening in her chest. Mason's betrayal was still difficult for her to both fathom and forgive.

"I'm sorry this happened to you, Skye." Tyler spoke softly. Sincerely. As if he understood and sympathized. Skye didn't want sympathy any more than she wanted him on the ranch.

She set what was left of the cinnamon roll aside. "It's done and I haven't lost the ranch." She propped her elbows on the table in front of her. "What else?"

"I got winter hay for a good price from Blaine. He'll deliver while I'm gone."

"That's good." Even though she hated feeling as if the ranch operations were being taken out of her hands.

"And, since you're working and I'll be gone a good deal of the time, I decided that we should hire out the fence and roof repairs."

"*You* decided." She couldn't help herself. She hated having all of the decisions taken out of her hands.

"Here's the deal, Skye. I have the money to do the repairs *now*. If I get hurt, then I won't have an income. My idea is to pour as much into the ranch as possible now, so that it can start making money and then I'll have something to fall back onto."

Talk about déjà vu. Mason had said the exact same thing when they'd first married and started planning their future. He'd meant what he said, until gambling took over his life and common sense. She was sure that Tyler meant what he said—for now. But how long would this aura of responsibility last before circumstances, and good times on the road, caused it to dissipate?

She swallowed her rising annoyance and said in a stony voice, "That makes sense."

It also made sense for her to get that second job and do everything she could to buy her ranch back as soon as possible.

"Since I'm paying for half of the repairs, maybe I should have half a say in matters."

"I planned to pay for the repairs."

"That isn't the way our agreement is written." It was very clearly a fifty-fifty deal for cash outlay.

"I want the repairs made soon."

"And I want to wait until I can pay fifty percent of those repairs."

"Realistically, Skye, how long will it be before you can do that?"

She shifted on the bench. "I think we both know it won't be this fall."

"Let me do this. It only makes sense, and because I'll be gone, all of the day-to-day stuff falls to you. It seems fair."

Skye's mouth flattened. "I don't—"

"Like to be beholden?"

"There's that."

"And the fact that you don't much like your business partner."

"How am I supposed to answer that, Tyler?"

"Let's try the truth."

She chewed the inside of her cheek. Debated. "All right…how comfortable do you think I am being partners with a guy I accused of…" She made a gesture instead of finishing the sentence. He knew what she'd accused him of. "A guy I never got along with all that well in the first place."

"Why is that, Skye?"

She couldn't help the incredulous stare. "You're really asking that?"

"Yeah. I am. Because I never understood."

Now who was kidding whom? "Where do I begin?"

He put his elbow on the table and propped his chin in his hand. "Anyplace will do." His tone was one of casual interest, but there was a hard glint in his eyes.

Skye closed her own eyes briefly. Where *could* she begin and how could it possibly help things now? It couldn't help, so she wasn't opening this particular can of worms. Wasn't going to risk showing any vulnerabilities to this man—like the fact that she'd been intimidated by him back in the day.

She opened her eyes and found him studying her

face, his expression intent, as if her response was important to him. For a brief moment she couldn't drag her gaze away, and the air between them became increasingly, unexpectedly charged. Skye abruptly pulled her gaze away, clearing her throat as she bought herself a little time. When she felt as if she had something of a grip, she met his gaze again. His expression was cool and businesslike for Tyler, making her half wonder if she'd imagined the crazy edgy vibe between them only seconds before.

"I have an idea," she said, annoyed that her voice was huskier than normal. "You pay for the repairs and we'll get them done right now. I'll manage the day-to-day operations, *and* I'll pay you back as I can."

He nodded his approval. "If we get roofs on those buildings before winter, we won't lose them, but they're in bad shape right now, Skye, and we don't need any more water running down inside of them."

"I know." She leaned back, half wondering if she was trying to put more distance between them. Suddenly, the picnic table didn't seem wide enough anymore. Annoyed at herself, she plopped her forearms on the table and leaned forward.

"As to the cattle—"

"I'll handle the cattle."

Tyler's mouth flattened before he asked in a patient voice, "You have some slick calves. When are you planning to brand?"

"About two weeks."

"I want to be here."

"Why? I've managed quite well without you in the past."

"I'm going to do my share."

"You're paying for the roofs." A stubborn expression settled onto his handsome face, but before he could speak, Skye said, "Cliff and his son help me brand in the fall and the spring. I don't have that many slick calves. We'll preg-check then and arrange to ship the empty cows. It'll all be done in one day." Or maybe two. Cliff didn't like doing everything in one day, but Tyler didn't need to know that. She leaned even closer toward him. "I want carte blanche on the cattle." Something that wasn't in the agreement. Something, judging from his expression, he wasn't going to agree to.

"Until the spring."

"Until the spring," she echoed. She resisted the urge to ask what happened then. She'd take things one day at a time, just as she'd taken them since Mason's death.

A gust of wind blasted over them, lifting and tipping the cinnamon roll pan. Both grabbed for it at the same time, and Skye snatched her hands back as Tyler covered them with his own. He righted the pan, meeting Skye's gaze before she got up and crossed the lawn to pick up the napkins that had blown away. She crumpled them in her hand and headed back to the table, where Tyler was already on his feet.

"You never answered my question," he said.

Skye tipped her chin up. "What question is that?" she asked, knowing full well what he was referring to.

"The one about why we never got along."

She gave a careless shrug. "I don't know…spiders. Snakes. The incessant teasing?" His knack for finding little weaknesses and insecurities and exploiting them. "You were merciless toward me."

"You mean I was acting like a preadolescent boy who liked a girl?"

She stared at him, stunned, as heat flooded her cheeks, which was ridiculous. But ridiculous or not, her cheeks were hot and she didn't know what to say.

Tyler gave a little laugh. "You didn't know?"

"How could I know?"

"I thought I was telegraphing my feelings pretty well back then."

Skye couldn't find words. He'd had a crush on her? "If that was how you showed that you liked someone, then I'd hate to see how you treated someone you didn't like."

"I ignored them." She gave him an uncertain sidelong glance, and he explained, "Our dad taught Jess and I not to waste energy on people who treat you poorly or people you don't particularly like."

"You didn't see what you were doing to me was akin to treating me poorly?"

He gave his head a simple shake, somehow looking sexy as hell as he said, "Nope. I was eleven years old and I was a courtin'."

Skye rolled her eyes as her cheeks warmed, thankful to have something to distract her from the other questions crowding into her head—such as why had he asked her out in high school?

Tyler hooked his thumb in his belt loop. "This isn't going to be easy, is it?"

"I see no way that it can be." Skye spoke truthfully, thankful that he hadn't cued into the direction of her thoughts. "But—" she had to say it "—I appreciate the fact that you've given me a chance to hang on to the ranch." She owed him for that. She might hate it, but the old cliché about beggars not being choosers came into play here.

"Seemed like the thing to do." He spoke without any hint of emotion. "You should know, too, that I'm leaving in two days."

"Will you be back anytime soon?"

"I might squeeze in a day or two—like when you brand—but for the most part, no. I'll be hitting it hard for the next three months." One corner of his mouth twisted in a rather grim smile. "So you'll have your ranch to yourself for the most part. The only person here will be the handyman fixing the roofs and fences."

"Do you blame me for feeling that way, Ty? I've been alone here for a year. Been my own boss forever. It's not easy having someone come in and take charge."

"No, I don't blame you, Skye. But it's something you have to get used to." His expression grew serious. "I didn't make your situation, so I'd kind of appreciate it if I wasn't on the receiving end of your frustration."

She had no defense. She couldn't deny her frustration and anger, and she couldn't deny that she was taking it out on him, even after determining that he was probably not responsible for Mason's gambling.

"Then let me continue to run my ranch."

"Not a problem...for now."

She tilted her chin up. "When might it be a problem?"

"When I'm living on the ranch full-time and want equal say...just like the agreement says I get."

She swallowed and gave a curt nod. She'd sold her soul to save her ranch and now she had to live with the decision. "I foresee future discussions."

"Peaceful ones, I hope."

"When has anything been peaceful between you and me?" The question sounded bitter, and Skye instantly regretted her tone. "Not to say that we can't make things peaceful." There. A save. Kind of.

Tyler's expression shifted and Skye found herself on the receiving end of a long, speculative look. "Do you think that's possible?" His tone was low and surprisingly serious. "I mean…will you allow that to happen?"

"Me?"

"Yes, Skye, you."

She started to speak, although she had no idea what she was about to say, then abruptly stopped. There was nothing worse than your nemesis bringing up a valid point. "I'll do my best," she finally said in a flat voice. "Will you?"

He smiled at her in a way that bordered on predatory, causing a small tremor to move through her midsection. "Yeah. I will, Skye. As I see it, that's the only way we're going to survive this partnership."

TY COULDN'T HELP but wonder if it was a coincidence that Skye worked double shifts at the café for the next two days, leaving early in the morning and coming home just before dark. When she got home, Tyler decided not to be a jerk, since he'd had the place to himself all day, and stayed in his trailer while she fed and cared for her many animals. The first day after completing her feeding chores, she went straight from the barn to the house, but the second day, after shooting a look at his trailer, as if to assure herself that he wasn't watching her, which he was, she crossed the pasture to the fresh grave there and stood for several minutes first staring down at the dirt, then off across the horizon.

Skye had known a lot of loss.

Tyler turned away from the window and walked

down the narrow hall to his bedroom, essentially giving her the privacy she deserved as she mourned her horse. She was never going to like him. He was going to have to get that through his thick skull. Maybe some year she'd loosen up, let him be a friend, but she was never going to be easy with him the way she was easy with his twin.

Just recalling the horrified look on her face when she'd realized that he'd picked on her because of a schoolboy crush hadn't done his ego one bit of good.

Well, fine, Skye. You may not ever like me, but you're going to have to learn to deal with me.

Tyler went back to tossing things into his duffel. He was flying out of Butte the next day for Albuquerque, where the tour kicked off its second leg. After that it was three weeks of travel, a week off, three weeks of travel. He'd head back to the ranch for the week off, see how Skye was faring without him. His mouth twisted at the thought.

She would be doing very well without him, but hey…the ranch was half his, and he was going to spend his downtime there.

Skye was going to have to learn to share.

TYLER LEFT WELL before daybreak—pulling his truck out of the drive just after she'd gotten out of bed for her early morning shift. They'd spoken briefly the night before after he knocked on her door and offered her the extra key to his trailer in case she needed to get in while he was gone. Skye thanked him and wished him luck.

"When you're good, you don't need luck."

"All bull riders need luck," she'd retorted. No matter

how much skill a rider had, there were circumstances beyond his control. He'd simply raised his hand and headed back down the steps toward his trailer.

Now he was gone. And Skye felt like she could breathe again.

She watched the dust from Tyler's truck die down, then walked down to the barn with Jinx trotting by her side. Her ranch was hers once again…until Tyler came back. She had his schedule tacked to the refrigerator so that she knew exactly where he was and when. If things went well, she wouldn't see much of him until the summer hiatus. She was hoping that he might try to pick up a few summer events, and then he'd be gone even longer.

Probably not a nice way to think about the guy who'd bailed her out, but she couldn't help it. Whether it was fair or not, she couldn't totally shake the idea that Mason would have fared better if he hadn't had wild friends. And Tyler was a wild one.

Well, she could maybe find comfort in the fact that if she went down, she was no longer going down alone. She'd have someone to discuss the matter with.

Yes. She'd grab on to that. She wasn't alone. Mason had been dead for over a year. She'd mourned and she'd fought to keep her ranch. Alone.

Maybe she needed to get out. Make a new life now that the financial burden had been eased and she no longer had to pinch every penny and worry about making that next payment. She was in no way in the clear, but she was better off than she'd been in over a year.

Like it or not, she had Tyler to thank for that.

She did not like.

Chapter Seven

"The big question tonight is can Tyler Hayward do it a third time?" The cheer that went up from the crowd in response to the announcer's question indicated yes, they believed that Tyler could take home the top money three times in a row.

And why not? He'd killed in Albuquerque, having drawn a bull that hadn't been ridden in over six months and just making the buzzer before going off over his hand. Then in Oklahoma City he'd drawn another rank bull and gave a crowd-pleasing eighty-eight-point performance. He'd landed on his feet that time. It didn't happen often, but when it did, there was nothing better.

His draw that day, Bad Carl, a Brahman-Charolais cross, was a big, seemingly sluggish bull with a spotty record. Sometimes he bucked like a dynamo, sometimes he didn't.

"You'd better give it your all today, because I need a score," Ty muttered to the bull, who rolled a dark eye and flicked a buttercream-colored ear at him in response. "Yeah. Right back at you."

Tyler carefully adjusted his grip, then pounded his glove. He shifted his weight, pushing down through his legs and feet, his free hand on the top gate rail as he found the middle. One quick nod and the gate flew open. Bad Carl quivered for a moment, then lunged out of the chute, kicking so high that he was inches away from doing a somersault, and then rearing up to throw Tyler forward and smack him square in the face with the top of his head.

Sparks, brighter than the LED headlights he hated so much, obliterated Tyler's vision. His free hand hit the bull's shoulder, and somewhere in the deep recesses of his brain, he registered that he'd just disqualified himself. But, that didn't matter, because the ground came crashing up at him, then he tasted dirt. The stars disappeared, but with his ear pressed hard against the ground, he could still hear the thunder of hooves hitting all around him. He automatically rolled into a ball as one came close to his back, then tried to get to his feet as the bull moved away, staggering a little. The bullfighter took hold of his left arm and helped him to his feet. He was wobbly, but the crowd cheered and he lifted his hand, only to wince as pain ripped through his right side.

The bullfighter steadied him, and together they walked a few steps, then the bullfighter fell back, allowing Tyler the last several yards under his own steam. As soon as he made it through the man gate, a paramedic escorted him to the medical station.

"Bad Carl lived up to his name tonight," the paramedic said in a cheerful voice as he sat Tyler down.

"From your tone of voice, I gather that I'm not going to die." His head was starting to clear.

"No. But you're going to hurt. You just ripped the hell out of this shoulder."

Tyler squeezed his eyes shut and let his head fall back against the wall. "Ripped. How badly ripped?"

"You did some damage."

Tyler's head throbbed. He'd gone for so long without a debilitating injury that he'd started to feel bulletproof. Never a good thing in bull riding.

"The good news is that you didn't break your nose."

Hard to believe, since he felt as if he'd been hit in the face with a fence post. "Then what's all this?" Tyler pointed at the front of his shirt, which was covered with blood and dirt, and he could still feel the stuff oozing down his face and out of his nose.

"I'd say the gash between your eyebrows."

"Sweet." Tyler tried to pull a breath in through his nose. He failed, and the effort hurt. "You're sure it's not broken?"

"Yeah. Swollen, but not broken."

"Small blessings." He moved his shoulder, winced again. Pain was no stranger to him, but this went beyond pain. The shoulder felt oddly weak. Useless. "You think I'm going to be out for a while?"

The medic stood back. "Talk to the doc, see what he says."

SKYE SIPPED HER coffee and studied the calendar on her refrigerator. She had fourteen days of peace before Tyler returned for a short break. With Cliff's help, she'd managed to get the branding and preg-checking done a few days after his departure, despite Tyler's insistence upon being there to assist. Skye couldn't help it—she felt territorial. Tyler could putter around the ranch to his heart's content as long as he stayed away from her and her cows. There was nothing about that in the agreement, but she was fairly certain she could get her point across without having it in writing. At the very least, they'd discuss the matter.

Yes—they would discuss. Partnership and all that.

Skye set down her coffee cup and gently rolled her neck, taking out the kinks and noting that her muscles weren't nearly as stiff as they'd been not that long ago. As much as she hated to admit it, she'd been sleeping better since Tyler bought into the ranch. She didn't like sharing control of her operation, especially with a man who'd driven her so crazy in the past, but she was no longer overwhelmed by fear of losing everything. For the first time in a long time, Skye felt free to make plans—to act instead of react. She had projects on the ranch that she'd ignored for too long as she struggled to hang on. Now she could tackle some of them.

Now she could build her chicken house.

She'd had chickens as a kid, but they'd roosted in the barn, thus making them easy prey for various nocturnal varmints. After her last hen had gone to the big chicken coop in the sky, she'd decided not to keep chickens until she had a proper house. There hadn't been a hen on the place for almost fifteen years.

It was time.

Jinx threw himself against her legs, and Skye set down her cup to get a kitty treat out of the ceramic container next to the flour and sugar. The cat was spoiled, and she didn't care. He'd been a steady companion during the rough times.

"Fourteen days, Jinxy. Can we get our chicken house done by then?" There was a lot of scrap lumber stored in the barn, but she'd have to buy wire and roofing—or perhaps she could finagle a deal from the roofing crew that had finally shown up the day before.

She wasn't familiar with the outfit—they'd driven over from a nearby town—but they'd given Tyler the best price and had seemed polite and professional as they spent the day ripping into the outbuildings. Tyler was right about the roofs—they should have been replaced years ago and a few more bad winters would destroy the buildings. It was hell keeping up with an aging ranch and even worse to see it falling down around her.

But at least the equipment was new—thank you, Mason. He'd done a good job around the place when he'd been there, even though his heart hadn't totally been into ranching and farming. He'd been a bull rider, pure and simple.

Skye had just poured the last of the coffee into her cup when she heard a truck pull in. The roofers were early. She picked up the cup and headed out to the front porch, only to almost drop it when she stepped outside. Dear heavens, no.

Tyler climbed out of his truck, his movements stiff and awkward. Skye closed her eyes, took a calming breath. He was back. Fourteen days early. That could mean only one thing. He caught sight of her then, gave a curt nod in her direction and headed around the bunkhouse to his trailer.

Skye couldn't help herself. She set down the cup on the porch rail and started down the walk. Tyler came back around the bunkhouse as she reached his truck, and even at a distance she could see that both eyes were black. He seemed startled to see that she'd moved into his territory. She was certainly startled by his appearance, although, having been married to a bull rider, she shouldn't have been. He had four stitches along the bridge of his nose. Both eyes were black. And his nose was swollen and bruised, as was the right side of his face.

"How long are you out for?" she asked flatly.

"Four to six weeks. If I behave myself, I may be able to compete for the rest of the season without surgery."

Skye lifted her eyebrows, unable to squelch the expression of disbelief. None of this was new to her. "Will you be able to hold off for four weeks?" Because she knew it would never be six.

"Going to do my best." He opened the truck door and pulled out his duffel with what must have been his good hand. Judging from the odd way he was moving, his right shoulder was probably bandaged under his shirt.

Four weeks. Four. Long. Weeks.

This is what you signed on for. You can do this.

"I see that the roofing crew showed up," Tyler said as he shut the truck door.

"They got here just before I left for my shift yesterday and were gone when I came home." In that amount of time they'd stripped half the roofing from three buildings, which seemed like an odd way to tackle the project, but Skye figured that as long as they got it done, she didn't care how they did things.

Tyler frowned as he studied the buildings. "I wonder why they aren't here now."

Skye shrugged, even though she'd been wondering the same thing. She had a more pressing question. "Why didn't you let me know you were coming home early?"

He smiled at her, but it was lopsided due to the swelling on the left side of his face. "Planning big parties when I'm not around?"

"Yes. I'm such a party person," she snapped.

"Maybe you should be," he replied easily, making her aware of how waspish she'd just sounded.

"Why is that?" Skye took care not to bite her words out.

Tyler closed the door to the truck, wincing a little as he did so. "If you let go every now and again, you might feel less stress. Right now you're a candidate for a heart attack."

Tyler Hayward was giving her life advice?

"Thanks for the judgment," she said. "Perhaps I should tell you that riding bulls is hazardous to your health. No. Wait. Maybe you already know that, yet you continue, even though it defies logic."

"What's your point, Skye?"

A sigh escaped her lips. "No point. I'm just reacting." As always.

His eyebrows lifted...or at least tried to go up. She was definitely going to have to find a video of his wreck—it had to be a good one given the state of his face.

"I'm not trying to bait you," he said. "I'm just... talking."

Stop being so reasonable. Skye sighed again, inwardly this time, and went with the truth. Partners should be truthful. "Sorry for being short with you. I thought I had two weeks of alone time and didn't expect you back so soon. I'm not used to sharing the place." She resented sharing the place, but she was better off because of it. For now anyway.

"Feel free to go about your business. I'll be passed out in my trailer."

"For the whole four weeks?" she asked innocently.

"I wish," he said, rubbing his shoulder.

"Pain meds?"

"Lack of sleep. I drove most of the night to get here."

For some reason the thought of him driving all night while injured bothered her. It was habit, of course. She was conditioned to worry about bull riders and their crazy ways, but damned if she was going to worry about another bull rider. "Look—"

"Skye. Stop." He met her gaze dead on, all traces of easy humor gone from his face, and the rest of her sentence died on her lips. The blue-and-yellow bruises around his eyes and the stitches between his eyebrows made him look all the more serious as he said, "You don't need to hammer the point home. I understand that you don't want me here."

"Then why are you living here?" she asked in a low voice, even as she told herself to just shut up. "You could have parked your trailer on Jess's property. It isn't that far away."

"Keeping an eye on my investment. Sorry you hate it so much." He gave her a nod before adjusting his grip on his duffel and heading for his trailer, moving stiffly as he crossed the short distance.

Skye watched him go, her mouth tight. If they were going to coexist, she really, *really* had to start thinking before she spoke.

She turned on her heel and headed back to the house. He was back for a goodly amount of time, and she had to deal. She'd still go to work on her chicken house, but she was taking the coward's way out and building it on the opposite side of the barn from Tyler's trailer.

TYLER WOKE WITH a start, then groaned as he pushed himself upright. Bull dream. He didn't have them too often, but every now and again, a bull stomped him good while he slept. He swung his feet onto the floor and sat a minute, waiting for his groggy thoughts to clear before getting to his feet and walking down the short hallway to the kitchen. Outside he could hear the sound of hammering. The roofing crew, no doubt. He'd have to see how it was going and get a time estimate. Once they were done, he was going to slap a fresh coat of paint on the siding—using his good arm, of course. How hard could it be to paint left-handed? Next year they'd tackle the barn, which wasn't in as bad of shape as the rest of the buildings. Mason had not been one for maintenance.

He guessed he could say the same thing for Skye, but she'd worked full-time while Mason had been on the road, pursuing his career, so when would she have had time? If Mason had been dipping into the ranch fund that he'd drained for as long as Tyler suspected, he'd probably discouraged Skye from hiring out any repairs.

Skye…beautiful, closed-off Skye, who had never been closed off with his brother. Tyler was not his brother, and Skye was not the fantasy woman he'd made her out to be…but there was something about her that continued to draw him in, made him feel protective even as she took potshots at him. She was his business partner, who resented him, yet needed him, which probably made her resent him even more. *Great situation, Hayward.* And not one that would be sorted out anytime soon.

Tyler turned on the tap and poured a glass of water, then took a couple of ibuprofen tablets to dull the aches in his shoulder and his head. He caught the sound of distant hammering and decided to check the roofers' progress, hoping the fresh air would help clear his head. He'd driven too far last night before pulling into a truck stop and catching two hours of sleep and then driving again. He wanted nothing more than to be unconscious, but the aches in his body were stronger than the urge to sleep.

The hammering from the other side of the barn stopped as Tyler stepped out of his trailer, and that was when he realized that the driveway was empty. No truck belonging to a roofing crew. The only vehicles were Skye's old ranch truck and her small car. The hammering continued on and off as he crossed the driveway and walked around the barn to the opposite side, where Skye was kneeling over a small two-by-four frame. She was about to swing the hammer again when she heard his footsteps and instead of smacking the nail, laid her hammer down and got to her feet.

"You didn't sleep long," she said, dusting her hands on her jeans and looking more than a little self-conscious. Secret project? "Did the hammering bother you?"

"I thought it was the roofers." As curious as he was, he didn't ask about her project. They'd keep things on business-level, because that was where she wanted them kept and right now he felt too foggy to hold his own.

"They haven't shown." She pushed tendrils of wind-blown hair off her face. "Seems kind of odd." She tilted her chin up as she spoke, and he wondered if she was making an effort not to say anything to start another argument. If so, he truly appreciated it. They could pick up again when he felt more himself.

"Yeah. It does." He checked his watch. Eleven o'clock. "I'll give them a call. See what gives."

"Let me know."

"Yeah. I will." He glanced down at the frame, then turned without comment and headed back to his phone in the trailer.

Skye shot Tyler a cautious look as he came back out of his trailer five minutes later, as if expecting bad news. She would not be disappointed.

"The number is disconnected."

She blinked. "As in…"

"Out of service."

"Maybe a glitch?"

"I have a bad feeling it's not." He looked past her to the roofs that now had no shingles. Roofs in worse shape than they'd been when he'd contracted the job.

"If it's not a glitch…" Her mouth tightened, as if she didn't want to acknowledge the alternative out loud. Neither did Tyler. He had money tied up in this deal—one-third of the cost of the job—and now that he wouldn't be riding for the next four weeks, this could turn out to be some serious stuff.

"I'd better go to town. See what's going on." She gave him a sideways glance, her gaze traveling over his banged-up shoulder in a speaking way. "Hey," he said. "It isn't like I didn't just drive seven hundred miles to get here from Reno."

"I'm coming with you." When he lifted his chin, she

met his eyes, a vaguely challenging light in her own. "Partners, remember?"

Twenty minutes later he pulled his truck to a stop in front of the building where he'd made the deal to roof the outbuildings. The windows were dark, the small parking lot was empty and there was an ominous-looking bright pink sign on the door.

"Not good," Skye muttered, reaching for her door handle.

No. Not good at all.

They came around their respective sides of the truck to walk together to the abandoned office to read the notice. Tyler stopped a few sentences after "Out of Business," but Skye leaned closer to read the rest of the smaller print.

When she was done she looked over at Tyler. "How much of your money do they have?"

"A couple grand."

She exhaled. "I have a feeling that we're going to be in a long line of creditors if they shut down just like this. How much research did you do before booking these guys?"

"Research?" He frowned at her. "I asked places for bids. These guys came in lowest."

"Did you check online reviews?"

"I don't see where reviews would have warned me that these guys were about to secretly go out of business."

"True."

He studied the Out of Business sign grimly. "They knew they were going out of business and they took my money."

"That stinks."

Tyler shot Skye a quick look and decided that she wasn't being sarcastic. He pushed his hands into his jacket pockets. "What stinks even more is that we have half roofs on all of the buildings." That and the fact that he felt stupid for dealing with these guys. The price they'd given him was so much lower than the lumberyard in Gavin that maybe he should have suspected something was up. Shaking his head, he headed back to the truck.

"What now?" Skye asked as she caught up with him.

"I buy shingles and do what these guys were supposed to do."

"You?"

She may not have meant to sound insulting, but all the same... "I'm not without skills."

"Have you ever roofed anything—?"

He scowled at her. "It's not rocket science."

"While incapacitated?" she continued smoothly, ignoring his interruption.

"Incapacitated?" He gave a scoffing laugh. "Nothing's broken."

"Which hand is your hammer hand?"

"So I learn to hammer left-handed. Big deal."

"Jarring your shoulder every time you take a swing? Yes. That will help your recovery."

He had a strong feeling that she was concerned about his recovery only because the sooner he recovered, the sooner he would be out on the road again. "What do you suggest?" he asked with exaggerated patience.

Her mouth flattened and she started for her side of the truck. "Let's go price shingles." She yanked the door open. "And we better start buying the newspaper, in case there's a notice of bankruptcy. Or maybe we can sue in small claims court."

"Yeah." But for all intents and purposes, the money was gone and he needed to focus on getting roofs on the buildings. "I'll see if Jess is available to help with the roofs."

She put the truck into Reverse, and an odd grinding sound came out of the transmission. He looked over at her with a questioning raise of his eyebrows. "Ignore it," she said as she shifted into a forward gear.

"I don't know how long you can ignore stuff like that before it gets you into trouble."

"I'll take my chances."

"I don't want you stranded somewhere."

"I don't go anywhere," she pointed out. "I go to work and I go home. Sometimes I go shopping in town on a day off. It isn't as if I'm heading out across the wilds of Montana." She checked for traffic, then eased out onto the road. "Besides, I couldn't afford to get it fixed if I wanted to."

"It will need fixed."

"Right now I'm more concerned about the roofs." She kept her gaze glued to the road, but he saw the corner of her mouth go tight. "If you're out of work for a while—"

"I still have some money." Enough to buy roofing and fencing anyway.

"But we're making a plan before we act. Right?"

"Oh, no way. Why make plans when you can shoot from the hip and compound your mistakes? I'm all about the impulse."

She shot him a dry look. "I figured."

"Here's the thing, Skye—we need to fix the roofs before the weather starts. I say we buy enough stuff to start now and plan later."

"Any idea what we need?"

"Tar paper. Shingles. Nails." A bunch of money. "I'll put it on my credit card until I can access my savings account."

"I don't know…"

"I do. We need to roof those buildings soon."

She put her hand on the edge of the door, narrowing her eyes at him. "Just so we're straight on this, when I eventually pay off the mortgage—" and he could see by her expression that she had every intention of doing that "—I reimburse you for the repairs. Are you keeping track? Or am I?"

"Half the repairs."

"Is that what the contract says?"

"That's what I say."

"That would give you a continued stake in the ranch."

"Don't worry, Skye—you'll eventually get the place free and clear."

She opened her mouth as if to argue, then seemed to think better of it…as in, she'd fight this battle at a better time than while sitting in a truck in the parking lot of the expensive lumberyard.

"I'll keep track," she said. "And maybe you'd better also keep track, to keep me honest."

"I'm not exactly worried about your honesty, Skye."

She shrugged nonchalantly as they walked toward the door. "You never know. I may be an accomplished liar."

Tyler managed a small smile, but his mouth hardened as soon as she looked away. No. She was not the accomplished liar. Mason had been.

Chapter Eight

Skye did some online research as Tyler spoke with a sales associate at the lumberyard. He was right—they had to deal with this mini-disaster as soon as possible, and if the prices here were close to those at the big-box stores in Bozeman, then they'd buy today. If not, then she voted for taking their chances with the weather. Years of frugality were not easily set aside—especially when her business partner was out of a job for at least a month—probably more if he insisted on hammering. Maybe he wouldn't do that. Bull riders lived to ride—although they had an unrealistic sense of what they were capable of. Ride with a broken leg? Why not? Two broken feet? Go for it.

Hammering shingles on a roof? Child's play.

Tyler and Mason were so very similar in that regard that it made her wonder if Tyler would finish the roofs before deciding he was well enough to go back on tour. Mason had started several projects—fence repairs, flooring repairs, corral cleanups—only to abandon them out of necessity and lack of time when he headed back out on tour to earn his living. But roofs were different. Roofs were necessary.

Tyler appeared at the end of the aisle and motioned

with his head for her to join him. She'd almost reached him when someone from behind her called his name, and she turned to see Paige Andrews approaching, looking as poised and confident as she had every day of high school, where she'd been student body president and the top scorer on the basketball team. She had a few debating and track honors, too. Paige was an achiever and she liked to be in charge, which worked out well, because she was very good at being in charge.

She came to a stop and smiled at Skye before getting a good look at Tyler's face and wincing.

"Been practicing your craft, I see," she said. Tyler's bruises were blooming, the black turning to blue and the blue to yellow. He looked like a Technicolor raccoon. And, interestingly, Skye noticed color rising in the nonbruised parts of his face as Paige studied him, a faint frown drawing her perfect eyebrows closer together.

"Some days are better than others," Tyler muttered.

"Bull riding is a crazy occupation." Paige gave her head a small shake.

"Pays the bills."

Skye noted that Tyler, who had the social thing down pat, didn't sound all that friendly. Who wasn't friendly to Paige?

The woman cast a glance in Skye's direction. "So you guys are out shopping together?" The unspoken question was obvious. Were they together?

"We're partners," Tyler said before Skye could answer.

"Partners?" Now Paige's eyebrows went up. "In the business sense?"

"Yes." Skye wanted to get that straight immediately, before the rumors started.

"What kind of business?" Paige seemed truly interested, and not in a gossipy sort of way.

"Ranching," Skye said simply.

"Ah." She eased her expensive leather bag off from her shoulder. "I just moved back from Dillon and I'm opening an accounting firm here in Gavin. If you need a ranch accountant—" she pulled a card out of a side pocket of her bag and held it out to Skye "—give me a call."

"Will do."

Tyler gave a curt nod, and Skye began to wonder just what the history was between these two. He might not be Paige's type—she'd always gone for the clean-cut-jock types—but he was gorgeous when he wasn't all beat up.

Although…yeah…Skye had to admit that he had a strong physical appeal even when he *was* beat up. He was a beautiful man, but she found wolves and cougars beautiful, too—that didn't mean she wanted to get close to them. Skye knew trouble when she saw it, and she had recognized Tyler as trouble from the tender age of eleven.

"I need to run," Paige said with an apologetic smile. "I hope to see you again sometime."

Paige walked toward the exit, and Skye felt a brief moment of envy as she watched her go. What would it be like to have things so together? When she looked at Tyler, she found him studying her with an odd expression, and she had no idea why. "What?" she asked, figuring if she challenged him, he wouldn't ask any questions. She was right.

"Nothing." He frowned and headed toward the counter, where the guy manning the register did a double take when he saw Tyler's black eyes and stitches.

"I ran into a door," Tyler muttered. "And I need to price shingles."

ONCE THEY GOT HOME, Skye helped Tyler unload the heavy bundles of shingles, dragging them off the bed of the truck into a stack, Tyler doing as much with one arm as she was doing with two. And while Skye knew better than to point out that he was pushing himself too much, she could think it…then remind herself that it was none of her business. She wasn't married to Tyler. She didn't need to keep him from hurting himself. But that didn't mean she didn't have questions.

"How are we going to get these onto the roof?" Because there was no way either of them could carry a bundle of the heavy, unwieldy shingles up a ladder. "A few at a time?" Which meant trip after trip after trip.

"I called Jess while you were in the house. He'll be here tomorrow."

"That's a relief. We'll pay him, right?"

"He's my brother. He'll get paid—it just may not be in cash."

Skye decided to let that one go, even though it meant being beholden to yet another Hayward. She pulled the tape measure out of her pocket and started measuring the dimensions of the buildings, jotting numbers in a small notebook as she took them, so that she could calculate areas and determine how many more shingles they needed to buy.

She was just starting to measure the granary when

she glanced up to see Tyler studying her with an odd frown. "What?"

"You're making me think that math really can be used in real life."

"Funny."

"Want me to hold the other end of the tape?"

She couldn't help the surprised look on her face. "I got it."

"You don't need to do everything alone, Skye."

She gave a small sniff as she snaked the tape out. "I'm used to it."

"The point is that you don't have to do everything alone."

She met his eyes then. Intense eyes surrounded by angry black bruising. "I'm not a twin."

"What does that have to do with anything?"

"You've always done things together. I'm an only."

Tyler let out a breath as he propped his hands on his hips. "Did you do everything alone when Mason was home?"

"Of course not." *Not much anyway...*

Tyler's eyes narrowed as if he'd just read something in her response that he hadn't expected—which meant she needed to work on her game face.

"He had his responsibilities and I had mine."

"Ah."

"Don't judge what you don't know about, Tyler."

"I'm not judging."

"I think you are."

"Because it's easiest to think the worst of me?" he asked, his easy tone of voice belying the hard look in his eye.

Do not react. Think first. Skye glanced down, took

her time jotting down the final measurement, then pushed the button to rewind the tape into its case. She hooked the tape onto her belt, carefully stowed the notebook in her pocket, then ruined the effect of total self-control by fumbling the pencil. It dropped to the ground and rolled to Tyler's boot. He bent down with a small grimace, telling her just how sore he was, and picked it up. He solemnly held it out, and Skye just as solemnly took it.

"I'm not trying to think the worst of you." She squeezed the pencil so hard that she was surprised it didn't snap.

"It just keeps happening automatically?"

She let out a sigh. "You rescued me. I owe you."

"That doesn't help matters, does it?"

She had to be honest. "No."

The word was barely out of her mouth when a blast of warm wind came out of nowhere, swirling around them. They simultaneously hunched their shoulders, stepping together as the moving air whipped their coats. Seconds later it was gone.

"Storm's moving fast," Tyler said, scanning the dark clouds on the south horizon.

"I have tarps." She started for the barn, not waiting to see if he'd follow, which of course he did. The tarps were old and covered with thick, choking dust. They worked together to drag them out of the barn, ignoring the hissing of her goose, who took exception to Tyler, a stranger, coming close to her sanctuary on the straw stack. Once outside they shook off the dust, both of them coughing as the dust rose around them, then hauled the first tarp to the granary and covered the grain inside, weighting down the old canvas with sledgehammers, bars and picks that Tyler brought from the toolshed nearby.

"I vote for roofing this building first," Tyler muttered.

"Yeah."

They went back for the other tarp and arranged it inside the toolshed. Tyler opened the door of the third half-roofed building, the tack shed, and shook his head. Without waiting for him to speak, Skye said, "Yes. We should move them."

Realizing that she'd just answered a question that hadn't been asked, Skye felt an odd rush of emotion. The only other person she'd ever done that with was Mason.

It was just a fluke. The question had been an obvious one. Skye stalked into the tack room and started pulling bridles off hooks and hanging them over the horn of the nearest saddle. She threw a couple of pads on top and hefted the saddle, edging past Tyler, who was doing the same, and headed toward the door.

The rain started as she started up the walk. She dumped the saddle in her living room and headed back for the next load. Three saddles later, her living room was full of tack and all that was left in the shed were the ropes and halters and grooming equipment—things that could get wet without major consequences.

Tyler dumped his load onto the floor just as the rain started hammering on the roof. He went to the door and pushed it closed.

"Need some help arranging this?"

Since her instinct was to say no, and she knew Tyler fully expected her to say no, Skye said, "Yes. Thank you."

Silently they carried the saddles to the edge of the

room, tipping them up so the skirts didn't curl and draping the blankets and pads over them. Skye brought in a laundry basket, and they filled it with bridles and breast collars.

"Lot of tack," Tyler said when they were done.

"A lot of it was my dad's," Skye replied. They stood side by side, studying the basket, because it was too unsettling to focus on one another—on her end anyway. She had no idea what Tyler felt, but an uncomfortable vibe was once again filling the space between them.

"I noticed that your slick calves have brands."

"They do," Skye agreed. Because they were her calves.

"I thought we were going to brand when I got back on break."

"I decided to do it earlier."

Her stubborn words hung in the air, but Tyler didn't engage. "Next year we'll make a schedule."

And there it was. Another glimpse of that reasonable side of him that kind of reminded her of his brother. She didn't want him to remind her of anyone she liked. She wanted to continue their safe, adversarial relationship. She gave a small sniff. "That makes sense."

His lips curved slightly, as if he knew how difficult it was to make that answer when she wanted to argue with him—to drive a nice deep wedge between them—then to her shock and amazement, he reached up and gently brushed his fingers over the side of her face. She went still as shock rippled through her, then she jerked back.

His hand dropped loosely to his side. "Your cheek is covered with dirt from the tarps."

"Oh." The word choked out as her hand went to her face. "I can get it."

"Yeah." His mouth tightened. "I'd better go."

Oh, yes. He needed to go. Because she could still feel the sensation of his hand brushing across her face, and worse than that, she felt herself reacting to his touch in a very unexpected way.

SMOOTH MOVE, HAYWARD.

Tyler shook his head as he walked through the rain to his trailer. What had he been thinking, touching Skye like that when she'd made it so very clear that she wanted no part of it?

He hadn't been thinking. He'd been acting on instinct. He wouldn't be doing that again.

The low-lying clouds made his small living room darker than usual, but Tyler didn't bother with the lights. Gray day, gray mood. He ate some leftover chicken, stared out the window, paced the short length of the hall. Finally, he made a quick call to his brother, then grabbed his hat and headed for the door. A little Shamrock time would lighten his mood, and he could bribe his brother into helping him with the roofs in exchange for…something.

It was almost dark by the time he parked behind the bar, which was nearly empty. Apparently nobody felt like coming out in the rain on a weeknight, but he was glad to be out of his trailer, off the ranch.

"You're a wreck," Jess said as he offered Tyler a chair by shoving it away from the table with his foot.

"It looks worse than it is." And it wasn't as if it was the first time he'd had a couple of black eyes and stitches, although this was the first time he'd had the two together.

"More like it could have been worse than it is."

"That, too." After hitting the ground, there was always that pregnant pause as the fates decided whether or not a bull rider was going to be kicked, crunched, stepped on or rolled.

"How's ranch life?"

Tyler tried to raise an eyebrow, but it didn't go too far. "Skye's not happy to have me back."

"Did you think she would be?"

Tyler pulled the beer his brother had waiting for him closer, but he didn't drink. "I got scammed by a roofing company. Now three of her outbuildings have half roofs and I have to finish them." He met Jess's gaze. "I could use some help. Will you be around?"

"Unfortunately, yes."

"Unfortunately?"

"I was supposed to have a job in Billings, putting up a big-ass metal building, but we're on the verge of losing the contract."

"Sorry to hear that. Maybe it's a sign."

Jess gave him a humorless smile. "You're not going to be happy until I'm as ugly as you are."

"I'm not going to be happy until you use your talents before you're too old to do so." He wouldn't encourage his brother to try for the tour if it wasn't for the fact that he knew that Jess loved the challenge of bull riding as much, if not more, than he did. But that cautious, build-a-stable-life thing always got the better of him. Being a decent brother, he didn't point out that the build-a-stable-life thing didn't seem to be working out all that well.

"It's supposed to rain on and off all week."

"And then there may be an early snow. I've been watching the forecast." He finally took a drink. "Will you help me?"

"Happy to." Jess smiled his then-you'll-owe-me smile.

They fell into silence, then Jess asked him about his shoulder and Tyler gave him the details—finish the season, consult with his doctor about surgery, hope for a full and rapid recovery so he didn't miss too much of the following season.

Jess soaked it all in, but Tyler had the feeling that he was also gnawing on another matter as he listened. Finally, Tyler said, "What?"

"You said Skye wasn't happy to see you."

"Yeah?"

Jess settled his forearms on the table. "Why did you move onto the ranch?"

"Because if either of us had gained an ounce of weight, we wouldn't have fit into your camp trailer."

Jess shook his head. He wasn't buying. Fine. "To keep an eye on my investment. Be a partner."

"And Skye was good with that?" Before Tyler could answer, Jess went on to ask, "Or was she in a position where she didn't have a lot of choices?"

"Are you saying I took advantage?"

"I'm asking about your motivation and goals."

One thing about it…a guy didn't need a conscience if he had a twin like Jess. "My motivation was to keep Skye from losing the ranch."

"Okay."

"And to invest my money."

"All right."

"I hadn't planned on being there all that often. You know that I'm gone more than I'm home." Jess didn't answer. Tyler pushed his beer glass back and forth between his hands, then raised his eye to meet his twin's gaze. "I'm not going to admit to unrequited love, if that's what you're waiting for."

"You don't know her well enough for that."

True, but he'd always felt that connection…and a couple of times recently, he'd thought that she might have felt it, too. Of course, she'd always seemed a little horrified afterward, which wasn't exactly promising.

He pulled in a deep breath and leaned back in his chair, dropping an arm over the back. "I've always cared for Skye. You know that. But she also made me mad by making out as if I was getting Mason out of bed and marching him to the blackjack tables."

"And by marrying Mason."

Tyler clamped his mouth shut. There was a limit to how much he would admit to. "I didn't save her ranch for revenge. I honestly needed an investment. And I… wanted to help her."

"Then give her a break."

"I'm trying." The words snapped out. "She's pretty much fighting me on everything."

"She feels powerless."

So did he in a lot of ways.

Tyler let out a breath and focused on his beer. Apparently he'd shared the womb with a psychologist. He took a long drink, draining a good part of the glass, then set it down carefully. "Here's the deal," he said. "Skye would have lost the ranch if it hadn't been for me. She agreed to this partnership, and I'm going to be an active partner, as *agreed*." He smiled darkly. "You can drop by every now and then so that she can vent about me doing what we agreed upon."

Jess shook his head instead of responding. "When do you want to start roofing?"

"Tomorrow."

"Unless I get an eleventh-hour call from my boss, I'll be there at eight or nine."

"Great. I appreciate it." Tyler drained his glass. "One more thing."

"Yeah?"

"I don't want to talk about Skye anymore."

A FEW DAYS ago she had roofs. Now she had sieves.

Skye paced through her living room, occasionally glancing out the window toward the county road. Tyler had headed off to town hours ago, leaving her in precious peace, except that Skye found she couldn't relax. Not when she knew he was coming back.

The character of the ranch had changed over the past few days. It was no longer her sanctuary, the place where she could hole up and let the world go by. The place where she could recharge after a day of dealing with people. Now, when she should be recharging, she was seething instead. And waiting for his inevitable return.

Skye pushed her hair back from her forehead with both hands. This was her reality, and only she could control the way she reacted to it. Jinx had not gone out that night, perhaps sensing that she needed both a snuggle buddy and an ally. Now he butted his head against her chin, insisting in his feline way that she chill.

She dropped a hand onto his back and stroked. The big cat's motor started, and Skye closed her eyes. At some point she dropped off, because when the throb of the diesel engine jerked her awake, her thighs were almost numb from the weight of the heavy cat. Her partner and adversary was home. Skye nudged Jinx off her lap and stood, shaking out her tingling limbs, then jumping a mile when the first footstep hit her porch. A moment later there was a knock on the door.

Skye checked the porch through the side window. Sure enough, it was Tyler.

Why?

She jerked open the door, did her best not to glare up at her business partner who'd woken her up.

"Your donkey is out. He won't let me near him."

Skye rolled her eyes, then reached for her coat. At least it wasn't raining. "Thank you. I've been meaning to string a lower wire, so he doesn't escape so easily, but he's been staying in lately."

Skye headed off across the drive to where she could see Chester standing on the opposite side of the fence from Babe, which explained why the mule had been so silent. Tyler hadn't followed her, so she took her time getting a halter out of the barn and catching the donkey. She put him back into the corral with Babe, then noticed that the sunflower patch near the barn had been decimated. That explained the escape. Chester would be on reduced rations the next day.

As she started back across the drive, she slowed as she saw that Tyler was waiting for her at the end of her walk.

"Thanks for the heads-up," she said.

"He probably would have been okay until morning, but like I said, your light was on."

"I fell asleep in the chair."

He gave a short nod, the light filtering out of the living room window accentuating his cheekbones. Even beaten up and swollen, his face was something. He was more handsome than Mason had been, and judging from his breath, just as fond of beer.

"Jess is coming to help me with the roofs tomorrow."

"Good to know."

An awkward silence settled between them—one in which it was obvious that he had things to say, but for some reason wasn't. Finally he gave her a single nod of dismissal and brushed past her, disappearing around the bunkhouse. She heard the trailer door open and then close, but she didn't move.

She hated how unsettled she felt around him. Hated that he could, just by knocking on her door and telling her that her escape-artist donkey was out, boost her adrenaline to the point that she didn't know if she'd be able to fall asleep again.

"I CANNOT UNDERSTAND why Paige Andrews and Tiffani Crenshaw are still friends," Angie said as the two women left the café after an early lunch. "It isn't like Tiffani cares much about anything except for Tiffani. Surely Paige has figured that out by now."

Indeed, the hair salon owner did have a reputation for being both self-centered and way too interested in the goings-on of everyone else in the community, but Angie also had a similar rep. She wasn't self-centered, but she was a gossip extraordinaire.

"Opposites attract?" Skye asked. And even though it was none of her business, she also wondered what the deal was with Paige and Tyler. Judging from the encounter in the ranch supply store, they'd been more than passing acquaintances, and even though it bordered on being irrational, given their situation, Skye couldn't say that she liked the idea of the two of them together. For Paige's sake, of course.

"Maybe." Angie looked unconvinced, but since she and Tiffani had had a few skirmishes over the years, Angie was predisposed to disliking the woman. "I thought that Paige would have figured out Tiffani by now."

"She might have figured her out a long time ago and accepted her as she is."

Angie made a face at Skye. "Do you have to keep being positive when I'm trying so hard to be negative?"

Skye laughed. "Sorry. I'll watch myself."

"At least they tip well," Angie muttered as she put bills into the tip jar. She looked over her shoulder. "I'm sure it was Paige."

Skye just smiled again and then headed out from behind the counter as a couple she didn't know came in through the door. She guided them to seats and set the menus on the table.

"Is the weather here always like this in the summer?" the man asked, sounding disappointed.

Skye bent to look out the window. The sky was overcast. Gloomy. "Sometimes, but we have our share of sunny days." Unfortunately, the forecast called for rain on and off for the next several days, but she didn't see any sense in passing that information along. "Where are you visiting from?"

"Alabama."

"You know," the wife muttered, wrapping her sweater around her a little tighter, "where it's warm."

"I've always wanted to visit Alabama," Skye said as

she poured water. "And I hope you have some sunny days while you're here."

The woman picked up her menu with a shake of her head, as if that was never going to happen, and her husband rolled his eyes at her before picking up his menu.

"Unhappy about the weather," she murmured to Angie as she went by.

"Well…it is Montana…"

"Shh."

It didn't rain, but the wind gusted so hard on Skye's drive home that she had to fight to keep her little car on the road at times. When she pulled into her driveway, there was no sign of Jess's truck, which meant the twins must have had the good sense not to try to work in this weather.

The sound of rapid hammering brought her eyes up, and she caught sight of Tyler on the opposite side of the granary roof. Okay. So much for good sense. A wind gust smacked into Skye, nearly knocking her off her feet.

Swallowing a sigh, she headed toward the far side of the granary, hoping to get there before the wind blew Tyler off the roof. If he hurt himself again, he may never leave the ranch.

Chapter Nine

"What are you doing up there?" Skye called when she reached the base of the ladder.

Tyler paused midswing and glanced down as if surprised to see her. "Learning to hammer left-handed." The wind was blowing so strongly that it was difficult to hear him.

Skye put a hand on her forehead to keep her hair out of her eyes. "Where is your brother?"

"On the other side of Montana. He got called out on a job."

"So you've been up there all day?" Obviously from the amount of work he'd gotten done. "Alone?"

"This needs done," he said.

Skye agreed. It did need done. "I have to change."

She turned and headed for the house. He might have called her name—it was difficult to tell over the wind—but she kept walking. Jinx came trotting out from under the porch, and she scooped him up and carried him into the house under one arm. Once inside, she set the heavy cat onto the arm of the sofa, then walked down the hall to her bedroom to change into jeans, running shoes and a sweatshirt. She took a few minutes to rebraid her hair, to keep it from beating her to death, then grabbed gloves out of the basket by the door and headed back out into the weather.

Tyler was coming down off the roof as she rounded the corner of the granary, climbing down the ladder one-handed and making Skye wish that she owned a more stable ladder. Hers was old and wooden and had a couple of loose rungs. In other words, it was an accident waiting to happen and Tyler had been using it all day—with a bum shoulder. Maybe it was because she'd lost her husband not all that long ago to a senseless accident that she was more focused on the possibility of danger than she used to be. Whatever the cause, she felt a flash of annoyance.

"What if you had fallen today?" she asked as soon as Tyler's boots hit the ground.

He frowned at her. "What if you hit a deer with your car while driving home?"

"Meaning?"

"Meaning," he said in a patient voice, "that just because something *can* happen, it doesn't mean that it will."

"So let's just tempt fate?"

He shook his head and then picked up a few sheets of shingles and draped them over his good shoulder. "I tempt fate for a living, sweetheart."

She knew he was being sarcastic, playing the cocky bull rider, but she couldn't help the way her spine stiffened. "Don't call me that."

"Sorry. That was a jerk move." He spoke with a sincerity that almost undid her. He hadn't intended to insult her.

She clenched her teeth for a moment, wondering if she was being unreasonable about not wanting him on a roof with a bad ladder and an injury. No. She wasn't. But he was a bull rider and looked at life differently than normal people. As for the "sweetheart"...

One corner of her mouth quirked as she muttered, "I get called sweetheart a lot at work. Along with honey, dearie, sweetie." She crossed her arms over her chest. "One guy calls me sweet cheeks, and I don't think he's talking about my face."

"Who calls you that?"

There was a note in Tyler's voice that made Skye decide that said guy should remain anonymous. "It doesn't matter. I can deal with it."

He gave her an if-you-say-so look and started up the ladder. The first big fat drops of rain hit just as he dropped the shingles.

"You better come down." The rain would make the roof slick, and it wasn't as if he could finish enough to keep the interior of the shed from getting wet.

"When I finish this row."

There was an open toolbox sitting at the base of the ladder. Skye went over to it, picked up the hammer sitting on top of the tools and closed the lid, then draped four shingles over her shoulder the same way he had. She'd barely started up the ladder when Tyler's face appeared.

"What are you doing, Skye?"

She held up the hammer and continued to climb.

"This roof is going to get slippery," he warned.

"Exactly. So I'll help you get done." She kept climbing. When she scrambled off the ladder onto the new shingles, Tyler frowned at her.

"Be sensible."

Skye laughed. She couldn't help herself. "Really?"

The rain was coming faster now. Tyler shifted his weight, and Skye could plainly see bull rider stubbornness battling logic.

His mouth tightened, then he picked up his hammer and the can of nails, before gesturing to the ladder. "Ladies first." He knelt down to take hold of one of the uprights while she eased herself onto the rungs. The ladder was already slippery, and she was glad to be heading toward earth—and she was glad that Tyler was coming down right after her. She held the ladder until he was halfway down, then stepped back just as his feet came off the rung and he plummeted earthward, grabbing wildly at the ladder, which Skye instantly took hold of.

The hammer missed her, but the nail can hit her on the shoulder as Tyler slid by, landing on his side in the wet gravel at her feet. Skye gasped and dropped to her knees as he pushed himself to a sitting position, pressing his palm against his chin. Blood flowed from between his fingers, dripping on his jeans.

Skye took hold of his fingers and pulled his hand away from his chin, wrinkling her nose as blood ran down his shirt. She instantly pushed his hand back up against his chin. Their faces were close enough that she could see that his pupils had dilated. Pain? Awareness?

Because despite the rain and the blood and the muck, he was studying her in a way that made her pulse bump higher. That was when she realized that she had a hand resting on his knee. Quickly she snatched it away and sat back. Even with another foot of space between them, she could still smell him—wet wool, denim and leather. Man.

"You might need a stitch there," she said as she got

to her feet. She hesitated then held out a hand, because that was what she would do for someone who wasn't making her insides turn small somersaults.

Crazy, crazy, crazy.

But she hadn't been with a guy in a while. Or even around a guy. Plus, Tyler was off-limits. Her business partner. Her former enemy. Forbidden fruit.

Although *enemy* was a strong word. *Nemesis* was better.

"Stitches are for sissies," he said, and Skye felt a bubble of laughter start to rise as she zeroed in on the stitches between his eyes. Great. On top of everything she was becoming hysterical. "I have some butterflies in my med kit," he said.

"Want help?" The last thing she wanted was to be in close quarters with him, touching him, but she was his partner and he was hurt.

"I'm good."

"I'm not squeamish. I've stitched up animals." Her father had taught her how.

He gave her a dark look. "You aren't offering to stitch me up, are you?"

"Maybe your mouth." He choked back a laugh, then grimaced, obviously in pain. Skye wrinkled her nose. "Go take care of that before I do. I'll get the tools out of the rain."

Tyler didn't argue. He turned and started for his trailer, and Skye watched him go for a second, before gathering the nails into the can and then stowing the tools in the barn. She was soaked by the time she was done, but there was still the feeding to do...or there should have been the feeding to do.

All the mangers were full. Even Vanessa the goose's troughs had been filled.

Tyler had fed the menagerie before she could. It made sense, since he'd been home and she'd been at work, but feeding was her time to connect with her animals, and she missed her evening ritual.

Both Chester and Babe were in one small stall that opened out onto the pasture. It was such tight quarters that the mini-donkey was practically standing underneath the tall mule as he ate. Skye noted that neither seemed to care who had fed them. The manger was full, and they were happy.

The rain had stopped by the time she left the barn, but there were so many puddles that Skye had to choose a path between them on the way back to her house. The lights were on in Tyler's trailer, shining golden yellow against the gray day, making Skye wonder how he was doing fixing up his chin. Tyler had to be a pro at doctoring himself up, meaning he'd do fine without her help. And maybe he'd stay off slippery roofs and ladders.

She'd just closed her front yard gate when she heard Tyler's trailer door open and the sound of his boots hitting the ground outside the door. Curious as to where he was going, she waited until he rounded the corner, holding a wadded-up washcloth to his chin.

"Hey," he said as he caught sight of her. "Do you have manicure scissors?"

Skye grimaced at the cloth, which was soaking up blood, before meeting his gaze. "In the mood for a mani-pedi?"

He didn't smile, but she had a feeling he wanted to.

"I want to take the stitches out of my forehead when I get done with my chin. It's time."

"Yes, I have sharp scissors."

"I'm also having a time finding my butterfly sutures. They might be in my truck."

"Or you used them all up the last time you split your face open." She gestured with her head toward her door. "Come on."

Why are you doing this?

No good answer sprung to mind. Maybe because it was the decent thing to do. Maybe to prove to herself that she could be near Tyler and maintain composure. Trial by fire, and all of that. She was going to have to get used to being around the guy—right?

"You have adhesive sutures?" Tyler let himself in through the gate and followed her to the porch.

"Was I married to a bull rider?"

He snorted in reply and Skye assumed that he caught her meaning. Blood and stitches were a way of life.

Skye led Tyler through her house and made him sit in a kitchen chair while she got the scissors, tweezers, gauze, butterfly adhesives and antiseptic cream. If it had been Mason, she'd have sat him down on the commode, but Tyler didn't need to see her newly washed lace bras hanging from the shower rod, or her makeup spread over the counter. Now that the bathroom was hers and hers alone, she left her stuff out where it was handy to get at. And she hung unmentionables wherever she so pleased.

Skye returned to the kitchen to put the supplies on the table along with a two-sided mirror on a stand.

Skye started peeling the covering off the adhesive suture, then handed it to Tyler after he'd wiped his chin clean with a paper towel. She had to admit to being impressed with the way that he quickly pulled the edges of the wound together and applied the butterfly.

"You need another."

"Probably," he agreed as he took the second suture from her. "I know this isn't as much fun for you as sticking me with a needle."

"I'm certain I'll get my chance."

"Looking forward to that?" he asked mildly.

She smiled a little. "You better believe it."

He reached out and picked up the scissors and then leaned toward the mirror to slip the tiny blade under the first stitch and snip. "Tweezers?"

Skye handed them to him and he pulled the first stitch. Skye was no stranger to stitches. She'd been raised around animals and she'd married a bull rider. She retrieved the small trash can from under the kitchen sink without a word and held it out for Tyler to drop the suture into. He gathered up the butterfly wrappers and dropped them in before tackling the second stitch.

Skye watched him work, standing close enough that she could see her reflection in the mirror and was glad that her expression rivaled that of a surgical nurse. Cool and impassive, as if her nerves weren't dancing, and as if she weren't on high alert.

After removing the last suture, Tyler met her eyes in the mirror and Skye suddenly felt as if she were standing a little too close to him, even though she was a good eighteen inches away.

"So what do you think?"

"About...?" she asked coolly.

"Am I pretty again?"

Skye forced a frown, because yes, he did look prettier, and she didn't want to notice those things about her ranch partner. "I'm sure the ladies of Gavin will think so."

He held her gaze for another split second before gathering the items she'd supplied him into a neat pile and getting up from the chair. And that was when Skye's theory that she might be standing too close to him became hard fact. She was too close now, but she wasn't going to move. Tripping over herself to put distance between them wasn't going to make her feel better.

"Thank you for the help."

"I don't think I did that much."

"Never underestimate the value of moral support."

She gave a small snort through her nose. "That's me. Ms. Moral Support."

Heaven knew that had been her role with Mason. One she missed…just as she missed being supported by her husband. They'd had a decent partnership and there were days when she was so tired of fighting the world alone that she felt like curling up and hiding. But that wasn't possible. The world was there, whether she hid or not, so that meant that she needed to face things head-on. Things like this ridiculously attractive man standing way too close to her in her own kitchen, making her feel all jumpy and aware.

He raised his chin, looking down at her from his superior height and Skye fought the urge to tilt her chin up to meet his gaze…mainly because that would bring her lips all the closer to his and she had no business—absolutely no business—wondering how he kissed.

Such thoughts were crazy and dangerous and not

allowed into her head. And if she couldn't get the thoughts out of her head, she needed to get Tyler out of her house. She'd underestimated the impact of having him there.

Tyler cleared his throat. "I'll let you be."

Without waiting for her to reply, he turned and headed toward the door, leaving Skye staring after him. Had he read her thoughts or something?

Or had he felt that same thing she had?

THE GROUND WAS moist and the grass squishy the next morning when Tyler came out of his trailer, his very sore chin tucked deep into his jacket. A fat robin yanked a worm up out of the ground and flew away as he rounded the corner of the bunkhouse, his shoulders hunched against the nip in the morning air. Clouds hung low, but the sun broke through on the far side of the pasture where Skye's cattle grazed. He shook the ladder that was leaning against the granary. Water splashed down on his hat. Slippery, no doubt, and since he hadn't felt like sacrificing his chin again, he wore running shoes to work in today. Hopefully the soles would give him better traction. As it was, he was going to get soaked climbing around on the wet roof, but so be it. More afternoon showers were forecast for that day, and he wanted to get as much done as possible.

He heard the door to Skye's house slam and the sound of her boots on the porch. The odds were that he would have help today, since it was Skye's day off. The woman was bound and determined to maintain as much control of her place as possible, and he was good with that—as long as she didn't put herself in jeopardy...like, say, by climbing a slippery ladder onto a slippery roof. She'd probably say he was being sexist, but it was more like being protective…of a woman who didn't want to be protected.

Skye crossed the gravel driveway, hands pushed deep into her sweatshirt pockets. She had on faded blue jeans and a canvas vest over her hoodie. Her hair was spilling out from under the hood she had pulled up over her head. As she got closer, she raised her gaze from the gravel to meet his, her expression cool, almost serene, as if she knew exactly what lay ahead that day and how she was going to handle it.

He, on the other hand, didn't have a clue. Would they talk? Not talk? Get into yet another argument about roofs and ladders? Would he notice her perfume and her hair and wish that things were different between them, just as he had in her kitchen last night? She probably wouldn't be thrilled to know he thought things like that.

"Morning," she said in a low voice. "How's your chin?"

"Sore as hell."

"As it should be." She stopped a few feet away from him, and he sensed the huge chasm separating them. Because of Mason? Because he was who he was? Because she was used to seeing him as the enemy?

Last night he'd felt a shift between them, then Skye had done a mental one-eighty, as if she couldn't handle the idea of being attracted to a guy like him.

"Do you like the way things are between us, Skye?"

A startled look crossed her face. "I don't—"

"I think you do," he interrupted. "I'm not your enemy, Skye."

"Of course you're not my enemy." She jammed her

hands back into her pockets and pursed her lips in a way that told Tyler that there were a lot of things she wanted to say, but that she was afraid of revealing too much. So he shifted his weight and waited. Sometimes stubbornness was a good quality. "We are not enemies," she said carefully. "But we aren't actually friends either."

"And why is that?"

"Friends feel easy around one another. I feel easy around Jess."

"You don't feel easy around me?" He knew she didn't, had seen more than enough evidence last night in her kitchen to confirm the fact—but he asked the question anyway. Maybe it was a jerk thing to do, but he wanted to hear her answer. Wanted to know where he was lacking.

She lifted her chin and met his challenge with the truth. "I feel edgy around you, Tyler."

"Yeah. I've kind of sensed that," he said drily. "My question is why do you feel that way?"

If her hands went any deeper into the pockets, they would come out the other side. "You're different from Jess."

"I'm the bad twin, you mean?"

"If that's the way you want to put it." She casually backed up a step or two, then stopped and shifted her weight to one side, hands still in her pockets. "Jess was friendly and supportive and never once did anything to make me feel self-conscious."

"Back to that, are we?"

"You've got to understand, Tyler… I spent a lot of years thinking of you as the…" Her mouth flattened. "I'm *not* going to say enemy."

"What synonym will you choose?" he asked grimly.

"Nemesis. You threatened me with reptiles, for pity's sake."

He took a step closer. "But I think we both know that it isn't the reptiles that we're dealing with now."

She let out a self-conscious sigh. "I made you out as the bad guy with Mason, and…well…I believed it. But I apologized."

"Do you still believe that I was the bad guy?" He needed to know.

"I…don't know. I no longer think you encouraged him to gamble."

"But…"

"You're two of a kind. I think you encouraged him to be wild."

"I did. Although he didn't need encouragement, Skye."

She took another step back, even though she was already a good distance away from him, and pulled her hands out of her back pockets, folding them over her chest. "I've lost my husband, I almost lost my ranch. I've been through hell this past year. I don't need to hear this."

"It's the truth, Skye. I liked Mason, but I accepted the truth about him."

"Because it didn't affect you." She moistened her lips then abruptly announced, "I hate feeling uncomfortable on my own ranch."

And there it was. He made her uncomfortable by just…being there.

"I guess you'll have to go back to the bank."

She swallowed. "You know I can't do that."

"Then I suppose you want me to move off the ranch?"

It was obvious she wanted to say yes, and he had no idea why she didn't, for no other reason than to show him how she felt about him. But instead she said, "We need a…treaty…or something. Rules. That's it. We need rules."

"Okay. Make some rules."

A pained expression crossed her face. "Why is everything so impossible with you?"

"Something to do with my winning personality, I guess."

She didn't answer immediately but instead studied his face closely, as if trying to find the answer to some mystery there. Even without the stitches, he wasn't pretty at the moment. He knew that. Not unless she was a woman who liked yellowish-brown circles around eyes and remnant suture marks above the bridge of the nose. But her gaze did not linger on his injuries. It traveled down to his mouth and held, and he felt his body stir in response.

"Skye?" Her gaze jerked up to his as if he'd just startled her out of a daydream. "Make some damned rules so that we can go work on the roof."

She gave her head a slow shake. "What good would it do? Bull riders are born to break rules."

"Except for Jess?"

"I have a feeling he's no angel either."

Tyler couldn't help it. He smiled. "I'd like to make a rule."

She shot him a startled look. "Which is?"

"We talk about everyday stuff. The kind of stuff

you would talk to Jess about. I look like him. It seems to me that you could pretend."

"You don't look like him," she said as she knelt to open the toolbox and take out a hammer.

"You mean the black eyes?"

She stopped with her hand on top of the box. "No. I mean you don't look like him."

"We're identical twins."

She shook her head and started toward the building with the ladder leaning against it. Tyler stood frozen, then started after her. He really wanted more of an explanation, but he'd just made a rule, and it seemed important not to break it—especially when she expected him to do just that.

THE SUN PEEKED out from behind a cloud as Tyler went to get the tractor. After a brief consultation, they'd decided to use the bucket to lift the bundles of shingles to the roof, thereby avoiding numerous trips up and down the still-damp ladder, and also avoiding any future ladder accidents.

As she waited, Skye climbed up to the roof and looked out over the ranch that she loved…loved and sacrificed for. It was a sacrifice having Tyler here, especially when she was becoming so aware of him in ways she hadn't expected, but she needed to stop taking it out on him. Therefore, she was going to do exactly as he'd suggested—talk about neutral stuff.

Pretend he was Jess. She didn't know how successful she would be, because he wasn't Jess. He was darker, more unpredictable. More attractive. But…she had to do something to create a more peaceful environment on her ranch. An environment that didn't have her feeling jumpy and defensive.

The tractor fired to life, and after allowing it to warm up for a few minutes, Tyler brought it out of the shed and headed toward the granary. He stopped and set down the bucket, then climbed down from the driver's seat and started pulling the bundles of shingles into the bucket before Skye reached the ground. She put a hand on his shoulder to get his attention, since the engine noise was loud, and his gaze jerked toward her, as if he was startled that *she* had touched *him* instead of the other way around.

"Let me," she said. She took hold of the shingles and pulled, groaning a little as she realized just how heavy a whole bundle was. When Tyler leaned down to help, she waved him off. "I can do it."

And she did. It took a little time, but at least Tyler wasn't ripping his shoulder up. She let out a breath and stood, dusting her hands off on her pants. "If you rip your shoulder again, you'll be here for six weeks instead of four."

"And we wouldn't want that, would we?"

"Just thinking about you and your career."

"Bull."

Skye straightened up and looked him square in the face. "I thought we were aiming for neutral. And, for the record, I was being truthful. I know how difficult it is for you guys to be off the circuit."

There'd been a big learning curve after she'd married Mason, but she'd eventually come to understand that her guy needed to ride the way some people needed to climb mountains. It was something deeply ingrained in his psyche, and she'd come to a place where she could support his needs. Understand them. And it worked. She went to events when they were close by, but mostly she stayed at home and kept the ranch running. Mason made it home more often than a lot of his buddies.

Tyler gave a curt nod and headed back to the tractor and revved the engine.

"Ready?" he asked over the noise.

"Yes," she called back and then started climbing. He waited until she was safely on the roof before lifting the bucket with the shingles and the tools. Fifteen minutes later, the bundles were deposited on either side of the roof and Tyler had demonstrated the not very complex task of laying shingles and hammering them into place. And since Skye refused to relinquish the hammer, Tyler flopped the shingles into place and she nailed them down. They continued their assembly-line work until Tyler called for a break about an hour in. They sat a couple of feet apart on the small roof and looked out over the ranch, just as Skye had done earlier.

"Your chicken house is coming along nicely," Tyler said as he gestured toward the single frame lying where she'd started working on it behind the barn.

"Funny," she muttered, but she took no offense. This was a good neutral topic—the first they'd hit upon. Until the break, they'd worked in silence.

"It's not very big. More like a chicken apartment."

"I only want four or five hens. Enough to keep me in eggs and to eat the bugs. I had a few hens when I was a kid and they roosted in the barn, but the raccoons and owls played hell with them. I promised myself that if I got chickens, they would have a safe place to sleep."

"Your goose sleeps in the barn unmolested."

"Vanessa is a tough old girl."

"I noticed."

She was about to ask what he meant when he pointed into the distance. "Are those our pastures there?"

"Yes. But the ones beyond...those belong to Cliff."

"Ah. We need to ride the boundary sometime soon. Check fences."

"I'll have to borrow a horse from my neighbor Lex." Lex—Alexa—was married to one of Mason's friends, and because of that had become her friend.

"There are two horses in the pasture," Tyler pointed out.

"Buzz is chronically lame."

"You're feeding a lame horse?"

She looked out over the pasture where Buzz and her other very ridable horse, Pepper, were eating. Buzz had a solid pedigree and had cost Mason a lot of money, but a bone spur had put an end to his usefulness. Skye loved him, just as she'd loved Mr. Joe. It made her feel good having him around, and at this point in her life, she was all about anything that gave her peace and good feelings.

Skye pushed her hair back again, a nervous gesture that was becoming a tell. "The alternative to feeding a lame horse is to put him down. The vet assures me he's in no real pain as long as he doesn't bear weight, and I'm not going to kill him."

The stark words hung for a moment, practically echoing between them. But Skye meant them with all of her heart. There'd been enough death associated with her ranch of late.

"I wasn't judging you," Tyler said in an unpcharacteristically soft voice, making her feel embarrassed for her own quick judgment.

"I'm sorry," she said. "It's…"

"A habit?"

She gave a nod. "A bad one, apparently." Tyler shifted his gaze to stare out over the distance, while Skye sucked in an audible breath. "Look. I'm sorry."

He turned his head to look at her. "Me, too."

"Why?"

"I forced my way onto your ranch."

Her mouth flattened grimly. "Thus allowing me to keep it."

A gust of wind swept over them, and Tyler reached for the shingles. "We'd better get back to work."

Deep blue-gray clouds were building in the distance, and even though, for reasons she couldn't fathom, Skye wanted to continue the conversation, settle things once and for all, she gave a nod of agreement and took up her hammer.

They managed to lay most of the roof before the rain started, and then there was no question of continuing as the skies opened and rain began hammering on the roof, fat drops bouncing and splashing around them. They scrambled for the ladder, Tyler going first, and then waiting at the bottom for Skye. His big hands settled on her waist as her foot slipped and stayed there until she was safely on the ground. Without a word, they dashed to the nearby safety of the barn.

"The nail can is still on the roof," Skye said after they had raced through the wide-open double doors.

"I'm not going after it," Tyler said in a serious voice.

In spite of herself, Skye smiled. Their gazes connected and Tyler smiled back, and suddenly there were butterflies beating inside Skye's chest. She'd never re-alized what a devastating smile Tyler Hayward had. And if she'd wanted to double-check her findings, she would have been out of luck, because it faded instantly and his usual cocky half smile took its place.

Self-protection?

The thought came out of nowhere.

"If you want, I can do the chores on the days you work afternoons."

"Yeah. About that…" Her hands went deeper into her pockets, stretching the heavy gray knit fabric. "You don't need to feed."

"It's not a problem."

"I like to do it. It's part of my unwinding."

Tyler smiled again, but it wasn't the same smile as before. It was…guarded. "Feeding that mean-ass goose is part of your unwinding?"

"What did Vanessa do to you?" Because it was ob-vious from his tone that she'd done something.

"Scared the crap out of me. I let myself into the barn, and she came at me flapping wings and hissing. She got me up onto the hay."

Skye laughed. "I can't say I wouldn't have loved to have seen that."

"Maybe she'll do it again." He jerked his head to-ward the wide doors at the far end of the barn where Vanessa was strutting back and forth as she watched the rain.

"She's not a big fan of strangers. She wasn't even that fond of Mason."

"But she likes you."

"I raised her. I found her as a baby at the creek. Something must have happened to the mother. I brought her home and put her under a heat lamp, and as you can see, she thrived. Mason was pretty surprised to find a little goose in our bedroom when he came home."

"You let her roam?"

"She was in a box. A really big box that took up most of the bedroom floor. I didn't want her to feel lonely. Also, I could monitor Jinx, my cat, until he came to realize that she was part of our family." Her expression brightened. "I have the cutest picture of the two of them curled up together in the yard." And then she seemed to remember that he was Tyler and not Jess.

"Maybe you could show me sometime."

"Yes," she said. "Maybe."

Translation: probably not.

"How much do you feed Goosezilla?"

She let out a small snort and shook her head, but didn't look at him. "A scoop of mash and some grain scattered on the ground. She likes to forage. If I have vegetable scraps, I bring them to her. Maybe you could give her some of your veggie scraps after one of your precisely portioned muscle-building meals and make friends." She smiled a little. "And then maybe she won't put you up on the hay."

"I will consider it."

She moved onto the haystack just inside the door, expertly rolled a bale down and pulled a jackknife out of her pocket to cut the strings. "So tell me more about this diet of yours." Safe topic.

"It's not a diet in the weight-loss sense. It's a diet in a nutritional sense. I have to do what I can to maintain muscle, so I don't waste calories on empty carbs."

"Do you do yoga?"

"Tried. Not my thing. I have some stretches and some balances." He gave her a quick look. "What kind of program did Mason follow at home?"

"He ate pretty normal, but liked steak that we could afford sometimes and not others. He did yoga." She gave him a curious look. "If you don't do yoga, what kind of balancing do you do?"

"I stand on a ball, try not to fall off."

"Interesting."

"Kind of funny to watch. You should have seen me when I started. Even with a medicine ball, I ended up on my butt a couple times."

"Yes, it's always good to have a program in which you can get hurt while practicing."

He gave her a crooked smile. "That's kind of what my profession is all about."

Chapter Ten

When it became obvious that the rain was not going to let up, Skye and Tyler went to their separate abodes to spend their evenings alone. Skye told herself she was good with this, but the truth was that after having a rather decent conversation with Tyler in the barn, her house seemed lonelier than usual. Which was crazy. Why would she be hungry for human contact when she worked in a very people-centered occupation?

It made no sense. And neither did pulling back the curtain before she went to bed to see if it was still raining and Tyler's lights were still on. The answers to those questions were no and yes. She had to work the morning shift the next day but fully intended to get back up on the roof when she got home. The quicker they got the roof done, the better.

She also thought about crossing the distance to Tyler's door and asking him not to get on the roof when she wasn't there.

She didn't.

He wouldn't agree, and she wasn't going to put herself in a position of arguing with him. Things were so much less stressful when they didn't argue. Could they possibly continue in this mode? Because it would probably be years before she could make a serious dent in what she owed him, so it really made sense to broker peace between them.

Yes. Peace.

And maybe that would help her deal with the edgy feeling she had whenever he got close to her.

Skye got off shift a little early the next day and arrived home to find that Tyler had finished one roof and had a start on the next. She changed her clothes, retrieved her hammer out of the toolbox and climbed up to join him on the roof.

"How was work?" he asked, as if having her show up to roof was a normal part of his day.

"Not very busy. I like it better when I'm busy." She reached into the nail can, grabbed a handful, then gestured for him to lay the next shingle. He did, and she nailed it into place.

They moved to their left. Tyler laid another shingle, and Skye hammered it in. "You know that I can hammer, right? That I hammered for a couple of hours before you got here?"

"Guess that makes it my turn." She hit a nail in with one satisfying blow. "You shouldn't be doing this at all while you're healing, but I know better than to argue with you."

"Know me that well?"

She leveled a look at him. "I know your species." She hit a nail wrong and sent it sailing off the roof, then put another in place and tried again. "When Mason and I married, I thought I understood bull riders, but I still had a few things to learn. Now I get it."

"And you were good with all the time he spent on the road?"

"I missed him." She couldn't say she was good with all the time she'd spent alone, but she understood it. Figured it was temporary. A guy's body could take the stress of bull riding for only so long. Once Mason retired, they'd have a ton of time together, working the ranch...that had been the plan anyway.

Skye let out a sigh. Plans. Yeah. She hit another nail.

Tyler flopped another shingle in place, and she moved toward him to hammer. They made a good team, covered some decent ground, but they would have done better had they been on separate roofs. She meant what she said about him not stressing his shoulder for at least one more day. Even hammering with his off hand had to jar his healing muscles.

"I hope I'm not treading into the land of things I don't want to know, but were you and Paige once close?" There. She'd said it as if she didn't care—and, of course, she shouldn't care. Paige was an impressive woman, and Tyler could do a lot worse. However, when Paige had questioned her that day about Tyler's role on the ranch, she'd rather resented it...and once again suspected that Paige had a thing for her ranching partner.

"We kind of started the journey, but it didn't go very far."

Ka-ching. "Ah. Well, I think she's interested in starting again."

"Huh."

Skye couldn't tell if that was a good *huh* or a bad *huh*. It was a purposely neutral *huh*, and perhaps that was a sign that she needed to keep to neutral topics, even if she wanted a more definitive answer. "What will you do when you retire?"

Tyler was silent for a moment. "You mean if I'm

not working the ranch here with you and bringing in huge profits?"

Skye laughed. Huge profits and ranching rarely went hand in hand. People ranched because they loved the land and the life. When she glanced over at Tyler, his cheeks were creased in a most pleasant way, and when he slowly turned his head to meet her gaze, amusement lit his eyes—eyes that were even more attractive without the stitches between them.

Something stirred low in Skye's abdomen as their gazes connected, but she did her best to ignore the sensation as she said, "Yes. Exactly. Let's say the unimaginable happens and the ranch is barely making enough to sustain us both…or I manage to pay off the paper and we dissolve the partnership. What are you going to do then?"

"Tough question, Skye."

Even though the nails were short, she managed to pound the next one in crooked. She was about to hit it hard and bury the bent head when Tyler held his hand out for the hammer. Without a word, she handed it to him and he pulled the nail, then handed it back. "We could have flattened it, but I like all my nails straight."

Skye gave him a curious look. "I'd never peg you as a straight-nail kind of guy."

"There is a lot about me you don't know, sweet…" His mouth tightened as the words trailed off. "…person."

Skye fought another smile, which was happening more frequently than she would have thought possible. "Sweet person?"

"Beats sweet cheeks." He shot her a look. "You need to tell me who that guy is."

"Not a chance." Todd Lundgren, local golden boy ex-football star, wouldn't stand a chance against Tyler.

"Back to what I'm going to do… I want to raise some cattle."

"Bucking stock?"

"No. I'll leave that to Hennessey. He seems to have gotten a good start. The young ones look good. I'll never ride one, but Cody might."

"Cattle won't support you—unless you own land outright…or you're still here."

"And you assume I won't be."

"Not when you're say…fifty."

He cast her a sidelong look. "You're saying you don't want to grow old with me?"

Skye sputtered and focused on hammering so she didn't nail crookedly again. That didn't require an answer. It also didn't require her insides doing a free fall. What was it about this guy? The forbidden-fruit aspect maybe?

"My plan," he continued on a serious note, "is to bank the money you pay me back. I get interest on the paper and I get interest from the bank. As long as no one I know gets too seriously banged up, I'll save the money and buy a new place where I will be able to be supported by raising and selling cattle." He flopped down a shingle. "That is my plan."

The part about no one getting seriously injured got her attention. Bull riders did tend to help one another. She and Mason had donated to medical funds when they'd been able. "You need to think about your own future, too." She reached in the can for another few nails. "But I know it's a thin line to walk."

"It could be me. I mean I have some bare-bones insurance, but it costs."

The sun came out from behind the clouds, and while it felt good at first, it wasn't long until it was beating down on them and both Tyler and Skye were shedding coats, vests and sweatshirts. Finally, she told Tyler that she needed a break to grab something to eat.

"Meet back here in fifteen minutes?" he asked as he wiped the back of his sleeve over his forehead and then put his ball cap back into place.

"Don't eat any Twinkies." She turned and headed back to the house, whistling under her breath. She, on the other hand, was totally going to eat a Twinkie. She loved them.

As Tyler watched Skye walk away, he wondered if she was aware of just how far her barriers had dropped that day. Neutral topics. Who would have thought it?

He felt as if he might have moved a few steps closer to convincing Skye that, beneath the bad-twin facade, he was just as good of a guy as Jess was. As good as her late husband, if not better, because at least he was honest.

Tyler shook off the thought. The past was the past.

When Tyler got to his trailer, he reached into his small fridge and pulled out the almond butter, opened it and dipped a spoon in, eating it straight out of the jar. Twinkie indeed. Although, truthfully? He'd eat a carton of them if they were available. That was why he didn't have cookies or sweets in his house. There'd be time to indulge later, when he wasn't so dependent on his body being the best it could be. When what his brother called "real life" started.

As if he wasn't living real life now.

The last roof was almost done. Skye worked again tomorrow, and he intended to have it finished by the time she got home. He rolled his shoulder, knew that while he might not be doing it damage, he wasn't helping the healing process any. But it was his fault that the buildings had no roofs, and he was going to make certain they were fixed before he left. When they were done roofing, he'd ride the property, check the fences... and for that he needed a horse. Or maybe a mule.

He dipped into the jar again. He'd have to ask Skye what the mule's infirmity was, because all her animals seemed to have one. She had a lame horse, a chronically mean goose, an escape-artist donkey and an oversize cat, who was the most normal member of her menagerie. As far as he knew anyway.

He and Skye had barely made it back outside before another storm started blowing in and he suggested that they call it a day. Surprisingly she agreed, so Tyler got into his truck and headed off to Hennessey's to watch the riders and shoot the breeze with his own kind.

When he arrived, he was surprised to see Angie Salinas standing close to Cody. The last he'd heard she'd been dating his cousin Blaine, but since neither Blaine nor Angie had a reputation for sticking with one person for too long, maybe it wasn't that much of a surprise to see her with Cody. "Hey, Angie."

"Tyler." Angie cocked her head at him. "Aren't you supposed to be putting a roof on a building?"

"We're done for the day," he said, coming to lean on the fence next to her.

Cody stepped closer as if Tyler were encroaching. *Fear not, kid.* Angie was a likable girl, but not his type.

"You're roofing?" Cody asked.

Angie shot Cody a look. "Tyler got scammed by a roofing company," she explained matter-of-factly. There were no secrets in this town—at least not between the women who worked at the café.

"Honestly?"

Tyler shrugged philosophically. "They took my money, started the job, then closed doors."

"Sucks."

"Yeah. It does."

Angie reached out to touch Tyler's arm, bringing his attention back to her. "Is Skye really helping you? On the roof, I mean?"

"Yep. Building a chicken house, too. She's good with a hammer."

"No kidding." Angie looked as if she didn't know whether or not to believe him. He decided to let her work it out for herself.

Tyler nodded at Cody and moved to the far side of the arena, where Jasper Hennessey and his brother, Bill, were talking to a couple of high school kids. They asked Tyler his opinion on the mandatory use of helmets, which he fully supported. After this last ride, he was going to become a helmet wearer, himself.

Angie continued her flirt-fest with Cody, so Tyler ambled over to where Trace Delaney and Grady Owen were standing near a gate, deep in conversation. He slowed his steps as he approached, not wanting to interrupt, but Grady waved him over.

"It looked like you guys were discussing important matters."

"Actually, we were discussing logistics," Grady said. "Annie wants to travel with Trace for a week, so Lex is going to watch the twins instead of coming with me. It's a matter of who stays where."

"Life seems to get complicated when you marry," Tyler said. It wasn't that long ago that both Trace and Grady were single and their only worry was staying healthy and getting to the next event.

Trace nodded. "Throw in twins and, yeah, it can get…interesting." But he smiled in a way which clearly indicated that he liked his new role as a husband and father. Tyler had to admit that Annie Owen was a sweetheart and her eight-year-old twin girls always made him smile.

"Even without twins, it gets interesting," Grady said.

Tyler snorted. "Yeah, but you married Lex."

Grady grinned. "Point taken." He pulled his phone out of his pocket and glanced at the time. "Speaking of which, I need to get going. We're painting the upstairs bedrooms, and I promised I'd be back in time for paint consultation."

"Yeah," Trace agreed. "Annie and I are taking the girls shopping for winter coats as soon as I get back. I'm better at coats than dresses."

"Not me," Grady said. "I'm a party dress shopping fool."

The guys laughed and Tyler smiled, feeling as if he'd just wandered into a new, strange land where he wasn't familiar with the customs and mores.

"Are things going okay on the ranch?" Trace asked.

"As well as can be expected. As you can imagine, Skye and I are working out a few things, but…you know. It's always that way when you start something new."

Trace and Grady exchanged a quick look, telling

Tyler that his arrangement with Skye had most probably been a topic of discussion in the Delaney-Owen
households. He expected no less. Bull riders kept track
of their own.

"Let us know if you need any help around the place,"
Grady offered.

"We have it covered for now, but thanks." He em-
phasized the word *we*, as if he needed to let these family men know that he wasn't alone in the world. He had
a twin on the other side of Montana and a business
partner who wanted him anywhere but on her ranch.

After Trace and Grady left, Tyler drifted back to the
rails and watched a few more rides, then said his good-
byes and headed to his home that wasn't really a home.

Meanwhile, Trace and Grady were going home to
women who wanted to see them.

What would it be like?

"I HAVE TO admit that I didn't believe you when you
said you were helping with the roof," Angie admitted
as she loaded glasses onto a tray. It was her last day of
work before she left for cosmetology school in Missoula for the next six months, and she was moving with
tortoise-like speed—not that Skye blamed her. Angie
had wanted to get out of the café forever, and Tiffani
Crenshaw had already offered her a position in her
salon when she'd finished her course of study, which
meant that the gossip capacity of the beauty shop would
be doubled by next spring.

Skye gave a small snort. "Why would I lie about
helping with the roof?"

Angie tossed her head. "To mess with me?"

There had been occasions when people had told

Angie a false story just to watch it spread. It was a lot like putting a dye marker in a lake.

"If I decide to mess with you, it'd be with a better story than that."

"Is roofing hard work?"

"Easy to do, but tedious and time-consuming." Especially when they kept having to break for weather. But if all went well, they would be done that afternoon.

"I'd spend a day on the roof with Tyler Hayward," Angie volunteered, still slowly transferring the glassware. "But Cody's pretty cute, don't you think?"

"Very." It was hard not to be with a bull rider's build, green eyes and longish blond hair. "Just…be aware of what you're getting into if you date a bull rider."

Angie set down the tray. "What?"

Skye held up a finger, indicating that Angie should hold her thought, before heading around her tables, checking on her customers. When she got back, she said, "It's hard to explain until you experience it, but a serious bull rider can't help himself. He lives for the ride. Most other things take second place."

"Like girlfriends?"

Skye didn't know how to answer that, because it depended on the bull rider and the relationship.

"Their careers are generally fairly short," she offered as a positive.

"And if they aren't?"

"Be prepared to pray and worry and leave things to a higher power for eight seconds several times a week during the season." Skye leaned her hip against the counter. "What I'm trying to say is that these guys are focused. If you can't live with their career, then don't date a bull rider."

"Thanks for the warning...I think."

"It's something you need to know." Skye reached out and touched Angie's arm. "Forewarned is forearmed and all that."

Angie blew out a breath. "Guess I'll find out what I'm capable of."

"Guess so. And, yes, Cody is adorable."

Angie smiled. "I know! And guess what he told me about Trace and Annie? They're thinking of trying for a baby."

"How does he...?" Skye shook her head as she held up a hand. "Never mind. I don't want to know. And maybe Trace and Annie want this kept quiet?"

Angie looked surprised at the concept. "Huh. Maybe."

The door opened, and a group of six teens headed for the booth in the back. "Better start the fries," Skye called back to the kitchen. "The after-school crowd is here."

Angie sauntered over to the table as Skye wiped the counter again. Angie was twenty-five and meant no harm...but her mouth was practically a lethal weapon at times. It'd certainly gotten Skye in trouble when Angie had mentioned that Skye thought Tyler was trying to buy a clear conscience by investing in the ranch. There was no way she wanted the same thing to happen to Annie Owen.

BABE'S HEAD WAS hanging over the fence, his long ears tipped forward, when Skye parked her car close to the house. As soon as she opened the car door, he gave a long, plaintive call. Chester was on the move again.

She grabbed her tote bag and crossed the driveway to the mule, stroking the side of his face as she told him that she'd find his little friend and bring him back as soon as she changed her clothes. Babe was not mollified by her response, and as soon as she turned to go to the house he let out another loud, creaky call for his little buddy.

Skye changed into jeans and flannel shirt, shoved her feet into running shoes and barely took time to tie them. Stepping out onto the porch, she stood for a moment surveying the immediate vicinity, looking for a furry gray bundle of trouble. Nothing. Tyler's truck was not in its usual spot, and all the roofs were completely finished. Maybe he was out looking for Chester, or maybe he'd left before the little guy had escaped. One thing she was certain of—now that the roofing disaster was over, they were going to work on securing the fence so that the donkey stayed put.

Skye trotted down the porch steps and started looking in all the usual donkey-hiding places—the barn where the hay was stored, the compost pile out back, the garden. No sign of a mini-donkey. Skye stood in the driveway with her hands on her hips. He'd never left the property, and she was certain he wouldn't leave it now, unless he'd been chased off. He had no fear of coyotes, but maybe a larger animal had passed through...

Her stomach was starting to knot, and for the first time since he'd arrived, Skye wished that Tyler was there. She could use the help scouring the property.

She started toward the large pasture, thinking he might be on the other side in the trees, then abruptly shifted course.

The orchard.

The apples were down due to the wind and frost, and

there was nothing Chester liked more than old apples. However, he'd never before gotten through the fence to help himself to any. Today, however, proved different... not only had he finagled his way through the fence, he was lying on his side at the edge of the orchard.

Skye started running when she saw the small gray heap lying just inside the fence. Her thoughts jumbled as she dashed the last few yards—he'd eaten too many apples, colicked, rolled, twisted his gut...her beloved donkey was dead or dying. Only he wasn't dead. Skye could hear his raspy, labored breath as she skidded to a stop at his side. If he was colicked, she needed to get him to his feet.

Within seconds she realized he wasn't colicked. Instead he was wrapped—tightly wrapped—in old barbed wire that was cutting into the skin of his neck and legs. Skye tried to loosen the wire, find the end. It was too tight, too tangled.

The sound of a motor brought her head up, and she jumped to her feet. Chester struggled, and she instantly sank back down next to him, stroking his neck and telling him it would be okay.

"I have to get tools," she murmured, hoping the little animal would understand her tone of voice. Rising to her feet, she started across the pasture toward the house. Tyler was on the way to his trailer when she shouted his name. She shouted again, and he stopped, then turned. As soon as he saw her, he started toward her with long, purposeful strides. She broke into a jog, and they met at the fence.

"What's wrong?" He was already climbing through the rails.

"We need nippers. Chester is rolled up in wire." She pointed to where she'd left him. "In the old orchard."

"I'll get the tools."

Tyler climbed back through the fence, and Skye started back toward where the donkey lay. The poor little guy was ripped and cut, and she needed to get him free. Tyler must have had his tools at the ready, because she'd barely reached Chester's side when she heard him running through the grass toward them. A few seconds later he was beside her. He knelt and began testing the wire wrapped around the little donkey's legs and neck. Chester took a painful breath, and Skye ran her hand over his wiry coat.

"Here, I think." Tyler struggled to get the nippers in between the wire and skin, then snipped. The wire loosened an iota, allowing him better access to the next strand. Skye continued to pet Chester, murmuring words of encouragement as Tyler moved around the little donkey, snipping wire and tossing pieces aside. When he got the last bit free, he sank down next to Skye and ran his big hand over the donkey.

"He has thick skin. Amazing that he's not cut up more than he is."

Indeed, a horse in the same circumstances would have had larger, more gaping wounds. "Small blessings," Skye murmured. "We need to get him up. If we can't, then I guess we'll get the tractor."

They didn't need the tractor. After a few more seconds lying on his side, Chester seemed to understand that he was totally free and lifted his head. With help from Tyler and Skye, he got to his feet, then stood, shaking, his head hanging down.

"Maybe I should try to carry him."

"He weighs more than two hundred pounds."

Before Tyler could argue the point, or sacrifice his shoulder, Chester took a shaky step forward and then another. With Skye on one side and Tyler on the other, they maneuvered the donkey back to the ranch proper. Skye opened the man gate, and Tyler urged the little guy through. After that he headed straight for his distraught mule buddy. Tyler nudged him toward the barn, and Babe trotted into his stall to keep an eye on his friend while Tyler and Skye doctored him.

Together they cleaned the cuts, gave the donkey a tetanus shot and big dose of penicillin, then turned him loose in a small pen in the barn where he was knee-deep in clean straw. Babe crowded as close to the dividing fence as he could get, nudging his buddy with his nose.

"I thought I'd lost him," Skye said. "When I found him lying still under that tree...I thought he'd colicked and died." She felt the sting of tears and swallowed hard. Reaction, pure and simple, but she wasn't giving in. The donkey was alive. She'd been terrified of losing yet another thing in her life, but hey—hadn't happened. A tear rolled down her face anyway, and Skye swiped at it with her sleeve.

"Are you okay?" Tyler asked.

"Fine. All's well..." Her voice thickened, and she let the words hang. Then, in a move that seemed ridiculously right, Tyler put an arm around her without taking his eyes off the donkey, who was thinking about bedding down, and pulled her close to his side. Skye didn't fight him. Not even a little. She leaned into his comforting warmth, closed her eyes, drew in his scent. Felt the need stir inside her.

Step away.

She did not. She was tired of fighting, tired of worrying. Tired of everything being a battle. Tyler didn't move, but his grip had tightened on her shoulder as she relaxed against him. He smelled good, he felt safe—which only proved how stressed and tired she was. And when he did move—when he looked down at her and then lifted her chin with his thumb and forefinger—she did not allow herself to think. Thinking would ruin everything.

Her eyes drifted closed again, and a second later his lips lightly touched hers, just as she'd known they would. She let out a soft breath, felt it move across his skin. Tyler hesitated, as if he were afraid of doing too much, too soon. A wise man, Tyler, because this was too much, too soon. Skye did not care. Her lips parted against his as she slid a hand up around his neck, felt the hair beneath her palm, the solidness of his chest beneath her other hand. The kiss deepened, and Skye lost herself. She hadn't kissed a man other than her husband in years and years, had forgotten the rush, the taste, the excitement...

She eased back, her lips lingering on his for another long second before she broke contact. Tyler dropped his arm, allowing his hand to slide down to hers before falling away. Skye drew in a breath and decided that the very last thing in the world she wanted to do was to address what had just happened. So instead she gave him a weary half smile.

"Strange day."

He hesitated, then smiled back at her. "That's one way to put it."

"I should get back to the house." For no reason other

than the need to escape while she could. "I'm on shift tomorrow, but when I get off, can we talk about beefing up donkey security?"

"You bet. I don't want this to happen again."

"Yeah." Chester was going to hate total confinement, but he was going to have to give up his Houdini ways for his own health and welfare—as well as Skye's. She couldn't take many more afternoons like the one she'd just had.

Chapter Eleven

Mason's ashes had been scattered on the mountains behind the ranch, so on the occasion of his birthday, two days after Chester's traumatic wire incident, Skye had no memorial to visit. Instead she walked into the pasture and stood for a long time staring at the gorgeous mountain range that was her husband's final resting place.

Last year, when she'd stood in this spot, she'd been raw with pain from her loss. This year...she felt differently. She missed him. But she was also angry at him for leaving her in the circumstances she was now in.

I supported you and you betrayed me.

He'd had a disease. Gambling addiction was like alcoholism. Mason hadn't been able to help himself because he hadn't yet admitted he had a problem. Skye believed in her heart that he would have...but she didn't know what it would have taken for him to make that admission. He'd drained their bank account and hadn't told her anything.

He thought he'd win the money back.

He was young and wild and with time would have settled.

Maybe.

Looking at the man his father had been, there was always the possibility that he would have maintained his wild ways. His father was a good man, funny and caring, despite the fact that he was less than dependable when push came to shove. He meant well...and he was married to a woman who managed his life for him.

Mason had been similar to his father in temperament, as she was very similar to Mason's mother. No relationship was perfect, and for the most part they had done well together, her and Mason. She loved him. She missed him. And she regretted that she never got the chance to discover what Mason might have been capable of after his bull-riding career was over. He was good on the ranch, when he had the time to do the work, finish his projects. He partied hard, he worked hard. He rode hard.

He'd lied to her and left her with nothing.

The conflict between anger and love was killing her. Would next year be any better? Would she have a firmer grip on things? Understand more than she did now...be able to fully and totally forgive?

And damn it, would Tyler still be on the ranch, tempting her and taunting her?

She left the pasture, because it seemed wrong to have thoughts of another man crowd her on the day she was contemplating her husband's day of birth, and walked to the grave of Mr. Joe.

Another loss. Devastating, but expected. Losing Mason—devastating beyond words. The discoveries that followed...also devastating. And then came Tyler—unexpected white knight. He'd had a crush on her way back when, and judging what had happened between them two days before, he still had feelings for her. Or felt sorry for her. Poor Skye. Another near-loss.

Her jaw muscles tightened at the thought of being an object of pity.

But this crazy feeling dancing around inside her wasn't one-sided and was not the result of pity—she was certain of that. She was also dead certain that this crazy feeling was dangerous. Beyond dangerous, because it could blow her peaceful existence to smithereens. Tyler was attractive—in a way his twin was not—and if she could do it with an iron-clad guarantee of no consequences now or ever, she wouldn't mind getting closer to him, playing with fire.

But consequences and bad circumstances had been coming at her over the past couple of years, and she was not going to tempt fate. Nope.

She and Tyler were business partners and nothing more, and she needed to make certain that he understood that…and she needed to make certain her errant hormones were aware.

The rain increased in intensity, running down her vinyl coat, soaking into her jeans, clinging to the ends of her eyelashes, but she couldn't bring herself to move. Tyler was almost to her when she finally heard his footsteps in the wet grass over the sound of the rain and turned to see him sloshing across the pasture.

He stopped a few feet in front of her. "Is something wrong?"

Nothing. Everything.

"It's Mason's birthday."

There was a slight shift in his expression, but he said nothing as he reached out to take her arm and start her moving toward the house. His hand slid down over the sleeve of her damp coat, and his warm fingers laced with hers. "Do you get some great joy out of getting soaked to the skin?"

"The rain makes me aware."

"Of what?" he asked without slowing his steps.

"Being alive." She felt his grip tighten on her fingers before it loosened again.

They ducked under the porch cover, and as soon as they were out of the weather, Tyler let go of her hand and brushed the water off his lower face. "I was worried about you. I didn't know it was Mason's birthday."

"I felt like I had to acknowledge," she murmured. "He was my husband."

"And left you in a bad situation." Her eyes flashed to his face, and Tyler said, "He was my friend, but it's true, Skye."

She folded her arms over her chest, pushing the damp sweatshirt beneath her raincoat into her bare skin, which in turn made her shiver. "*Here's* the truth, Tyler—I'm still dealing with stuff. And until I'm done…" She had no idea how to finish the sentence, no idea how to tell him that as attractive as she found him, she was not hooking up with a bull rider—not even on a temporary basis—so she shrugged.

"Deal away, Skye. Just don't paint me as the bad guy."

"I'm not." To her surprise, she meant it. She no longer saw Tyler as a bad guy…but she did see him as dangerous, which might be worse in some ways. "You're my business partner."

My dangerous business partner.

She cleared her throat before tackling the hard part.

"Which means that we should probably act like partners, instead of manhandling one another."

"Manhandling?"

"Okay. Maybe that was a stretch." The rain started to pound on the porch roof, and small rivulets were running down the driveway. "No more kissing."

"Because…"

She pushed her wet hood back. Her hair was damp around the edges, sticking uncomfortably to her face. "It makes for an uneasy partnership."

And would continue to make for an uneasy partnership for long as she was who she was and Tyler was who he was.

"I think we need to keep an open mind, Skye."

The intensity of his expression made her insides tumble. "I don't think that's wise. I'm not ready to jump into anything. Especially not…with a friend of Mason's. We can't be…attracted."

His eyebrows lifted. "I don't think we have much of a choice."

Skye swallowed as an odd emotion stirred somewhere inside her as she tried to explain. "Since Mason died, I don't feel like I've had much of a choice in anything. I do have a choice here. I choose peace of mind." A gust of wind blasted over them, bringing the rain with it. "We should get out of the weather."

His mouth opened, as if to argue, then closed again. "Agreed."

He waited for a moment, as if wondering if she was going to invite him into her house. She couldn't do it. "I'll see you later."

He stepped back, teetering for a moment on the edge of the porch. Skye reached for him, but he got his balance before she could touch him and she dropped her hands. He forced a smile. "You can't hurt a bull rider."

She begged to differ, but kept the thought to herself.

DON'T PUSH THINGS.

It was so hard not to. Tyler had spent his life pushing boundaries, but he wanted to get back out onto the road, so he was doing his best to stop doing whatever it was he was doing when his injuries started hurting instead of pushing through it. Not easy to do when he'd always pushed through the pain, but this was the first time he was looking at surgery, or maybe not finishing a season, so he needed to change his mind-set.

Again, no easy task, but Skye was helping. She was downright strict about what he could and could not do on her roof—even if technically it was their roof. Tyler had let her call the shots when she was around, and they finished the final side of the last roof that morning, before the rain.

Twilight was setting in by the time he left Skye's porch and headed for his trailer through the rain, still battling frustration. Mason had left a mess behind him, and Tyler was suffering the consequences.

Reality really sucked at times.

Yet another long evening stretched ahead of him, and he thought about calling his twin as he headed up the mucky path to his trailer. Instead he decided to head to town and see who was at the Shamrock. It was Friday night and there should be action there—any action was better than hanging in his trailer alone.

He showered in the tiny shower stall, wondering as he always did how a guy with some size on him would manage in such a small place. Not a worry of his. His body was about as lean as it could be. After he towwled off, he found a clean, albeit somewhat wrinkled shirt and decent jeans, and, since he was going out in public, he put on his good boots with the teal green uppers. Then he pulled his pant legs down over the boots so that no one could see the tops. It was the way things worked in his world. He knew about the green teal leather, and anyone who got him out of his pants would know about them.

He smiled grimly as he shrugged into a canvas vest. No one would be seeing his boots tonight. He wasn't in the mood for something quick and meaningless. Hadn't been for a while now.

The Shamrock was hopping when he got there. It didn't take him long to locate his bull-riding buddies— Cody, Trace Delaney and his cousin, Blaine. Even Jasper Hennessey was there, but he set his hat on his head as Tyler approached the group.

"Just leaving," he said, clapping Tyler on the good shoulder. "Do some howling for me tonight, okay?"

"You could stay and do your own."

Jasper gave his head a shake. "I don't get the same thrill out of it as I used to. I'm only here because the kids dragged me."

The "kids" were all well over legal age, with Cody being the youngest. Tyler smiled and wished Jasper a good night, then pulled out a chair.

"You should have seen Trace today," Cody said with a laugh. "Landed face-first in a pile of—" He abruptly stopped when Trace raised a finger in a mock warning.

"Sounds entertaining."

"When are you heading back out on the road?" Tyler

asked Trace after ordering two pitchers of beer from the server who cruised by.

"Annie and I leave day after tomorrow. She wanted to travel a little before I settle."

"Settle?" Tyler asked.

"It's my last season," Trace said. No one else at the table seemed surprised at the announcement.

"No kidding."

"Embracing my new life," he said. "I'm going to work for Jasper. Won't pay that much, but I'll be home at night."

"Congrats, man."

Tyler went on to ask Trace about his shoulder surgery, since he was looking at nearly the same operation, then after hearing the cold hard facts, he settled in for some drinking. Trace left not long after they finished their conversation, leaving him with Blaine and Cody.

The two bull riders kept the beer coming, but Tyler drank slowly, seemingly one to their two. Cody and Blaine both had family within walking distance of the Shamrock, while he would be sleeping in his truck if he didn't watch himself.

Cody was getting downright funny as he described the latest goings-on at the practice pen and gossiped about his fellow bull riders' love lives. Tyler made a mental note to keep his mouth quiet around Cody in the future and was still smiling at the kid's story about Jasper's wife coming to the practice pen and telling him off for not doing the laundry on "his" day when he became aware of someone coming to a stop close to his chair. He looked up, straight into Paige Andrews's very green eyes. He'd seen her and her friend Tiffani

Crenshaw when he'd first come in and had been glad that their table was on the opposite side of the room.

"Hello, Tyler."

"Paige." He tipped his hat back as Cody's chair scraped across the floor before he excused himself with a polite nod at Paige.

Tyler felt very much like telling the kid to come back, even if it meant being ribbed later, but the kid was already long gone, and Blaine was nowhere in sight, either.

Paige settled in the chair that Cody had just vacated. "How long will you be home?"

"A couple of weeks."

"And, obviously, home is Skye Larkin's ranch?"

He worked up an easy smile. "It is. We're partners in the ranch."

Paige's eyebrows rose. "How did that come about?"

Tyler leaned his elbows on the table. "Through a string of circumstances." He glanced down at his clasped hands for a moment, then back up at Paige, meeting her gaze dead on. Her mouth, which tilted up naturally at the corners, tilted even more.

"Tiffani has to leave soon. Why don't you join me for the rest of the evening?"

"Because I don't think that's a very good idea." If she wanted company, there were any number of guys in the bar who would be happy to oblige. She was pretty and polished and had an air of cool confidence that was extremely sexy. The problem was that she had a very hard time taking no for an answer, and that had ultimately been the answer Tyler had given her six months ago. It wasn't an answer she liked.

Paige gave a measured shrug. "Maybe at some point

in the future, then." She smiled at him as if it were only a matter of time until he came around to her way of thinking and gracefully rose to her feet. He thought about telling her that there wouldn't be a future time—that they'd dated and it hadn't worked—but kept his mouth shut.

Yes, they'd had some fun, but she wanted too much control—of everything. Tyler didn't mind compromise, but he wasn't interested in being managed...although he had to admit to kind of liking it when Skye managed him.

Paige sauntered back across the room to the table she shared with Tiffani, who'd been watching with interest, and then the two women picked up their purses and headed for the door. Tyler let out a long breath just as Cody came back to reclaim his chair.

"She's hot."

"Ask her out," Tyler suggested as he poured them both more beer.

Cody shook his head. "I know my limitations, man. That woman would eat me alive. Besides... I kind of like Angie."

Probably because they both enjoyed passing along good gossip. Tyler just smiled and lifted his drink in a salute before promising himself to watch his mouth around his friend. Cody was bad enough on his own, but if he passed things on to Angie with her connections to the beauty shop and café...watch out.

SKYE JERKED AWAKE as Tyler's pickup drove past her window, and then she settled back against her pillow, heart pounding. Not since Mason had been alive had someone driven in during the early morning hours.

She exhaled deeply and closed her eyes again.

No use. She was awake, but it was close to the time her alarm was set to go off. Since the bars closed at one o'clock, she could only imagine where he'd been until now.

You do not want to know.

Although a small part of her did. She wanted to know if he'd been doing what she'd been thinking about, then in turn wondered why such a thought made her feel jealous. She got out of bed and went into the bathroom, where she turned on the shower. She took her time making coffee, reading the news on her phone as she ate toast with jam and drank two cups of coffee. A normal morning...except that she kept wondering about Tyler.

When she let herself out of her house, she was surprised to see Tyler sitting on the steps of the granary, drinking a cup of coffee in the watery morning sun. She set her purse in her car, then crossed the driveway.

"Decided not to sleep?"

"I slept," he said.

"When?"

"After the bar closed. I climbed into my truck and got a whopping four hours." He took a drink of coffee. "I don't drive after drinking. No good ever comes of that."

"You're sober now?"

"Wasn't that drunk to begin with."

"Your eyes are red."

"Lack of sleep?" She shook her head and started for her car, but Tyler caught up with her before she'd gone more than a couple of steps. "Stop thinking the worst of me, Skye."

"I don't." The denial was automatic and not quite true. She did think the worst of him, and as time passed she was becoming convinced that she did it as self-protection mechanism.

"Yeah. You do." He pushed up the brim of his ball cap. "If you let me use your horse, I'll ride the summer pasture perimeter today."

"That sounds good," she said stiffly, even though she'd been looking forward to the ride. It had been a while since she'd been out. Life had kind of beat up on her for a while, and she'd pushed small things like riding and knitting to the side.

"Easier than borrowing a horse from the neighbor."

"Totally." She gave him a quick apologetic smile. "I have to get going."

"Come out with me tonight."

Skye stopped so fast that she almost left divots in the gravel at her feet. "What?" she asked, startled and half-convinced she'd misunderstood.

"I said, 'Come out with me.'"

"Like…out?"

"Yeah."

"Not like a…date?"

"Maybe."

She tilted her chin. "Weren't you listening yesterday when we talked?"

"It'll be a business date."

She frowned at him, wondering if he was messing with her, but he seemed totally sincere. "Where are we going on our business date?"

"The Shamrock."

"So it's a drinking business date."

"Kind of the Montana version of the three-martini lunch."

"I thought that was two-martini."

"We go big or go home here."

"No."

"Mason is gone, Skye. I'm here. I agree that it's not good practice between business partners, but we haven't exactly had a smooth business relationship thus far, have we?"

"Uh...no."

He smiled at her. Not the cocky bull rider smile, but the one that she'd seen only a handful of times when he let down his guard—as he was now. "Then we don't have much to muck up, do we?"

She hated a logical argument that made it all the easier to get herself into trouble. Skye kicked the gravel at her feet. "I should say no."

"But you aren't."

She gave a snort as she met his eyes. "Yes."

He cocked his head and asked cautiously, "Yes, you *are* saying no? Or yes, you're saying yes?"

"Ty..." It was the first time she'd ever used the shortened version of his name, and it felt oddly intimate coming off her tongue.

"Skye..." The rhyme made it possible for him to exactly mimic her tone. His expression became serious. "How long has it been since you went out and had fun, Skye?"

"You mean like cut-loose fun?"

"Yes."

"Believe it or not, I haven't felt like having that kind of fun. Life kind of smacked it out of me."

"Then we need to get you up to speed again."

"And you think you're the guy to do that?"

He gave her the cocky smile. "Kind of sure." Despite the attitude, she could see a trace of uncertainty in his expression. "Trust me, Skye."

Trust him. Oddly, at a gut level, she did. And it was time for a change in her life. Time to move on. She'd never expected Tyler Hayward to be the guy to help her out there, but why not?

"Fine. I'll have a business date with you—not a cut-loose date. We'll discuss our partnership and our goals for the future."

"Pick you up at seven?"

Chapter Twelve

What did one wear on a business date? Which really wasn't a business date, but she was pretending it was, and Tyler was playing along. That right there told her that Tyler Hayward wasn't the guy she'd thought he was.

Skye mentally flipped through her closet, which hadn't seen anything new in well over a year. What would she have worn if she and Mason had been going out to the Shamrock? As opposed to what would she wear when she went out as a single woman for the first time?

You are single.

Skye twisted the simple wedding band on her finger.

Not an easy thought, but an honest one. She was single and she was young. For the past year she'd stayed close to the ranch when she wasn't working, had turned down tentatively offered social invitations until they eventually dried up, and then it was just her and Jinx hanging out alone at night. And she'd been happy with that existence until Tyler had come into her life.

In just a few short weeks, things had changed due to finances, unforeseen circumstances and a stubborn, hard-to-manage bull rider.

And now she had nothing to wear…nothing that didn't bring back a boatload of memories anyway. She debated about asking Chloe if she could borrow one of her blingy tops, but she decided against it because she didn't want to answer questions. Yet. She'd be answering them soon enough. Gavin was a small town in every sense of the word. Just working one shift in the café earned her more gossip than she knew what to do with.

It was a good tip day, and as soon as Skye got off shift, she decided to splurge and buy something new. How comfortable would she feel in her old memory-laden clothing as she took this new step in her life?

Besides, she wanted something new. It had been a long, long time since she'd spent money on herself. She stopped by the new Western clothing boutique two blocks from the café and, after pricing things, decided she'd skip the new jeans and buy a fancy shirt. Then she saw the dresses on the sale rack. The first thing she pulled off the rack was a red sheath. Perfect to wear under a short denim jacket with boots. She had the jacket. She had the boots. Fifteen minutes later she had the dress, and then, on impulse, she walked into her favorite store, Annie Get Your Gun, on her way by.

Danielle Perry Adams looked up from where she stood behind the counter and smiled. "Hey, stranger."

"I think I just saw you a few days ago," Skye said with a frown.

"That was in your territory, at the café. I haven't seen you in the store since Christmas."

"Been pinching pennies."

Danielle came out from behind the counter. "Are you looking for another gift?"

"No. I'm looking for one of those big necklaces."

"A statement necklace. Lex just brought in some cool pieces. Do you want to see them?"

"Are they in my budget?"

"Why don't we take a look?" Danielle led the way to an antique table in the rear of the store where several silver and stone necklaces were tastefully arranged in a display of antique spurs.

"Wow. I don't even have to turn over a price tag…" Her eye caught a more delicate piece draped over a polished piece of sagebrush. "I like that one." It wasn't what she'd come in to buy. She'd been thinking funky. Something different. But the oddly shaped lapis stone set in silver on the simple chain spoke to her.

Danielle picked up the piece and turned it over. Skye looked at the price and nodded, pursing her lips together. It would take a couple of days of decent tips to pay herself back. Or she could pull another double next time Chloe had a doctor's appointment and not put the money in the mortgage fund.

She drew in a breath and said, "I'll take it."

Danielle smiled. "Shall I wrap it?"

Skye shook her head. "I think I'll wear it."

"I'll cut the tags for you." Danielle took the necklace and then pulled a pair of small scissors from beside the cash register. "Let me help you."

Skye lifted her hair, and Danielle fastened the necklace and then stood back. "I know I say this all the time in the course of my day, but Skye…that necklace is gorgeous on you. The stone and your eyes are almost the same color."

Skye touched the stone. "Thank you." She dug into

her purse and pulled out a wad of small bills. "I hope
you don't mind me paying you in tips."

"I could use the small bills," Danielle said with an
easy smile as Skye smoothed out the bills. "Everyone
from out of town seems to pay with a hundred-dollar
bill. I get tired of dashing to the bank."

Skye's stomach was tight as she left the store—
she'd spent money on herself, and she was moving
forward into uncharted territory life-wise. She took a
deep breath and told herself to get over it. Life went
on. The ranch wouldn't fail because she'd spent forty
dollars on a necklace that she loved. It had been a long,
long time since she'd bought anything she loved. Now
she had a dress and a necklace. More than that, she had
an occasion to wear them.

And she was darned well going to enjoy herself
while she did so.

Ty wasn't certain what exactly had prompted him to
ask Skye out early that morning, because it certainly
hadn't been on his list of things to do that day. Maybe
it was because of the way she'd been looking at him, as
if he were something that both aggravated and attracted
her. Maybe it was because he honestly thought a night
out would do her good. Whatever the reason, when
Skye came out of the house that evening and crossed
the driveway to his freshly washed and vacuumed
truck, he was glad he'd made the move. She looked
both grimly determined and wildly uncertain, and he
knew that this was a huge thing for her—her first date
since losing Mason. A business date, of course, because a real date would have been too threatening. It
was common knowledge that one did not get involved

with one's business partner, but Tyler had made a career out of bucking expectations.

Whatever happened, he was going to make certain Skye had a good time. After calling around, he'd managed to get together a mellower crew than usual. Trace had found a sitter, so he was bringing his new wife, Annie. Cody was bringing Angie who he promised wouldn't get drunk and dance on the pool table as his previous girlfriend had done. Blaine was supposed to show, but he was coming alone. Tyler had given him a heads-up about Cody and Angie being part of the group, but Blaine had assured him the breakup had been both mutual and amicable. Blaine was always mellow, so Tyler wasn't concerned about him. He halfway wished his brother, Jess, could have been there, because Skye felt comfortable with him, but another part of him said no, he did not want to share.

"You look good," Skye said as she approached. Well, he had ironed his white shirt and dug out his newest jeans.

"As do you." He was not being polite. She wore a slim red dress under a short jean jacket that made him want to swallow when he first saw her. And the tops of her boots—red—did show, unlike his. He smiled as she got closer. "I like the necklace." The blue stone looked good on the red, but more than that, it seemed to reflect the color of her eyes.

She touched it self-consciously, then let her hand drop. "You realize this is my first time out in a long time."

"It's just the Shamrock. We're meeting people there for our business date."

"And I haven't been single in about six years." She

held his gaze as she spoke, and Tyler reached up to lightly brush his knuckles across her cheek.

"Yeah. I know. Let's just go have fun. We can come home super early if you want."

She smiled a little. "Thank you. And please realize that if I don't make small talk as we drive, it's because I'm really bad at small talk."

"We'll discuss ranch business as we drive." He opened the door for her, and she climbed into the cab of the truck, hiking her dress up over truly beautiful thighs in order to make the big step up. She smoothed her dress down and looked straight ahead as he shut the door, tipping up her chin as if mentally girding herself for the challenge ahead.

He blew out a breath as he walked around the back of the truck. He was not going to screw this night up. No, he was not.

SKYE FELT AS if a spotlight was on her when she walked into the Shamrock with Tyler. Heads literally turned. Not that many heads, but enough to tell her that no one expected her to be there, wearing a new dress and jewelry, on the arm of Tyler Hayward.

She felt like announcing that it was a business date and nothing more, but that was so not true. It was a turning point. Her first date since her husband's death, and it was with a guy she'd once ducked behind trees and bookshelves to avoid.

A guy who now had his hand comfortably resting at her elbow as he guided her to the bar.

"Hey, folks," Gus Hawkins said with an easy grin. "What can I get for you?"

Tyler glanced down at Skye, and there was something in the way he looked at her that made her throat go dry.

Business date. Business date. And there would be more people joining them. She was safe. For now.

"What would you like?"

"Beer would be nice." And would perhaps help calm her overactive nerves.

Tyler ordered two drafts, then picked up both glasses as Skye led the way to a table toward the back where it felt more private.

"Feel well hidden now?" Tyler asked,

"More hidden anyway." She pulled her glass closer. "This is a big step for me."

"I know."

Surprisingly, she believed that he did know. "I feel self-conscious."

"And like you're cheating on your late husband?"

She met his eyes. "A little."

He reached out and covered her fingers with his, gave them a quick squeeze, then pulled his hand away again. Skye took hold of her glass but did not drink. Instead she took a moment to study the man sitting across the table from her. His face was entirely healed now, but for how long? How many times had Mason left home pretty and come back swollen and broken?

Did she want to get back into that again?

As a bull rider's wife, she knew fear, and she knew prayer. Ultimately she'd relied on the latter along with a healthy dose of optimism. Things would be okay. And as far as bull riding went, they had been.

Tyler sipped his beer, allowing Skye her silence. Mason had never been comfortable with prolonged silence, and she'd assumed without thinking that Tyler was the same. But no. Instead of forcing conversation, he seemed content to give Skye time to decide her next step. That, too, surprised her.

So what was she going to do now that she was out with an attractive man whom three months ago she would have refused to share a table with? A man she'd once thought was to blame for a lot of her misfortune?

She had no idea what she was going to do, and she was surprisingly okay with that. They were out for a drink. There wasn't even a dinner involved. There could have been, but she nixed it, and Tyler had gone along with her wishes without an argument.

Imagine that… Tyler Hayward without an argument.

Was she getting in over her head?

No…she wasn't even knee-deep yet, and, if she took care, she wouldn't slip into deep water.

"A penny for your thoughts?"

"Fat chance," Skye murmured before meeting his gaze. "I told you I wasn't a great conversationalist."

He smiled at her. "Maybe you can pretend that we're on the roof in a storm."

"Maybe." She pressed her lips together thoughtfully. "This is harder than I thought it would be."

"We can leave anytime you want." Tyler reached for her hand, when a commotion started at the door and they both looked that way. Gus was already at the door, coolly suggesting that the rowdy couple find another place to drink.

Skye tucked her hands into her lap before looking back at Tyler. "I didn't expect to feel this conflicted."

"Things take time."

"It's been eighteen months."

"Everyone has their own schedule. Why don't I take you home?"

She shook her head and picked up her drink. "I have to start somewhere, and I may as well start by being out with someone who gets it."

"Bet you never thought you'd say those words."

"No," she said with a small laugh. "I never did." She set the drink down. "I like you, Ty. And that scares me to death."

"Because you know it's the first step toward being forever smitten?" he teased.

"Exactly." She picked her drink back up.

"It's a problem I have."

"I bet you do."

This time when he reached for her hand, she didn't pull hers away. "I'm not asking for anything, Skye, except for an open mind. Don't talk yourself in or out of something for the wrong reason."

"What," she asked softly, "might be considered a wrong reason?"

"Guilt. Fear." He waggled his eyebrows. "Lust."

Skye nearly spit out her drink. She dabbed a napkin at her mouth. "Unfair."

He grinned back unrepentantly. "Hey... I gotta be me."

Skye laughed in spite of herself, and after that the mood lightened. She finished her drink and ordered another as Tyler talked about life on the road, life as a twin. Life in general. He seemed happy to carry the conversational burden, until Skye relaxed enough to lean her elbows on the table and ask, "Do you see us becoming friends?"

"Like you and Jess are friends?" He shook his head.

Skye moistened her lips. "Then what?"

"I don't know." He spoke with an honest intensity that made Skye's cheeks begin to feel warm. Not from embarrassment or self-consciousness but rather from raw awareness. "But whatever it is, it'll be something mutually agreed upon."

"That sounds very...civilized."

"For a rough-and-ready bull rider?"

"Something like that," she admitted.

"You compare me to Mason."

It was a statement, not a question, and it gave Skye pause. "It's that apparent?"

"It's logical. We were friends in the same profession."

Skye lightly cleared her throat. "I can't help it."

"I'm a different kind of guy than Mason was."

She didn't ask how, maybe because she was afraid of the answer.

Oh, deep water, here I come...

Tyler suddenly raised his chin and Skye turned in her chair to see a group of familiar people crossing the room—Angie and her new bull-riding beau, Cody, as well as Trace and Annie Delaney.

Tyler raised a hand to greet them, then shifted his chair so that it was closer to hers, thus freeing up space for the newcomers.

Skye smiled and said hello as people settled in chairs, then jumped as Tyler touched her knee under the table. He leaned close and said, "We'll continue this business conversation later?"

Skye held his gaze for a moment, wondering if he'd made her jump on purpose because she wasn't in a position to call him on it. Or had he simply wanted to touch her?

She waited for him to casually raise his beer before reaching out to settle her hand on his knee. He coughed and she smiled a little before pulling her hand away and turning toward Angie to ask how she liked school.

REALLY, SKYE?

Tyler had almost choked on his beer when Skye touched his leg. The touching, in itself, was no big deal, except that it was Skye, making physical contact with him of her own accord. Maybe it was payback for him touching her...or maybe it wasn't.

He wasn't certain, but he was looking forward to getting the answer later that evening. In the meantime, Skye pretty much focused on everyone at the table, except for him. When Grady and Lex showed up they scooted their chairs even closer and Tyler slid his arm along the back of Skye's chair. She turned to look at him, her expression making him feel like a junior high kid who'd been caught doing the arm-around-the-girl-while-yawning move.

He gave her a mock frown and lightly caressed her bare arm with his fingertips. A shiver went through her and her eyes widened ever so slightly. Then she turned back to Angie, her hair sliding over his arm like a smooth silken sheet.

Tyler felt his body stir at the sensual contact, then told his body to knock it off. Not the time or place and he was thirty freaking years old. He continued to stroke Skye's arm ever so lightly and she did not move away. Nor did she move closer—not until she leaned in to say, "This is not the way I do business."

"We might have to discuss your technique."

"Fat chance," she whispered sweetly.

"We'll see," he murmured back. He looked up then, caught Grady studying him with a slight frown and had the craziest feeling that his fellow bull rider wanted to offer him some advice. He looked away. He was doing okay, considering the circumstances. He'd gotten Skye out on a date, hadn't he? She'd touched his leg. Major headway.

The group broke up early. Trace and Grady and their ladies had duties at home and since Tyler had a feeling that Cody and Angie were itching to ramp up their evening, he and Skye left with the married crowd. The couples went their separate ways in the parking lot and after opening Skye's door for her and helping her into the truck, Tyler walked around and got into his own side.

Skye sat close to the window, her face turned slightly away from him, as if being alone with him without the protection of a crowd was suddenly too intimate.

What happened to the woman who'd patted his leg under the table?

She certainly wasn't there in the truck with him.

Tyler did Skye a favor and left her alone in her thoughts on the short drive out of town to the ranch.

Once they'd parked, he'd half expected her to bolt from the truck, but instead she opened her door and made her way to the ground, taking care not to tear her tight-ish red dress. A dress that didn't cry out "business date."

Tyler walked Skye to her door, maintaining the silence until she'd put her key into the lock. Then he reached out to put his hand on top of hers, stopping her from turning the key. Her startled gaze jerked up to his and he saw color stain her cheeks. He eased back, dropped his hand.

"I was just wondering if tonight was…okay."

"Tonight was fun." She seemed sincere, but still distant.

"What's wrong?"

She glanced down ever so briefly before raising her gaze first to his mouth, then to his eyes. She moistened her lips. "As we spoke about before…a lot of firsts."

Tyler tipped his chin up and looked down at her. "Have you ever heard of fear fantasies, Skye?"

She gave her head a slow shake.

"It's when you think about all the things that could go wrong and worry about them, just as if they had gone wrong. Your body reacts accordingly."

"But…isn't it a good thing to anticipate problems? Be prepared?"

"Yes. But it isn't a good idea to obsess over things that could happen, but haven't."

Her eyebrows drew together and he abandoned his intention of keeping his hands off her. Gripping her lightly by the shoulders, he moved a step closer, bringing her close enough to feel the heat of her body, breathe in her wonderful scent, but not close enough for their bodies to touch. "Skye," he said patiently, "you can be prepared, but you also need to understand that you can't control the future. You can kind of control the moment you're in…unless, of course, you're on a bull. Then it's a totally different thing."

She bit her lip, fought the smile. He smiled at her

and it broke through. She shook her head one more time and then leaned it on his chest.

"You drive me crazy."

"In a good way?"

"For the most part."

He reached down and tipped up her chin, then took her lips in a soft, sweet kiss. It was all he would allow himself, because he was not going to mess this up. Skye's lips clung to his, making it all the more difficult to pull away. Somehow he did.

"I will not push things, Skye. Slow and steady. No fast moves."

"You make me sound like a green colt."

He smiled a little. "No. Just someone who needs some practice living in the moment without imagining awful consequences in the future."

LIVE IN THE MOMENT.

The words had become Skye's mantra, and now, as she put the finishing touches on the lasagna she was making for dinner—hopefully to be shared with Tyler, if she could find him to invite him—she repeated them again. She could control the moment. She couldn't control the future.

She went to the window and peered out across the field where Tyler had taken the four-wheeler to check on cattle in a far pasture. No sign of him. She picked up the heavy pan and put it into the oven.

They'd fallen into a routine of sorts after their date at the Shamrock. During the day, they kept things businesslike. Tyler did his thing—the fencing and the maintenance—and she did hers—the feeding and the cow management. They didn't spend that much time together—they were at work, after all—but in the evening, Tyler would knock on her door, invite her out for a walk. Or a drive to town. And sometimes she invited him to dinner, as she was doing tonight.

They moved forward cautiously, both ultra-aware of the fact that Tyler would be leaving soon, and sometimes he would kiss her good-night before leaving her to go to his trailer. A gentle kiss that left her wanting more.

Part of his plan? She thought not. He was honestly trying not to spook her. To allow her time to come to terms with the fact that attraction didn't mean disaster… and that she could trust him.

Skye was going a little crazy with it all. She wanted more. She was afraid of more. She didn't want a fling, but she didn't want commitment. But she wanted Tyler.

And that seemed like a good way to totally screw up her life.

Live in the moment.

A truck pulled into the driveway, and Skye wiped her hands on a towel as she walked to the door. The guy was already halfway up the walk, carrying a vase of daisies and small rosebuds.

"Who're they from?" she asked, even though she could think of only one person who would send her flowers.

The guy shrugged. "Read the card."

She did and smiled. Flowers. Other than for her proms, she'd never received flowers. Mason hadn't been a flowers type of guy, but apparently Tyler was.

Who would have thought?

And what did she do about it?

Say thank you, and continue as usual. The only problem was that she wasn't certain about what usual entailed. They couldn't continue as they were indefinitely—but Tyler was leaving, so they could continue until then... unless she gave in and did what she really wanted to do. With him.

She was afraid—not of him, but of herself. Of needing someone and losing them.

But she couldn't stop thinking about the guy and... well...possibilities.

AT SIX O'CLOCK, after the lasagna had been out of the oven for almost half an hour, she started to suspect that something was wrong. Tyler was rarely this late getting back to the ranch when he worked the perimeters. At six thirty, as it was growing dark, she kicked off her heels and slipped into her barn boots. She grabbed the flashlight off the charger on the wall, pulled a hoodie on over her dress and headed outside, wishing she'd acted earlier. Something wasn't right.

She was tired of things not being right and she was tired of knee-jerk fear reactions, but if something had happened to him...

When she reached the middle of the driveway, she stopped as a flash of light in the middle of the pasture caught her eye and relief slammed into her. The light came bobbing closer and Skye realized it was from a cell phone. Tyler was almost to the pasture gate by the time she reached it.

"Did you get my flowers?" he asked as she undid the latch. His crooked smile almost did her in.

"I did. What happened?"

"The four-wheeler ran out of gas."

Her eyes widened, more out of anger than relief now

that she knew he was safe. Out of gas? "Damn it, Ty, I was scared to death—"

He reached for her and pulled her closer, bringing his hands up to frame her face before leaning down to touch his forehead to hers. She let out a ragged sigh as she felt the reassuring contact. He was close and he was okay. She took hold of his upper arms, felt the tightly bunched muscles beneath her palms. "Sorry," she murmured.

"The last thing I ever want to do is scare you, Skye. It was a stupid mistake. I was in a hurry this morning... I'm sorry."

Skye nodded against his forehead. "It's okay. I'm... easily triggered." But then, when she thought he was going to kiss her, he stepped back, dropped his hands.

She hated losing the connection.

Hated that she was afraid to move forward with anything. *Really, Skye? You can't go after what you want...what you* need?

He took her hand, and together they crossed the driveway to her porch, where he stopped. "I'm a mess," he said.

He was pretty muddy. Skye looked him over, then gave her head a shake. "I guess you need a shower."

"Yeah." He leaned in and gave her a quick kiss, before turning to start down the steps.

"Where are you going?" Her voice didn't sound like her own.

He shot her a frowning look over his shoulder. "To shower?"

She sucked up her courage, then gestured toward her front door with her head. "Would you like to use mine?"

The emotions that chased across Tyler's face would have been comical under other circumstances, but Skye didn't feel like laughing. She waited, her heart beating too hard, too fast, until he said, "Are you sure, Skye?"

She gave a small nod. "I've never been surer."

SKYE WAS SURE, but she was also nervous. Tyler could feel her pulse racing beneath his fingers as he took her hands and ran his thumb over her wrists. Too soon? He didn't want to push things.

She pulled a breath in over her teeth before pulling her hands out of his and Tyler felt a swell of disappointment, coupled with acceptance. Half a heartbeat later her arms were around his neck and her lips were on his, demanding what he'd been holding back for so long.

Tyler met her kiss, asking for more. Skye was where she belonged, in his arms, her soft curves pressing into him. He pushed one hand up into her soft hair as his other slid lower, over her firm bottom. Perfect. Utterly perfect. He deepened the kiss, bringing her even more tightly against him. He wanted her and now she was aware of just how much.

"I really do need a shower," he murmured against her mouth.

"So do I."

"How big is your shower?" he asked in a low voice, his hands running gently up and down over her back.

She smiled slowly. "Big enough."

And it was—big enough to allow the two of them to get wet, soap up, slowly explore one another's bodies. Before things got out of hand—just barely—Tyler cranked the water off and opened the glass door, allowing Skye to exit before him. Then he took a towel and slowly dried her off.

Her eyes went closed and her breath caught, but he continued to wipe away the moisture that clung to her perfect body.

He sensed that she was still nervous…but so was he.

Skye opened her eyes and held out her hand for the towel. "My turn."

"I…"

"Shh." She put the towel on his head and briskly dried his hair, smiling a little as she did so, but the smile faded as she began working the towel over his shoulders, his chest, his stomach…

Tyler was barely aware of moving, but the towel dropped to the floor as he swung Skye up into his arms, cradling her against his chest. There was so much he wanted to say, but more than that he wanted to act. To show Skye exactly how much he cared for her.

Skye gave a gasp at the intimate contact, then wound her arms more tightly around his neck. She touched his lips with hers before whispering, "My room is straight across the hall."

Chapter Thirteen

In less than forty-eight hours, Tyler would be on the road again. His shoulder felt good, probably because Skye had been nuts about not letting him use it over the past several weeks, and he hoped that he could finish the season, bring in some more money.

The ranch buildings were roofed. The cattle moved. The fence was fixed as well as he could fix it, and it was definitely good enough to keep the cattle—and a donkey—in until he got back, unless of course the cattle decided they really wanted out. Then there would probably be no stopping them. Blaine had already agreed to be on call if Skye needed help on the ranch, although he pointed out that she'd run the ranch just fine without him or Tyler until a few weeks ago. Tyler agreed, but he felt better knowing that someone was there when he and his brother were not around.

For the first time in his life, he wasn't practically jumping out of his skin in anticipation of getting back out onto the circuit. Yes, he wanted to ride, but he didn't like leaving Skye behind.

It was only for a matter of a few weeks, and then he'd have a break and be able to come home for a few days.

Home. Wow.

Things were moving rapidly, but he was good with that. He'd cared for Skye forever, and now it seemed as if she was allowing herself to care for him. They now shared her bed, and more and more of his belongings had made their way into her house.

They lived together and worked together and it seemed to be working. They didn't talk about the future, but Tyler had faith they were on the same page… that they were working toward a commitment.

She came out of the house and crossed the driveway to where he waited in the truck, looking great in slim-fitting jeans and a scoop-neck blue T-shirt, carrying a covered bowl for the potluck they were attending. The Founders Day picnic was a big community event, but he hadn't been to one in years, since he was usually on the road during the weekend it was held. Skye had told him she'd missed only one—last year's.

The parking lot was packed when they pulled in, and after he found parking, Skye hurried across the lot to put her pasta salad on the table with the other side dishes. Trace hailed Tyler from a table at the edge of the park, and as soon as Skye rejoined him, he took her hand and they crossed over to join the group at the same time that Grady Owen and his bride, Lex, approached from the opposite direction.

Lex had always scared Tyler a little. She was about as no-nonsense as a woman came and called things the way she saw them. Grady was smitten by her, which was funny, since for the longest time he'd considered her a sworn enemy. Very much as Skye had considered him to be the enemy. Funny how things worked out sometimes, even though he and Skye were still in the very early stages of nailing something down between them.

Trace and Annie's twins raced by with several kids in hot pursuit, one of them swinging a small lariat. Tyler gathered from the twins' laughs and whinnies that they were wild horses and the other kids were trying to capture them. Good game. He remembered playing it a time or two himself back in the day.

"Be careful!" Trace yelled to the kids as the boy swinging the rope tripped over the end and went down. He jumped back to his feet, and the chase continued.

"I wish I could bottle that energy," Annie said as the kids circled the swing set.

"You'd be rich," Skye agreed, taking a seat beside her.

Tyler sat next to Grady, and they discussed the standings in the tour as well as Tyler's chances of gaining enough points to make the finals.

"I'd like to final," he admitted, "but I think that's unlikely. Mostly I'd like to earn enough to cover my road expenses and the surgery, so I can start fresh next year."

"You mean fresh in April," Grady said.

It would take that long to recover, so yes, that was what he meant. And while he was recovering, he'd work the ranch. Not exactly a win-win, since surgery was involved, but close. He glanced over at Skye, who was deep in conversation with Lex and Annie, and smiled to himself. She was more relaxed than he'd ever seen her, and when she glanced up unexpectedly and caught him studying her, she smiled a little, then focused back on Lex.

Things were good. He hoped they stayed good.

SKYE HAD RARELY ever stayed at the Founders Day celebration after the cleanup, but this year there was a dance and fireworks and she wanted to stay. Tyler would be gone in less than two days, and she was going to indulge in her fantasy world for a little longer.

Was it really fantasy?

More like idyllic, and that would change as real life happened. If she and Tyler continued their slow process toward a relationship, they would eventually argue and learn to work out compromises. Life wouldn't be all roses...but it was all roses at the moment, and there wasn't one thing wrong with enjoying the present without worrying about the future.

Lex and Annie worked with her to clear the tables, placing the bowls on a long table in the kitchen facility where the owners could claim them before they left. When Skye came out of the kitchen with a bucket of warm water and a sponge to wash the tables, she caught sight of Tyler close to where the band was setting up, talking to Paige.

"I don't like her," Lex said as she came to join Skye in table-washing detail. There was no question whom she was talking about, since she gestured in the direction of Paige and Tyler with her chin.

Skye gave her a surprised look, but maybe it wasn't all that surprising. Lex didn't make friends easily. "Why's that?"

"Gut instinct."

Tyler smiled briefly at Paige then and turned and walked back to where Trace and his twins were sitting.

"She wants our ranch account for her new business."

"Just the account?" Lex asked.

"Well, no," Skye confessed. "But it's a small town

and exes have to see one another, and I don't think Ty's in the market." The important thing was that no matter where they were in their relationship, she trusted Tyler. He'd never lied to her—if anything he told her more truth than she wanted to hear. She needed to improve her breeding program—her fields were in rotten shape—and Vanessa was not the sweet goose Skye thought she was.

"Yeah. I think you're right there." Lex shot a look at Tyler. "He's as nailed down as I've ever seen him. Good work."

"Thanks," she said drily. She and Tyler had agreed to keep their budding relationship under wraps, but Cody had talked to Angie, who'd talked to the world, and there was now no such thing as being under wraps.

"No problem."

Skye and Lex finished the tables and then dumped the water. "I'm heading back out," she said as two guys came in with fresh black trash bags to reline the kitchen garbage cans.

"Tell Grady I'll be out shortly."

"Will do."

But when Skye started toward the table where Trace and Grady sat with Cody and Angie, who'd driven down from Missoula for the weekend, Tyler was gone.

"He's in the parking lot," Angie said before Skye could ask his whereabouts. "Talking to Paige." She gave Cody a tight-lipped sidelong look that made Skye's insides shift uneasily.

Things suddenly felt awkward at the table, as all eyes shifted toward Angie and then away again, and it appeared as if everyone was in on a deep, dark secret. What the heck?

Skye forced a smile and turned to head back to the kitchen, thinking she'd find Tyler later, when he was done talking to Paige in the parking lot. She'd only gone a couple of steps when she heard Cody ask Angie why she hadn't keep her mouth shut.

"I don't want that…thing…to happen to her again," Angie muttered in her quietest voice, which wasn't quiet at all.

It was all Skye could do not to turn on her heel and march back to the small group to discover what that "thing" was, but she continued her forward path. She'd talk to Angie later. Or better yet, she'd talk to Tyler, who was coming toward her from the direction of the parking lot. Paige's brand-new car backed out of a parking space and roared past them, out of the lot.

"What was that about?" Skye asked as Tyler looped an arm around her shoulders.

"I told her we weren't going to use her services." He gave her a look. "She might be good at what she does, but too much potential for complications."

"Must be rough being irresistible."

"A burden," he agreed. As he steered them toward the table where the bull riders sat, Skye slowed her steps. "Is something wrong?"

"I don't know."

"What does that mean?"

She shifted her position so that she was facing him. The uneasy feeling had yet to abate, and she decided that maybe an answer or two was in order. "Do you know of any secret thing that could happen to me… again?"

"What?"

"When you were in the parking lot with Paige,

Angie whispered something to Cody about not wanting that thing to happen to me again."

Tyler's gaze instantly jerked over to the bull riders' table, and she saw Cody give a small shrug. The knot in her stomach tightened. There was something she didn't know. Paige. Tyler. The "thing."

Her lips parted as a wild idea struck her. Crazy thought. It couldn't be.

"What don't I know?" she demanded.

His expression clouded, and she could see that he was fighting to find a response—one that she would find palatable.

"Tyler...explain this to me."

The look he gave her was both dark and pained. He shook his head. "It would be better if we just went home."

"Better for whom?"

He didn't answer. Skye glanced behind them, saw the three bull riders and Angie staring at them as if waiting for the aftermath of the events just set into motion. She looked back at Tyler, her stomach so tight that it was all she could do to hold nausea at bay as her theory continued to form.

It couldn't be.

"Tell me," she repeated.

He looked past her. "Not here." Tyler reached down to take her hand and interlace his fingers with hers. "Let's go."

Skye stood frozen for a moment and then nodded. They walked to his truck, and as always, Tyler opened the door for her. She climbed in but could see by Tyler's set expression that he wasn't about to discuss anything until they got back to the ranch.

It was not a long drive home, but tonight it felt never-ending. Angie hadn't been talking gambling. If she had, Tyler would have told her back in the parking lot.

By the time Tyler parked next to the barn, Skye's heart was beating as if she'd just run a couple of fast miles. He turned off the ignition and shifted in the seat so that he was half facing her.

"Yes or no, Tyler...did Mason cheat on me?" His mouth was a hard flat line that gave no sign of budging. "Tell me."

"Yes."

Arrow to the heart.

She couldn't breathe. Couldn't talk. Couldn't cry. She was...frozen.

She never suspected. Never, ever, ever. And how stupid did that make her?

"Skye."

She blinked at Tyler. "Who knows?" she asked lowly. "Does everyone know?"

"No."

"How did *you* know?"

"Because he wasn't that good at sneaking around."

"So...anyone who was on the circuit with him..." She swallowed, unable to finish the sentence.

Tyler stretched his arm along the seat, let his fingertips brush her shoulder, but she jerked away from his touch. "Grady, Trace and Cody are the only people in Gavin who know."

"And that explains Angie."

"Cody must have told her."

Skye closed her eyes, drew in a painful breath. This was close to how she'd felt when the sheriff's deputy had come to her house eighteen months ago with the unthinkable news about her husband. Very, very close.

"I know you're hurting."

Her eyes came open. "You have no concept. My entire relationship with my dead husband was a lie."

"Not all of it."

"Oh yeah? What part was real? The part where I trusted him? The part where I thought he had integrity?"

Tyler had no answer to that. She could see that he wanted to touch her, and she hoped beyond hope that he didn't. If he did, she would shatter. As it was, her skin seemed to burn and her throat was closing, but tears...there were no tears. Mason deserved no tears.

"He—"

"Do *not* tell me that he loved me." Skye clamped her teeth together then, so tightly that it seemed a miracle that they didn't crack and break.

"Let me stay with you, Skye."

She stared at him. Company? Now? No freaking way. She reached for the door handle and jerked it open. "No."

He flattened his mouth again, as if afraid that words she didn't want to hear were somehow going to escape. She shut the door and marched around the front of the truck and up the walk to her house. Once inside she snapped on the porch light but didn't bother with the interior light. Darkness. It was crowding her soul, so why not welcome it? Revel in it.

She sank down onto the sofa and sat, numbly staring across the room as her eyes adjusted to minimal light.

Her husband, her trusted husband, had lied to her. And Tyler had, too. And...so had everyone else who knew and didn't tell her. How stupid had she looked? The supportive wife who managed the ranch. Did extra duty so that her husband could follow his dreams.

She gathered a pillow to her middle, squeezed it hard, then threw it across the room, jumping a mile when a light rap sounded on the door. Without pausing to think, Skye jumped to her feet, crossed the room and yanked the door open.

"What?" she demanded.

"I don't have to go tomorrow."

She gaped at him through the semidarkness. "Why would I want you to stay?"

His chin jerked as if she'd just struck him. She couldn't help that. "Skye—"

"Why didn't you tell me?"

"Because there was no reason to tell you. Nothing could be changed or fixed. How would knowing have helped anything?" He took a step closer. "How is it helping now?"

"I'll tell you how it's helping," Skye said. "It's helping me understand that I can't trust my own instincts. That I don't know what I think I do. And that things that seem right can be very, very wrong."

He lifted his hands, as if to pull her into his embrace, and she took a step back. "Don't touch me."

"All right."

"I want…no, *I need*…to be alone."

"I understand."

"And I want the ranch to myself. When you come back on break, we'll talk. But tomorrow… I don't want to see you before you leave."

"Right." There was a clip to his voice now, as if he was also getting angry.

"I'm going to bed." She took hold of the door, and Tyler was wise enough to simply step back and allow her to close it.

Once the door was shut, Skye waited until she heard Tyler's boots head down the porch steps. That was when she felt the liquid fire running down her cheeks, dripping onto her chest.

Tears ran like rain, and she did nothing to stop the flow. She was a mess. Her life was a mess.

How was she ever supposed to trust herself or anyone else again?

Chapter Fourteen

Tyler paced through his trailer, unable to sleep. Skye's kitchen lights had come on not long after she'd shut the door on him and had yet to go off. What was she doing?

It was killing him to have to hang back and let her deal with Mason's betrayal on her own, even though logic told him that was the only way she could deal. What he hadn't expected was that she would lash out at him.

How was he supposed to head out on tour with things like they were? But he had to go. She needed time. He needed to make some money. She said they'd talk when he got back, and he was going to hold her to that, even though he hated the thought of her dealing with this alone.

Why couldn't Angie—and Cody—have kept their mouths shut? He was having a hard time tamping down his anger. Neither of them meant Skye any harm, but…

Tyler finally fell asleep sprawled on his small sofa sometime after 2:00 a.m. When he woke up, it was daylight and Skye's truck was gone. He shoved his feet into his boots and headed outside. The animals were fed, and the gray cat was sunning himself near the barn. He went back to his trailer and sat on the step. He didn't have to leave to catch his flight to Portland until after Skye got home from shift, and he was waiting until the last possible moment. Yeah, she wanted to be left alone, but he had a few things he wanted to say before heading out on the road.

Things he had to say.

He loaded his truck, checked everything on the ranch he could think to check, paced his trailer. Waited.

When Skye's usual arrival time came and went, he paced more. It was close to the time when he had to leave to catch his flight in Butte when he called the diner and asked what time Skye had left.

She'd left two hours before her shift was over. Chloe had covered for her. Tyler hung up, his gut tense with worry, when he heard the sound of her truck. He grabbed his keys and headed to the door. If the traffic was with him, he might still make the flight. Skye was getting out of the truck when he came out the door.

"Why are you still here?" she asked.

"I was worried about you." She looked sideways as if it pained her to hear that answer. He crossed the distance between them. "Nothing has changed between us, Skye."

Her eyes narrowed as if she couldn't believe he'd either said that or believed it.

"Things have changed with me, Tyler."

"How so?"

"Have you ever been betrayed?"

"I didn't betray you."

She gave him a look that clearly said she wasn't so certain about that before saying, "That wasn't the question."

Fine. He'd answer the question. "Not in a big way."

Skye pushed her hands into her pockets, the way she did when she was stressed. "If you ever had been, you'd understand that it makes you question everything."

"You don't need to question me, Skye."

"I don't know that."

He took a couple of paces closer, stopping when she gave him a warning look. "You do know that. I love you."

Her chin jerked up. "Don't."

But he did. He came forward and put his hands on her stiff shoulders. If anything, they stiffened even more. He hung on anyway, bringing his face closer to hers as he said, "I. Love. You. I understand that you don't want to hear it, but you need to know it before I leave." He let go of her and took a step back.

"Mason said he loved me, too. You saw how that turned out."

Anger flashed, catching him off guard. He sucked in a breath before saying in a deadly voice, "Don't *ever* put me in the same class as Mason. I did not make him gamble, I did not make him cheat and I'm in no way like him." He looked away, then brought his gaze back to clash with hers. Yeah, she was hurting. Lashing out. Well, he was starting to smart a little, too. "For the record, I hate that you would lump us together."

"Mason lied to me, you lied to me—" He started to cut her off, but she raised a finger in a warning gesture. "By omission, but it still feels like betrayal."

"So what now?"

"Things go back to the way they used to be. When our lives were very much separate."

"And you didn't have to take any risks?"

"If you were me, would you take risks?" Before he

could answer, she said, "Risks are not working for me. I want my nice, solitary life where no one slips a knife between my ribs when I'm not looking."

"And just like that, we're done?"

"No, Tyler. We're not done. We're business partners."

"And that's all?"

She gave a nod, and her voice was crisp and cold as she said, "Do not ask for more."

TYLER CAUGHT THE tour in New Mexico, where he had an okay ride. The bull he'd drawn wasn't the meanest bucker in the bunch, and even though he'd ridden for eight, his score didn't put him in the money. His shoulder had held up, though, so he was glad he'd followed doctor's orders and taken the time off—at least in the sense of having healed his body. As far as his personal life went, well, that was about as screwed up as it could get.

Should he have told Skye about Mason?

Why inflict pain when it wasn't necessary? Why destroy memories and the illusion of trust? He might have been wrong, but it still killed him to think of Skye's expression, which was freeze-framed into his brain, when she'd figured out what Angie had meant. What had been the chances of Skye ever finding out? Before the Founders Day celebration, before Cody had taken up with Angie, he would have said close to zero.

After Albuquerque, he caught a ride with another bull rider, Caiden Craig—aka CC—first to Phoenix, then to Bakersfield. Both of those rides were good, and he earned some money in Bakersfield. The next leg started in Denver, moved on to Salt Lake City, then Billings and Spokane, but he had three days before Denver—enough time to fly home, get his truck and drive down. He'd promised CC rides between these legs, so he'd have company he wasn't certain he wanted. It all depended on his reception when he went back to the ranch.

It'd been difficult staying in radio silence over the past two weeks, thus giving Skye time to work through issues. And maybe time to miss him? A guy could only hope.

And he did hope...even while a small part of him said that it was going to take her a long time to trust anyone again.

He had time. He was her business partner.

Tyler's flight landed in Butte at 11:30 p.m. He tossed his duffel into the back of his truck, paid the parking ransom and started driving to Gavin. His plan was simple—get some sleep and whenever Skye was available, they'd discuss the ranch—the safe topic. The last thing he expected was for the lights in her house to be blazing when he drove down the long driveway in the early hours of the morning. When he parked, he saw her pull the curtain back and then drop it again.

Let it be.

He headed past her house and around the bunkhouse to his trailer, stopping when he heard the distinctive sound of her screen door shutting and her footsteps on the porch. Turning back around, he met her at the corner of the bunkhouse.

"I didn't expect you back," she said in a low voice. "Not yet anyway."

"I wanted to drive to Denver."

"Ah." She hugged her arms around herself.

"What are you doing up so late?"

For a moment he thought she wasn't going to answer, but since it was past 2:00 a.m. and she was still fully dressed, she must have figured she had to give some kind of explanation. "I was cleaning."

"Why?"

"It's what I do when I can't sleep."

His lips parted, and he wanted to reach for her. Pull her into his arms and make everything all right—or as right as he could. Skye read his face, took a step back, hugging her arms around herself more tightly.

"How long are you home?"

"I take off on Wednesday." The day after tomorrow. "Is everything okay here?"

"Yeah. Good. I got the chicken house built."

"Can't wait to see it." He hesitated, the duffel growing heavier in his hand. "Can we talk tomorrow before I have to go?"

She let out a soft sigh. "I'm off tomorrow. We can talk. About the ranch."

He glanced up at the starry sky. Things were no better than when he'd left. Maybe now that she'd had time to stew, they were even worse. "Understood."

She turned, but before she made it around the corner, he said, "I am not the enemy, Skye."

He had no idea whether she'd heard him or not.

SKYE AWOKE TO a buzzing text message. Feeling as if she'd gotten a whopping thirty seconds of sleep, she grabbed her phone, noted the time to be 10:30 a.m. and then flopped back against the pillows, bringing the phone with her to read the text. She sat up a little when she saw that it was from Tyler.

Have to take off early for unexpected promo event.

Maybe she had heard a knocking on her door a while back. She thought for a moment, then texted back.

Meet in half an hour?

Sure.

Skye threw back the covers and went to the bathroom to start the shower, then headed to the kitchen to make a new pot of coffee. The one that had been simmering since five thirty, her normal wake-up time, would probably not be all that drinkable. She checked the clock again before she went back to the bathroom. When was the last time she'd overslept?

She showered quickly, dried her hair, then twisted it into a knot on the back of her head before dressing in jeans and an oversize baseball jersey. No one could accuse her of trying to look attractive today, but when she answered the knock on her door ten minutes later, she could see that it didn't matter what she wore. Tyler's gaze zeroed in on her face.

"When do you have to leave?" she asked.

"In about an hour. It's for a local television appearance in Denver. I'm getting interviewed before the event."

"Ah." Skye poured coffee and set two cups on the table, but neither of them sat down. It became obvious after a few seconds that she needn't have poured. She folded her arms and leaned back against the counter. "You did well, I see."

"So far so good."

"The shoulder is holding up?"

He nodded. "I miss you, Skye."

She pressed her fingers against her forehead. "I miss what I thought was true." Her entire foundation had been rocked, and at this point, she didn't know if she had enough foundation left to rebuild. She was hurting. She was numb. And so not ready to slip back into what she and Tyler had started to explore.

"What do you want, Skye?"

She gave a short humorless laugh. "Honestly? To have my ranch back. My life back."

"I wish I could do that for you," Tyler said, getting to his feet. "Unfortunately, I have too much money sunk into the place."

"I know."

She spoke without looking at him. He said nothing and when she glanced up, she found him studying her with a faint frown, and for a moment it was all she could do to breathe correctly.

"Hiding from life isn't going to help, Skye. It's only going to make things worse."

Her chin lifted. "I'm not hiding from life. I'm living it on my terms."

An expression of disbelief combined with something that looked like pity crossed his handsome face, which in turn sparked anger deep inside her. Before she could speak, he said, "I am not Mason."

"I need time, Tyler."

"And you, more than most, should know that time is not guaranteed." He looked as if he wanted to say more, then instead he turned and strode out the door, letting the screen bang shut behind him.

Skye didn't move. She barely breathed.

This was for the best. Tyler could live his life and she could live hers. They might have some awkward moments on the ranch, but it appeared that she'd finally gotten it through his thick bull rider skull that she wouldn't risk getting smacked down again. Not for a long, long time.

WHAT DID IT say about Skye's life that her only confidant was a cat?

It said that she'd gotten exactly what she'd asked for.

At least Skye could vent to Jinx and he wouldn't spill her secrets. Chloe very much wanted Skye to spill her secrets. She didn't know what was wrong, but, because Skye had been unable to hide the fact that *something* was wrong, Chloe was clucking around her like a mama hen. If Angie had still worked there, then Chloe and the world would have known everything, but Cody must have come down hard on his girlfriend, because not one person seemed to know what had transpired between her and Tyler and her dead husband. And Sara Sullivan, the temporary new hire, pretty much kept to herself. She was dealing with an upcoming wedding and an overbearing mother, and it appeared that she had enough issues in her life without concerning herself with those in Skye's life.

"You're worried about your bull rider, aren't you?" Chloe asked seven days after Tyler had left for the second time, and somehow Skye refrained from telling her that Tyler was not *her* bull rider.

"He's a professional and good at what he does," Skye replied evenly. Then, to keep Chloe from continuing to question her, she said, "But of course I worry." She did, and Tyler's comment about not knowing how much time one had didn't help matters.

Chloe seemed happy to have a verified reason for Skye's preoccupation, and Skye was glad she didn't have to explain further how her life had been turned upside down and why. Upside down and inside out. It didn't seem fair that she kept getting hit by stuff, but what could she do except buckle down and deal with matters?

In the week that Tyler had been gone, she had finished her chicken yard and painted the chicken house bright red with white trim. Cliff had some laying hens he was willing to part with, and Skye planned to stop by his place on her first day off. Chickens would make the ranch cheerier, give her something new to focus on. Something to keep her from thinking about the big hole in her life.

She'd felt much the same after Mason died, and, in a way, it was as if he'd died again. How long was it going to take her to get over the fact that he betrayed her in ways she hadn't suspected?

Had there been clues?

She couldn't remember any, but she hadn't been looking. And every time she tried to think of reasons why her husband would stray while on the road, the knife in her heart twisted just a little more. She wanted to rage at Mason. To verbally beat on him. To tell him how he'd destroyed everything that had been good about their relationship with his lies. That she could have forgiven him the gambling, the lies of omission… but not cheating.

She couldn't forgive him, couldn't forgive herself for being so patently unaware.

It was too bad that Tyler was caught in the cross fire, but their relationship had been young. He'd said he loved her. Had practically shaken while he'd said the words, but all they'd done was freeze her up. Mason had professed to love her and she'd believed him, because she wanted to.

She wanted to believe that Tyler loved her, too—and maybe he did. But she was too afraid to believe it. To trust him...or herself.

Tyler did not contact her after leaving. She knew about his rides because she looked them up on the bull-riding sites. He was doing well in the standings, although it would be nip and tuck as to whether he'd make finals after his hiatus. Regardless, he was in the money, which made her feel good. He would be solely dependent on the ranch to see him through the winter financially. Maybe if he earned enough, he'd become an absentee partner. Surely that would be better than the two of them bumping into each other over the course of their days.

And what if he got a girlfriend?

No matter what she told herself, that wouldn't be easy to handle.

Tough. You will handle it.

SKYE WAS GETTING ready to drive to Cliff's farm when she heard the sound of an engine and looked out her bedroom window to see a familiar truck park next to her car.

Skye's stomach lurched, and she instantly headed for the door. Why would Jess be there unless something had happened to his twin?

"Hey," he called easily as she walked out onto the porch, and her hammering heart slowed.

"Hi." She stopped at the newel post and set a hand on it, hoping she looked calmer than she felt. "What are you doing here?"

"Checking in on my brother's investment."

She frowned. "How so?"

He stopped at the bottom of the stairs, propped his hands on his hips. "I drove to Billings to watch Tyler ride last night, and he asked me to stop by."

And a small part of her had secretly hoped that since he was so close, that he would spend a night or two on the ranch—a very small part that was quickly beaten into submission.

"To check on me or the property?"

"He was pretty clear about it being just the property. He wanted me to have a sit-down with you. Make sure everything is all right, because he probably won't be back for months."

Skye's heart did a double beat. Months. That was what she wanted. Right? Time to recover, get her footing back.

"I didn't see that coming," she said, gesturing for Jess to follow her into the house.

"Neither did I," Jess said as he closed the door behind him. "Tyler always comes home when he's close." He gave Skye a look that she couldn't say she felt comfortable with—as if she were to blame. A second later she decided that she'd misinterpreted, because he smiled at her and asked if she had any coffee left.

After pouring two cups, she sat at the table and Jess sat on the opposite side. "Have you bought hay?"

"I need Tyler's half of the money if we're going to go without a loan this year."

Jess pulled a notebook out of his shirt pocket and jotted down a few words, then looked back up at her. "When are you shipping cows?"

"Two weeks." She cupped her hands around the heavy coffee mug. "Will Tyler be back for that?"

"I don't see that happening. He wants Blaine and me to help you."

"I see." But she didn't. What was with the rock-in-the-pit-of-her-stomach feeling? She forced the corners of her mouth up.

Jess flipped the notebook page. "Tyler wants to buy a few registered Angus to replace the empty cows you're shipping."

"Maybe he and I should talk about that."

Jess looked over the notebook. "As I understand it, talking isn't going that well between you two."

"He told you?"

He smirked at her. "I know my brother."

And what did she say to that?

He closed the notebook. "You know I love you, Skye." When he said it, it didn't feel threatening at all. "But you're ruining my brother."

She was ruining *him*? Right.

Jess reached across the table and pried her hand off her coffee cup, gripping her fingers hard. "My brother has been in love with you forever."

Skye started shaking her head before she was even aware of moving. "I can't help that."

"Yeah?" Jess sounded unimpressed with her adamant tone. "I think you could, if you had the guts."

"Guts?" Skye pulled her fingers out of Jess's grip

and clasped her hands together tightly. "How dare you?" She asked the question flatly, grimly, with no hint of dramatics.

"I dare because I care about both of you."

"That doesn't make things any easier."

He put his hand on top of her clasped hands. "I'm not trying to make things easier for you. I'm looking out for my brother."

Her chin jerked up and she met his gaze. "Did you know about Mason? Not the gambling, but…"

Jess gave a slow nod.

"For how long have you known?"

"Probably since it started." Jess's mouth hardened. "Tyler was so damned angry when he found out." He rubbed his forehead, as if somehow feeling his brother's pain, then set his palm flat on the table. "There was nothing he could do about it."

"He could have told me," she snapped.

Jess leaned forward. "When, Skye? Before Mason died? After? When could he have told you? How would you have taken it?"

Instead of answering, Skye dropped her gaze to her tightly clenched hands, closed her eyes, attempted to gather her thoughts so that she could battle on. She'd been over the same questions a couple hundred times, and there were no easy answers.

"Skye?" Jess's voice softened as he spoke, as if he recognized that she was on the edge of breaking. She wasn't, and she needed to tell him that…but she didn't.

Instead she raised her eyes and said, "This is a complicated matter, Jess."

Complicated and messy and hurtful. She hated being duped and feeling like a fool. She hated that people had known things—bad things—about her husband that she hadn't known.

And…she hated that she totally understood why no one had told her about Mason's behavior.

As much as she wanted to lash out and blame someone, there was no one to blame except for Mason for cheating and herself for not picking up on it—and for blindly trusting her untrustworthy husband.

Where did that leave her?

It left her afraid to trust her own judgment. And she certainly didn't trust those close to her to let her in on secrets that impacted her life in a big way. Angie had known about Mason before she had, and that was simply wrong.

"I agree," Jess said. "It is complicated. But it doesn't need to be impossible." The understanding note in his voice brought her closer to breaking than his accusatory tone had.

Skye swallowed, drew in a breath. Confessed. "I'm afraid."

"I know."

"I thought Mason and I had a good marriage. I could forgive the gambling. But the other… I didn't have a good marriage." Jess nodded and squeezed her hand. "But I thought I did. That's what scares me to death."

"Legitimately so." He cleared his throat. "I know you've been blindsided and I know you have to work through things, but…"

She pressed her lips together, then let loose with the truth. "I've been applying for bank loans again. To buy Tyler out. Things can't continue like they are. It will make us both miserable." Jess scowled at her and Skye frowned back. "It's what I have to do."

"And if you can't get a loan?"

"Then I guess we continue like this, with you as the go-between, until I do get a loan. You said yourself that Tyler didn't want to see me."

"He's doing that for you."

"And I appreciate it."

Jess pushed his untouched coffee aside and got to his feet. "Can you answer me one question?"

"It's probably not a question I want to answer," she said. "But I'll do my best."

"Do you love my brother?"

"It's not a question of love, Jess. It's a question of trust."

"You didn't answer my question."

No she hadn't. And that, in itself, was an answer.

After a few beats of silence, Jess shook his head. "I'll pass the information on to Tyler."

"Thank you."

He went to the door, opened it, then turned back. "One more thing, Skye…"

"What's that?" Her stomach tightened.

"I want you to think—really think—about what you're sacrificing…and what you're gaining."

"And what I'm losing?" she asked lightly, playing the game, thinking that it was so easy to give advice when one's own future and emotions were not involved.

"Yeah."

Chapter Fifteen

Skye hadn't seen Angie since the Founders Day celebration when her world had been turned upside down, and she assumed that was no accident, since it was common knowledge that Angie traveled to Gavin on the weekends to stay with Cody. Therefore, it came as a surprise to see the former waitress sitting in a booth on her side of the café early Thursday morning. Skye picked up her coffeepot and headed over to the table.

"How are you doing?" Angie asked in a subdued voice as Skye poured the coffee.

"I'm doing okay." Most of time anyway. Normally she enjoyed her job, and she was good at it. Today she wasn't enjoying it so much. An out-of-town couple had been rude and demanding, and now Angie was here and Skye had to remind herself that the woman's only crime, other than partaking in rampant gossip, was whispering too loudly. "How's cosmetology school?"

"I like it. I think I'll be good at it."

"And think of how much gossip you'll pick up," Skye murmured. She was done tiptoeing around people's feelings.

"About that… I'm sorry I was the one who made you realize that—"

"My husband had cheated on me? I'm better off knowing." Skye held the coffeepot close to her chest. "Don't you think?"

"Cody dumped me after that."

"I didn't know."

"We're back together again...but he made me see some things I hadn't realized before. Like..."

"Gossip hurts?"

Angie pressed her lips together and nodded. Skye gave a casual shrug. "It hurt me, but I'm thankful that I know the whole truth now. So maybe in this case, gossip was a good thing."

"If you say so."

Skye bit her lip and then, after scanning the room to make certain all of her tables were doing okay, slid into the booth across from Angie. "I do say so, and no hard feelings, okay?"

Angie's eyes were getting red. "Cody told me that I'm the reason you and Tyler broke up."

Skye shook her head. "Circumstances did that. I'm..." What? "...not ready for a relationship."

Only a partial truth, that. She'd been ready to ease forward slowly. Tyler had been good with not rushing matters, and then...bam! The truth had smacked her in the face. Scared her back into her hidey-hole.

"I needed to know the truth," she said firmly. "I may not have wanted to know it, but I'm better off." Unless there were other lies out there, but she was fairly certain that her late husband held no more secrets.

Angie reached across the table and touched her hand. "I'm not trying to gossip here, but I think you and Tyler were a good couple and I think you should know that Paige is still following him around."

"Following him?"

"She's been traveling to bull-riding events. Casper. Billings. I've seen her."

Skye sat back against the booth cushions, surprised at how much she hated the idea of Paige being anywhere near Tyler.

"Is that gossip?" Angie asked in a low voice, as if afraid that Cody might find out she'd been telling tales out of school again.

Skye shook her head. "No. It's just the truth, and if she's not keeping things secret, then there's no need for you to do so."

Angie's face brightened. "Yeah. I guess that's the way to measure things."

Skye reached out to pat Angie's arm, then slid out of the booth and picked up the coffeepot. "I agree. The truth isn't gossip, unless there's a reason to keep it secret. Then it's not your place, or mine, to tell the tale."

Angie finished her coffee, then came to the counter to pay and say goodbye. "I hope things are better between us," she said.

Skye gave her a quick hug. "Things are fine. Come see me next time you're in town."

Angie was smiling when she left the café. Skye, not so much.

Paige was following Tyler around?

Well, that had to stop…even though it wasn't really her business. Was it?

It sure felt like her business. Skye glanced around the dining room. Everyone was happily engaged in their meals, so she slipped back to the pantry, propped hands on a shelf and dropped her chin to her chest.

She had no right to be jealous of Paige, but she was.

She wanted Tyler, but she was of terrified of losing again, terrified of trusting and being emotionally backhanded. So freaking scared that she was willing to give up the possibility of happiness for the safety that came of hiding from life.

So what was she going to do about it?

Or better still, what *could* she do about it?

"Excuse me...?"

Skye's head jerked up at the customer's voice and she quickly stepped out of the pantry and headed across the café to her patron. Real life called.

DESPITE HIS SHOULDER INJURY, Tyler was on a roll. He made the semifinals in Denver, the final round in Casper and had won Billings. Even if his shoulder had slid in and out of the socket during the ride, he had every intention of winning again in Spokane. Injury was not an option. He needed the sheer physicality of riding to help battle the frustrations in his life. As long as he was focused on the bull, he was fine. It was during the long drives and the social functions associated with the events that the frustrations built and he found himself getting antsy.

Jess phoned while he was on the road to Spokane with his friend CC sleeping in the passenger seat, head bobbing against the window. Everything was fine on the ranch. No set date for shipping cows, and, well... Skye was looking for financing to buy him out.

That stung.

If he'd done her wrong, if he'd messed up like Mason, or if they'd dated and she'd decided he wasn't her type, he could have lived with it. But that wasn't how it was. He was collateral damage in Skye's battle with fear of loss. She hadn't come out and told him that, but it was too big to miss.

As he saw it, he had two choices—fight back, or walk away gracefully. Give her what she wanted.

"She's doing all right," Jess said. "In a walled-off way…the way she was after Mason died."

Because she was mourning another loss. This one probably almost as devastating as the first. Now she didn't even have fond memories. She had nothing.

Ty had a strong feeling that she also wanted nothing, except to maybe be left alone.

"You won't be making Spokane, will you?"

"Wish I could. I have to be in Kalispell the next day." A short silence hung between them, and then Jess said, "If you want to move your trailer onto my lot, there's room."

"Yeah. I know." He'd already done his figuring there, and now, once again, his question was should he stay on the ranch he owned part of, move to his brother's place or maybe head down to Texas, where, even if he couldn't put Skye out of his head, he could at least put some distance between them?

The one thing he did know was that he needed to dissolve their partnership, so that if he and Skye ever did try to hash things out between them, there wouldn't be a ranch hanging between them.

THERE WERE FRESH tire tracks on her driveway when Skye drove in but no vehicle and no sign of a package delivery. Someone needing directions, perhaps?

No. It had been Tyler, there and gone while she'd been at work. He'd left a note on her locked front door telling her that he'd left something for her in his trailer.

Skye folded the note and carried it with her as she retraced her steps down the path and around the bunk-house to the trailer. It was unlocked, so she opened the door and stepped inside.

It smelled like Tyler.

She pressed her lips together after inhaling deeply, then crossed to the table where a large envelope with her name on it lay. She opened it and pulled out the single sheet of paper.

The mortgage agreement. At the bottom he had printed PAID IN FULL.

What the heck?

Skye sank down on the hard cushion of the futon-like sofa. There was only one reason he would have done this. He was leaving. Going to Texas as he'd once said he was. In fact, there was a Texas road map lying on top of a stack of books.

Skye closed her eyes, feeling ridiculously close to tears. Things were happening too quickly. Yes, she'd thought she wanted to end things before they became too serious, but now she feared they already were too serious.

She felt like her stomach was turning inside out. *I love him...and I'm a coward. I'm using Mason's betrayal as an excuse to hide from the normal risks one takes in life.*

What was it Tyler had said to her? You never know how much time you have. Skye put the agreement back into the envelope and slid in the note Tyler had left on her front door.

Then she reached into her pocket for her phone, pulled up her contact list, drew in a deep breath and yet again prepared to eat humble pie. When the line picked up, she said, "Hello, Jess…I need a favor."

THE LAST TIME Skye had been in Nampa, Idaho, had been with Mason, just after they were married. She'd traveled to several events with her new husband before settling in to run the ranch and earn their one steady paycheck by working at the café. Skye hadn't loved living alone for weeks at a time, but it wasn't something she hated, either. It was the reality of their existence, and she knew it would last for only a matter of years before Mason retired from bull riding and ranched full-time.

Little had she known…

But Skye wasn't going there. Yes, she was borderline terrified, but letting the past color her future to the extent that she embraced the idea of rattling around in an empty life because it was "safe" bordered on wrong. And cowardly.

Face the truth.

Her seat was not the best, but what could she expect for minimum dollar and last minute? She was squeezed between a family with four children happily eating gooey cotton candy and an elderly couple wearing very large cowboy hats. Twice Skye had cotton candy stuck in her hair before the child's mother intervened and changed seats with her daughter.

"Sorry," she murmured.

"Not a problem." Skye sat up straighter as the show began. The arena lights dimmed, smoke swirled and the bull riders walked out into the arena as colored LED lights danced over them. She instantly recognized Tyler by his walk, and her heart swelled.

She was not giving this guy up.

She only hoped that giving up the ranch didn't mean that he was giving up on her. He was a bull rider. Stubborn.

Then the lights went low and the show began. Skye dodged another wallop from the cotton candy as the little girl squeezed past her to head for the restroom with her mother, then settled in to watch her guy do what he loved.

She didn't have long to wait. Tyler was up fourth, and after the usual fanfare, the gateman pulled the rope and Little Biscuit, a big Charolais-Brahman cross, exploded out of the chute and she realized that, just as he'd once promised, he was wearing a helmet. No more stitched-up face. Not unless he got clocked really good.

Little Biscuit spun to his left then flipped his hind end the opposite direction, throwing Tyler over his hand. He pushed deep, recovered and was well settled by the time Little Biscuit did his opposite spin. Four seconds left. Three…

The bull did a high buck and looked as if he was going to sunfish, but instead came down with a jarring front-end landing as the buzzer rang. A cheer went up from the crowd, but Skye stayed where she was, gripping the seat on either side of her until Tyler disembarked and rolled as the bull bucked past him toward the gate.

Only then did she lean back and let out the breath she'd been holding for fifteen long seconds.

HE WAS A winner and a loser. Tyler hadn't taken home the top check, but he'd scored third, and that made him a winner. Walking out of the arena alive made him a winner. It was having no one and nowhere to go home to that gave him the loser feeling.

He'd have to see about moving his trailer off the property. His parents had assured him they'd love to see him in Texas. He imagined they would.

Problem was…he was a Montana guy, and it was hard to change that.

He'd been interviewed, along with several other riders, immediately following the event, and then he'd had to get his shoulder bandaged up to immobilize it—just a precaution, since once again it had felt as if it had slid in and out of the socket.

Just a few more months…like four. He could do this.

He left the arena by a side door, stepping into an almost empty parking lot. The next event was on the other side of the Mississippi, and he was flying. He'd park his truck at Jess's, see what he could do about his current living situation. His boots echoed on the pavement, and as he approached his truck, he slowed.

Maybe he'd been hit in the head harder than he'd realized when he'd gone to the ground, because the woman leaning against his truck, head down, hugging her arms around herself, looked just like Skye, about five hundred miles from where she was supposed to be. As he started walking faster, and his footsteps began echoing on the pavement, her head snapped up, and his heart tumbled.

"Skye?"

She stepped away from the truck, and then her spine stiffened as she took in his bandaged arm. "Is it bad?" she asked.

"Depends." He stopped a goodly distance away from her. If she was here, that was good. But his gut told him to move slowly. Find out the whole story. "Did you get my note?"

"I did."

"And?"

She took a couple of steps toward him, arms still crossed over her body as if she were protecting herself. But when she stopped in front of him, she dropped her arms to her sides and tilted up her chin. "Thank you for the gift, but I don't want it."

"That makes no sense at all."

"It does if I want to keep you around."

His heart did a couple of hard beats against his ribs. He turned his head to look at her sideways. "You better take this offer while you can." The fair-play part of him insisted that he say those words. "I may be bankrupt by this time next year."

She shook her head.

"Why do you want to keep a broken-down bull rider around?"

"I love him."

Another double beat of his heart. Tyler wanted to move closer but instead stayed put. No more jumping ahead of himself, buying ranches and the like. "Do you trust him?"

"Yes," she said simply. "If I don't have trust, then I have a ranch house with just me and a cat in it. Which was fine a couple of months ago, but it's not fine anymore." She exhaled, and it sounded shaky, as if her voice was on the edge of breaking. "I need you, Tyler."

That was when he moved, ignoring the pain as he pulled her against him, found her lips. Every time he kissed the woman it felt like a homecoming, and it was no different tonight.

"So," he murmured against her lips, "you want to keep things as they are?"

"Yes. As they are. We're partners." She eased back a little, so that they could see each other clearly.

"Let me make certain I totally understand." Because he wanted this carved in stone. "You want to be with me."

"Yes."

His eyes narrowed as he thought of Annie and Trace and Lex and Grady.

"Maybe you could travel with me?"

She brought her hands back up to frame his face. "Maybe…but I have chickens in addition to my job. It's a big responsibility."

"Jess has often expressed a deep interest in chickens."

"Funny thing—that's kind of what he's doing now. Watching my new chickens."

"You're kidding."

"His trailer had plumbing issues, and I'm letting him stay in the house." She let her hands slide down to the front of his chest. "I wanted to watch you ride. I never have, you know. I only knew you by reputation."

"What did you think?"

"It stirred my blood."

Tyler laughed even as he continued to grapple with the fact that Skye was here. She wanted him. She trusted him. "I can think of other ways to stir your blood."

"I know…and don't think I don't love that about you. I just need one promise from you."

"Name it."

"I need the truth. No matter what. If I know the truth, then I'm dealing with reality. Not illusions and not fears. Can you do that for me? Even when it's hard?"

He kissed her so gently and tenderly, his palm caressing her cheek as he made his promise to her. "Yes. I will always tell you the truth. You can depend on me."

* * * * *

Be sure to check out the
other books in Jeannie Watt's
MONTANA BULL RIDERS *series,*
THE BULL RIDER MEETS HIS MATCH
and
THE BULL RIDER'S HOMECOMING,
available now from Mills & Boon Cherish.

And look for a new **MONTANA BULL RIDERS** *story*
coming soon, wherever Mills & Boon books are sold!

MILLS & BOON®

Cherish™

EXPERIENCE THE ULTIMATE RUSH OF FALLING IN LOVE

MILLS & BOON®

EXCLUSIVE EXTRACT

When Greek tycoon Alex Mikhalis
discovers Adele Hudson is pregnant
he abandons his plans to get even and
suggests a very intimate solution:
becoming his convenient wife!

Read on for a sneak preview of
CONVENIENTLY WED TO THE GREEK

'What?' The word exploded from her.

'You can't possibly be serious.'

Alex looked down into her face. Even in the slanted
light from the taverna she could see the intensity in his
black eyes. 'I'm very serious. I think we should get
married.'

Dell had never known what it felt to have her head
spin. She felt it now. Alex had to take hold of her elbow
to steady her. 'I can't believe I'm hearing this,' she said.
'You said you'd never get married. I'm not pregnant to
you. In fact you see my pregnancy as a barrier to kissing
me, let alone marrying me. Have you been drinking too
much ouzo?'

'Not a drop,' he said. 'It's my father's dying wish that
I get married. He's been a good father. I haven't been a
good son. Fulfilling that wish is important to me. If I
have to get married, it makes sense that I marry you.'

'It doesn't make a scrap of sense to me,' she said.

'You don't get married to someone to please someone else, even if it is your father.'

Alex frowned. 'You've misunderstood me. I'm not talking about a real marriage.'

This was getting more and more surreal. 'Not a real marriage? You mean a marriage of convenience?'

'Yes. Like people do to be able to get residence in a country. In this case it would be marriage to make my father happy. He wants the peace of mind of seeing me settled.'

'You feel you owe your father?'

'I owe him so much it could never be calculated or repaid. This isn't about owing my father, it's about loving him. I love my father, Dell.'

But you'll never love me, she cried in her heart. How could he talk about marrying someone—anyone—without a word about love?

Don't miss
CONVENIENTLY WED TO THE GREEK
by Kandy Shepherd

Available May 2017
www.millsandboon.co.uk

Could he trust her?

Beneath wild-
ness. It ec itting
from her

Michelle Smart's love affair with books began as a baby, when she would cuddle them in her cot. This love for all things wordy has never left her. A voracious reader of all genres, she found her love of romance cemented at the age of twelve, when she came across her first Mills & Boon® book. That book sparked a seed and, although she didn't have the words to explain it then, she knew she had discovered something special— that a book had the capacity to make her heart beat as if she were falling in love.

When not reading, or pretending to do the housework, Michelle loves nothing more than creating worlds of her own, featuring handsome, brooding heroes and the sparkly, feisty women who can melt their frozen hearts. She hopes her books can make her readers' hearts beat a little faster too. Michelle lives in Northamptonshire with her own hero and their two young sons.

THE RUSSIAN'S
ULTIMATUM

BY
MICHELLE SMART

Published in Great Britain 2015
by Mills & Boon, an imprint of Harlequin (UK) Limited,
Eton House, 18-24 Paradise Road, Richmond, Surrey, TW9 1SR

© 2015 Michelle Smart

ISBN: 978-0-263-24828-9

Harlequin (UK) Limited's policy is to use papers that are natural,
renewable and recyclable products and made from wood grown in
sustainable forests. The logging and manufacturing processes conform
to the legal environmental regulations of the country of origin.

Printed and bound in Spain
by Blackprint CPI, Barcelona

THE RUSSIAN'S
ULTIMATUM

This book is dedicated to my wonderful parents
and their equally wonderful spouses.
I love you all xxx

CHAPTER ONE

Emily Richardson ducked under the scaffolding over the entrance of the smart building in the heart of the city of London, strolled through the spacious atrium and headed to the wide staircase. When she reached the second floor she took an abrupt left, walked to the end of the corridor and pressed the button for the lift. Only once she had stepped inside and the door had slid shut did she allow herself to expel a breath.

Catching sight of her reflection in the mirrored wall, she raised an eyebrow. Power suits were really not her thing, especially ones dating back to the eighties. She felt suffocated —and her feet, in their patent black stilettos, were already killing her.

She had to fit in, she had to look as if she belonged in the building, so no one would give her a second glance. Her usual attire made her too noticeable—she would have been recognised before she'd got her foot over the threshold of the building. Even with the suit, she'd have to be careful. She'd timed her entrance to perfection—not too early to be conspicuous but not so late that the people she needed to avoid would be in yet. So far, so good.

For this particular lift to work, a code had to be punched in. She duly obliged and was carried all the way to the top floor and the private offices held by the senior management team of Bamber Cosmetics International—or, as it had now been renamed, Virshilas LG.

The largest of the offices was held by Mr Virshilas himself. But not today; today Pascha Virshilas was in Milan.

Unlike in the rest of the building, renovation work had yet to begin on the top floor. She imagined it wouldn't be long before it was remodelled into Pascha Virshilas's idea of an executive suite of offices.

She walked up the narrow corridor to an unassuming door that required a swipe card to open. As luck would have it, Emily had such a card, slipped from her father's wallet...

The door opened into a large, open-plan office. It appeared empty and for that she expelled another breath of relief.

Holding her chin aloft and forcing her back straight, she walked through the central hub of the floor, gently swaying her empty black briefcase.

The place really was deserted. Excellent; she'd beaten the executive secretaries in.

It surprised her to find Mr Virshilas's office unlocked. Given how security-conscious the man was, she'd assumed it would be rigged with explosives in case an intruder made it through the security measures.

Maybe he wasn't as paranoid as she'd been told.

All the same, she paused after she'd opened it an inch, put her ear to the door and tapped on it. If the fates were conspiring against her and one of the cleaners was in there emptying his rubbish bin, she would apologise and say she was lost. She hadn't come this far to wimp out on a 'maybe'.

Her knock elicited no response.

She pushed the door open another inch, then another. Heart racing, she entered the office, softly closing the door behind her.

She was in.

Time being of the essence, she scanned her surroundings quickly whilst reaching into the back pocket of her skirt and pulling out a state-of-the-art memory stick.

According to her source, Pascha Virshilas kept a laptop in all his worldwide offices. If her source continued to be correct, the laptop sitting on his desk was a centralised hub containing every file created by every department of every holding owned by Virshilas LG. This laptop contained the means of clearing her father's name.

Looking around, Emily could see that Pascha kept the neatest office in history. Not a single item looked to be out of place, not a single speck of dust or tiny crumb to be found. Even the intricate pencil drawings on the wall seemed to have been placed with military precision. All that lay on the highly polished ebony desk beneath the large window was the laptop and what looked to be a document file.

Flipping the laptop open, she pressed the button to switch it on. To her surprise, it fired up immediately.

Her eyebrows drew together. Had he forgotten to turn it off after his last use? From everything she knew about the man, this seemed out of character.

All the same, she wasn't about to look a gift horse in the mouth. For once it seemed the stars were aligning in her favour. The laptop being turned on had saved her an estimated two minutes' worth of hacking time.

Sticking the memory stick in the side portal, she pressed a few keys and the process began. Now all she had to do was wait.

If her hacking-whizz of a friend's estimates were correct, all the data contained within the laptop should be copied within six minutes.

The blue document file beside the laptop was a good

inch thick. Emily opened the cover. The top sheet of paper had *Private & Confidential* stamped on it in angry red.

Pulling the thick sheaves of paper out of the file, she turned the top sheet over and began to read…

'Who the hell are you and what are you doing in my office?'

Emily froze. Literally. Her mind went blank, her brain filling with a cold mist. The sheets of paper held between her fingers fell back into place while her immobile hands hovered inches above the file.

Her gaze still resting on the papers before her, she forced her chin up to meet the stony glare of Pascha Virshilas.

Cold grey eyes narrowed. 'You,' he hissed, his chiselled features contorting.

She didn't know what was the greatest shock—that he'd caught her in the act, or that he recognised her. The one time she'd met him she'd looked completely different, so different she would have been hard pressed to recognise herself in the mirror.

With great effort, she forced her features to remain neutral. Now was not the moment to reveal her utter loathing of the man; she had to stay calm.

She'd met him six weeks ago at an event, optimistically billed as a party, thrown to celebrate the acquisition of Bamber Cosmetics by Virshilas LG and to allow the employees to meet their new boss. Emily had only attended as a favour to her father who, since her mother's recent death, became crippled with nerves at social events. Being a senior executive, his presence had been a requirement.

When she'd been forced to shake Pascha's hand, his only response had been a slight flicker of disdain before he'd looked through her and moved on to the next person. If he'd bothered to wait and talk to her, she could have apologised for her inappropriate attire and explained that she'd rushed over from work without having time to change. She'd been busy at a fashion show and it was mandatory for the designers of the house she worked for to dress the part.

Emily and her father had stayed at the party for a polite hour before making their escape.

She doubted her escape from Pascha's office would be as successful.

'I asked you a question, Miss Richardson. I suggest you answer it.'

'But you've just answered the question of who I am yourself,' she answered with more bravado than she felt. Her memory of Pascha Virshilas was vivid, yet in this office he appeared magnified. Impossibly tall and broad, even the crispness of his white shirt and impeccably pressed grey-striped trousers couldn't hide the muscularity of his physique. If anything, it enhanced it. And that face... Chiselled perfection a sculptor would struggle to replicate.

'Don't play games with me. What are you doing in my office?'

Her gaze flickered to the small stick poking out of the side of the laptop. From Pascha's vantage point, he would only be able to see the upright lid. He might not see the stick at all. If she was lucky, she might just be able to escape with the data.

Using all the nonchalance she could muster, Emily leaned forward so her chest rested on the desk. 'I was passing and thought I would pop in to see how you're settling in.' As she spoke, she inched her fingers forward, placed her knuckles either side of the memory stick and tugged it out, enfolding it into the fist of her hand.

If he saw what she'd done, he gave no visible sign.

She got to her feet and casually placed her hand in her

back pocket, releasing the stick into its tight confines. She had no choice but to brazen this out, whatever its conclusion may be. 'As I can see you've settled in fantastically, I shall leave you to it.'

'Not so fast. Before I let you go anywhere, empty your pockets.' Pascha's English was delivered with curt precision but with a definite trace of his Russian heritage in its inflection. Deep and rich with a hint of gravel, it sent the most peculiar tingle whispering over her skin.

'No chance,' she said, inching her way round his desk, slowly closing the gap between herself and the door to her side. She silently cursed herself for not paying more attention to the internal door Pascha had appeared through. She'd seen it when she'd first stolen into the office but had barely registered it; she certainly hadn't given it more than a cursory glance.

'I said empty your pockets.'

'No.' Her eyes darted to the door. She might be twenty-six but she'd been a nimble runner in her school days. She was half his size and figured she must be quicker than him…

It didn't surprise Pascha in the least when Emily made a run for it, shooting to the door and tugging on the handle.

'It's locked,' he informed her calmly.

'I can see that,' she snapped.

'It won't open until I press the button to release the lock, and I won't do that until you give me what's in your pocket.'

Her pretty heart-shaped face glared at him, defiance pouring off her.

It was hardly surprising he hadn't recognised her from the camera that piped to a small screen in his private room. When he'd met her at his buy-out party, she'd been dressed in a long, black lace dress with ruffles, complemented by a pair of black biker boots and dark, dramatic make-up. All the black had contrasted sharply with her porcelain skin.

While the other women at the party had made an effort with their attire, Emily had deliberately set out to subvert. All she'd needed was a black veil sitting atop her long, dark ringlets which had spilled out in all directions and she'd have been the perfect gothic bride.

Today, though, she had tamed her curls into a bun—although tendrils were falling round her face—and was dressed in ordinary business attire of a knee-length navy skirt with a matching blazer and a delicate cream blouse. On her feet were ordinary, businesslike black court shoes and her face was make-up free. No wonder he hadn't recognised her, not until she'd raised those dark-brown eyes to meet his.

He would have recognised those eyes anywhere, dark but with flickers of yellow firing through them. Under the light of the function room the party had been hosted in, the colours had melded together, glimmering like a fire opal.

Those same eyes were staring at him now, loathing radiating from them.

He held his hand out and waited. If necessary, he would wait all day.

It wasn't necessary. Emily slipped her hand into her back pocket and pulled out a small silver device. She dropped it into the palm of his hand and stepped straight back, away from him.

As he'd suspected: a memory stick.

He strolled round to his seat, still warm from her bottom, and folded his arms. 'Sit down.'

After a beat, Emily grabbed the chair opposite him and dragged it to the other side of his office, literally as far away from him as she could get it.

'So, Emily, it is time for you to start talking. Why were you trying to steal the files from my laptop?'

'Why do you think? I'm trying to prove my father's innocence.'

'By stealing my files?'

'I had to do *something*. According to my sources, you haven't even started the investigation into the missing money you've accused him of taking. The stress of it all is making him seriously ill.'

Emily would do anything in her power to clear her father's name. Anything. She had to give him something that would make his life—make *him*—feel as if it were worthwhile again.

As much as it pained her heart, Emily knew *she* would never be a good enough reason for her father to go on.

She'd watched him go through these dark times as a child, long periods where he wouldn't get out of bed for weeks on end. It had been terrifying. Back then, her mother had held them all together: had held *him* together. But now her mother was dead. The rock they'd all relied upon was gone.

In the space of three months her father had lost the wife he'd adored and been suspended from the job he'd taken such pride in. The threat of the police knocking on his door and a subsequent prison sentence loomed over him. With hindsight, it had been obvious he would try to kill himself. He'd very nearly succeeded.

Losing her mother had been the single most devastating thing that had ever happened to her, a fresh, open wound that couldn't begin to heal while her father's mental and physical health were so precarious. If she were to lose him too...

Pascha gathered the file Emily had been reading when he'd caught her. So she had sources within his company, did she? That was something to think about later on. There was a much more important factor to consider first, namely how much of the file she'd read. He had no way of knowing how long she'd been in his office before he'd caught sight of her on the monitor. No longer than ten minutes, that was certain, as that had been the length of time since he'd left it. But long enough to read about things she had no business knowing.

'We will move on to the subject of your father shortly,' he said. 'In the meantime, tell me what you read in this file. And don't say you didn't read anything, because you were engrossed in it.'

For long moments she didn't answer, simply stared at him, her eyes squinting as if in thought. As if she were weighing him up… 'Not much. Only that a company called RG Holdings is buying out Plushenko's.'

Plushenko's was a Russian jewellery firm whose trinkets were regarded as some of the most luxurious in the world and came with a price tag to match, the Plushenko brand rivalling that of the other famous Russian jeweller, Fabergé. At least, it *had* been regarded as such. In recent years the jewels had lost much of their lustre and sales were a fraction of what they had been a decade ago. Amidst the highest secrecy, Pascha was gearing up for a buyout, using a front company.

'Oh, and I read that *you* own RG Holdings but that your name is being kept off all the official documents between RG and Plushenko's.' Her brow furrowed, as if she were trying to remember something, then her lips twisted into something resembling a smile. 'What was the phrase I read? Something along the lines of, "it is imperative that Marat Plushenko does not learn of Pascha Virshilas's involvement in this buyout". Was that it?'

Only with the greatest effort did Pascha keep his features still. Inside, his stomach lurched, his skin crawling as if a nest of spiders had been let loose in him.

Her brown eyes held his, as if in challenge, before her lips curved upwards—amazing lips, like a heart tugged out at the sides. Her eyes remained cold. She leaned forward. 'It's obvious this buy-out is important to you and you need to keep it a secret. I suggest we make a deal: if you agree to withdraw the threat of legal action towards my father, I will keep the details of the Plushenko deal to myself.'

Pascha's fingers tightened on the document in his grasp. 'You think you can blackmail me?'

She raised her shoulders in a sign of nonchalance. 'You may call it blackmail but I like to think of it as us making a deal. Clear my father's name. I want it in writing that you'll exonerate him from any potential charges or I will sing from the rooftops.'

Emily could see by the whitening of Pascha's knuckles that he was fighting to keep his composure.

How she kept her own composure, she did not know.

She'd never been a wallflower, not by any stretch of the imagination, but she'd never been one for making war before either. To stand up against this powerful man—a man capable of destroying her father; of destroying her too—and know she was winning… It was a heady feeling.

From despair and anger at getting caught and failing her father, she'd found a way to salvage the situation.

'I can have you arrested for this,' Pascha said, his voice low and menacing.

'Try it.' She allowed herself a smile. 'I'll be entitled to a phone call. I think I'll use it to contact the firm Shirokov —is that how you pronounce it?—and see if they'd be interested in representing me.'

How Pascha stopped his tongue rolling out the volley of expletives it wanted to say, he did not know.

Shirokov was the firm representing Marat Plushenko in the buy-out.

She dared to think she could threaten and blackmail him? This little pixie with a tongue as curling as her hair dared to think she could take him on and *win*?

He'd spent two years trying to make this deal happen, had even bought Bamber Cosmetics a few months ago as a decoy to avert any suspicion.

And now Emily Richardson had the power to blow it all to hell.

If Marat Plushenko heard so much as a whisper that Pascha was the face behind RG Holdings, he would abandon the deal without a backward glance and Plushenko's, the business the late, great Andrei Plushenko had built from nothing, would be ground to dust. His legacy would be gone.

And so would Pascha's last chance at redemption.

Could he trust her? That was the question.

He had no doubt her actions in stealing his files had been driven by exactly what she claimed—to prove her father's innocence. He almost admired her for it.

But beneath the collected exterior lurked a wildness. It echoed in the flickers of light emitting from her dark eyes. He could feel it.

This was a woman on the edge.

That, in itself, answered his question.

No, he could not trust her.

In exactly one week, the Plushenko deal would be finalised, the contracts signed. Seven whole days in which he would be wondering and worrying if she really was capable of keeping her mouth shut, if something innocuous could set her off to make a phone call to Marat's lawyer.

Beneath Emily's bohemian exterior, which even the plain suit she wore couldn't hide, lurked a sharp, inquisitive mind. A sharp mind on the edge could be a lethal combination.

An old English phrase came to mind: keep your friends close and your enemies closer.

This deal was everything. It *had* to happen.

It had been eight years since he'd walked out on his family. It was too late to make amends with the man who'd raised him as his own, but he could restore his legacy and, maybe then, finally, his mother would forgive him.

And for that reason he needed to make Emily disappear…

CHAPTER TWO

EMILY DID NOT like the thoughtful way Pascha appraised her, leaning back in his chair with his arms folded, his long legs stretched out beneath his desk, ankles crossed, handmade brogues gleaming.

She'd never seen such stillness. It was unnerving. Almost as unnerving as her attempt to blackmail him. But then, she'd never thought she would break into an office with the sole intention of stealing data from a billionaire's laptop.

After what felt like an age, where Emily's skin became tense enough to snap, Pascha leaned forward to rest his elbows on the desk and draw his fingers together.

'So, Miss Richardson, you think you can blackmail me to get what you want? I will not be threatened and I will not have the deal I've spent two years working on be destroyed.' The grey in his eyes glittered with loathing. 'I will not capitulate to your demands. No. *You*, Miss Richardson, are going to disappear.'

That made her sit up straight. She shook her head, as if unsure she'd heard him correctly. 'What? You're going to make me *disappear*?'

'Not in the sense you're thinking,' he said shortly, aggrieved to see her face had turned white. What kind of a man did she think he was? 'I can't take the risk of you disclosing the specifics of this deal, so I need you to disappear for a week.' And he knew the perfect place to take her.

Emily stared at him with wide, disbelieving eyes that held a hint of relief, probably at the confirmation he wasn't going to make her disappear via a wooden box. 'You can't be serious.'

'I am never anything but serious.'

'I don't doubt it. But I'm not going anywhere.'

'Yes, you are. I will agree to clear your father's name but in return you must agree to go into hiding for a week.'

He had to give her something in exchange, that much he knew. And, seeing as it was her father's name she wanted to clear, then that was what she would have. It was hardly a trivial sum either. One-hundred-and-fifty-thousand pounds had gone missing on her father's watch. He was the only person who could have taken it.

Her stomach roiling, Emily forced her mind to think clearly. As deftly as a professional tennis player, Pascha had regained control of the court. But this wasn't a game. Not to her. And, she knew, not to him either. What he was demanding of her was unbelievable, yet the set expression of those cool, grey eyes and the line of those wide, firm lips showed he wasn't bluffing. 'I can't just leave… I have commitments…'

'You didn't think of those commitments when you entered my office for illegal purposes.'

'Yes, I did, but I only planned on losing a couple of days if I got caught. Not that I expected *you* to catch me. I was told you were in Milan.'

'You really are remarkably well-informed.' Those gorgeous lips curved into the semblance of a smile. *Gorgeous lips? Had her anger addled her brain…?* 'But have no fear—I *will* learn who your mole is.'

She threw him a tight 'that's what you think' smile.

Emily would never sell out a friend, especially to a man as dangerous as Pascha Virshilas, who ruined people's health and reputations for fun. She would bet that was the extent of any fun he had. He was so buttoned up, he probably even treated sex with the utmost precision.

And now she was imagining his sex life—where on earth had that come from? He'd unnerved her more than she'd credited.

Pascha rose to his feet and looked at his watch. 'I will give you five minutes to make your decision: your father's freedom in exchange for yours.'

'But where will I go? I have nowhere to go *to*.'

'I have somewhere to take you. It's safe and out of the way.'

Leaving her standing there to glower at his retreating figure, Pascha opened the inter-connecting door and stepped into his private space.

Emily would agree. Complying would give her exactly what she'd come here for.

He pulled out his phone and fired off an email to his PA, telling her to rearrange all his appointments for the next two days. As he wrote, he ruminated over the arrangements needed to get Emily out of the country and then immediately fired half a dozen more emails to the people and organisations he paid to make things like this happen.

Not that he'd ever done something quite like *this* before. And, if he felt any discomfort over what he was doing, he was quick to remind himself that she'd thrown the first ball. Emily had broken into his office to steal his company's data and then had tried to blackmail him. She didn't deserve him to feel any guilt.

Everything was in hand with regards to the Plushenko buyout. All the negotiations had been finalised; now it was just a case of dotting every 'i' and crossing every 't'.

His lawyers were in the process of doing just that. There was nothing more for him to do other than sign the final contracts in exactly one week.

Escorting Emily to Aliana Island wouldn't affect anything. He could accompany her there and be back in Europe within thirty-six hours. And yet…

Pascha didn't like leaving anything to chance. He wanted to be there on the scene should any unexpected crises be thrown up, not halfway round the world with a blackmailing thief.

The inter-connecting door opened and Emily burst into his private space, a space not even his executive secretary or PA were permitted to enter. More curls had sprung free from the bun she'd wedged her hair in, ebony tendrils falling over her face and down her back.

Without any preliminaries, she launched straight in. 'If I agree to effectively be kidnapped by you, I want it in writing that you'll exonerate my father from any and all charges.'

'I've already agreed to that.'

'I want your *written* guarantee. I doubt he'll ever be in a position to return to work, so I also want you to back-date the money he's been denied since being under suspension. And I want you to give him a decent pay-off of, say, a quarter of a million pounds.'

Pascha shock his head, almost laughing at her nerve. 'Your demands are ridiculous.'

She shrugged mutinously. 'That's what I want. If you agree to *my* demands, then I will agree to *your* demands.'

'I think you forget who is in the driving seat. I'm not the one whose father's future hangs in the balance.'

'True. But your wish for secrecy over your involvement in the Plushenko deal *is* in the balance.' Here, her face transformed, lighting up with faux sweetness. 'Either you agree to my demands or I whistle it to the world. We can call it a deal of mutual benefit or, if you prefer, mutually beneficial blackmail.'

Emily had never been on the receiving end of such pure loathing before. It radiated off him like a rippling wave.

She refused to cower.

She didn't care what the motivation was for his buy-out, knew only that it had to be something more than a simple business deal. Either that or the man was completely insane because no one went to such great lengths to secure a business deal.

No. For Pascha Virshilas, this buy-out was, for whatever reason, personal. And if he could use her emotions for leverage then she could certainly use his emotions for her own benefit—or, in this case, her father's.

Now the ball was back in his court.

After what felt like an age, he gave a sharp nod. 'I will agree to your demands with regards to your father, but you *will* disappear until my buy-out is complete. If at any point you find an opportunity to talk and are stupid enough to take it, our deal will be null and void and I will personally ruin the pair of you.'

Pascha pulled up outside the house in the London suburb Emily had given him as her address.

'You live here?' The cosy, mock-Tudor house was nothing like the home he'd imagined she would have. 'This is my father's home,' she answered shortly. 'I rented my flat out and moved back in a month ago.'

'That must have been a come-down, moving back in with your parents.'

She fixed him with a hard stare. 'Do not presume to know me or know anything about my life. Give me twenty minutes. I need to arrange some matters and get my stuff together.'

He opened his door before returning the stare. 'I'm coming in with you.'

'You certainly are not.'

'I'm not giving you a choice. Until we get to your destination, you're not leaving my sight.'

The fire running in her eyes sparked. 'To be clear, if you say or do anything to upset my father then our agreement can go to hell.'

'Then you will be the one dealing with the consequences.'

'As will *you*.' Before his eyes, her face transformed, the hardness softening to become almost childlike. 'Please, Pascha. He's in a very bad place. You probably won't even see him but, if you do, please be kind.'

He'd never had any intention of upsetting her father. All the same, he found himself agreeing to her heartfelt plea. 'I will say nothing to upset him.'

And, just like that, she went back into her hard shell and jumped out of the car. 'Let's go in, then.'

He followed her through the front door and into a spacious yet homely house.

'Dad?' she called, shouting up the stairs. 'It's only me. I'll be up in a minute with a cup of tea for you.' Not waiting for an answer, she headed into a large kitchen-diner, put the kettle on and reached for the house phone.

Pascha grabbed her wrist before she could dial the number. 'Who are you calling?'

'My brother. I told you, I have things to organise. Now, take your hand off me.'

Not trusting her an inch, he complied, stepping back far enough to give them both a little space, but remaining close enough to disconnect the call should she try anything.

'James?' she said into the receiver. 'It's only me. Look, I'm sorry for the short notice, but I need you to come and stay with dad for the next week and not just tonight.'

From the way she sucked her angular cheekbones in, and the impatience of her tone as the conversation went back and forth, she wasn't happy with her brother's responses.

Emily was clearly a bossy big sister but beneath it all he heard genuine affection. He could well imagine her ordering her brother around from the moment of his birth.

His mind turned to the man he'd always regarded as a brother, the same man who would sooner drive Plushenko's—the business he'd inherited from their father—into the ground rather than sell it to Pascha.

While Pascha had openly hero-worshipped him, Marat had never made any secret of his loathing for Pascha. When Pascha had been seriously ill and death had been hovering, real, Marat had *wanted* him—the boy he'd liked to call the cuckoo in the nest—to die.

Emily's conversation ended with her saying, 'Mandy's around during the day if you need to go into the office. I'm only asking you to come for a week—you'll be fine. Amsterdam will still be there when you get back.'

She disconnected the call and immediately put the receiver back to her ear, dialling yet another number. This time, she relayed that an emergency had come up and asked whoever was on the receiving end to tell someone called Hugo that she needed to take a week's leave of absence.

'Are you done?' Pascha asked when she'd replaced the receiver.

'Yes.'

'No boyfriend to call?' He didn't even attempt to hide his sarcasm.

In response, she threw him the hardest look he'd ever

been on the receiving end of, and in his thirty-four years that was saying something.

'No.' With that, she went back to the freshly boiled kettle.

'I take my coffee black with one sugar,' he informed her as she tossed a teabag into a mug, poured hot water onto it, followed by a splash of milk, and gave it a vigorous stir.

'That's nice.' She picked up the mug and swooped past him.

'It is good manners to offer guests refreshments.'

She came to an abrupt halt and spun around, somehow managing not to spill a single drop of tea. 'You are *not* a guest in this house and you never will be.'

For a moment, Pascha seriously contemplated forgetting his promise to send Emily somewhere safe and simply lock her in a sound-proof cupboard for a week.

Keeping close to her tail, he followed her up the stairs. When they reached the top, she turned back to him. This time she whispered, although she still perfectly managed to convey her hatred towards him. 'This is my father's room. Do not come in. Seeing you might just tip him over the edge.'

'Then keep the door open. I want to hear what you're saying.'

'You'll find our conversation scintillating.' She rapped her knuckles on the door, pushed it open and stepped over the threshold into a dusky bedroom, curtains drawn.

'Hi, Dad,' Emily said, speaking in such a gentle voice he could easily have believed it was someone else talking. 'I've made you a cup of tea.'

Pascha watched as she went to the window and drew the curtains back.

'Let's get some air in here,' she said in the same gentle voice, opening the window. 'It's a beautiful day. Honestly, Dad, you would love it out there. It really feels like autumn now.'

The daylight streaming into the room allowed Pascha to spot the full-length mirror on the wall, which gave him a perfect view of the still figure in the bed.

With Emily keeping up a stream of steady, gentle chatter, the figure slowly rolled over and lifted his head an inch before slumping back down.

Pascha's jaw dropped open to see him.

Malcolm Richardson was unrecognisable from the man he'd suspended just a month ago.

He looked as if he'd aged two decades.

A stab of something Pascha couldn't place jabbed in his guts.

It wasn't long before Emily re-joined him. 'Get a good look, did you?' she shot as she sidled past and over to a room on the other side of the landing.

'Don't be facetious,' he snapped, speaking through gritted teeth. 'When will your brother be here?'

She hadn't been exaggerating. Her father really was in a bad way.

'As soon as he finishes his meeting.'

'And he can care for your father?'

'Yes. He runs his own business—he's a financial advisor and sets his own schedule. The next-door neighbour pops in during the day when she can.'

'We need to make a move soon,' Pascha said, trying to ignore the new insistent jabbing in the pit of his stomach. However much his conscience might be turning on him, he couldn't let Emily stay. The risk was too great. 'We have a flight slot to fill.'

'You're taking me abroad?'

'Yes.'

'I expected you to leave me in a dungeon somewhere.'

'That's a very tempting thought.'

She opened the door with a scowl. 'You can come in, but only because I don't want my dad finding you out here.'

Emily took a deep breath and admitted Pascha into her room.

He made no comment, just stood there taking it all in.

To her chagrin, she was embarrassed for him to see it. She'd done her best, but comparing it to the sterility of his office made her see all the flaws. It was as tidy and as organised as she'd been able to manage but it was hard cramming an entire life into a childhood bedroom.

She thought with longing of her cosy flat, could only hope her short-term tenants were treating it with respect.

She pushed the thought aside. It could be months before she was able to move back. Torturing herself wouldn't change her circumstances.

'It's going to take me a while to get my things together,' she said, mentally shaking herself. 'Feel free to take a seat.'

'And where am I supposed to sit?' he asked. The small armchair in the corner was piled high with old clothes she planned to recycle into something new.

'On the floor?' she suggested with faux sweetness, yanking open the wardrobe door, glad she could hide her flaming cheeks.

Her room wasn't messy but it was filled with so much *stuff*. A lifetime's worth. If she didn't need to keep James's room free for the times he came to stay, she would appropriate it.

She would rather rip her own heart out than use her mother's small craft study. How many hours had they spent together in that room, working together, her mother teaching her how to create her own clothes? Too many to count.

Ignoring her suggestion, Pascha gathered the pile of clothes and placed it on the floor atop a neat stack of magazines, which promptly fell down under the weight. He raised an eyebrow then gingerly took a seat.

'Seeing as you're shunting me off abroad, what kind of weather should I pack for?'

'Hot.'

She pulled a face.

He leaned forwards slightly, resting his elbows on his thighs and exposing the tops of his golden forearms. 'You don't like the heat?'

'It makes my skin itch.' Disconcerted that a tiny glimpse of his *arms* made her blood feel thick and sluggish, she opened a drawer, gathered an armful of underwear and dumped it unceremoniously into the suitcase. Feeling Pascha's eyes watch her every move was even more disturbing, making her feel dishevelled and strangely hot.

Wanting to get out of the close confines of her bedroom as soon as possible, she packed quickly, throwing armfuls of garments into the case.

'I need to get changed,' she said, once she was satisfied she had enough suitable clothing for a week in the sun.

Pascha eyed her coolly before inclining his head and turning his chair so his back was to her.

In any other circumstance he would have left the room and given her the privacy she needed. In this circumstance, he could not.

He tried to tune out the sound of a zip being pulled down, the rustle of clothes being shed.

Determinedly, he focused his mind to running over the day's stock prices. Anything other than think about what was happening behind him where Emily was undressing…

He swallowed, trying to bring moisture into a mouth that had run dry.

He would not allow his thoughts to stray into such inappropriate territory.

Emily was leaving the country with him unwillingly, through circumstances neither of them could have wished for. That she was a single female should not mean anything.

All the same, the air trapped in his lungs didn't expel until she said, 'I'm decent.'

He twisted his chair back around.

She'd changed into a long, floating black dress with thin sleeves and was placing the business outfit she'd worn onto a coat hanger.

'So you *do* know to hang clothes properly,' he said as she hooked it into her wardrobe.

Her dark-brown eyes caught his and narrowed. 'These belonged to my mother. She did the occasional temping work.'

Belonged…? 'Your mother is…?'

'Dead. Yes.' The way her gaze fixed on him, it was as if she held him personally responsible for her loss. But there was something else there too, a flash of misery, quickly hidden but sharp for all its briefness.

'I'm sorry.' He truly meant it, too.

'So am I.' Her mouth set in a straight line that he understood to mean *this topic is not open for discussion*, Emily undid the bun holding the few tresses that had not already escaped before scooping the mass of curls back up and shoving a tortoiseshell comb high on the top, ringlets spilling over her face in a style that accentuated her high cheekbones.

'Is this really necessary?' he asked when she sat on the dressing table chair and began applying make-up.

'Yes,' she said, cleverly darkening her eyes. While she didn't go as far as she had at his party, there was more than a little hint of the theatrical when she'd finished.

He hated to admit it but the look really suited her.

He looked at his watch. 'If you're not ready in two minutes, I will carry you out of the house.'

'Good luck with that.'

Her stony gaze met his through the reflection in the mirror. For the briefest of moments, something sparked between them, a look that sent a wave of heat sailing through his skin and down to his loins.

Emily broke the look with an almost imperceptible frown.

'What's the weight limit for my luggage?' she asked, packing cosmetics into a large vanity case.

'We'll be travelling on my jet so there are no limits.'

'Good.' She dived back into her wardrobe.

'Now what are you getting?' His irritation had reached maximum peak, both at her attitude and the unfeasible reaction she seemed to be igniting within him.

The sooner he left her on Aliana Island, the better.

'My sewing machine.' She pulled out a large square case and dumped it on the bed beside the suitcase.

'Would you like me to un-plumb your kitchen sink for you while you're at it?'

The ghost of a smile curled on her cheeks, but she ignored his comment and slid under the bed.

Exasperated beyond belief, Pascha was suddenly distracted by the sight of dark-blue nail varnish on her pretty toes…and a small butterfly tattoo on her left ankle.

He couldn't say he liked tattoos but he couldn't deny that Emily's was tasteful. Delicate, even.

When she re-emerged, her hair having escaped the tortoiseshell clip and fallen down her back, she pulled out four large cardboard tubes.

'What's in those?'

'Fabric.' At his questioning look, she added, 'Well, it's

pointless taking my sewing machine if I have nothing to make with it.'

'Have you got your passport?'

'It's in my handbag.'

Gritting his teeth, Pascha got to his feet and lifted the weighty suitcase. If he'd known she kept her passport on her, he could have taken her straight to the bloody airport without any of this ridiculous carrying on.

Think of the reward at the end, he reminded himself. In one week this would be over. It would all be over.

In seven days, his redemption would be complete.

CHAPTER THREE

EMILY SIGNED HER part of the agreement before they boarded the plane, refusing to climb the metal steps until Pascha had signed his part too. He'd typed it on his laptop on the drive to the airport, printing it off in the executive lounge. She'd also insisted on getting it witnessed by one of the flight crew.

One week of her life and her father's good name would be restored. He'd receive a quarter of a million pounds too, enough to see him through to old age. If he made it to old age, that was. At that moment, she wasn't prepared to take anything for granted when it came to her father. He was too fragile to look beyond the next day. Surely the anti-depressants would kick in soon?

She pushed aside thoughts that when her week was up she would likely find herself without a job. The odds were not in her favour. Hugo was temperamental at the best of times. All the leave she'd had to take at the last minute recently, coupled with her request not to travel outside the UK for the foreseeable future, were strikes against her name. A further week's leave without warning would be the final straw.

The moment they were airborne, she ignored Pascha and tried to immerse herself in the fashion magazines she'd brought with her. Normally she loved flipping through them, finding inspiration in the most obscure things, but today she couldn't concentrate. Her brain was too wired, as if she'd had a dozen espressos in a row.

She'd known getting caught in Pascha's office would have basic risks attached to it but she'd assumed the worst that could happen would be a night in a prison cell. She'd arranged for James to spend the night with her father in that eventuality. That particular risk had been worth it for the chance of clearing her father's name and giving him something that might, just might, give him some form of hope to cling to. Something that might prevent him from sinking another bottle of Scotch and throwing dozens of pills down his throat again.

Her father was broken. He'd given up.

She hadn't been a strong enough reason for him to want to live.

By the time they embarked onto the small luxury yacht in Puerto Rico that would take them on the last leg of their trip, Emily's brain hurt. Her heart hurt.

Leaving Pascha to talk safety issues with the yacht's skipper, in much the same way he'd discussed safety issues with the flight crew before they'd taken off from London, Emily settled onto a sofa in the saloon and closed her eyes, blinds shading her from the late-afternoon sun.

She must have fallen asleep as a tap on her shoulder made her open her eyes with a snap.

Pascha loomed over her. He wore the same outfit he'd been in when he'd caught her in his office hours earlier, but still looked as fresh as if he'd just dressed.

'We'll be there soon,' he said before turning round and heading back outside, leaving his dreadful citrus scent behind him. Okay, maybe it wasn't dreadful. Maybe it was actually rather nice. Too nice. It made her feel…hungry. She didn't want to like anything about him, not even his scent.

Despite her worry and lethargy, she couldn't help but experience a whisper of excitement when she joined him on deck and felt the warmth of the sun beat down on her face. It really was a picture-perfect scene. Not a single cloud marred the cobalt sky.

Pascha pointed out the tiny, verdant island before them poking out of the Atlantic—or was it the Caribbean? They were right at the border between the two watery giants. In the far distance she could see a cluster of larger islands, seemingly surrounding the smaller one like sentries.

'That is Aliana Island.' It was the first time he'd put a name to her final destination.

Aliana Island: even its name was beautiful.

Emily reminded herself that it should make no difference whether her prison for the next week was an under-stairs cupboard or a virtual paradise. Her reasons for being there were the same. She was there against her will.

All the same, the closer they got to their destination, the more her spirits lifted. The island didn't appear to get any bigger, but she could see more detail. The deep blue sea beneath them lightened, turning a clearer turquoise than she could have dreamed of, the sandy beach before them sparkling under the beaming sun.

'We have to be careful getting to the island,' Pascha explained in that clipped manner she was becoming used to. 'It's surrounded by a coral reef.'

'Aren't they dangerous for boats?' She didn't know much about coral reefs but that was one thing she was fairly certain of.

'Exceedingly dangerous,' he agreed. 'Only a fool would navigate coral waters without any prior knowledge of them. Luis has been navigating these waters for years.'

'That's good to know,' she murmured without surprise. In the short time she'd known him, Pascha had proved himself a man who took security and safety extremely seriously.

'Is that a temple?' she asked, spotting what looked like some kind of Buddhist retreat set back a little from the beach.

'No. It's my lodge.'

'*Your* lodge?'

'Aliana Island belongs to me.'

Despite herself, Emily was impressed. Looking carefully, she could see other, smaller buildings with thatched roofs branching off the main one. 'It's beautiful. How did it get its name? Was Aliana the person who discovered it?'

'No. Aliana is my mother.'

'Really?' Something flittered over her face, a look he couldn't discern but made him think his answer had pleased her somehow. 'You named an island after your mother? What a fabulous thing to do. I bet she was delighted when you told her, wasn't she?'

'She...'

He struggled to think of the correct wording to describe his mother's reaction—the slap across his face and the words, 'You think an *island* can repair the damage you caused?'

He decided on, 'She wasn't displeased.'

He'd bought the island three years before. The ink on the purchase contract had barely dried before he'd changed its name.

He'd had it all planned out. He would visit his mother and Andrei after five years of estrangement. As part of his atonement, he would invite them to spend a holiday with him on the island. He would give them their own keys and tell them to think of it as theirs too—a special place for them all to share and use however they saw fit.

Time and distance had given him a great deal of perspective. When he closed his eyes, all he saw was the worry etched on his mother's face as she'd watched over the small son she hadn't known whether would live or die. He'd seen the stress Andrei had carried with him but had never shown his adopted son. The thick, dark hair had thinned and whitened too quickly; the capable hands had calloused seemingly overnight.

Fate had worked against him. Shortly before the lodge had been completed, before Pascha had been able to make things right between them, Andrei had died. He'd gone to bed and never woken up. A heart attack.

The man who'd raised him as if he were his own, who'd worked his fingers to the bone to give Pascha the chance to live, the man Pascha had walked away from…had gone. He'd lost the opportunity to apologise and make amends. He'd lost the opportunity to tell him that he loved him.

His grief-stricken mother…

Pascha's apology and remorse had washed right over her. His words had come too late. He should have said them when Andrei was alive. Aliana Island was just a possession; it meant nothing to his mother, not when she no longer had her beloved husband to enjoy it with.

But, while he might never be able to make amends with Andrei personally, he could secure his legacy. It was the *only* thing he could do. And if he was successful…maybe then his mother would forgive him. Their relationship could be repaired—he had to believe that.

'Do you spend much time here?' Emily asked, thankfully moving the conversation onto safer territory.

'Not as much as I would like.'

The yacht had been brought into a lagoon and moored

alongside a small jetty. A panelling in the side of the yacht unfurled to reveal metal steps for them to disembark from. Pascha strolled down the steps and made his way up the jetty.

He was sorely tempted to get Luis, the man he employed to skipper his yacht, to take him straight back to Puerto Rico so he could take his jet directly to Paris, his next destination. However, he'd been awake for over a day, having flown from Milan to London in the early hours. He needed sleep. If there was one thing Pascha did not mess around with, it was his health, and sleep was instrumental to it.

The odds of the illness which had threatened his life as a child returning was miniscule, but a miniscule chance was worse than no chance at all. Sleep, exercise and a healthy diet were all things he could control. Controlling them lowered that miniscule chance, putting the odds even more in his favour.

He'd planned to sleep on the flight from London but for once had been unable to, his awareness of the proximity of his guest having made it impossible for him to relax. He kept catching wafts of the perfume Emily had applied before he'd finally got her out of her bedroom. Her scent was delicious, an earthy smell with a touch of honeyed sweetness his senses responded to of their own accord, much to his annoyance.

He needed rest, and for that he'd need space. He would have a quick meal then get his head down— eight solid hours to recharge his batteries—then leave at first light.

He followed the pathway, traversing the beach up to the main entrance of the lodge, aware of Emily following behind him. Valeria, his head of housekeeping, was there to greet them.

After exchanging pleasantries, he said, 'Please show

Miss Richardson to her guest hut and show her where everything is. Are we okay to eat in an hour?'

Valeria nodded. His unplanned visit hadn't fazed her in the slightest. Under normal circumstances Pascha would give proper notice of a planned visit so she could prepare for it. Today she'd had roughly twelve hours to get everything ready, but from what he could see everything was in hand.

When he stepped into his hut, everything was exactly as it should be, not a speck of dust to be seen. Before heading to the bathroom, he stepped out onto the veranda and breathed in the salty air, closing his eyes as he willed the usual peace he found on Aliana Island to envelope him.

With Emily Richardson there, he suspected peace would be a long way off.

If Emily's eyes were capable of widening any further, they would have. Connected to the main house by a set of dark hardwood stairs, her hut looked more like an enormous high-end luxury cabin than anything else, with floor-to-ceiling windows that opened up to give a panoramic view, not just of the island but the surrounding ocean. The entire front section of the hut was one huge sliding door. Steps led out to a private veranda with a dining table, then down to a balcony with an abundance of soft white sun-loungers. More steps led down onto the beach.

After a quick discussion about Emily's dietary requirements—apparently there were three chefs on site to prepare whatever she wanted, whenever she wanted—Valeria left her to settle in.

Alone, Emily tried to take it all in, but she was so overwhelmed by her hut, her surroundings, the fact that Aliana Island was a private paradise...

And this was her prison. A jail with a four-poster bed.

It felt as if she'd been plunged into the middle of a fantastical dream.

In the far corner of her hut was a roll-topped bath. She longed to get into it but felt too exposed with all the surrounding glass. Instead, she opted for a shower in her bathroom, which was mercifully private, then changed into a pair of three-quarter-length skinny black trousers with silver sequins running down the lines and a silky grey vest top. She applied her make-up with care. She'd always adored wearing make-up, loved the way it could enhance a mood. Today it felt as if she were applying battle armour.

Her appearance taken care of, she set about unpacking then padded out barefoot onto the veranda. Her spirits soared further when she found her own small private swimming pool. She'd caught a glimpse of the long pool that snaked around the main house, but to find she had her own one too…and one that was entirely private.

Now that she really took stock of everything, she could see she really did have complete privacy. No one could see into her space. She decided that she would definitely use the bath in the morning.

She checked herself, forcing a curb on her excitement. This was not a holiday. Not by a long mark. She must not forget that.

It wasn't until she leaned over the pebbled wall separating her balcony from the steps down to the beach that she caught a glimpse of another hut overhanging to the left of hers. Craning her neck for a better look, she jerked when she saw Pascha leaning over his own wall talking into his mobile phone, the top part of his naked torso visible…

He must have sensed her gaze for he suddenly looked down. For the briefest of moments their eyes locked before she tore her eyes away and stepped back, out of sight.

She inhaled deeply and placed a hand to her chest. Her heart raced, her skin tingled and, much as she tried to blink the image away, all she could see was the hard chest with a smattering of dark hair over taut muscles.

Utterly unnerved by her reaction to semi-naked Pascha, Emily resolved to stay in her hut for the rest of the evening, using its phone to call down to the kitchen and request her dinner be brought up to her.

It felt safer to keep out of his way. Much safer.

In the meantime, she needed to call home. But picking up the receiver proved a fruitless task. The phone in her hut connected to the main house but nowhere else. As soon as she dialled any other number, a beep rang in her ear. She was disappointed, but she wasn't surprised. The whole point in Pascha keeping her there was to stop her communicating with anyone. All the same, she decided to try her mobile phone. She curled up on an outdoor sofa that was completely hidden from view and switched it on. Nothing. No signal bars, no Internet access. Nothing. No wonder Pascha hadn't bothered trying to take it from her.

She muttered a curse just as a soft buzzer went off in her room.

'Come in,' she called, assuming it was her dinner being brought to her. Rising to her feet, she gave a sharp intake of breath when she found Pascha in her hut.

'How have you settled in?' he asked, stepping out to join her on the veranda. He'd changed into dark linen trousers and an open-necked light blue shirt. Were it not for the fact his attire had been ironed to within an inch of its life, and his hair styled to such an extent that not a single strand dared depart from the slight quiff, she would have said he looked casual. But then, casual was a state of mind. Emily doubted he ever switched off.

'I've settled in fine,' she replied, resisting the urge to

push him back into the hut and shove him out through the French doors. It wouldn't make any difference if she did; they'd only be separated by the windows. She held her phone out to him. 'I need to call home.'

He didn't even look at it. 'There's a block on all electronic communications without an access code.'

'I gathered that. I need to call home. Is there another phone I can use?'

'You only left this morning.'

'A lot can happen in a day.' At his narrowing eyes, she quickly added, 'You can hover by my side while I make the call and satisfy yourself that I'm not revealing any state secrets. I just want to make sure my dad's okay and that my brother's got there.'

Silence hung between them while Pascha contemplated her request. After what felt like an age, he inclined his head. 'You can use my phone.'

'Seeing as *my* phone is useless here, I'll need a number my dad and brother can reach me on too.' She'd assumed he would take her phone and keep it on him, had assumed her family would be able to reach her even if she couldn't contact them.

When it looked as if he would refuse, she folded her arms. 'Look, you either let me give them an emergency contact number or I will make it my business to be the most difficult guest you've ever had here.'

'You're already the most difficult guest I've ever had here.' Was it her imagination or was that a glimmer of humour in his eyes?

'You haven't seen anything yet.'

'I can well believe it. You can call home and give my number as an emergency contact, but it can wait until after we've eaten.'

This time it was her eyes that narrowed.

His cheeks formed a semblance of a smile. 'Yes, Emily, you will be dining with me tonight.'

'I was planning on eating on my veranda. Alone,' she added pointedly.

'You can dine alone on your veranda for the rest of the week but this evening I require the pleasure of your company. My staff have set up the beach table for us.' From the way he enunciated the word 'pleasure', it was obvious he found the prospect of her company nothing of the sort.

'Why not?' She threw him a brittle smile. 'You and I are clearly ideal candidates for a romantic meal for two.'

His lips tightened. 'Circumstances are what they are. I'll be leaving for Paris first thing in the morning and there are a number of things we need to discuss before I leave.'

'Excellent.' She grinned at him without an ounce of warmth. 'Let's get this over with, then—with any luck it'll be the last time we have to suffer one another's company.'

CHAPTER FOUR

THE LONG TABLE on the beach had been set up for them just metres from the lapping waves of the ocean, tea-lights in lanterns glowing under the dusky sky.

'We're sitting on mats?' she asked, nodding at the thick cushions on the sand.

'Do you have a problem with that?'

She shrugged. 'No. I'm just surprised—I imagined you'd be averse to getting sand on your expensive clothes.'

'I find the sound of the ocean soothing,' he answered shortly. Emily's antagonism towards him was becoming trying. She had no one to blame for her predicament but herself. 'After the day I've had, I could use some respite.'

She settled onto a mat, tucking her bare feet beneath her. They really were the most delicate feet, he noticed: petite, much like the rest of her. Except her luscious mouth, of course.

He'd followed behind as they'd descended the stairs, holding onto the rail while she bounded down the steps without support, her long black hair, free from confinement, springing in all directions.

Emily had an energy about her that zinged. He found it intriguing. He found *her* intriguing. Any other woman in her predicament likely would have resorted to tears to get her own way. Emily had only become more defiant.

For the first time in a long time the image of Yana came into his mind, startling him. He never thought of his ex, had ruthlessly dispelled all memories of her so she was just a hazy figure in his past.

Yana and Emily were polar opposites, in looks and temperament.

The more time he spent with Emily, the more he was reminded of an uncut fire opal, passionate and vibrant. Yana was as polished as a Plushenko diamond. But by the time he'd ended their relationship she'd been a diamond without the lustre. And it had all been his fault.

He'd never had a problem attracting women but since he'd broken away from Andrei and set up on his own, building a multi-billion-dollar business in less than a decade, the feminine attention had become altogether hungrier. They were all wasting their time, something he spelt out at the outset of any fling. Sex was the most he could offer, the most he could give.

He'd destroyed the cut and polish of one woman. He would never put another in that position.

His thoughts were interrupted by a member of staff bringing out their starter of grilled squid and topping their wineglasses with chilled white before disappearing.

Pascha watched Emily take a bite, her lips moving in a way he could only describe as sensual. She really did have the sexiest of lips.

'What?' she asked a few moments later, looking at him quizzically.

To his chagrin, he realised he'd been too busy staring to take a bite of his own food.

He speared his fork into the delicate flesh of the squid. 'While you're staying here, I don't want you feeling you have to hide yourself away.'

'That won't be a problem when you've left. I'm looking forward to exploring your island.'

'Good.' It shouldn't bother him that she didn't want to be in his company. It *didn't* bother him. 'You'll find the island a place of hidden treasures. My staff are highly trained and able to cater for any wish you might have, which leads me to the next item on the agenda.'

'Do you want me to take minutes?'

'Excuse me?'

'You mentioned items on an agenda.' She put her knife and fork together and pushed her plate forward. 'Would you like me to act as secretary and write a set of minutes so neither of us forget what's discussed?'

Were it not for the unexpected spark of light that flashed in her eyes, he could have believed she was serious. 'I'm sure you'll remember it all without any problem.'

'A near compliment? I'm touched.'

His smile loosened a fraction. 'Onto my next item—my staff. I hand-picked them all and I do not want them upset in any shape or form.'

The spark of light in Emily's eyes vanished. 'My problem is with you, not your staff.'

'So long as you remember that. They follow my directives and know not to help you communicate with the outside world. Don't embarrass yourself or them by asking for their help.'

'I can go along with that so long as you promise to pass on any message from my family straight away.'

'If they get in touch once I've left the island, I will let Valeria know and she will pass on any message.'

'You'd better,' she muttered, becoming mute as staff inconspicuously cleared their starters away before returning with their main course. Soon, an array of fresh lobster, salads and spicy rice dishes was placed before them.

Emily heaped her plate with a little of everything then, using a bare hand, gripped the body of the lobster. Her eyes met his, insolence ringing from them as she reached for a claw with her other hand and twisted it off with a snap.

Pascha winced. While Emily attacked her lobster with relish, only using her crackers when absolutely necessary, Pascha used a more methodical approach, taking great care with the hard shell. By the time they'd finished eating, he was as clean as when he'd started, while her lips and fingers were slippery with butter.

His blood thickened as an image came into his mind of those slick fingers touching him...

What was it with this woman? Since he'd given Yana her freedom, he'd had more than his share of brief encounters, all with highly groomed, beautiful women who looked good on his arm. Not one of those women had roused him in anything other than the most basic of fashions. They certainly hadn't roused his senses. Not in the way Emily was doing at that moment and she wasn't even trying.

'Anything else you want to discuss?' she asked, pulling him out of his wayward thoughts. Bowls of hot flannels were placed before them and she took one, dabbing at her mouth, that beautiful, sensual mouth, and wiping her hands.

'No. That's everything.' There had been other issues but at that moment his brain felt as if a hazy fog had been tipped into it.

It was time to step away from this situation.

He should have got his staff to set up the dining hall, which had a table large enough to seat thirty. He should have stuck her right at the other end from him, all communication via megaphone.

If he hadn't wanted to eat by the ocean, he would have done just that, but in the morning he would leave for Paris, unlikely to return for a few months. There was something soothing about the sound of the gentle, rippling waves. It brought a contentment he'd never found anywhere else, a knowledge that whatever he did and wherever his future lay the tides would still turn.

'In that case, let's move on to "any other business": my phone call home.' She held a hand out, palm up. 'You gave me your word.'

He had to admire her devotion to her father. Such intense loyalty, she'd been prepared to spend a night in a police cell for it. It almost made him forgive that it had been *his* office she'd broken into and *his* data she'd attempted to steal. Almost.

Where had his own loyalty been eight years ago? He'd put his pride first and now it was too late. Andrei had died estranged from the adopted son he'd once adored. Was it any wonder his mother couldn't forgive him?

Snapping himself out of the settling melancholy, he pulled his smart phone out of his pocket and keyed in the password. 'What's the number?'

She recited it from memory. As soon as he heard the tone connecting the two lines, he passed it to her. She practically snatched it from him and pressed it to her ear.

'James?' Emily couldn't hide her relief. Her brother was there.

After hearing that her father had refused to get out of bed for his dinner, never mind eat it, Emily's eyes darted back to Pascha, who was watching her.

There were so many more questions she wanted to ask, but she resisted.

Now was not the time, not with Pascha listening in so closely. It was one thing for people to know how ill her father was, but his suicide attempt… No; that was between James, her and the medical profession. When her father recovered—and he would; whatever it took to get him better she would do it—she didn't want him living with the stigma of being the man who'd tried to kill himself. He wouldn't want it for himself. When he was well, his pride was everything. It had always been that way.

'My phone hasn't got a signal here,' she lied to her brother. 'So use this number if there's an emergency. It's right there in front of you on caller display—write it down, James. By the way, has Hugo called?' She didn't know if it was relief or dread she felt when James replied in the negative.

Disconnecting the call, she handed the phone back.

Her chest felt full and heavy and she suddenly realised she was on the verge of tears.

'Who is Hugo?' Pascha asked. 'You mentioned him earlier.'

Emily sighed.

'Hugo is my boss. Or perhaps I should say *was* my boss.'

Pascha arched a brow. *'Was?'*

'Unless Hugo's had a new heart transplanted into him, I won't have a job to go back to. Most employers wouldn't be happy about a key member of staff taking off for a week's leave on a whim, especially when that member of staff has already been given an official warning for taking too many unauthorised absences.' Stopping herself, Emily clamped her lips together. Pascha didn't care about her or her job. All she was to him was a potential threat that had to be hidden away.

Fashion design was all she'd ever wanted to do. But she shouldn't complain about Hugo. He'd been incredibly supportive through what had been a horrific time, at least initially, but he had a business to run—something he'd made abundantly clear when he'd given her that official warning less than a month ago.

After a long, thoughtful pause, Pascha said in a softer tone, 'I'm certain that if you explain the situation when you return Hugo will understand. He must know how ill your father is.'

Emily felt her heart lurch at the unexpected kindness from Pascha. Heartlessness she could cope with, but not that. Not now when her stomach felt so knotted she was having trouble holding down the beautiful food she'd just eaten.

Her mother had adored lobster, had been the person to teach her how to demolish one so effectively.

A wave of despair almost had her doubled over, lancing her stomach with a thousand thorns.

Her darling, darling mother; oh, how she *missed* her.

Emily fought to control her emotions. She couldn't let him see it. She just couldn't. He had enough power over her already.

'I...I need to get some sleep,' she said, backing away from him. 'Was there anything else you wanted?'

He shook his head, a strange, penetrative expression in his eyes.

She gave a brief nod and turned on her heel, forcing her rubbery legs to walk.

By the time Emily slid the door of her cabin shut, the grief had abated and her sudden tears had retreated back into their ducts.

Sinking onto the bed, she gazed up at the ceiling.

She could still feel Pascha's gaze on her skin.

The next morning, fortified by a huge breakfast that had been brought to her room, and armed with mosquito repellent, high-factor sun-cream and bottles of water, Emily set off to explore the island. It had been a long evening and an even longer night. She'd gone to bed far earlier than she usually did. As hard as she'd tried she'd been unable to sleep, her mind a cacophony of faces clamouring for attention: her mother; her father; her brother. Pascha…

She'd felt trapped in her guest lodge. She might be free to go anywhere on the island but knowing she could bump into Pascha had kept her firmly inside. She couldn't even get her sewing machine out. Such was the absolute silence of the island, the noise would have woken everyone up.

Making her way out of the main living area, she passed dozens of workers bustling around cleaning the house and grounds, the place a hive of activity. First she traversed the beach, smiling to see a couple of small children chasing each other over the sand. She waved politely at Luis, who was at the bow of the yacht at the jetty. He must have returned from taking Pascha to Puerto Rico.

Now she knew Pascha was off the island she could breathe a little easier, and was already plotting ways to convince Valeria to let her phone England and check on her father. So what if she embarrassed herself? Some things were more important than saving face.

She'd even tried to crack the code used to block her mobile again. It had been a complete waste of time. She doubted even her old housemate, the whizz who had taught her how to hack into Pascha's laptop, could have cracked it.

Finished with the beach, she set off up through the dense foliage. The further inland she went, the greater the humidity, and the trail she followed seemed to go nowhere in particular.

On the verge of turning back, she heard the sound of rushing water.

A couple of minutes later, she was awestruck with wonder.

'Oh wow,' she whispered under her breath.

She had reached a vast, open area with the middle missing, as if a huge circular section had been dug out of it. On the other side of the bottomless circle ran gushing water, pouring over the edge like a sheet. A ledge jutted out on her side. She stepped onto it and peered over. She'd found the bottom. The drop was at least forty feet, the waterfall pouring into a large, round pool.

Almost hugging herself with joy, she sat with her legs dangling over the ledge and took a long drink of water. She wished she'd taken Valeria up on her offer of a packed lunch. She could happily spend the next week in this little spot of paradise.

She'd found a spot very similar to this a few years before, on a holiday in Thailand. She and the friends she'd travelled with had taken it in turns to jump into the pool, exulting at the weightlessness of the fall. Emily hadn't had a care in the world. Not then.

Whipping her flip-flops and T-shirt off, leaving just her bikini top and shorts, she slathered herself in sun-cream and rested back, happy simply to soak it all in. Her solitude didn't last nearly long enough.

The shuffling of movement made her start. Turning her head, all her contentment died to see Pascha standing behind her.

'What are you doing here?' she asked rudely. He should be snug in his jet, flying away across the ocean.

Dressed in a pair of knee-length, dark-beige canvas shorts and an unbuttoned black polo shirt, he really was incredibly handsome. Even with his hair perfectly in place, and his clothes pressed to within an inch of their lives, he looked far more human than in his business attire. Her eyes drifted down to his calves, something hot flushing through her at their muscularity and the fine, dark hairs covering them. 'I thought you'd gone to Paris.'

'Never mind that, come away from the edge.' Speaking of edges, there was a definite one in his voice.

'I'm perfectly happy where I am, thank you.' Well, she had been.

'Where you're sitting could break away. It isn't safe.'

'Worried I might fall? At least it will save you having to worry about keeping me here.'

'Don't be infantile.' His face contorted into something resembling anger. 'While you're on this island your safety is my responsibility.'

'Actually,' she said, adopting an airy tone, 'I think you'll find I'm a fully grown woman and perfectly capable of taking responsibility for my own safety.'

'Not on my watch.'

'Have you jumped into the pool yet?' she asked, although she already suspected what the answer would be.

'That's a ridiculous question.'

'It feels like flying.' She couldn't help the wistfulness that came into her voice. 'It feels like nothing else on this earth.'

'I couldn't care what it feels like. It's dangerous. Now, come off that ledge—you won't be of any use to your father if you hurtle to your death.'

Damn him.

For a few brief moments she'd forgotten what her life had become, had slipped back into a life that had been free of worry and responsibility.

But he was right. What *would* become of her father if anything were to happen to her? What would become of James? James was more than capable of caring for their dad with her instruction, but when it came to working the practicalities out for himself he was useless.

Only a year ago she would have held her ground and refused anything other than taking a running jump off the ledge and plunging into the deep pool below.

As she now knew, through painful experience, a lot could happen in a year. A lot *had* happened. Her whole world had been ripped apart.

Pascha watched as a host of emotions flittered over Emily's pretty face. It had been a low blow using her father to make her see sense, but until she came away from that ledge he knew his racing pulse wouldn't rest. Perspiration ran down his back that had nothing to do with the soaring temperature.

But, when she shuffled back and got to her feet, the heat he felt under the collar of his polo shirt surged. Suddenly, now she was safe, the bikini top and shorts Emily wore came firmly onto his radar.

Her ebony hair was piled on top of her head, ringlets spiralling, but she'd left her face free of make-up, her beauty shining through in a wholly disturbing way. And that body... Skin that looked like silk...

As quickly as the snap of his fingers, his pulse raced anew, his blood thickening.

There was nothing immodest about Emily's khaki bikini; compared to the scraps of candyfloss most women of his acquaintance liked to wear, it was demure. The black shorts she wore with them were figure-hugging but modest. She wasn't wearing anything he hadn't seen hundreds of women wear on beaches around the world, yet she was the only one he reacted to with such force.

Breathing slowly through his teeth, he willed away his completely inappropriate reaction to her. 'Get your shoes on—we're going back.'

Dark-brown eyes narrowing, she folded her arms across her delicious chest. 'I've moved away from the ledge but I'm not prepared to let you order me around any further. If you want to go back, then go ahead. I'm staying here.'

'You haven't eaten for hours. My chefs are preparing

a late lunch for us. You can come back here later if you must.'

Something sharp pierced into Emily's chest.

'Give me a sec,' she said, looking away from him and slipping her toes into her silver sparkly flip-flops.

Had he *really* tracked her down just to make sure she had something to eat?

The last person to care that she ate three square meals a day had been her mother. During their daily phone calls she would always ask what Emily had eaten that day, what she was planning for her dinner...

Shaking her head to clear it of despondency, she shrugged her rucksack over her shoulder and followed Pascha back through the trail.

'So why are you still here?' she asked after a few minutes of silence. Despite his much longer strides, he never went too far ahead. She took a swig of water. The heat within the dense canopy of trees was fast becoming insufferable.

He ducked under an overhanging branch. 'There's a problem with the engine of the yacht. We need to wait for a part to be delivered from the mainland.'

'How long will that take?'

'It should be here by the end of the day.'

'Excellent. So you'll be leaving for Paris before the evening?'

'Sorry to disappoint you, but the part needs to be installed and then checked for safety before I allow anyone to go anywhere in it. I should be able to get away in the morning, depending on what the weather's like. There's a tropical storm heading for the Caribbean. I won't leave until it's passed.'

Emily didn't like the sound of that. 'Are we in its path?'

'No. We're likely only to get some high winds and rain at some point this evening, but it's an uncertain situation...'

Before he could finish his sentence, Emily lost her footing, practically skiing down a particularly steep incline.

Her cheeks were crimson; the only saving grace was that she hadn't fallen flat on her face.

'Are you okay?' Pascha asked, surefootedly hurrying to her side.

'Yes, yes. No harm done.' Feeling like the biggest fool in the world, she accepted his help, allowing his large, warm fingers to wrap around her own and pull her back to her feet.

'Thank you,' she muttered, knowing her cheeks had turned an even deeper shade of red that had nothing to do with embarrassment.

She snatched her hand away from his, as if the action could eradicate the effects of his touch. It felt as if he'd magically heated her skin, his clasp sending tiny darts of energy zinging through her veins, making her heart pump harder.

Pascha was still staring at her intently.

'Are you sure you're all right?' he asked after too long a pause.

'Honestly, I'm fine.' To prove it, she started walking again. It was with relief that she spotted the roof of the main cabin of the lodge poking through the foliage.

'Are you sure you haven't hurt yourself?'

'I *said* I'm fine.'

Before he had a chance to quiz her further, the theme to a cartoon she'd adored in childhood rang out. To her utter amazement, she realised it was his phone ringing.

Pascha had the theme to *Top Cat* as his ringtone?

He pressed it to his ear. 'Da?' His eyes immediately switched to her face. 'Yes, she is right with me. One mo-

MICHELLE SMART57

ment.' He handed the phone to her, mouthing, 'Your brother,' as he did so.

Her blood turned to ice.

'James?' The coldness quickly subsided when she learned the reason for her brother's call. He couldn't work the washing machine. Their mother had always done it for him, even after he'd left the family home. Since she'd died he'd used a laundry service—after failing to cajole Emily into doing it for him.

By the time she ended the call, irritation suffused her. She'd explicitly told him only to call in a genuine emergency—one call too many and for all she knew Pascha might decide not to bother passing on any messages. It was pure luck that she'd been with him at that moment.

Still, she consoled herself, at least she wouldn't have to badger Valeria for use of the lodge phone for another day. James had assured her their father's condition was the same, so that was one less thing to worry about.

Pascha had listened to Emily's side of the conversation with increasing incredulity. 'Your brother called about a *washing machine*?'

Judging by the way she inhaled deeply and swallowed, it was obvious Emily was carefully choosing her words. 'James isn't the most domestic of people.'

'Doing the laundry does not require a PhD.'

'In my brother's eyes, it does. Anyway, how would you know? I bet you've never used a washing machine in your life.'

'I make a point of learning how to use all the domestic appliances in my homes,' Pascha told her coldly. He understood why she made so many assumptions about him but it needled all the same. He hadn't been born rich— quite the opposite. Everything he had he'd worked damned hard for. Just being here, being alive, had been the hardest battle of all.

'Why would you do that?' For once there was no sarcasm or anything like it in her tone, just genuine curiosity. 'Surely you have a fleet of staff in all your homes?'

'I like to take care of myself,' he said tightly. 'Aliana Island is different—I come here to get away from the world and switch off.'

The lodge was only a few yards ahead of them now. Emily slowed down to adjust her rucksack. 'I can see why you would do that,' she admitted. 'I think Aliana Island might be the most beautiful spot on the planet.'

'I think that too.'

She gave him something that looked like the beginning of a genuine smile, her eyes crinkling a touch at the corners. It sent the most peculiar sensation fluttering in his chest. Before he had a chance to analyse it, he spotted Valeria waving at him in the distance.

'Excuse me,' he said, 'But work calls.'

As he walked, that same strange fluttering sensation stayed with him.

CHAPTER FIVE

EMILY HAD A quick shower, then steeled herself before setting off to the main lodge. But, when she stepped in the dining hall, the table was set for one.

A curious emptiness settled in her stomach when a young girl—she was certain the girl was Valeria and Luis's daughter—brought a bowl of bisque and some warm rolls through to her and gave a garbled apology about something important Pascha needed to attend to.

She ate mechanically then retired back to her hut, distantly aware the island's staff was now out in force. Though they weren't bustling in the sense that people bustled in large cities, the speed with which they were working had increased dramatically.

Back at her lodge, Emily dragged her sewing machine out and placed it on the table then got her tubes of fabric and her A5 pad of designs. What she really needed but had forgotten to bring was a mannequin on which to pin the dress she wanted to make. She wondered if Valeria's daughter—she must learn her name—would model for her.

Finally she had enough time on her hands to turn her own designs into something. Her own creations. Her own visions. No Hugo demanding she focus solely on *his*.

Disregarding the lack of mannequin and model, Emily laid the fabric on the long table and began to make her marks. How long ago had she designed this dress? Over a year, at the very least, before the bottom of her world had dropped away from her and she'd been left floundering, clinging on to anything that would give her a purpose.

The past year had been a constant whirl of hospital trips and visits to the family home. She'd been desperate to care for and spend as much time with her mother before the inevitable happened. All of this on top of holding down a demanding job and looking after her own home. When the inevitable had happened, life had continued at the same pace, this time a whirl of funeral arrangements, form filling and taking care of her increasingly fragile father. There had been no time to switch off. There had been no time for herself.

She placed the fabric chalk under her nose and inhaled, squeezing her eyes tight as memories of sitting in her mother's craft study assailed her. Her mother would have loved the opportunity to be a seamstress but it had never been an option for her. She'd married at eighteen and had had her first child at nineteen, devoting herself to being a good wife and mother.

And she had been. Even if Emily had been given a city of women to choose a mother from, Catherine Richardson would be the one she'd have chosen. Always supportive, always loving. When Emily had won her place at fashion college, she doubted there had been a prouder mother alive.

She wished her mother was here with her to see this beautiful island. But of course, if that awful, awful disease hadn't claimed her mother, Emily would never have seen Aliana Island either.

Catherine Richardson's death had unhinged the entire family and, no matter what Emily did or how hard she tried, she couldn't fix it back together.

She couldn't fix this dress either. She'd finished her

markings but without a model or a mannequin she would be sewing blind.

How could she not have thought to bring a mannequin with her when she'd remembered everything else?

Sighing, she gathered all her stuff back together and put it neatly away before wandering out onto the veranda.

As she leaned over the wall, she couldn't help but peek up to her left, where Pascha's hut jutted out. Nothing. If he was in there, he was out of sight.

She forced her attention onto the calm blue lagoon before her and breathed in the salty air which, mingled with the mass of sweet frangipani growing everywhere, created the most magical scent. If she could bottle it, she would make a fortune. She wanted to be out there in it.

She'd been shown a huge wooden hut that held a host of items for outdoor entertainment. She'd been told she could use whatever she liked when the mood took her. It was kept unlocked. She skipped down from her cabin and let herself in. Tennis and badminton rackets, sets of boules and kites all lay neatly shelved amongst kayaks and surfboards. So orderly was it all that she found what she was looking for with no effort at all: a row of snorkels and flippers.

Kitted out, she headed for the lagoon, delighting to feel the warmth of the fine white sand between her toes and the beam of the sun heating her skin, a breeze tempering it enough to make it bearable. In the distance, a boat sailed away from the island, going quickly enough soon to be a speck on the horizon.

Just one day in paradise and she had to admit she was already revising her opinion of the sun. Beneath the top heated layer, the water in the lagoon was deliciously cool, and she waded out in her flippers to waist height before donning the snorkel and diving under the surface.

What a sight there was to behold. She'd seen so many

pictures in the media of coral reefs dying, but here it thrived—blooms of colour in all shapes and sizes, an abundance of fish and other marine creatures, their individual colours and features clearly delineated.

Utter heaven.

Sitting on the ledge earlier overlooking the waterfall, she'd felt a sense of peace. She felt that same tranquillity now. It was just her and the lagoon. Nothing else. Down here, the rest of the world might not exist, and she was going to revel in the feeling. Even if just for a short while.

Emily's hut was still empty.

Pascha swore under his breath.

He'd searched the rest of the lodge. He needed to speak to her and she'd done another disappearing act. The only place now he could think she might be was at the waterfall she'd been so enamoured with. It was a good forty-minute walk, which wasn't the greatest length of time, but with the latest weather developments every second was precious.

Stepping out onto her veranda, he spotted the figure far out in the lagoon. He didn't even have to blink to know it was her.

Pascha cursed again, descending the outdoor stairs that led to the beach at a much quicker rate than usual.

In an ideal world he would send someone else out to her, but to do so would be to tear a member of his staff away from jobs that were now being undertaken as a matter of urgency.

As soon as he reached the sand, he kicked his deck shoes off.

After far too long standing, waiting vainly for her to notice him, he sat down and stripped off his polo shirt, ready to swim out to her. Except during that small action she'd disappeared from view.

Where was she?

Eyes narrowed in concentration, he scoured the area she'd been but could see no sign of her. His heart thudded harder. Where was she?

And then she emerged feet from the shoreline.

For the briefest of moments, his heart stopped.

Emily was wearing the same modest khaki bikini she'd worn earlier but she'd removed the shorts to reveal brief bikini bottoms. She'd donned a white T-shirt—sensible in this heat; he would give her credit for that—but the water made it transparent, the material clinging to her like a second skin.

He didn't think he'd ever witnessed such an erotic sight. Her dripping hair was longer than he could have imagined, the water pulling her curls out so it hung in a long sheet down to the small of her back.

Unable to tear his eyes away from the tantalising sight before him, his mouth went dry and heat pooled in his groin.

It wasn't until she started wringing water from her hair that she noticed him.

Something that was a cross between a scowl and a smile played on her lips as she removed the flippers and headed over to him.

'Come out to play?'

Mouth dry, he swallowed and shook his head, partly to refute her question and partly to clear it from the haze that had engulfed it.

He wanted to reach out a hand to her waist and pull her down to him. He wanted to roll her onto the sand and...

'Next time you decide to go out into the lagoon, make sure you let someone know,' he said in a far harsher tone than he'd intended.

Suddenly he felt furious. He should be in Paris finalising the documents that would make the completion of the Plushenko deal a formality, not worrying about the safety of the woman whose actions had been the catalyst preventing him from being *in* Paris. He certainly shouldn't be fantasising about making love to her, and *certainly* not right now when there was an emergency afoot.

She eyed him coolly before a tight, emotionless smile formed on her face and, so quickly that he had no time to react, she gathered her thick hair together and wrung it out again, this time over him, cold droplets falling onto his chest.

He jumped back. 'What did you do that for?'

'Because I felt like it,' she answered with a shrug. 'And because I've possibly just spent the most relaxing, wonderful hour of my entire life and you've ruined my mood completely with your irrational sanctimony.'

'I am being neither irrational nor sanctimonious.' He gritted his teeth together. He would hold on to his temper if it killed him. 'Anything could have happened to you out there. You might have got cramp...'

'Anything *could* have happened, but it didn't.'

'But if it had there would have been no one there to help you. In future, I would appreciate it if you let someone know when you're planning an activity with danger attached to it.'

Her eyes held his, narrowing, studying him, before he caught an imperceptible shift in them, as if they'd melted a little. Her clamped lips relaxed, a wry smile playing on the corners. 'Message received.'

'Good.' All the same, he made a mental note to warn his staff to keep an extra eye on her. Emily had a reckless streak in her. He would not have anything happen to her when she was on his island and under his protection.

'Was there a particular reason you sought me out? Or

are you just stalking me? Only, it's the second time you've come looking for me today.'

He ignored her flippancy. 'The tropical storm I mentioned earlier has changed paths—only slightly, but it's now heading for us.' He'd been given the news on his way to the dining hall.

She blanched and tilted her face upwards. 'I thought it felt a little breezy.'

The wind was slowly picking up speed, a few tendrils of her drying hair lifting with the breeze.

'These storms can turn from nothing to something very quickly.'

A sharp breath escaped her pretty lips. 'Okay, so what do we do?'

'What we do is go to safety,' he said grimly.

'Are we leaving the island?'

'No. We have the necessary shelter and provisions here.'

'The way you were talking, it was as if we had to move to safety now.'

'We do. The ocean currents are already strengthening. I've sent the last of my staff who live on the neighbouring islands home so they can be with their families, but the rest of us need to move to higher ground.'

Emily had been a touch sceptical about Pascha's insistence that they head straight for the shelter. Now she understood. The weather was changing far too quickly, even for her liking.

When they'd started walking the trail, a different path to the one she'd followed to the waterfall, the sun still blazed down on them. They finished guided by Pascha's powerful torch.

He'd insisted she carry a torch too, which she'd nestled in her rucksack with the few other items he'd permitted her to bring to the shelter. He'd chivvied her along in her hut, glaring at her while she'd debated what she needed to take.

In the end, he'd snapped with exasperation, 'The lodge and its huts are designed to the highest of standards. The chances of it sustaining any significant damage are very slim. Your possessions will be fine.'

'Then why are we going somewhere else for shelter?' she'd asked.

'Because a slim chance is worse than no chance. The shelter's on high ground and is designed to withstand the worst the weather can throw at us. I can guarantee your safety there.'

The wind had picked up as they walked but had no more strength than a mildly blustery English day. She knew this would increase, could feel it in the air around her. And she could see it. It wasn't yet full sunset but thick, black clouds covered what was left of the sun, the previously cobalt sky now a dismal dark grey.

Yet, now she saw the fortress he'd brought her to, she felt total confidence they would make it through the night unscathed, at least in terms of any damage by the storm. The shelter was a small concrete building in a small clearing, close enough to be protected by the surrounding trees but far enough not to sustain any real damage should any of them fall. When she followed Pascha inside, she was further encouraged that no damage could befall them, the interior walls of the shelter being reinforced steel.

But whether or not a night spent here presented dangers of a different sort…

'Where's everyone else?' The lodge had been deserted when they'd set off up the trail.

'They've gone to their own shelter.'

'What, this one is just for you and me?'

Pascha nodded, his mouth still set in the grim line it had held for the past couple of hours.

'Why didn't you tell me it would be just the two of us sharing?' she asked, not bothering to hide her irritation.

'I didn't think it important.'

'Well, *I* do. If you'd told me, I could have camped out with Valeria and the rest of the staff in their shelter.'

He raised a bored brow. 'My staff are all, in one way or another, extended family to each other. I deliberately built them their own shelter so in events like this they could be together *as* a family. You might be a guest, and I might be their boss, but they deserve their privacy away from us.'

How could she possibly argue with that? Although, she wanted to. She *really* wanted to. Sharing a confined space with Pascha for the foreseeable future could only bring trouble.

The interior of the shelter was practical but luxurious, with a large double bed, a plush sofa, a dining table and a small kitchenette with a bar at the end. The only privacy came in the form of a bathroom which was, by anyone's standards, opulent.

When Pascha shut the door of the shelter, the silence was total, making Emily realise just how loud the wind had become.

She peered through a small round window which reminded her of a ship's porthole, the only source of natural light in the shelter.

Shelter? It was the same size as her London flat.

Turning her head, she found him opening cupboards and rummaging through drawers.

'Can I get you a drink?' he asked, not looking at her.

Taken aback at the offer, she stared at him. 'What have you got?'

'Everything.'

'Rum and Coke?' she said flippantly, wanting to test him.
His grey eyes met hers. 'Do you want ice in that?'
'Seriously?'

He reached under the bar and pulled out a bottle of rum,
arching a brow as he displayed it for her.

She had to admit, she was impressed. And an alcoholic
drink might take the edge off her angst. *Might.* 'No ice for
me, thank you.'

'A thank you? You shock me.'

'I like to keep you on your toes.'

'You're doing an excellent job of it.'

While Pascha mixed them both a drink, her curiosity
overcame her and she wandered into the kitchenette to
rifle through the cupboards.

Amazing. There was enough food here for them to live
like kings for at least a fortnight. A month, if they down-
graded to princes.

'I take it there's a back-up generator?' she said.

'Of course.'

Something in his tone made her look at him. He looked
furious. 'What's the matter?'

'I've left my phone charger at the lodge.'

'And?'

'And I don't have enough battery left to get through
the night.'

'I would suggest going back for it but looking at the
trees through the window I can see it wouldn't be the
brightest of moves.'

'Finally she says something sensible.'

'*I* didn't leave the charger behind so don't take it out on
me.' She wasn't any happier about it than he was—what if
there was an emergency at home? James wouldn't be able
to get hold of her.

She forced herself to think practically. If an emergency

did occur, she wouldn't be able to do anything about it anyway, not from Aliana Island.

A whole evening of peace.

She couldn't even bring herself to feel guilty about it. Peace had become such an elusive thing in her life.

It was just a shame she had to spend it with Pascha Virshilas. It would be more relaxing to spend it with an angry bear. Though she had to concede that an angry bear wouldn't have the sex appeal…

Where had *that* thought popped out from?

No, no, no. If she was going to get through the night with even a semblance of sanity left, she had to tune out the fact she was in a confined space with the sexiest man alive.

Sexiest man alive?

Ten minutes in the shelter and she was clearly suffering from cabin fever.

'I'm not taking it out on you,' Pascha said.

'Good,' she shot back, the scowl on her face still evident.

He expelled a long breath and ran his fingers through his hair. Technically speaking, it wasn't Emily's fault, but if he hadn't been so determined to get her to the safety of the shelter, and wasted all that time at the beach with her, he would never have forgotten something as vital as his phone charger.

He could kick himself. He *should* kick himself.

Pascha should be with his lawyers. They'd spoken and corresponded throughout the day, none of them prepared to leave anything to chance, but it wasn't the same as being in the same room. There was too much that could go wrong and scupper the Plushenko deal, and he was thousands of miles away. And soon he'd be totally cut off from all communication.

He finished mixing her drink and handed it to her.

'Thank you.' She turned away and strolled into the living area. Her behind really did sway beautifully when she
walked, he noticed, curving nicely in her modest shorts
and causing a whole heap of improper thoughts to race
through him. Those improper thoughts were not helped by
her silver top with its slanting neckline, which displayed a
whole heap of porcelain shoulder, transparent enough for
him to see the bikini she wore beneath it.

'So, what is there to do for entertainment in here?' she
asked briskly, curling up on the sofa.

He held back the answer that formed on his tongue by
the skin of his teeth. 'I'm sure a resourceful woman like
you can make her own entertainment.'

She took a sip of her drink. 'Maybe enough of these
will send me to sleep and then I'll be able to wake up and
the storm will be over.'

'You'll have a headache if you drink too many of them.'

'Then I'll take a headache tablet.'

The woman had an answer for everything.

'Are you hungry?'

Her face scrunched up. 'A bit.'

'I'm not the greatest of cooks but I know how to make
eggs on toast. Do you want some?'

She jumped back to her feet. 'I tell you what, I'll cook.'

'Can you cook?' Why did that surprise him?

'Yep. It'll give me something to do.'

'Are you bored?'

'Yep. Anything you don't like to eat?'

'I'll eat anything.'

She practically skipped to the kitchenette. Opening the
cupboards and the fridge, she started examining ingredi-
ents, selecting some, rejecting others.

'Don't get too excited,' she warned. 'I can cook but it
won't be the *haute cuisine* you're used to.'

'I didn't grow up eating *haute cuisine*,' he said drily.

'Someone with three chefs at his holiday island is not someone who eats simple food.'

He'd followed her to the kitchenette and his huge form blocked her way to the utensil cupboard. A masculine scent with a hint of citrus filled her senses.

'Excuse me,' she muttered.

He shifted to the left.

Emily knelt down and snatched at a saucepan, tugged it out and immediately lost her grip, the pan clanging to the floor.

She picked it up and shoved it on the work surface. 'Look, you're getting under my feet. Why don't you sit down while I get on with dinner?'

What was *wrong* with her? Her entire body was flushed, as if she'd been heated from the inside out; her hands and fingers were refusing to cooperate with her brain.

The only thing she knew with any certainty was that this was going to be a long night.

CHAPTER SIX

EMILY DID HER best to eat her dinner but she struggled to swallow.

Her body just wouldn't relax.

What she needed was noise. She liked noise. It was comforting. If she'd been eating at her flat or at her parents' house—correction, her dad's house—the radio would be humming in the background.

Here, in the shelter, there was nothing but silence. Heavy, oppressive silence.

'Are you not enjoying your meal?' Pascha asked her.

Looking down, she found she'd been pushing her pasta around her plate.

'I'm not very hungry,' she confessed, adding with forced brightness, 'They always say the chef loses their appetite when it comes to the actual eating.'

'Well, I think it's delicious,' he said, popping a heaped forkful of her pasta concoction into his mouth to make his point.

She couldn't help but smile, but as the corners of her mouth lifted nodules in her belly tightened.

How could she eat when Pascha sat so close, near enough that if she moved her foot forward an inch she would graze his leg?

She was softening towards him. She could feel it. And

she didn't like it one jot. It felt disloyal, as if she was some-how betraying her father by finding the enemy to be so human. *And so damn sexy...*

However it was dressed up, be it mutual blackmail or force, Pascha had given her no choice but to come to Ali-ana Island. There had been no option but for her to com-ply. Her desperate attempt to help her father had backfired so spectacularly, a firework could be made in its honour.

And yet in the short time they'd been together Pascha had shown more consideration towards her than she'd ever known. He'd sought her out at the waterfall because he'd been worried she would be hungry. He'd sought her out at the lagoon because of the storm, because he'd wanted to take her to safety. Even his anger at her snorkelling alone had been provoked by his concern for her well-being.

When had anyone last worried about her safety? *When had anyone last worried about her full-stop?*

For her own sanity she needed to hold onto her anger towards him.

But how could she hold onto her anger and hate when every time she looked up at him she found magnetic grey eyes holding hers and the nodules in her belly tightened that little bit more?

She waited until he'd cleared his plate before rising.

'Sit down and relax,' he said, gathering the plates to-gether. 'You've done your share. I'll clear up.'

Only when his back was turned to her at the kitchenette did she exhale. It felt as if she'd been holding her breath the entire meal.

As she watched him load the dishwasher, admiring the tautness of his buttocks against the heavy cotton of his shorts, the strangest feeling crept through her veins, a fizzing, as if her blood had awoken and started dancing.

Disturbed by all these strange feelings being evoked

within her, and determined to pull herself together, Emily decided she might as well take Pascha's advice and relax. Taking another sip of wine, she put her bare feet up on his recently vacated chair.

'You would make an excellent house-husband,' she commented idly. He was wiping the work surface down with such thoroughness, she wouldn't be surprised if the top layer was scrubbed away.

He gave a grunt.

'I take it the thought of being a house-husband does nothing for you?' Saying the words made her realise she knew nothing about his private life. Nothing. Was there a woman? Surely there must be? Regardless of his wealth, a man who looked like Pascha would attract pretty much any woman he fixed those grey eyes on.

Another grunt.

'Do you think you'll ever marry?' she asked.

Pascha paused from wiping the side down to pin her with a stare. 'What's with all the questions?'

'I'm bored,' she lied with a shrug. 'You're the one who dragged me to a shelter where there's nothing to do to pass the time.'

'Can't you be bored quietly?'

'Why? Am I annoying you?'

'Yes.'

'Good.'

His glare turned into a half-smile and a rueful shake of the head.

'So are you going to answer my question?'

'The answer is no. No, I don't think I'll ever marry. In fact, I know I won't.'

'That sounds pretty emphatic.'

'That's because it is.'

'Why don't you want to get married?'

He turned his head to spear her with a glance. 'Why don't you have a man in *your* life?' he countered. 'How long have *you* been single?'

'Seven years.'

He leaned back against the work surface and folded his arms. 'That long?'

'Yep.'

'Any flings?'

'Nope. I work in the fashion industry. The vast majority of the single men I work with are gay. It's rare I meet an eligible straight man.' She tried her best to keep her tone light and nonchalant. Okay, so she was exaggerating, but it was the old tried and tested response she'd been using for years. Anything had to be better than admitting she'd given up finding anyone who didn't make her feel inadequate. Who didn't make her feel second-best.

She'd long accepted love would never happen for her. She'd grown tired of trying to find it. When her father had sunk into the dark depressions that had blighted her childhood, it had always been her mother who'd lifted him out of it, never his daughter. When he was at his lowest ebb, Emily might not exist. She'd never doubted his love for her but it had never been enough. *She* wasn't enough. His suicide attempt had only reinforced that feeling. If she wasn't enough to make her own father want to live, how could she possibly be enough for someone else?

And, just like that, the lighter mood she'd been trying to create darkened, making her stomach cramp.

Time to move onto safer territory, far away from relationships of any form.

'Seeing as the subjects of marriage and relationships bring us both out in a cold sweat, why don't you tell me why you want to buy Plushenko's instead? My guess is that it has to be personal.'

'What makes you think that?'

'You don't force a woman to travel halfway round the world simply to salvage a deal without it being personal.'

Although the very mention of the word Plushenko was enough to tighten his chest, Pascha found himself grinning. 'Were you a journalist in a previous life?'

'You would know the answer to that yourself if you'd bothered to ask about my job,' she said tartly.

'I couldn't get a word in,' he said, raising his brow. 'You ask more questions than the old KGB.'

'That's because I'm incurably nosy.'

Picking up the wine bottle, he headed back to the table. 'Tell me about your job first and then I'll consider telling you about my relationship with Marat Plushenko.' He topped both their glasses up then deliberately tugged his chair out from under her feet and sat down.

For half a moment he thought she might put her feet back up and onto his lap.

For half a moment his skin tingled with anticipation.

What, he wondered, would she do if he were to lean a hand down and gather those pretty feet onto his lap…?

Emily took a sip of her wine. 'You want to know about my job?'

'I do.' It dawned on him that he wanted to know a lot more than that. Emily Richardson was the most intriguing person he'd met in a long time, maybe ever. A seemingly fearless woman without limits when it came to those she loved. 'You say you're in the fashion industry?'

'I'm an in-house designer for the House of Alexander.'

'Ah.' He nodded. 'You work for Hugo Alexander?'

'Yep.'

'All the pieces fall into place.' The House of Alexander was one of the UK's foremost fashion houses, famous for its theatrical, off-beat designs. Hugo Alexander's designs had captured the eye of fashion editors around the world and the imagination of the public. It was one of the fashion houses to buy on his radar.

'What, you mean the sewing machine and the rolls of fabric I brought here with me?'

'And all the fashion magazines littering your bedroom.' *And the way you dress*, he almost added. He couldn't think of a more suitable fashion house for her to work for. Not that she was dressed that way now. Since arriving on the island, all her theatricality had been stripped away.

'You could have been Sherlock Holmes in a previous life.'

Pascha didn't want to laugh. He didn't want to find Emily amusing but the truth, as he was rapidly finding, was that he did.

He couldn't remember the last time he'd found anyone fun to be around. It was not a trait he sought. Yes, many of the companies he'd bought over the years were run by flamboyant characters, but these were not people he mixed with on anything but a professional level.

'Do you remember that party you had when you first bought Bamber?' she asked.

'I remember it,' he said, surprised at her turn of the conversation. Throwing a getting-to-know-you party was something he always did when he bought a new company, wanting to meet his new staff on a more human footing than at their work stations.

'I was only dressed that way because I'd come straight from work—we'd just had a show and Hugo had steered us all in a gothic focus.'

He looked at her. 'So you don't normally dress as the Bride of Frankenstein?'

She laughed. 'Not to that extent. If I'd had the time, I

would have changed into something a little more appropriate.'

'I thought you'd dressed that way deliberately.'

'If I'd had the time to change, I would have, but you know what fashion shows are like; the days just don't have enough hours in them.'

Pascha did know. When he'd bought his first fashion house he'd felt obliged to attend New York Fashion Week. He'd stayed for approximately one hour before boredom had set in and he'd made his escape. He'd felt the energy all the designers, make-up artists and all the other people involved had expelled, like a hive of creative bees working in perfect harmony. He could easily imagine Emily fitting into the hive with ease. 'How did you get into fashion?' he asked, curious to know.

'When I was a kid the only clothes available for little girls were "pretty" clothes and always in pink.' She pulled a face. 'I *hate* pink. I used to draw the clothes I wished I could wear. Eventually I badgered my mum enough that she taught me how to use her sewing machine.'

'Your mother was a seamstress?'

'If she hadn't had kids at such a young age, she probably would have been. Maybe if she'd lived a bit longer she might have gone on to do it.' She reached for her glass of wine and took a sip. Was it his imagination or was there a slight tremor in her hand?

Despite her threat to drink herself into a stupor, she'd had only the one rum and Coke, and had hardly touched her second glass of wine.

'Mum was so proud when I got the job with Hugo,' she said wistfully. A flash of pain crossed her face before she took another sip of her wine and then visibly braced herself, fixing a smile onto her face to say, 'Anyway, your turn.'

'My turn for what?'

'To tell me why you want to buy Plushenko's.'

Briefly Pascha considered batting the question away.

'It's not as if we've anything else we can do other than talk,' she pointed out, those meltingly gorgeous eyes fixing themselves on him, waiting.

His eyes dropped to her bare shoulder, his skin heating as he considered a different, far more pleasurable way in which they could pass the time…

He gave a brisk shake of his head.

He needed to get a handle on himself.

They might be getting along in the shelter better than he had hoped but it didn't change the facts. They had blackmailed each other. It was the only reason either of them was there.

'Marat Plushenko is my brother.'

Emily gave a low whistle. 'I didn't see that one coming. You're trying to buy your own brother's company? In secret?'

He sighed. There was little point in trying to cheat her with part of the story. 'We're not biological brothers. I never knew my biological father—he abandoned my mother before I was born. Marat's mother died when he was a toddler. Our parents married when I was eighteen months old and Marat five. Andrei adopted me, my mother adopted Marat.'

'Right…' She nodded slowly. 'So you were raised together as brothers?'

'Yes. We were raised together as brothers but Marat never accepted me as a brother.' He gave a rueful smile. 'He always hated me.'

A groove formed in her brow. 'Why?'

He rubbed his face. 'Marat never wanted anything to do with Plushenko's or with me—'

'Back up a minute,' she interrupted with a shake of her head. 'I've just got it—Andrei Plushenko is your adopted father, therefore you're part of the Plushenko dynasty?'

'A dynasty conveys a sense of longevity. Andrei founded the company.'

'I see.'

'Are you sure *you* weren't Sherlock Holmes in a previous life?'

She laughed. 'You were telling me about Marat,' she prodded.

'He set up a number of failed businesses—I think it was five in all. Eight years ago he decided he should join the family firm, except he wasn't prepared to work his way up and learn the business. He wanted to join at executive level.'

'You didn't agree with that?'

'No. To me, it was a ludicrous idea. I was happy for him to join us, almost as happy as Andrei was, but I thought he should learn the intricacies of the business first, just as I did.' He shook his head. 'Our father didn't see it like that. He was desperate for Marat to come aboard, would have given him anything he desired. It came to a head when I made the mistake of giving Andrei, our father, an ultimatum—if Marat joined the board, I would resign.'

'Did Andrei choose Marat?'

'Not in so many words.' He fixed suddenly bleak eyes on her. 'What he said was, "But, Pascha, he is my blood". I handed in my resignation the next day.'

'How did Andrei react to that?' Her voice was low, soft.

'He was very upset with my decision. My mother was too. But I was…' He almost said 'devastated' but stopped himself just in time. 'I was very angry about the situation, angry enough to change my name from Plushenko to my mother's maiden name. I'd joined the business straight from school, pushed for the international expansion, the new state-of-the-art workshop…'

He blew out a breath and shook his head as more memories assailed him. 'It took five years before I began to see things clearly but I never got the chance to make amends with Andrei—he died in his sleep three years ago. Marat took the reins. Since then, Plushenko's has gone to the dogs. Marat won't sell it to me so I formed RG Holdings as a front company, spent two years building it up and investing in companies so he wouldn't be suspicious.'

'*Why* does he hate you so much? You're his *brother*.'

His chest expanded to see her outrage on his behalf.

You're his brother.

He'd always wished that to be true.

'I don't know. I don't have any memories of life without him. But he was older when our parents married. He has memories of life without me.' He shook his head and raised his eyes to the ceiling before leaning back into his chair some more and placing his feet on the chair beside her. 'Maybe a more pertinent question to ask is why I'm telling you any of this.'

Her gaze still resting on him, she raised a shoulder in a rueful shrug, the expression on her face indicating she didn't know the answer to that any more than he did.

He breathed heavily and got to his feet. 'More wine?' As a rule, he didn't drink much alcohol, too conscious of the effects it had on the body. Tonight, he was prepared to make an exception.

She covered her glass with her hand. 'Not for me, thank you.'

'Have you abandoned your idea of drinking yourself into a stupor?' he asked lightly.

'I'd only get really giggly and annoying, and we both

know I'm annoying enough as it is,' she replied, her light tone matching his.

'In that case, how about I get you a glass of milk?'

She laughed but her eyes remained troubled. 'I might take you up on that later. Right now, I think I need a shower. My hair is still full of sea salt.'

'Okay, well, while you do that I'm going to check in with my lawyer.' He didn't hold out much hope that his battery would last long but he needed something to distract him.

Sharing his past did not come easily to him, but then he'd never found himself in this kind of situation before, where talking really was the only way of passing the time. The only way apart from the obvious, that was, which categorically could not happen. It just couldn't.

No matter how tempting he found her: a bundle of sin with porcelain skin and ebony hair.

CHAPTER SEVEN

EMILY SPENT A long time in the shower, clearing her muddled thoughts.

Pascha Virshilas was the enemy. She had to remember that.

But she was hanging on to her hate by the tips of her fingers, the threads she'd gripped her loathing onto loosening to such an extent she couldn't keep a proper hold on them.

Simply enjoying his company felt like stepping into enemy territory. This was the man who hadn't given her recently widowed father the chance to defend himself before suspending him without pay; the man who'd left her father to flounder in a pit of despair rather than start the investigation which would have cleared his name. This was the man who had left her father to rot.

He'd looked out for *her*, though.

Donning a knee-length black dress—when had her wardrobe become so *dark*? She really needed to inject some more colour into it—she went back into the main part of the shelter and found Pascha sitting on the sofa reading a book.

'I thought there wasn't any form of entertainment here,' she said mock-accusingly.

He held the book up. 'I'm afraid all the reading material in here is in Russian.'

'Never mind.' She wandered past him and over to the kitchen.

She needed something to do, something to keep her mind occupied so it wouldn't be so full of *him*.

'If I'd known I would be having an English guest, I would have arranged for some books of your own language to be stocked.'

'I'm hardly your guest, though, am I?' She said it for her own benefit as well as his—a reminder to them both.

He put his book down and raised a brow. 'While you are on this island, you are my guest and you will be treated as such.'

It was on the tip of her tongue to rebuke him, to point out that guests were generally allowed to communicate with the outside world. And that, oh, as a rule, guests weren't usually forced on to their host's island.

For once she kept her tongue still.

They both knew the facts. There was little point rehashing them.

They had a long night ahead of them. Better to try and sustain the strange kind of harmony they'd managed to establish.

As long as she continued to keep her guard up, she would be fine.

Rooting round the kitchenette for something to do, she found a large tub of vanilla ice-cream in the freezer. There was nothing better than ice-cream to aid harmony.

'Do you want some?' she asked, holding it up for him.

'Sure,' he replied with a shrug, closing his book and placing it on the arm of the sofa.

Grabbing two spoons, she took it over to the table.

Pascha pulled out the chair opposite her and nodded at the tub. 'No bowls?'

'Saves washing up.'

'It'll melt.'

'No, it won't. I guarantee that in ten minutes it will all be gone.' She might not have been able to manage much of her dinner, but ice-cream…now, *that* she could happily eat, however fraught her emotions. 'If you want a bowl, help yourself.'

Rolling his eyes, he got himself a bowl, sat down and methodically scooped some ice-cream into it.

'Is that all you're having?' she asked with incredulity. He'd only put two scoops into his bowl.

He quelled her with a look. 'It's hardly a healthy food.'

'It's ice-cream. It's not supposed to be healthy. It's supposed to be comforting.'

'I'll be sure to tell my arteries that.'

They ate in silence but, unlike over dinner, this silence didn't have an uncomfortable edge to it. Probably because no one could be uncomfortable whilst eating divine vanilla ice-cream. The sweetness was soothing.

While they ate, Pascha checked his phone.

'Did you manage to get hold of your lawyer?' she asked.

'Just. The battery died after a couple of minutes.' He gave it a shake, as if hoping it would miraculously charge itself.

'You do realise you're torturing yourself by checking it?' she said.

He pursed his lips. 'It's pointless, I know. I just find it incredibly frustrating.'

'Have some more ice-cream.'

'Will that help?' he asked mockingly.

'Nope. But it will make the frustration taste a bit sweeter.' To make her point, she put a delicious spoonful into her mouth.

His lips twitched.

She grinned to see him scoop a little more into his bowl, but only a little. 'Have you always been a control freak?'

His eyes narrowed a touch. 'I like to control the environment in which I live,' he answered slowly.

'We all do that to an extent,' she agreed. 'But you seem to be quite extreme about it.'

He put his spoon down. 'I had leukaemia as a child,' he said simply.

Startled, Emily felt her eyes widen.

He'd had *leukaemia*…?

'Being so close to death so young…' He raised a shoulder. 'It shapes you. It shaped me.'

'I don't know what to say,' she said starkly. 'Are you okay now? I mean…'

'I know what you mean and, yes, I am in good health.' He hadn't escaped unscathed, though, Pascha reflected with a trace of bitterness. Five years of chemotherapy and all the other associated treatments had given him a future but had also come with one particular cost, a cost that no amount of money could ever fix.

'But I do not take my good health for granted. I freely admit I like to take control of my life, but when you have spent five of your formative years with no control over your body or your treatment, and no control over how it affects those you love…' He shook his head and scraped out the last of the ice-cream in his bowl. 'Now I am in control. Just me. To use business jargon, I will not outsource it.'

Emily had stopped eating, her spoon held in mid-air. 'I'm so sorry.' She shook her head, a dazed expression on her face. 'That must have been awful for you. Terrifying. And your poor parents. It doesn't bear thinking about, does it? It's hard enough watching your parents suffer but when it comes to your own child…' Her words tailed off and she seemed to give herself a mental shake, sticking her spoon back into the tub.

'Yes, it was hard for them,' he agreed, his voice dropping, his mind wandering back to a time when his mother had seemingly aged overnight. One minute she'd been a young mother with an easy laugh, the next a middle-aged woman with lines on her face.

The memories had the power to lance his guts.

His mind drifted back to those—literally—dark days, when they'd been so poor his parents could only afford to heat his bedroom. That had been when Marat's disdain for his younger, adopted brother had turned ugly. How clearly he recalled Marat whispering to him when their parents had been out of earshot, 'Why don't you just die and save us all this trouble, Cuckoo?' Pascha might have been only seven years old but he'd known his brother meant it.

'Cuckoo': Marat's secret nickname for him.

He looked down at his empty bowl.

To hell with it.

He could allow himself one night of sweetness.

He stuck his spoon into the tub and ate straight from it.

Something flickered in Emily's eyes as she did the same, their spoons clashing as they dived into the tub a second time.

The flickering darkened and swirled, their eyes locked.

She really was incredibly beautiful. And incredibly easy to talk to.

With a stab, he realised he'd shared more of his past with her this evening than he had ever done with anyone. His childhood illness was history, not something he talked about.

He looked at his watch. 'Half an hour.'

A groove he was starting to recognise formed on her brow. 'Half an hour...?'

'That's how long it's taken us to finish this tub of ice-cream. You said ten minutes.'

'Too much talking, not enough eating. And it's not finished.' She yanked the tub up and peered into it. 'There's at least a spoonful left.'

'You finish it.'

'How very magnanimous.'

He watched as she seemingly scraped out every last drop of the by now melted remnants.

His blood thickened at witnessing her pink tongue dart out to lick the spoon.

Mentally taking a deep breath, he got to his feet. To-night he was also going to say to hell with his strict diet and limited alcohol consumption. 'How about we open another bottle of wine?'

'Why not?' she agreed, pushing the tub away from her. 'It's more exciting than milk.' She placed a hand on her middle. 'Do you think it's any good for stomach-ache?'

Why did that action automatically make him think of a pregnant woman rubbing her swollen bump?

He blinked the image away, unsettled at the imagery.

'Has someone eaten too much ice-cream?'

'Mmm…maybe,' she said, elongating the first syllable.

'I hate to say I told you so…'

She pulled a face. 'I know, I know, too much ice-cream is unhealthy. That didn't stop you from eating half of it.'

'Not quite half,' he said with a wry smile, pushing his chair back. He'd eaten more ice-cream in one sitting than he'd consumed in the past decade.

Emily was right. It made bitterness much easier to swallow.

Or was it that she was such a good listener that it made it easier to spill the secrets of his past?

When he sat back down with the bottle and two clean glasses, she leaned forward and rested her chin on her hands. 'Being stuck in here with me must be a nightmare for you. First the engine of the yacht breaking, then the storm… It must be driving you mad, all these things occurring that are out of your control.'

He laughed. 'I'm coping.' To his surprise, he realised, he was coping remarkably well.

Under normal circumstances, an event like this would elicit a vigorous amount of pacing the room, waiting for the danger of the storm to pass. But instead he was content to sit back, relax and just…talk.

When had he ever taken the time just to *talk*?

No wonder he wasn't going mad when he had Emily to distract him, something she managed to do effortlessly.

He gripped the stem of his glass, fighting a sudden compulsion to reach over and touch her hair. She'd left it loose. Her curls had dried since her shower, a mass of long ebony ringlets springing here, there and everywhere.

What did that gorgeous hair smell of? he wondered. What, he wondered, would she do if he were to capture one of the locks and wind it around his finger?

Every sinew in his body tightened.

He took a large swallow of his wine, watching as she reached for her glass and did likewise, running a finger over the flesh of her bottom lip to wipe a drop away.

He took another swallow and forced a smile at her questioning look.

He wished there was another tub of ice-cream in the freezer. Maybe he could spoon it straight onto his lap and kill the heat simmering in him.

Emily sat curled up in the armchair she'd dragged over to the wall so she could peer out of the porthole-like window. Only the dim glow from the outside lights enabled her to see the trees bending under the assault of the wind. Rain lashed down like a sheet, more powerful than anything she'd ever witnessed.

She shivered.

'Are you cold?'

She shook her head, keeping her face pressed to the window.

'I'll get you a blanket.'

'I'm not cold.' It was looking at the storm that had made her shiver. All the same, when Pascha gave her the soft fleece blanket, she wrapped it around her shoulders with gratitude, murmuring her thanks.

By the time they'd finished their wine, the atmosphere between them had shifted. A growing charge had sent her away from the dining table to where she was now, holed up by the window.

If she couldn't look at him, she couldn't notice how utterly gorgeous he was.

If she couldn't talk to him, she couldn't feel the richness of his voice seeping through her veins…

How long would the storm go on for? It seemed interminable.

They'd been in the shelter for six hours. The time was really stretching now, and so was the tension brewing between them. She could feel it with every breath. And what made it worse was that she knew he felt it too.

She didn't know much about leukaemia other than that survival rates had improved dramatically in recent years. How old was he? Thirty-four? When he'd had it, the survival rates had been dire. The battle would have been immense. She kept imagining the small child he'd been and the desperate worry of his parents. She wanted to travel back to the past and hug that small child.

It explained so much about him.

For the first time, she tried to think from his point of view. There he was, pouring all his energy into buying the firm his adored adopted father had founded, having to do it amidst the highest secrecy, when he'd learned a sum of money had gone missing on a senior executive's watch. He hardly knew this employee. The sum was significant by any normal person's standards, but to a billionaire it wasn't significant enough to warrant an immediate investigation, not when priorities lay elsewhere.

Twirling a curl absently around her finger, Emily sighed. However much she might disagree with his methods, she understood the reasons.

If only she wasn't so aware of him. Her attention might be firmly fixed on what was going on outside but still she sensed every move he made.

He was back on the sofa, his nose buried in his book.

Even if there had been a book in English she wouldn't have been able to concentrate. There was too much energy racing through her veins. More than that, she was too consumed with *him* to concentrate properly on anything.

She heard every page he turned. She knew every time he ran his fingers through his hair. She knew when he stretched his long legs out.

After another hour of silence had passed, during which the storm hadn't abated at all, she heard him close his book.

'I need to get some sleep,' he said. 'You can have the bed. I'll take the sofa.'

'Don't worry about it—I'm a night owl. You take the bed. I'm happy watching the storm.' Before he could open his mouth to argue, she turned her head and threw him a wry smile. 'I'm half your size and probably need half the sleep you do. It's more logical for me to take the sofa.'

Pascha wanted to argue with her but, studying Emily's expression, he could see she didn't look remotely tired.

He wasn't tired either.

His body clock, usually so good at regulating his sleeping patterns, appeared to have gone on strike.

But he had to sleep—at least had to try to—even if Emily *was* sitting mere feet away from him.

'If the sofa is too uncomfortable, feel free to join me in the bed,' he said in as casual a tone as he could muster. 'You have nothing to fear from me.'

His veins thickened anew at the thought of her climbing in beside him, her sweet scent inches from him, close enough for him to reach a hand out, touch her skin and discover for himself if it was as silky as it seemed. Close enough to discover for himself exactly what her glorious hair smelled like.

With iron will, he forced the torrent of desire away.

'I know.' She turned her face back to the window before he could read what was written on it.

After brushing his teeth, he poured himself a glass of water and padded around the shelter turning off all the lights bar the small lamp near where Emily sat curled like a cat.

Her concentration was firmly focussed on the storm outside, yet he could feel her awareness of him as keenly as he felt his own awareness of her.

Did she realise she'd been twirling that same curl round her finger for the past hour?

He stripped to his boxers and slid under the covers. Usually he slept nude but tonight he felt it more appropriate to wear something. He didn't want her feeling uncomfortable with him. 'Goodnight, Emily.'

She didn't look at him. 'Night.'

His eyes wouldn't close. Try as he might, he couldn't stop his mind drifting into what would happen if she *did* join him in the bed. He didn't think he'd ever felt the blood running through his veins so keenly, a thick desire that, if he'd been alone, he'd be able to do something about. If he'd been with any other woman, he'd have been able to do something about it too. Since making his fortune, he'd never been rebuffed by a woman. But he'd never felt a woman's disinterest in his money as keenly as he did with Emily. His wealth meant nothing to her.

She was only here on Aliana Island with him, in a storm shelter, out of sufferance.

No, he corrected himself. She was here out of love. Love for her father.

She was also a thief, he reminded himself. However good her intentions, she'd stolen her father's pass key, incited someone into giving her the code—he would find out who as soon as he returned to the UK—and had intended to steal every scrap of data from his hard drive. If he hadn't returned earlier from Milan than intended, she would have got away with it.

And yet...

Her actions had been born out of desperation. Born out of love.

As sleep continued to elude him, he cursed that he hadn't sent her to the staff shelter. Forget all his good reasons not to have done; for the amount he paid them, his staff could have put up with Emily for one night. Sleep was an essential function of his life. He'd never forgotten the words of his doctors when he'd been a child. *Sleep will help you get better,* they'd told him. And he *had* got better. He'd recovered. He'd beaten the odds and he'd survived.

He heard movement—Emily quietly making herself a hot drink before settling back on the armchair.

Pascha willed sleep to come quickly.

CHAPTER EIGHT

SLEEP DIDN'T COME. Time dragged ever more slowly. But Pascha must have drifted off at some point, for one minute Emily was there and the next she was gone.

Rubbing his eyes, he sat up. The armchair she'd been sitting in was empty. The small lamp still glowed.

He checked his watch and saw it was three a.m.

He looked through the porthole. It appeared the worst of the storm was over. The trees still swayed but the rain had stopped.

Stopping only to pull on a pair of shorts, he turned the handle. The door was unlocked. Stepping outside, he found her huddled up in the fleece blanket on the bench in front of the shelter.

The chill of the breeze hit him immediately. Not all the storm clouds had disappeared but right above Aliana Island they had cleared enough to reveal a black night sky alight with stars.

She turned her face to him. Under the glow of the outside light he could see her desolation.

'It's three o'clock,' he said gently, crouching down to her height, noting that she'd taken the padded mats off the dining table chairs and placed them along the bench to sit on.

She nodded, blinking rapidly. She cleared her throat.

'I needed some air. I'll come back in if the wind picks up any more.'

She isn't a child, he reminded himself. If she wanted to sit out in the cold wind, then that was her business. But the look on her face reminded him of a child. Emily looked lost.

He sat next to her, thankful for the mats she'd placed on the bench.

At first she didn't acknowledge him, simply kept her deadened gaze on the starry sky.

After long moments of silence, she opened her mouth. 'When I was a little girl, my mum told me the stars were our dead ancestors looking down on us.'

'That's a nice thing to believe,' he answered carefully.

'I want it to be true. I want to believe she's up there looking over us all.' She hugged the blanket tighter around herself. 'You know you asked me why I went into fashion?'

He nodded, a pointless gesture with her eyes still staring upwards.

'It was because of her. It was a way to spend time with her, just me. She loved us all but so much of her time was spent managing Dad's depression and trying to limit its impact on me and James that sometimes it was hard to get her to myself. We'd hole ourselves up in her study and design and make our own clothing. I kept trying to talk her into going to my old fashion college as a mature student, but she kept putting it off, saying she would do it one day. And now it's too late. She'll never do it. All the dreams she had…all gone.'

'When did she die?'

'Three months ago.'

The jolt this information gave him felt like a physical blow.

Three months?

That meant Malcolm Richardson had lost his wife only weeks before the money had gone missing...

He lost his train of thought when he felt her slump beside him, saw her drop forward to wrap her arms around her knees and bury her face.

For too long he stared at her shaking body before placing a hand on her back.

She shuddered. He thought she was going to shrug off his ineffectual attempt at comfort; instead she twisted into him, placing her head on his chest as she sobbed, her tears falling onto his naked skin.

Pascha didn't think he'd ever felt as inadequate as he did at that moment. All he could do was stroke her hair with the palm of his hand, his guts a tangled knot.

His mind raced, a confusion of thoughts he couldn't begin to decipher.

Only three months...

'I miss her so badly.' Emily spoke in gasps, her breaths warming his stomach. 'I can't believe she's gone. I just want her back.'

What could he say? Nothing.

'When she was diagnosed we knew she wouldn't have long but it happened so *quickly*. Seven months. That's all we had—that's all *she* had. Seven months. All the time in the world would never have been enough.'

It was as if a floodgate had opened. Emily's anguish spilled out, unable to be contained.

'What happened to her?' he asked quietly, nestling his hand into her hair and cradling her scalp protectively.

It took a few attempts for her to get the words out. 'She had Progressive Bulbar Palsy.'

'What's that?'

'A form of motor neurone disease. Very aggressive. So cruel....' Her words tailed away.

'Is that why you took all that time off work?' he asked, his stomach clenching. He'd assumed it had all been tied to her father's recent mental breakdown; he'd had no idea it stretched back so long.

She rocked into him. 'I had to be there. So little time.' Emily couldn't speak any more, her vocal cords choked by her grief.

Since the diagnosis, Emily had worked on autopilot, on the go all the time, never sitting still long enough actually to face what was happening to her mother full-on. It had been the same when she'd died.

She hadn't cried since the funeral, too worried about her father to grieve for the woman they'd all adored.

'Let me ask you something.' Pascha spoke in a gentle tone that soothed her as much as the tender movements of his hand in her hair, massaging her scalp. 'When your mother died, did she know how much you loved her?'

She tilted her face to look at him. His face was crinkled, his eyes a litany of emotion. She nodded in response, still unable to speak.

'Then you did have enough time, *milaya moya.*' His finger brushed against her cheek, his grey eyes swirling with emotion. 'I know it doesn't feel like you did and you're right—all the time in the world would never have been enough. But for your mother to go to her grave knowing how much you all loved her is the greatest gift you could have given her. For that, you were blessed with all the time you needed.'

Even through the pain of her grief, Emily could feel the sorrow beneath the empathetic tone of his words. Her hand moved on its own accord to touch his face. Dark stubble had slowly spread along his jawline throughout the evening, a roughness to the touch that felt impossibly comforting.

She shifted a little, moving her face up his chest so her cheek rested on his shoulder. 'Are you thinking of your father?'

His jaw clenched but he nodded. 'I never got the chance to say goodbye or to—' He cut his own words off, tilting his head back to look at the sky thickening with clouds once again. 'I never told him how much he meant to me.'

'I'm sorry,' she whispered.

He looked back down at her, his usually composed features raw.

Emily had been there at the end, holding her mother's hand when she'd slipped away. They'd all been there. It was a comfort knowing her mum had been with the people she loved most when the end had come, that she hadn't left this life alone.

All Pascha had was regrets. She could feel them as keenly as she felt their mutual sorrow.

She had no idea how long they sat there gazing at each other, his hand nestled in her hair, her fingertips tracing his stubbly jawline.

She wanted to kiss him. She wanted to feel those wide, firm lips upon hers and learn for herself what they'd feel like upon her mouth. And from the deepening of Pascha's breath and the growing intensity in his eyes she could tell that he wanted it too.

His head dipped at the same moment she raised her chin, their lips coming together in a whisper of movement. He exhaled at the same moment she expelled the breath she hadn't realised she'd been holding and, inhaling again, she breathed him in, a dark, masculine essence that filled her with such deep longing.

She pulled back to stare at him, recognising the same puzzlement in his own stare as she knew must be in hers.

But then their lips came together again, his strong arms

enveloped her and he was kissing her properly, his tongue sweeping into her mouth, filling her senses with his exotic taste.

As if they had free will, her arms wrapped around his broad shoulders and she pressed her hands to his skin. It was smoother to the touch than she could ever have imagined and she traced her fingers over it in circles.

The deeper his kisses, the more she wanted, soaking in as much of his taste and touch as she could consume.

Time slipped away, the world shrinking just to them, a mesh of hungry lips and tongues devouring each other.

His hand swept down her back to clasp her thigh over the restriction of the blanket she was nestled in.

Her blanket.

For the first time, she considered how cold he must be in the whipping wind.

While she was all snuggled up in the fleece blanket, Pascha was sat in nothing but a pair of shorts.

It wasn't just the wind lashing around them either; the rain had started again, not as fierce as earlier but picking up quickly, big, fat droplets of it.

'We should go back inside before we get pneumonia,' she said, disentangling her arms from around him, swallowing hard.

Pascha hadn't noticed the rain. He'd stopped feeling the cold.

One kiss and he'd forgotten himself.

He'd forgotten his health.

For the first time since the age of five, he didn't care.

How the hell had that happened?

Emily slipped off his lap—when had she climbed onto it?—and got back to her feet in such an unsteady fashion he grabbed her arm to stop her falling.

'Thanks,' she muttered, stepping back with wide, pained eyes before disappearing back into the shelter.

Pausing only to collect the seat covers on the bench, he followed her in, locking the door behind him.

She'd disappeared into the bathroom. He took the moment of solitude to inhale deeply and calm his racing thoughts.

Never had he felt desire so strong.

Or so wrong.

To allow anything more than a kiss to develop between them was to take the first steps on the road to madness.

Emily was nothing like the women he usually entertained for his gratification. She was all too real. All too human. And she was vulnerable.

But his good intentions died when she reappeared from the bathroom, a white towel wrapped around her, accentuating her feminine curves.

All the moisture left his mouth. All the words he'd planned to say left with it.

She passed him a hand-towel with which to dry himself. Wordlessly he accepted it, rubbing it over his hair and face.

She closed the gap between them and placed a hand on his chest. The heat from her skin warmed him more than any fire ever could have.

Slowly Emily traced her fingers over him. It was every bit as beautiful as the tantalising glimpse she'd caught on the veranda had promised, his chest hard and golden, the dark hairs covering it soft.

His chest rose, as if he were struggling for breath. He caught her wrist. 'Emily, I do not want to take advantage of the situation.'

She could see the pain on his face as he spoke the words. As she closed the final gap between them, pressing herself so her mouth was against his collarbone, she could feel the strength of his erection through his shorts, a movement that sent a bloom of heat straight between her thighs. 'You might not want to take advantage of the situation, but *I* do,' she whispered.

How could she not? The whole day felt like a dream. So many emotions had been churned up, so much desire. And right then it was the desire that burned the strongest, enough to drive out all the other emotions living within her, all her fears.

Stepping back, she tugged at her towel and let it fall to the floor, watching as his eyes widened, the grey darkening.

It was her turn for eyes to widen when a strong hand clasped her waist and wrenched her to him. Before she had time to breathe, Pascha's hot mouth had found hers, his hold on her the only thing keeping her boneless legs upright.

She wound her arms around his neck and clung to him, kissing him back with everything she had, her tongue winding around his, dancing a tune she never wanted to end.

When Emily had been a child she had always adored watching couples kissing on the television and had eagerly anticipated her own first kiss. In her head, she'd envisaged it would be just like the movies and would send her into a frenzy on the spot. Needless to say, her first kiss had been a disappointment. It was nothing she could put her finger on but kissing had never sent the shockwaves through her that she had always secretly hoped for.

She could kiss Pascha for a lifetime. His kisses were everything she had yearned for and more, sending ripples of pleasure careering through her veins and tingles of electricity zipping through her skin. His kisses were perfect.

She wanted to cry out when he broke away and stepped

back. Without any preamble, he slid his shorts off and kicked them away.

He stood before her, fully erect.

Her breath caught in her throat. He was beautiful in every way.

He reached out a hand and placed it on her breast, simply resting it there, his fingers gently cupping the swollen skin. Fresh desire shot through her and she sucked in a breath, fighting the urge to close her eyes. She wanted to see everything. She wanted to feel everything. Beneath his touch, her nipples puckered and hardened and she arched slightly into him, her mouth filling with moisture, the heat between her legs growing and bubbling.

Mirroring his movement, she splayed a hand on his chest and tugged the silky hair between her fingers, adoring the feel of his warm skin beneath her touch, the hard satin-smoothness of it.

His free hand clasped her neck and began a lazy trail over her collarbone and down past her breasts. Down his fingers trailed, skimming lightly over her belly before slipping further down still.

A gasp escaped her throat and their eyes widened, mirroring each other. Pascha was dumbfounded. He'd known she wanted him but he'd had no idea how deeply her desire ran or how closely it matched his own throbbing need.

Jaw clenched, he fought to keep his head, to keep some basic control.

Snaking one hand around her waist, he used the other to capture her chin and gaze deeply into those mesmerising eyes, the flicker of fire burning from them; they were like precious jewels. Slowly he brought his mouth down and kissed her, her lips parting at the first touch as they forged back together in a fury that threatened to unravel his restraint.

Emily's fingers skimmed up his chest and her hands hooked around his neck. She pressed into him, moving against his erection, her breasts crushed against him.

Unable to bear the thought of breaking contact with her luscious soft flesh, Pascha half-dragged and half-carried Emily to the bed. There, they fell onto it in a heap, her melodious easy laughter like music.

He gazed in wonder, taking in all the features of her face, from the large brown eyes that glowed with sensuous promise to the heart-shaped lips curved in a half-shy, half-wanton smile. He took in the faint smattering of freckles the sun had exposed on her delicate skin and wondered if a more beautiful woman existed—but, no; in his eyes, that would be impossible. Perfection was lying beneath him hooking an impatient arm around his neck and tugging his head down to capture his lips in a deeply passionate kiss that made his blood burn into a fever.

'You're beautiful,' he whispered before burying his face in her neck and kissing his way down to her perfectly ripe breasts.

Moving his lips over each of them in turn, his need deepening with every second, he forced his mind to detach. He was close to the edge. He could feel it.

Reluctantly he abandoned the softness of her breasts and snaked his way down her body, smiling at her jolt as he moved lower. How many more of her secrets were there to uncover?

Casting his head lower still, over her dark, downy hair, he felt her body tense slightly when he gently prised her thighs apart and laid between her parted legs. Gazing up at her through hooded eyes, he was gratified to see her head thrown back, her breathing shallow through her parted lips.

He dipped his head, his tongue immediately homing in on the nub of her pleasure. She tasted wonderful, of musky, sexy woman. Her breathy, responsive whimpers only served to fire him further, and when her fingers clasped his hair, and she raised her buttocks and writhed beneath him, he feared his own peak was nearing.

And then he felt her stiffen, her whole body lifting from the mattress, her fingers digging into his scalp as her orgasm rippled through her.

The white light flickering behind Emily's eyelids slowly dispersed. The deep pulses flowing through her body dissolved into a trillion tiny tingles that burrowed from the tips of her toes all the way up to her scalp. Dazed, she lifted her head up and opened her eyes. Pascha's chin now rested on her abdomen and he was gazing at her with something akin to wonder.

Wordlessly he crawled up the length of her body until he was on top of her, his nose touching hers. Their lips came together and she wrapped her arms around him, the bodies pressed together so tightly it was impossible to know where she began and he ended.

A whimper of panic flew from her mouth when he pulled—ripped—away from their embrace.

Placing a tender finger to her lips, he smiled crookedly. 'I must get some protection.'

She twitched a nod and attempted a smile in return. As she watched his retreating figure head to the bathroom, she took deep breaths, trying desperately to contain the ragged beat of her heart.

Pascha was back by her side in less than thirty seconds yet those beats seemed interminably long.

Her gaze moved to the square silver packet in his hand.

He gathered a handful of curls and moved them aside to place a solitary kiss on her neck. Looking back at her, his eyes burned, sparkles flying into her and liquefying her core all over again. 'Do you want to put it on?'

But Emily's hand was shaking. It was nothing but anticipation, she frantically told herself. She was a twenty-first-century woman.

So why, then, did she suddenly feel so vulnerable?

She wanted this more than she had wanted anything in her life. And that was terrifying.

He leaned forward and kissed her, a kiss full of passion and hunger, a kiss that blew everything else from her mind. She slipped a hand down his arm and caught hold of his fingers. Together, their lips still locked, they rolled the condom on. Done, Pascha smoothly manoeuvred her onto her back and pushed her legs apart, his big hands stroking her thighs before curving up her sides, up the sides of her breasts, up to her neck, before resting on the pillow either side of her head.

Her lips suddenly cold as he broke the kiss, Emily's eyes fluttered open and locked onto his.

The sensation of drowning flooded her. She could feel the strong thud of his heart hammering against his chest, reverberating through her skin and burrowing through her ribcage to match the unsteady tempo of her own.

Pascha placed his lips on her mouth, just a light pressure, his breath flowing into her pores and filling her mouth with sweet heat and moisture. Every nerve-ending in her body burned, demanding his possession, and when he finally entered her she had no control over the high-pitched moan that flew from her mouth.

Keeping her eyes wide open, she raised a hand to his cheek, savouring the feel of him inside her, filling her completely.

His movements were torturously controlled as he began to move, his kisses intensifying as he deepened the penetration, their bodies fusing into one pulsating, rhythmic mass.

Emily was helpless in his arms, unable to do anything

but clasp tight to him and repeat his name over and over in a desperate voice that was not her own, taking every ounce of the pleasure he was bestowing. Pascha began to drive harder and faster into her and still all she could do was cling to him, nothing but willing putty in his hands until, finally, the tension tightening in her core exploded. Waves of pulsating ripples tore through her into a crescendo of colour that blinded her in its brilliance.

Dimly she was aware of his movements becoming more frantic, his groans deepening until he gave one last powerful thrust and crashed on top of her.

For long minutes her head was nothing but mist. Pascha's breath was hot on her neck. Her fingers idly caressed his scalp and the nape of his neck, her eyes locked on the ceiling.

As the mist began to clear and the sensations absorbing her body started to lessen, the world came back into focus. But it was all wrong. It was nothing she could put her finger on; it was like looking at the world through a different lens, a tiny shift in the spectrum.

But that tiny shift was enough to tell her she would never be the same again.

CHAPTER NINE

THE STORM HAD cleared when Emily awoke, a beam of light pouring through the small porthole.

Pascha's side of the bed was empty.

She looked at her watch. It was only eight a.m. and she'd only had minimal sleep but it had been enough to see her through what she already knew was going to be a long day.

The bathroom was empty. She dived inside and locked the door. A minute later she stood under the steady stream of the shower. For an age she did nothing other than let the hot water pour over her body. The same body that had woken barely two hours before to make love to him all over again.

She could still feel the press of his lips to hers…

She could still taste him…

A flush swept through her that had nothing to do with the steam of the shower.

Every atom of her body danced with an energy she had never experienced before.

But mixed with the dancing was a deep feeling of dread right in the base of her stomach, a warning that she had made what could be the biggest mistake of her life.

However much she wanted to, she couldn't hide in the shower for the rest of her life. She had to face him under the light of day sooner or later.

Dressing in a clean black bikini and a sheer viridian-green sarong, she made herself a cup of tea then opened the door of the shelter.

The early heat of the day hit her immediately, warming her skin. She breathed it in, eyeing her surroundings, looking at the destruction from the night before. Dozens of trees had been felled, the clearing in front of the shelter littered with leaves and snapped-off branches. The shelter appeared to have escaped unscathed. She doubted the lodge had got off so lightly.

There was no sign of Pascha.

She sat back on the same bench from the night before; it was bone-dry, as if the rain had never lashed it. In the daylight she saw it had been welded to the concrete beneath it, a sign of Pascha having taken no chances, not even with a bench. The thought brought a wry smile to her lips.

The man thought of everything.

Inhaling deeply, she looked around. All the stars had gone; the sky was bright and cloudless. For the first time she was able to appreciate the view, a vista even more spectacular than the one from her veranda. In the distance were the neighbouring islands cresting out of the calm, sparkling ocean. She hoped they hadn't suffered too much in the storm.

She sensed rather than heard movement. Holding her breath, she waited as Pascha sat next to her, keeping a respectable distance between them. Her heart hammered painfully beneath her ribs.

'What's the damage?' she asked. At least her vocal cords worked. That was something.

'I haven't been to the lodge yet. I was waiting for you to wake.'

She supposed this was her cue to get to her feet and get her stuff together.

Closing her eyes briefly to brace herself, she fixed a nonchalant look on her face and turned her head to look at him.

At some point that morning he'd shaved. His hair had resumed its usual immaculate state. Somehow the chinos and polo shirt he'd changed into were properly pressed.

An ache bloomed low in her abdomen, climbing all the way up to tighten in her chest.

Pascha stared at the beautiful face he'd woken up to.

He'd had possibly the worst sleep of his life but also, somehow, the best. He'd listened in the dark as Emily's breathing had deepened and slowed into a regular drawn-out beat. At one point she'd turned in her sleep, her face just inches from his own. He'd gazed at her lips, barely visible in the darkness, and had pressed the lightest of kisses to them. His body hardened at the memory of her taste, a sultry sweetness that fired his loins anew.

Her hair smelt like raspberries.

Everything inside him tightened.

Mingling with his desire was guilt. It plagued him.

If he'd known Malcolm Richardson's wife had died only a few weeks before the money had disappeared, he would have handled the matter differently. He wouldn't have suspended him summarily without giving him a chance to put his side across. He would have been far gentler in his approach.

Pascha had been so wrapped up in the Plushenko deal that he'd put everything else on the back burner, including the internal investigation into the missing money. So wrapped up had he been that not one employee who knew Malcolm Richardson had dared tell him of his recent widowhood.

He put himself in Emily's shoes. If it had been Andrei accused of stealing money...

He would have done anything to clear his name. He would have believed in his father's innocence every bit as fiercely as Emily believed in Malcolm's.

'I'm sorry.'

A groove appeared in her brow that he wanted to smooth away. 'I should have known your father had been so recently widowed.'

Her gaze remained steady but something flickered. 'Yes; yes, you should have.'

He sighed heavily. 'I really am very sorry. I wish I'd known about your mother. I would have handled things a lot differently if I had.'

She nodded and sank her teeth into her lips before saying, 'Please, do me a favour and clear his name. I know you're going to drop the suspension and everything, but he still needs to be cleared properly for his peace of mind. I swear he never took that money.'

'I will get it prioritised.'

'Thank you.' Her eyes held his, something swirling in them that disappeared before he could read it, and she straightened, as if giving herself a mental shake-down.

'I'll get my stuff together and we can go back to the lodge.' She didn't wait for his response before disappearing back into the shelter.

'What's that place?' Emily asked shortly after they started the walk back to the lodge, spotting a pretty concrete hut through the foliage.

'One of the guest shelters.'

'Like the one we stayed in?' She mentally applauded her outward nonchalance. So long as she kept the conversation impersonal she would be fine. Her stomach felt all knotted and twisted, though, and she inhaled deeply, trying to loosen all the constrictions within her.

She was reading too much into her jumbled emotions. So they'd made love; that didn't have to mean anything. People made love all the time. Well, other people did.

She'd been single for too long, that was her problem. Her emotional state made her vulnerable too. It was no wonder her heart raced when she was around him.

'It's identical. There are three of them for guests to shelter in if a storm hits so they can retain their privacy.'

'Why didn't you put me in one?'

He turned his head to look at her. 'I didn't want you sitting through that storm alone.'

The warm glow his words evoked in her made her feel flustered.

Why, oh why couldn't he be the evil monster she'd assumed him to be at the beginning?

But then, if he had been that evil monster, she would never have made love to him. She would never have clung to him for support and comfort when her grief had threatened to drown her with its strength.

The further down the trail they went, the more the wreckage from the storm became apparent. The majority of the pathway was covered with felled trees, branches and tiny twigs sharp enough to cut into flesh. Pascha enfolded her hand in his, helping her clear it all, his care expanding her heart so much it threatened to smother her lungs and stop them working.

The main house of the lodge appeared to have survived the storm without any damage. It was lucky. Devastation abounded everywhere else.

Half of the roof was missing from the hut where all the game paraphernalia was stored, a yellow cordon already erected around it. A tree had fallen onto the roof of the dining hut and had cut straight through it like a hot knife slicing through butter. Everywhere the eye could see lay scattered debris.

But it was at the jetty that the real destruction had occurred. Pascha's yacht, the beautiful vessel due to take Pascha back to Puerto Rico later that day, and her ticket home in five days, had toppled over in the storm and beached on its side.

Pascha held onto his temper by a thread.

Were the fates conspiring against him? How else to explain the run of luck, all of it bad, that had blighted him the past couple of days?

Until Emily had stolen into his office, everything had been running smoothly. Marat had been too taken with the number of zeroes on the buy-out offer to look closely into the provenance of RG Holdings. Not that it would have mattered if he had. So complex was the structure disguising Pascha's involvement, he was certain it would withstand any vigorous scrutiny. And yet…there was always room for doubt. Marat was lazy but there was no telling how deep his lawyers would dig.

There always existed the possibility something could go wrong.

Emily, who had kept her distance while he'd spoken to his staff, joined him and gave a sympathetic grimace. 'Is it salvageable?'

'It's on its side and filling with water as we speak. The chances of getting a crew here within the next few days to attempt a rescue are remote at best.'

'So what happens now?'

He dragged a hand down his face. 'I don't know.'

He moved away from her, crossing over to Luis, who was speaking on his mobile phone. When he got a minute, he would get his charged. For the moment the yacht was taking all his attention. Once he'd got this sorted he would go back, check the dozens of messages that would undoubtedly have piled up and call Zlatan, his lawyer. One thing at a time. Right now it was the loss of his only means of getting off the island that was his priority.

'Any news?' he asked Luis when he disconnected the call he was on.

'The soonest we can get a boat to you is likely to be two days. The other islands took a real battering—the few boats that aren't destroyed are needed to get the injured to the mainland hospital.'

One consolation Pascha could take was that none of his staff here on Aliana had been injured. They'd all escaped with a solitary scratch between them.

He nodded curtly. 'Keep trying,' he said, doing his best to keep his tone moderate. He could easily pull some strings and get any number of boats to come for him from the mainland. If he were to do that, he could be off the island within a couple of hours. But the real issue was the coral reef. The local islanders knew it well, knew which sections were safe to sail through and which would rip the hull to shreds. Outsiders, the yachtsmen that could come to his rescue, did not. To call them would be to place lives at risk.

For the first time he cursed his refusal to build a landing strip or heliport on the island. He hadn't wanted to destroy the qualities that made Aliana Island so special. It just went to prove that sentimentality got you nowhere.

'Is there anything I can do to help?' Emily asked quietly, appearing at his side.

'Speak to Valeria. At the moment, it's all hands on deck.' He shook his head at the inappropriateness of his comment. The deck of his yacht was submerging by the minute.

It suddenly occurred to him that Emily would want to hear news of her father.

'Let's go to my hut and check my phone for messages.'

However much he would like to blame her—blame anyone—none of this mess was Emily's fault.

There was nothing else he could do here at the jetty. The clean-up was under way. The storm had knocked the power out but the generators were working and would keep them going for at least a fortnight.

They made the short walk to his hut in silence.

He unlocked the door and held it open for her. Her petite figure brushed against his as she passed.

His jaw clenched.

With everything that was going on, the adrenaline pumping through him—the urge to bury himself in her softness, even if just for a short while—was strong.

Instead he sucked in a breath, plugged his charger in and turned his phone on. It lit up immediately, two dozen beeps ringing out in rapid succession.

He listened to his voicemail messages first. Six missed calls: two from his lawyer, one from his PA and three from James. He listened to the latter first.

'Well?' Emily asked, her arms folded so tightly across her chest a sliver of paper would have struggled to get through. Worry was etched all over her face.

'Three messages from James. One asking how to work the dishwasher, one asking if it's okay to cook a pizza in a microwave and one asking where the iron is.'

She relaxed her stance slightly. 'At least we know they're alive.'

'If your brother hasn't killed them both with food poisoning.'

'My dad's not eating anything so he'll be safe.'

He saw straight through her vain attempt at humour. 'He's not eating?'

'All he does is sleep.' She shrugged helplessly. 'Sleep

is good. Eventually he comes out of the darkness. Well, normally he does.'

'And James is capable of caring for him?' Now he knew the man microwaved pizza, real doubts had set in.

'Yep. All he has to do is make sure Dad takes his pills and keep an eye on him throughout the night.'

He could see how badly she was struggling to keep herself together and he admired her efforts. There was so much he admired about her. 'I'm surprised James didn't ask you to pop home and iron for him.'

'He can ask all he likes—I'm happy to cook for my brother but when it comes to ironing he can jolly well do it himself.' She grinned, a forced smile that tugged at his heart. 'I swear, if I ever have a boy I'm going to train him to do every domestic chore going before I let him loose on the world.'

Of course Emily wanted children. A woman as devoted to her family as she was wouldn't think twice about it. It was in her DNA.

A lancing pain settled in his guts. Once, a long time ago, he'd dreamed of having children. A family linked by his blood.

'So you don't completely baby him, then?' he said, forcing his own grin.

The groove in her brow deepened. 'I never baby him. He's just hopelessly undomesticated.'

'I understand that it's normal in a lot of families for the baby to keep the baby role even into adulthood.' That didn't apply to him, though—Marat had gone to great lengths to ensure Pascha never felt like a brother to him, younger or otherwise. Pascha had grown up feeling like an only child with a stranger living in the room next to him. A stranger he had wished with all his heart would accept him.

'James isn't the baby of the family,' she said, sounding offended. '*I* am. He's three years older than me.'

'Really?' He stared at her, looking for a sign that she was teasing him. All he saw was indignation. 'Then why have *you* taken responsibility for your father?'

'James and I share the responsibility.'

'If that's the case, why didn't he move back home to be with your father too? Why was it only you?'

A look he struggled to discern flitted over her face. The closest he could come to describing it was confusion. 'I offered.'

'And James was happy with that? He didn't offer in turn?'

'What is this? Are you trying to turn me against my brother?' Her brown eyes were wide, the rest of her features tight, and she took a step back.

'Not at all. I'm just trying to understand why you're the one doing everything—*risking* everything: your job, your home—while your brother gets to live his life as normal apart from occasionally acting as a babysitter.'

She looked as if she'd been punched. 'You haven't the faintest idea what you're talking about or what we've been through, so keep your opinions to yourself.'

She left his hut without a goodbye.

Pascha could have kicked himself. He hadn't wanted to upset her, but nonetheless he was glad he'd said what he had.

He would bet every last cent he had that James's job wasn't at risk. The man ran his own business, could take all the leave he needed with no one to answer to.

Emily had been the one to take all the time off, enough to have been given a final warning for it. Emily had been the one to leave her flat and move back into her childhood home.

James might be the elder sibling but it was the younger of the two who had taken the role of leader.

It was the younger of the two who'd effectively given up her life for their father.

CHAPTER TEN

EMILY SAT AT the table of her hut—which had mercifully escaped the storm with no internal damage—carefully sewing sequins onto the hem of the dress she'd spent the afternoon making, a different dress from the one she'd marked out a couple of days before. So what if she had no mannequin or model? That she was doing something practical was enough.

She remembered the first dress she'd made. She'd been seven. Naturally, her mother had done the majority of the work, but once the work was done she had let Emily raid her button box. Emily had spent hours sewing all the pretty, sparkly ones all over the dress, being very careful not to stab her seven-year-old fingers too often.

She'd loved wearing that dress, had got every ounce of wear from it, leaving a trail of fallen-off buttons wherever she went. More than anything, she'd loved the closeness she'd felt with her mum at that time, a special time only for them.

After her heated exchange with Pascha in his hut, Emily had buried herself in the clean-up, working until long after the sun had gone down, doing everything she was physically capable of. It had been therapeutic. It had left her no time to think.

Today was different.

Today, when she'd shown up at the main lodge at the crack of dawn, Valeria had given her a hug and told her there was nothing else for her to do. All that was left was hard manual work.

Emily had spent the day alone with her thoughts.

She'd thought about a lot of things, especially about what Pascha had said about James; the truth it contained. And, as she'd thought, she'd wandered back to the waterfall and sat on the ledge, gazing at all the bright colours glistening under the sun.

She might loathe the colour pink but she'd always adored bright, happy colours.

When had she stopped designing bright clothes? When had she stopped wearing them? It was working with Hugo, his love for the gothic and theatrical. His control over his designers was absolute. She'd moulded herself into what she believed he wanted her to be and, worse, had let it spill into her private life. Yes, she adored dressing up, loved wearing make-up, but when had she last worn clothes she felt were for her and not some image she was trying to live up to?

Armed with a determination to fix it, she'd hurried back to her hut, grabbed the roll of Persian Orange cotton, drawn a quick sketch as a guide and got to work.

So what if the finished product was a shambles?

So what if it didn't fit properly?

This was for *her*.

When had she lost the essence of herself?

Had she ever found it in the first place…?

A tap on the door caught her attention and she tilted her head to find Pascha standing there. With all the activity involved in fixing and straightening everything affected by the storm, they'd spent hardly any time together since leaving the shelter.

He'd come to her hut, though, late in the night, so late she'd almost given up hope.

Not that she'd been hoping. She'd been too angry and hurt by his words about James to want him to come to her.

She'd been lying in her bed wide awake when he'd tapped on the same glass door he was currently standing at. That one tap had been enough.

However much she'd wanted to deny it, she'd carried with her a deep, inner yearning, an intense almost cramp-like feeling of helpless excitement.

He'd stood at her door, hands in his pockets. He'd looked shattered.

He'd said two words. 'I'm sorry.'

She'd been in his arms before he'd crossed the threshold.

There had been no more conversation. All their talking had been done through their bodies.

He'd left early.

Now, he stepped into the hut bringing with him a cloud of citrusy manliness.

She closed her eyes, hating the way her heart raced just to see him.

The night was bewitching. Everything felt so different in the daylight, her emotions so much more exposed.

'Everything okay?' she asked, forcing graciousness as she resumed her sewing.

'I thought you'd want to know—James has called. Your father got out of bed today.'

She turned her head to look at him so quickly she wouldn't have been surprised if she'd given herself whiplash. 'You're joking?'

His eyes were steady. 'No joke.'

While Emily tried to digest this unexpected news, Pascha took the seat opposite her.

She could feel his stare resting on her but suddenly felt

too fearful to return it, too scared of what he would read in her eyes. Scared of what she would read in *his* eyes.

Her father had got out of bed. A small step, yes, but one with huge implications. In theory this meant the worst of it was over. She should be celebrating.

So why did she still feel so flat?

'Why didn't you tell me your father tried to kill himself?'

The needle went right into her thumb. 'Ow!' Immediately she stuck her thumb into her mouth.

'Have you hurt yourself?' he asked, his eyes crinkled with concern.

She shook her head before pulling her thumb out of her mouth and examining it. A spot of bright red blood pooled out so she put it back in her mouth and sucked on it.

She was going to kill James.

They'd made a promise to each other. Yes, it had been an unspoken promise, but it was an unspoken promise they'd carried their entire lives. They didn't speak about their father's severe depression outside the family home, not to anyone. It was kept between them. Their father's attempted suicide came under that pact.

So why the hell had James told Pascha Virshilas, of all people?

'Do I take it by the horrified look on your face that you're angry I know?' Pascha asked.

'Yes, I am *very* angry,' she said, her fury so great she could barely get her words out.

'Why? Are you ashamed of him?'

'Of course not! But when my dad's well again I know *he* will be ashamed. He won't want anyone to know.'

'Has he done this before?' Pascha asked quietly.

'What? Tried to kill himself?' Her voice rose.

'I know this is painful for you to talk about but I must know—when did he take the pills?'

'Didn't James tell you that?'

'No. And, before you turn your anger on your brother, he didn't tell me, not directly. It was a throwaway comment about stopping his watch on the medicine cabinet. I don't think he even realised he'd said it.'

Slightly mollified, Emily put the fabric down and made a valiant stab at humour. 'Your powers of deduction astound me.'

To her alarm, Pascha saw right through her attempt to lighten the mood and placed his hand on her wrist. 'I'd already guessed something bad had occurred. This just confirmed it. Now, please answer my question. When did he take the pills?'

Finally she met his gaze head-on. 'When do *you* think he took them?'

He sighed heavily, as if purging his lungs of every fraction of oxygen contained within them.

'He tried to kill himself the same day you suspended him on suspicion of theft. Two months to the day after we'd buried my mother.'

The obvious remorse that seeped out of him as she spoke her words had her feeling suddenly wretched.

She tugged her wrist out of his strong grip but, instead of moving her hand away, rested it atop his. 'He was a man on the edge before you suspended him,' she explained with a helpless shrug. 'What you did pushed him over that edge, and I'm not going to lie to you Pascha: I've spent the past month *hating* you for it.

'But the truth is, my father had just been waiting for an excuse. James and I knew how bad he was becoming. It's like watching a child cross a road with a lorry rushing towards them but not being able to run fast enough to push the child away, or scream loudly enough for them to hear. We couldn't reach him. *I* couldn't reach him. I've never been able to. The only person who could reach him when he fell into that pit was my mother, but she isn't here any more.'

Did Emily realise she had tears pouring down her cheeks? Pascha wondered. Or that her fingers were gripping his hand as if he were the anchor rooting her? His chest hurt to see such naked distress.

'This depression, it's happened before?'

She nodded, running her hand over her face in an attempt to wipe her free-flowing tears away. 'He's always suffered from it but can go months—years—without succumbing. And I know I shouldn't say succumbing, as if it's his fault, because I know it isn't. He can't help it any more than Mum could help getting that monstrous illness.'

Despite her impassioned words, Pascha didn't think she believed them, not fully.

He tried to think how he would have felt if he'd been a child and his father had shut himself away for weeks on end. Children were sensitive and felt things more deeply than most adults credited.

His illness had been devastating for his parents, but they were adults and understood there was nothing they could have done to prevent it. Children were liable to blame themselves.

Just as he was considering which of his contacts would be best placed to recommend a psychiatrist at the top of their field, his phone vibrated, the *Top Cat* tune ringing out loudly.

Emily laughed, tears still brimming in her eyes. 'I love that tune.'

He grinned in response and swiped his phone to answer it.

It was his lawyer, Zlatan.

'I'll call you back,' he said, disconnecting the call. He got to his feet and looked down at her. She'd stopped crying. Her eyes were red and swollen, her cheeks all blotchy. She looked adorable.

'Are you going to be okay? I need to call Zlatan.'

She sniffed and nodded. 'I still can't believe that's your ring tone. *Top Cat* was my favourite cartoon as a child.'

'And mine,' he admitted. 'My father got some black market videos of it from one of his clients. When I was too ill to do anything else, I would watch them over and over.'

Their eyes held and he was taken with the most powerful urge to lean over the table and scoop her into his arms.

Yesterday he'd sworn to himself that whatever was happening between them had to stop.

All he could offer her was money. He knew without having to be told that she didn't want it.

Emily needed someone to love her—someone who could give her a family all of her own to heap her love on.

And that was the one thing he could never give her.

Despite his best intentions, he'd climbed the stairs leading up to her hut in the dead of night, exhausted after the clean-up and little sleep, and found himself rapping on her door before he'd realised his legs had taken him to her door. Even then, he'd tried to convince himself he was there to apologise, nothing else. Certainly not to make love to her again.

He needed to put some distance between them. Things were becoming too... He didn't know what the word was to describe the growing connection between them, knew only that nothing could ever come of it. 'I need to get going. I have a lot of work to do.'

'I'm going to stay in here and finish this off,' she said, picking up the bright material she'd been working on when he'd walked in. 'And then I might take another walk to the waterfall.'

'It will be dark soon,' he pointed out. 'I would prefer it if you held off until the morning.'

He was rewarded for his concern with a soft smile. 'If it makes you feel better, I'll wait until the morning.'

'Thank you.'

'And I'll hold off jumping into the pool until I can see the bottom.'

'Very funny.' Not even Emily would be crazy enough to jump into that pool. 'I'll see you later.'

He could feel her eyes following his movements all the way to his own hut.

Emily assumed she would spend the evening in her hut alone as she had the night before. The clean-up was still ongoing, with most of the staff concentrating on clearing the felled trees and other manual jobs.

When Pascha turned up at her hut not long after sundown, he looked more relaxed than she'd ever seen him, the lines around his eyes and mouth softened. Even his clothes were casual, dressed as he was in faded jeans and a white T-shirt. She would never in a million years have guessed he owned a pair of jeans. Or that they would fit so well…

'We're eating on the beach tonight,' he said, not bothering with any preamble.

On the beach…

Had it really only been three days since they'd eaten on the beach, her first night on the island?

It felt a lifetime away. *She* felt a lifetime away.

She'd placed the dress she'd spent the afternoon making on a hanger. It wasn't quite finished; it was missing embellishments she wanted to add to it. But…it was done. A little rough, considering there was no mannequin or model for her to use, but it was done—the only item of real colour in the room.

She was fed up of the dark.

'Give me a minute,' she said, yanking the dress off the hanger and diving into her bathroom. In no time at all, she'd stripped off the black vest and black shorts and donned her creation.

She turned before the mirror, staring critically at her reflection.

Deviating from her original sketch, she'd made it sleeveless, the bodice smocked and elasticated to hold it in place, the skirt flaring out into a 'V' that fell to her knees. She plucked out a couple of loose threads from around the hem then pulled her tortoiseshell comb loose—really, why did she bother with it? Her hair always fell out.

She dashed back into the main room of the hut. 'Two secs,' she said, lunging at the dressing table. Not bothering to sit down, she applied a little eyeliner, some mascara and a dash of coral lipstick.

There was no need for war paint. Pascha had seen her stripped bare, in all senses of the word. And he'd still wanted her. Just as she'd wanted him. Just as she still wanted him, more than she'd ever dreamed possible.

When she turned to face him, the grey of his eyes glittered.

Her thundering heart soared.

'You look…' He raised his shoulders as if to find the word he searched for. 'Like a fire opal.'

Her voice broke. 'Thank you.'

He edged back towards the door. 'We need to go.'

Her skin dancing, she followed him down the steps to the beach.

The staff were already there, setting up long bench tables which were being covered with crockery, cutlery and plentiful bottles of wine and beer. Some of the felled trees and branches had been placed in an A shape to make a bonfire a little further down the beach from where they would be eating.

'I thought everyone could do with a night off to let their hair down,' Pascha murmured into her ear.

Startled, she tilted her face to look at him. His arms were crossed over his broad chest but there was nothing defensive about his stance. It was more a look of a man surveying all he owned and taking immense pride in it.

'What can I do to help?' she asked.

He gave a brief flash of his teeth. 'You can help me with the barbecue.'

'You're cooking?'

'We all muck in but the barbecue is my domain.'

'You've done this before?'

He raised a shoulder. 'A few times.'

He never ceased to surprise her.

It wasn't long before laughter was the predominant sound, laughter and a whole heap of chatter, the two-dozen staff all determined to forget their worries about family and friends on the battered surrounding islands and mainland for one evening. Plates of food and condiments had been brought out and the wine was in full flow. The balmy weather and black sky with stars glittering like tiny jewels only added to the party effect.

The good humour was contagious and spirits were high. Even Pascha, set apart from the rest of them at the barbecue, had a smile on his face. Emily went backwards and forwards from the industrial-sized barbecue to the tables, delivering trays of ribs, chicken breasts, king prawns, skewer kebabs… The list of food was endless.

So busy did she make herself, and so many conversations did she strike up, that she spent hardly any time with Pascha. That didn't stop her awareness of him.

For a man desperate to get off the island, he was clearly in his element. No one looking at him would think he wished to be elsewhere.

Noticing his glass of beer was empty, she poured another for him and took it over. 'Are you coming to sit down?'

'I'll get these chops finished and then I'll be over,' he promised, taking the glass from her. 'Thanks for this.'

'You're welcome.' His smile made her belly flip over and her heart soar. She hurried back to the benches with a skip in her walk.

Pascha watched as Emily sat down with his maintenance guys, an animated conversation breaking out.

He wished he could build a rapport with people as easily as she did but he was not one for making friends. He'd missed so much of his schooling due to illness that by the time he'd been well enough to return he'd become an outsider. Five years was a long time in a small child's life. He'd been an outsider ever since, never knowing or learning how to fit in. If it hadn't been for Andrei taking him under his wing, giving him confidence enough not to care when peers had parties to which he was never invited, who knew where he would be today? He'd found his own niche to fit into because he'd always been aware there was nowhere else he *could* fit. Even being tucked under Andrei's wing had come at the price of Marat's hatred for him increasing exponentially.

Was that why he'd been so desperate to hold on to Yana—because he'd felt he'd found a niche with her and had wanted to hold onto it at any cost?

He tried to imagine what his life would have been like if he hadn't, finally, recognised that the cloudy diamond she'd turned into had been a mask for her misery. What kind of a couple would they have been if he hadn't set her free?

The icy clenching in his guts told him the answer to that.

He looked back at Emily. Had he even stopped looking at her?

That dress she'd made...

His fire opal had come to life, dazzling him with her vibrancy. If she were to tread the same path as Yana, and be emotionally blackmailed into forgoing her most basic desires, would her lustre fade too?

He would never know. He would never allow her to set off on that path.

He took a seat at the end of the table and looked at her anew, watching her be dragged to her feet to dance around the bonfire with a bunch of his younger staff. The skirt of her gorgeous dress swirled as she moved to the music being played by his gardener, Oliver, who was singing reggae songs as he strummed on his guitar. Her delicate arms clapped and swayed, her black curls fanning in all directions. He could feel the warmth radiating from her.

It drew him to her.

An ache formed in his chest and he swigged at his beer, as if the act of swallowing could loosen it. It didn't.

From the distance of the bonfire where the embers lit her up, making her beautiful face seem almost ethereal, she caught his gaze. She stilled for a moment before one of the girls grabbed her hand and pulled her into a dance that involved lots of hip-shaking.

He could watch her for hours.

His heart seemed to stutter when she scooped up little Ava, Valeria's two-year-old niece who lived on the island with her parents, who also worked for him.

He couldn't hear Ava's squeals of delight but he could feel them. They hit him deep in his guts.

Emily would be a fantastic mother, fierce and loving, just as his mother had been to him before he'd thrown all her love back in her face.

He could still see the ashen hue of her skin when he'd walked out that final time.

'Pascha,' she'd said. 'Andrei loves you. He would never put Marat above you, only equal to you.'

'You weren't there,' he'd sneered, his anger and hurt turning outward. 'He thinks Marat is deserving of a place on the board by virtue of his *Plushenko blood*.'

'He didn't mean it like that…'

He hadn't let her finish. 'So now you're taking his side? I thought I could expect support from my own mother.'

'It isn't a case of taking sides…'

'From where I'm standing it is. And I can see you have made your choice. I might have wished for your support but I certainly do not need it. I'm finished with this excuse for a family and its obsession with bloodlines. This cuckoo is leaving the nest.'

He could still see the confusion in her eyes at his parting comment.

Would he have reacted differently if he hadn't received the test results mere days before, if his dream of having his own blood family hadn't been crushed?

He didn't know. All he remembered feeling was hopelessness as he realised that his life meant nothing. That *he* meant nothing. The woman who had borne him, the one person in the world he shared a bloodline with, had failed to take his side. He was alone. Isolated. So he'd forced Yana to stay, desperate to hold onto something to validate his life.

It had taken almost two years of misery, as he threw

himself into work, determined to make a success of himself on his own, before he'd seen what he was doing to her and set her free.

Luis joined him, forcing him to switch his attention away from memories that speared his heart and onto easy talk of boats and island life. By the time Luis had slapped his back and wished him goodnight, Emily was no longer dancing.

Automatically he looked out to the lagoon, his lips curving into a smile to see her paddling out to calf height.

He got to his feet.

At the water's edge, he removed his footwear and rolled his jeans up.

'I knew that was you,' Emily said, turning her head to smile at him. There hadn't been an atom of doubt in her mind that the person wading into the lagoon behind her was Pascha.

'I'm just making sure you're not planning on going for a swim.'

'I was thinking about it,' she admitted. 'Maybe later when everyone's gone to bed. You should join me.'

She'd come out for a paddle because she'd needed space. She'd needed to put a little distance between her and Pascha before she ran over and dragged him onto the makeshift sandy dance floor.

She'd felt his eyes on her as she danced. Whenever she could no longer resist, she'd peeked back, her heart tugging to see him alone nursing his beer, setting himself apart while the party he'd instigated went on around him.

'Wading to my calves is enough for me,' he said. 'Not all the marine life in the lagoon is friendly, especially at night.'

'Is that your way of telling me not to go for a midnight swim?'

'It's my way of asking you to consider the dangers of doing it.'

She laughed softly. 'I've probably had too much to drink to swim.' Not that she was drunk. A little merry, maybe, but probably more than was safe to go swimming alone.

Pascha standing beside her made her feel giddy in a completely different way; her blood fizzed at his closeness.

'I'm glad to hear it,' he said, his voice dry.

'I'll save my swimming for the waterfall tomorrow,' she couldn't resist saying before laughing. 'Do you have any idea how lucky you are, owning this island? You've got your own lagoon and your own waterfall!'

'I do know how lucky I am.'

Something in his tone made her stare at him, made her realise that up to that point she'd avoided his gaze.

With the darkness of the sky enveloping them it was impossible to read his eyes; she knew only that something glittered there that made her heart double over.

In the distance, Oliver was singing a Bob Marley classic, the remaining partygoers singing along, the music blurring with the gentle lapping of the waves around them.

Pascha's chest rose and he looked up to the stars before staring back down at her. He reached out a hand and caught a ringlet.

All the breath rushed out of her body as he leaned his head forward.

She had no idea what profound comment he would say next, and certainly didn't expect the mirth that spread over his face. 'You smell like a bonfire.'

His fingers still played with her curl. He'd moved closer to her, near enough for her to feel the heat of his body.

The amusement left his face. He dropped her curl and dragged his fingers down the mane of her hair to her shoulders, then brushed up her neck to gently cup her throat.

His breath was hot on her skin. She closed her eyes. Her lips tingled, anticipating his kiss…

'You could make a man lose himself, Emily Richardson,' he murmured into her ear, before releasing his hold.

She snapped her eyes back open to find him striding through the water back to shore.

She spent the night in her cabin alone.

CHAPTER ELEVEN

EMILY SAT ON the ledge watching the sun make its ascent, the moonlit silver slowly vanishing, shades of blues and greens emerging. The only sound was the steady rush of the waterfall opposite. It glistened in a multitude of colours.

At best she'd managed a few hours of sleep. Every time she'd closed her eyes all she'd been able to see was Pascha's face. He'd been there when she'd opened them too. He was everywhere.

She'd been so sure he was going to kiss her. When he'd walked away she'd felt such rejection despite the strange words he'd uttered. Those feelings were still there but also in the mix was the euphoria of a whole evening with no worries. The impromptu party had been exactly what she had needed. Pascha had made it happen. It hadn't been for her, it had been for his staff, but it was all down to him. All the anxiety that had held her in a noose for the best part of a year had slipped away.

But now, here at the waterfall, her head felt crammed.

Her father was going to be all right. She could feel it. Such a small thing, getting out of bed. Given the state he'd been in, though, it was a huge thing. It showed willingness.

The road ahead wouldn't be easy but for the first time

she allowed herself to believe the road ahead would have him travelling on it.

The relief was indescribable.

But mingled with the relief was something else. It shamed her. As childish and selfish as she knew it to be, she couldn't help feeling despondent that it was for James that he'd made that first step. Not for her. It didn't matter what she did or how hard she tried, it was never for her.

It shouldn't matter. It *really* shouldn't matter. That he was treading the first steps on the path to recovery was enough. She'd done everything she could to help him, given up so much. Surely now...

Surely now it was time for her to start living again?

And she knew just the way to start.

She got to her feet and peered over the edge. A thrill of anticipation rushed through her. She unwrapped her sarong and placed it on the grass, then slipped her flip-flops off.

Another image of Pascha came into her mind. If he knew what she was about to do, he would probably tie her to a chair for the rest of her stay. It was one of the reasons she'd started the trail before the sun had come up.

She forced his image away.

Adrenaline pumping, she took a few paces backwards and then ran, jumping high into the air right at the very last second.

Those few moments of weightlessness were indescribable, exhilarating: the heady rush of flying combining with the hint of danger at what lay beneath the clear water.

Keeping the presence of mind to point her toes and hold onto her neck, she entered the cool water at incredible speed. Down she went, lower and lower into the pool, waiting to hit the bottom.

* * *

The sun had not long risen when Pascha awoke with a start.

He'd slept well enough but his dreams had been fitful. He'd woken to the vivid image of Emily jumping off the ledge and into the waterfall.

He threw on a pair of shorts and raced to her hut.

It came as no surprise to find it empty.

His subconscious had been telling him something.

He made it to the waterfall in a third of the usual time, his body drenched in sweat.

Her possessions were at the base of the ledge. Blood pounding in his head, he peered cautiously over it.

He caught a flash of ebony hair.

Squinting to get a better focus, he saw her properly, legs stretched out, arms resting back atop a crop of rocks at the edge of the waterfall, the stream of water pouring over her steadier than the torrent flowing in the centre.

She must have sensed him for her head lifted and she raised an arm in a wave. She called out but her voice was muffled by the waterfall.

It was not until she beckoned him that he realised she was asking him to join her.

He cupped his hands around his mouth and yelled, 'Don't be ridiculous.'

Shaking her head, she got to her feet and dived into the pool, staying submerged for so long the breath caught in his throat.

When she resurfaced she swam to the other end of the pool and hauled herself out. 'Jump in,' she called up to him, now far enough away from the waterfall for her voice to carry.

'No!'

'I promise you, it's the most exhilarating feeling in the world.'

She was too far away for him to see her features clearly but there was a definite air of elation about her.

Pascha did not take risks. Having come so close to death at such a young age, when the question of whether he lived or died had been completely out of his control, he had determined always to decide his own fate. He did not compromise his safety and he *never* put it solely in the hands of others.

Less than ten hours earlier he'd been tempted to throw off his clothes and swim into the lagoon in the dark. *She'd* made him want to do that with the sparkle in her eyes as she'd looked out over the lagoon, the sense of an adventure waiting to happen.

The temptation he'd felt had been real. But not half as real or as consuming as the temptation to pull her into his arms and taste those delectable lips all over again. He'd wanted to taste all of her all over again. He still did.

If it had been just the two of them at the beach, he doubted he would have had the presence of mind to hold himself back. His staff surrounding him had kept his control—his sanity—in check. He'd lain in his large, lonely bed and fought the greater temptation to take himself to her, as he'd done the night before, and slip beneath her covers; to make love to her all over again. Because that was exactly what it felt like: making love. And that was the greatest danger of all.

And now she wanted him to jump forty feet with only her word that it was safe.

'Pascha, trust me. Keep your feet together and hold onto your neck. You will love it, I promise. Trust me.'

Trust her? Put his control and safety in the hands of another?

Despite all his self-imposed safety mechanisms, his body zinged, as if it were trying to take possession of his mind.

Her madness must be contagious.

Focusing solely on the raven-haired beauty perched like a mermaid on the pool's edge, he removed his boots.

All you have to do is run and jump.

He hadn't run on anything other than a treadmill since he'd been fourteen.

His legs had had enough of his procrastination.

Almost as if it were happening to someone else and he was watching from afar, he took the short run and jumped.

Those few seconds of flying felt like nothing else in the world.

As gravity sucked his body down to the clear blue abyss, all Pascha could think was that she was right: this was the most exhilarating feeling in the world.

He hit the water, landing with an enormous splash. It consumed him, as if he were being dragged to the centre of the earth.

He refused to panic, keeping a clear head through the enormous shot of adrenaline the jump had produced. Pointing his arms upwards, he propelled his body up until he broke the surface.

The first thing he saw was the relief on Emily's face, a look that was immediately replaced with the brightest, most beautiful smile he had ever seen.

'You did it!' She laughed, a sweet, lyrical sound that warmed his heart. 'You really did it.'

He swam over, caught hold of her thighs and pulled her down into the water, using his arms to trap her against the edge of the rocks. He tried to catch his breath, tried to suck oxygen into his burning lungs, but all he could focus on was the beam of her smile.

The swell of her breasts pushed against his chest but she made no move to escape the confinement. Instead, she rested her hands on his shoulders and gazed at him, her chest hitching, an intensity swirling in her eyes that drove into his veins and paralysed him.

Her thighs brushed against his. A charge careered through him, so powerful he could feel it singe his blood.

He wanted to lose himself again in the wonders of her—the woman who made his senses come alive. The only woman capable of making him forget himself.

Her eyes had transformed into liquid. Her lips parted.

And then there was no more staring.

There was no slow build and no tentative caresses either. They simply fused into one, plundering each other's mouths with scorching fierceness.

Her fingers dug possessively into his scalp, her legs lifting and wrapping around his waist, whether by his instigation or her own volition he could not say.

She moaned into his mouth and wrapped her thighs ever tighter, the movement making him realise he'd lost his shorts during the jump. The only barrier between his rampaging erection and her welcoming warmth was the flimsy material of her bikini bottoms.

For the first time in nearly two decades he had to grit his teeth to stop himself losing all control.

He needed air. He needed to feel the ground beneath his feet before he lost all contact with reality.

In one motion he lifted her out of the water, pulled himself out and tumbled down onto the grassy bank, pinning her beneath him.

The expression in her eyes… Never had he seen such openness reflected back at him. No inhibitions, nothing except honest, naked desire.

Her hand snaked around his head to cradle his skull and pull him down for another kiss. Devouring the sweetness of her mouth, he roved a hand down her side, exploring the soft, creamy skin. Her bikini top was secured by a tie around her back. It took no effort to untie it and whip the top away.

The feel of her naked breasts crushed beneath his chest fired him anew and he dipped his head down to capture a dusky nipple in his mouth.

She responded to his caresses with more passion than he could ever have dreamed.

He needed to kiss her again and, as he lost himself in the headiness of it all, Emily twisted from beneath him and climbed on top, straddling him.

For what felt an age in which his heart beat a thousand times she did nothing but stare at him, her eyes scanning every inch of his face.

She traced a thumb over his lips, a feather of a movement that was both tender and erotic, before replacing her thumb with her mouth.

His hands reached round and held her tightly against him as she ground against his erection.

She gave a low moan followed by the breath of a sigh, then nibbled at his neck, teasing, painless.

Covering his face and neck with kisses, tasting the muskiness of his skin, Emily slipped a hand between their meshed bodies, running her fingers down his lightly haired chest all the way to his mass of dark, wiry hair.

A deep pulsation seeped through her when she encircled his erection. She closed her eyes and thrilled at its heavy weight, the silken feel of its length.

Never, never had she imagined she could feel like this, feel such a need to be possessed. And it was all him: Pascha. He *did* something to her, ignited feelings—sensuous and emotional—she had never known existed within her. And those feelings were growing.

When she opened her eyes, she found his gaze locked upon her, his magnetic eyes stark with his desire. For her.

Whatever his reasons for keeping his distance last night, at that moment it didn't matter. All that did matter was this moment, and this moment was with Pascha, the man who made her body come alive and her heart sing.

He cupped her cheeks and half-rose to meet her mouth, devouring it with his hot tongue, their kisses becoming increasingly desperate.

His fingers played with the ties holding the sides of her bikini bottoms together. She raised her hips a touch, her gasps deepening when he untied them and pulled the scraps of material off, discarding them on the grass beneath them.

Now they were both naked, the burn inside her turning to lava.

His mouth closed back over hers, large hands running over her back, tracing the arch of her shoulder blades and up, digging into her scalp, dragging through her hair. And all the while the tension within her grew. She'd never known desire could be a living thing.

And then she remembered where they were. And remembered that Pascha had lost his shorts in the pool. Even if he carried condoms with him they would be gone.

It took every ounce of her control to break away from his kisses and the heavenly things he was doing to her, grab his wrist and pin him to the grass.

Still straddling him, she gazed down at the face she could never grow tired of staring at. 'I'm not on the pill.'

The intensity in his eyes concentrated, a pulse firing from them that made her belly somersault.

'Emily, I can't…' He swallowed. 'All my treatment as a child left me sterile. I promise I am clean and I promise you'll be safe.'

Her heart twisted. She returned the strength of his stare, trying to reach through and read his mind. Read his heart.

He was sterile…?

He was asking for her trust…?

She *did* trust him.

She might have been forced to the island but he was doing everything in his power to keep her safe while she was there.

Pascha did not take risks. Making unprotected love definitely constituted risky by anyone's standards, but doubly so for him.

Her heart twisted again as she realised that this promise meant that he must trust her too.

He'd trusted her enough to make the jump…

He'd trusted her enough to share his secret—one which, instinct told her, haunted him.

Unable to stop herself, she released his wrists and planted her lips on his, a hard yet tender kiss that he responded to with a growl, his arms snaking around her waist.

The tip of his erection pressed against her opening, almost teasing her. She raised her groin a little higher, consumed with the need to *be* consumed.

The strong thud of his heart hammering against his chest reverberated through her skin, matching the unsteady tempo of her own.

Slowly she sank onto him, finding his lips, his breath flowing into her pores and filling her mouth with his heat just as he was filling her.

Skin on skin.

There were no words.

Nothing could ever describe the total bliss filling her.

With Pascha's hand steadying her, she started to move. Gripping the sides of his head, her sensitised breasts brushing against his chest, she ground against him, a steady, almost lazy tempo, the pulsations within her deepening.

A glazed look came into his eyes but the total connection between them remained, fusing them so deeply that she lost any sense of where he began and she ended.

Pure, pure pleasure.

Her orgasm started out as a low surge rippling through her, setting alight every atom of her being. Higher and higher it climbed until it peaked in an explosion of colour.

A strangled groan escaped his lips and he bucked into her, holding her tight against him, prolonging the moment for them both.

She rode the crest for as long as she could before floating back to earth, the softest landing.

Emily expelled a contented sigh.

Her face was buried in his neck, his strong hands stroking her back, holding her tight to him,

Pascha twisted onto his side so he could look down at her.

A lock of ebony hair lay damp across her forehead. He smoothed it away, pressing a kiss to the newly exposed skin.

'Why are you staring at me like that?' she asked, tracing a lazy finger up and down his forearm.

'Because I like staring at you. You're beautiful.'

'I think *you're* beautiful.'

'A very macho description,' he said with a laugh, and rolled onto his back, pulling her with him

The sun's rays were increasing, bathing them in a warm pool of light. Pascha could almost imagine it was just the two of them on the planet. If it were just the two of them left on Earth, Pascha reflected, he doubted he would ever be bored. Emily kept him on his toes.

'What possessed you to make the jump?' he asked after long, serene minutes had passed. 'Anything could have happened to you.'

'But it didn't.'

'But it could have.'

She raised her head and smiled. 'Pascha, this water-fall has clearly been evolving for hundreds of thousands of years, and the pool with it. I knew it would be deep.'

'But you couldn't have known what was beneath the waterline. There could have been rocks or anything. You could have killed yourself.' A coldness crept into his bones at the thought.

'But I didn't.'

'But what if you had? Where would that leave your father? Your brother?' *Me*, he almost added, the thought coming from nowhere.

'I don't know.' She bit into her lip and stared at him. 'They have each other. It was on James's watch that my dad got out of bed.'

'You've been there the rest of the time.' From what Pascha understood, Emily had been there the whole time. She'd given up the independence of her home and put her job in jeopardy for her father.

'From what's happened since I left, it's obvious that the only person my dad needed was James. Not me.' She broke the stare and tugged herself out of his arms, sitting up. 'I've tried so hard. All my life I've tried.'

'Tried for what?'

She turned her face back to him and raised her shoulders. 'To be enough.'

'Enough for what?'

'For him to hold on to.' She shook her head. 'In all honesty, Mum was the only one he really responded to when he was ill, but James would tell him a joke and sometimes Dad would smile. I'd tell him a joke—normally the same one as James—and he never responded. Never. When he was well, he was wonderful with me, but when he was ill it was as if I didn't exist. I was never enough. I guess I'm still not.'

'I don't believe that,' he said carefully, rubbing a hand over her naked back. She had the softest skin. 'Your father loves you.'

'I know he loves me.' Her voice was sad. 'It's just not enough, is it? Not if I can't help him.'

He placed a kiss to the small of her back. 'You've done more for your father than anyone could have wished. It is time for you to forget about your relationship with him as a child. Focus on the future.' He kissed her again, a little higher. 'I would sell my soul if I could have a future with my father.'

'I know. You're right.'

'Of course I'm right.'

'Your arrogance never gets old.'

He swiped at her nose before wrapping his legs around her and pulling her so she leant back against him.

'Can I ask you something?'

'You're asking my permission?' He was certain she was going to ask about his sterility. As if there was anything to be discussed. It was a fact of life—a fact of *his* life— something he'd long ago accepted. Just as he'd accepted it prevented him from having the future he'd always craved.

'It was something you said before about you and your father building Plushenko's between you. I always thought it was a really old firm, like Fabergé.'

'That was clever marketing—we wanted people to believe that.' He breathed in a sigh of relief as he realised it wasn't the subject he'd thought she was going to broach. At that moment, wrapped around Emily, he was as close to peace as he'd ever been.

He couldn't regret making love to her again. He would

never regret it. For now, all he wanted was to hold onto it for a little longer.

As he inhaled, he captured the scent of her hair. Even with her swim in the pool and the spray of the waterfall he could still catch the faint scent of the light, fruity shampoo she favoured.

'In a way, you can thank my leukaemia for the founding of Plushenko's,' he said. 'I had to undergo five years of chemotherapy and steroids and a host of other medicines. To keep me alive cost money. The only way to afford it was for Andrei—the man I called Papa—to work all the hours he could. At the time he was earning minimal wages as a jewellery maker for a middle-of-the-road Russian jeweller. He started to produce his own bespoke pieces, working every spare hour in the workshop he built at the back of our house. Those pieces paid for my medications and, unwittingly, formed the basis of the company known today as Plushenko's.'

'He sounds like an amazing man.'

'He was,' Pascha agreed.

'Do you think all the attention Andrei paid you, and all the hours he spent working to earn money for your treatment, made Marat jealous?' she asked.

He breathed her in deeply. 'I don't remember Marat ever liking me.' Knowing how much Marat loathed his very existence had done nothing to stop Pascha's idolisation of him. For years he'd wanted nothing more than Marat's acceptance. A part of him still longed for it.

'Have you thought of trying again with him?' she said. 'I know you said you offered to buy Plushenko's a number of years ago, but you were probably both feeling raw; it was so soon after your father had died. Maybe time has mellowed him.'

'I can't take the risk.'

'Why not?'

Because if it blows up in my face I will lose the chance to save Andrei's legacy. And if I lose that I will never be able to convince my mother how sorry I am.'

'Are you still estranged from her too?'

He nodded. 'I sought her out after Andrei's funeral. I apologised for our estrangement. I told her about the island I'd bought in her name but she didn't want to know.' She'd rejected him, just like Pascha had rejected her.

'Words aren't always enough,' she said softly. 'It's our actions that prove our love.'

'Is that why you went out of your way, at your own risk and with a real possibility of arrest, to help your father?' he said with more acid than he would have liked. 'Is that why you've given up your home and sacrificed your job, so he has living proof of how much you love him?'

She froze in his arms. When she next spoke, her words were measured but had a definite catch to them. 'The one thing I know with any certainty is that our time on this earth is limited. And you know it too.'

She didn't say anything else. She didn't need to.

They'd both lost people who'd meant the world to them.

But Emily's situation was different and not just because she'd been secure in her mother's love. Emily had never wounded someone she loved so badly that forgiveness was only an elusive dream. And, if she ever did wound someone she loved to that extent, she would be forgiven without having to prove her worth. Whatever darkness resided in her father's head, he did love her. She wasn't inherently unlovable. She didn't have something missing like he did. The blood that ran through the Richardson clan's veins tied them together, made them a part of each other.

He shared his mother's blood but still she couldn't forgive him.

With a start he realised it had been almost three years since he'd asked her forgiveness at Andrei's funeral.

Emily had lost her mother three months ago and the pain was still very much there on the surface.

He'd lived through a dark fog for at least a year after Andrei had died.

His mother and Andrei had been soul mates. Was it any wonder she'd lashed out at him when he'd said, five years too late, that he was sorry?

'I'm sorry,' he whispered, brushing her hair with the flat of his hand. 'I know your need to help your father comes from the love you have for him.' She had more love in her heart than anyone he'd ever met before.

Emily rubbed his arm in silent understanding then leaned forward slightly to swipe a small bug off her thigh. As she did so, his attention was captured by a tiny blue blur on the base of her spine. 'Sit forward.'

She shifted a little and he was able to see it clearly: another butterfly tattoo, smaller yet more intricate than the one on her ankle.

'I got it done just after my mum died,' she explained, craning her neck to look at him. 'We had our ankle ones done together.'

'Your mum had a tattoo?'

She nodded with a whimsical smile. 'She'd always wanted one. When we got the diagnosis that her illness was terminal, we went to a tattoo parlour and had identical ones done. I wanted this one as my own private memory of her.'

Pascha stared at the private memorial a beat longer, feeling like he had just had his own butterfly let loose in his chest.

He gently pushed her forward some more so he could kiss the butterfly. She truly tasted like the honey scent she carried.

A gasp escaped her throat as he trailed his tongue up her spine, all the way to the base of her neck.

'Enough talk.' He knelt behind her and cupped a breast, savouring its creamy weight. He felt as if he could savour it—savour her—for ever.

CHAPTER TWELVE

HE MUST HAVE dozed off. Totally spent, Pascha had gathered Emily into his arms and lain back down on the grass with a heart hammering loudly enough to frighten any wildlife.

He'd held her close, inhaling the musty scent of their sex, and a solid form of contentment had stolen over him.

For the first time in his life, he'd truly let go of himself. Emily did that to him. Somehow she was able to tap into parts of him he'd hidden for so long he'd forgotten they'd ever been there.

As a child he'd dreamt of driving fast cars. Now, as an adult, he owned more fast cars than his childhood self had known existed—but he drove them cautiously, all too aware of what other drivers on the road could do.

His childhood self would have been disgusted that he'd never taken one of his fast cars onto a track and put his foot down just for the sheer hell of the ride.

He had no way of knowing the time but, judging by the position of the sun almost directly over them, it must have been getting on for midday.

Emily looked so sweet curled on him with her hair spread across his chest that he felt cruel waking her. But he had no choice. He should have headed back to the lodge hours ago. Before he'd made love to her. Before he'd been foolish enough to go against everything he believed in and jumped off the ledge.

Both were equally dangerous in their own way.

He had a sudden image of his small childhood self, fist-pumping at seeing him fly off the ledge and into the pool. Yes, younger, childhood Pascha would have approved of *that*. But that was before he had learned how precarious life could be.

'We need to go back,' he said, kissing her shoulder before giving it a gentle shake.

She opened her eyes and smothered a yawn. 'Already?'

'I should have word if someone is available to get me to the mainland.' For all he knew, someone knowledgeable about the coral reef might have already made the trip to Aliana Island and, unable to locate him, returned to their own island. Try as he might, he couldn't bring himself to care. He wanted to hold onto this moment while he was living it. Before he had to say goodbye to her.

Emily got to her feet and tied her bikini bottoms back together.

'Where's my top?' He didn't have a chance to look for it before she spotted it and walked a couple of feet to retrieve it. Keeping her back to him, she put it on, tying it together at the back in a bow. Done, she turned back to him. 'So, Sherlock, how do we get out of here?'

'You mean to say you jumped into the pool without an escape route planned?' He didn't know whether to laugh or shout.

'You jumped too,' she pointed out with a grin.

'I assumed you'd already thought of a way out before *you* jumped.' He'd thought no such thing. At the time he hadn't been thinking of anything but her. If he'd been thinking a fraction more coherently, he would never have made the jump.

As they scanned their surroundings, he caught sight of his shorts floating at the edge of the pool. He fished them out and wrung as much water as he could out of them. He was stepping into them when Emily pointed to the right of the waterfall.

'Look,' she said, 'that incline there seems to have some natural gradients—we should be able to climb up it.'

'It's the most plausible way out,' he agreed, not seeing any other way.

He'd barely finished speaking before Emily darted over to it. She didn't even pause when she reached it.

Open-mouthed, his heart seeming to stop, he watched with a combination of horror and admiration as she began to scale the incline, her bare feet white against the rock.

Where did she get this fearlessness from?

And did he follow in her wake or wait at the base to catch her if she should fall…? Not that she showed any sign of falling; her movements were focused and assured.

From his vantage point he had an excellent view of her bottom and couldn't help the half-smile that twitched on his lips.

'Come on, slow-coach,' she called down to him, pausing for a moment. 'After a couple of feet it's more scrambling than climbing. Honestly, it's fine.'

She'd said similar words right before he'd jumped. Despite himself, and all the protection he placed around himself, he'd believed her. He'd trusted her. He still did.

He trusted her completely.

Taking a deep, steadying breath, he placed a hand on a ridge and carefully began to climb.

He refused to look down until he made it to the top, which came a lot more quickly than he'd expected.

'Do you have no fear?' he asked, catching his breath. Who needed to work out in a gym? A morning with Emily

Richardson provided enough exercise and adrenaline to last a month.

'Of course I do. I just don't feel the need to do a full risk assessment first.' Emily flashed him a half-grin. 'Don't get me wrong, I'm not a die-hard thrill-seeker or anything, but when the opportunity comes to experience something new or different I want to take it.'

It was just another part of herself that she'd suppressed in recent times. Well, no more.

She wrapped her sarong around her waist and slipped her feet into her flip-flops, all the while wishing they didn't have to leave this spot. Not yet.

But the time was inching closer.

In a few short hours Pascha would be leaving the island. Leaving her.

The thought made her throat close and her heart constrict.

She didn't want him to go. Not without her.

His pace was slower than the long strides he usually took. With his hand clasping hers firmly, hope began to stir.

She hadn't been with a man for more years than she could count. It was for a whole host of reasons that she'd avoided relationships and one of them—probably the most minor reason of the lot—was because she'd been waiting to find a man who made her heart beat faster just to think of him; a man who made her go figuratively weak at the knees.

Pascha did all that. He made her feel more than she'd ever felt in her life.

He wasn't the monster she'd thought him at the beginning. He was just a man, a mortal with his own demons to conquer, trying hard to make amends for a past it hurt her heart to think about.

In his office, she'd imagined sex with him would be perfunctory and proper. How she wished she'd been right. Maybe then the need within her would have been extinguished with disappointment, not quadrupled and morphed into something so huge her brain struggled to comprehend it.

But, what her brain struggled to recognise, her heart knew.

Her heart knew she was falling in love with him…

'When we get back to the lodge we'll learn if there's a boat available to take us back to Puerto Rico,' Pascha said, breaking through her dumbfounded thoughts. 'If there is, you will need to pack.'

'I'm coming with you?' That little bit of hope stirred a little stronger.

He gave a rueful smile. 'I have no good reason to keep you here, not any more. I know you won't say anything about the Plushenko deal.'

Stunned at this unexpected development, Emily stopped walking. 'Thank you.'

'I will speak to Zlatan, my lawyer, as soon as we return to the lodge and get the money transferred into your father's bank account. I will also have an official letter drawn up exonerating him of any wrong-doing and leaving the door open for him to return to his job if and when he feels able to.'

'Have you had the case investigated?' she asked hopefully.

'I do not believe your father took that money deliberately. We still need to trace exactly where it went and make moves to retrieve it but that's nothing for you to worry about.'

'That's—'

She tried to speak but he cut her off by cupping her

cheeks with his strong hands. 'I want you to know how sorry I am that I didn't get this situation resolved when it first occurred. I like matters of theft, which is what I believed it to be, to be investigated by my personal legal team. Because I had them working flat-out on the Plushenko buyout, your father's case was put to one side. I can't express how deep my regret is for what your father's been through. I am very much aware that I have contributed to his mental decline. Please let him know that if he chooses not to return as my employee I will give him an excellent reference.'

Emily was at a loss for what to say. Pascha's words were like music to her ears. In the end, all she could do was rise onto her toes and place a gentle kiss on his lips. 'Thank you.'

'Don't thank me. It should never have come to this in the first place.'

'You've had a lot on your plate.'

'And don't make excuses for me.' She caught the fleeting ghost of a smile on his handsome features before he released his hold on her and stepped back, running a hand through his hair. 'Come; let's get you back to the lodge and see if we can get you home. I know how badly you want to return to your family.'

Did she? Did she really? She was certainly anxious to see for herself that her father had made an improvement, but did she really want to go back to that same life, a life where she lived for everyone else rather than herself?

She'd been like that in all her relationships.

With a jolt she realised that Pascha was the first person ever to have really known her, stripped back. When they'd first met she'd been too anxious and angry to put on any kind of face for him.

He'd seen *her*, the rawness, all the components that made her Emily, and he hadn't rejected her.

No wonder her few relationships had failed. She'd moulded herself into what she'd thought her boyfriends wanted her to be. And they'd seen through it, become bored with a woman who agreed with everything they said and was always obliging, doing what they wanted.

She'd been right: she hadn't been enough for any of them. How could she have been when she'd never been enough for herself?

Pascha had only ever seen her as herself and still he'd wanted her.

The question now was whether he would still want her when they were away from this spot of paradise.

Emily stood at the back of the yacht watching Aliana Island shrink away, blinking back hot tears. This could be the last time she saw it.

In less than a week her world had changed irrevocably.

The island had become little more than a speck on the horizon when Pascha joined her on the deck.

When they'd got back to the lodge, his hair had been mussed, his jaw covered with dark stubble. He'd looked wild and devilishly sexy.

Since their return he'd showered and shaved, styled his hair and dressed into a beautifully ironed open-necked white shirt and dark-grey trousers. Even his black belt looked as if it had been pressed. Add a tie and blazer, and he could step into any boardroom.

His wildness had gone but he still looked devilishly sexy.

'Am I going to see you again?' she asked, staring up at him and taking the bull by the horns. One thing she had learned during the past few days was that she needed to control her own destiny. If there were changes to be made then she had to be the one to make them.

She saw rather than heard him draw in a breath, his mouth compressing, his features contorting into something that looked like pain. That same pain shot straight into her heart.

'Do I take that as a no?'

Pascha watched as a whole swathe of emotions flittered over Emily's face. The one that struck the strongest chord with him was the fleeting anguish she hadn't been quick enough to conceal. It hurt him to see it.

He should never have given in to his desire, should have fought it harder. And now he had to hurt a woman who had already been through too much pain. But the alternative would only cause her far more.

'Emily, I'm sorry; you and I can never be together.' He needed to spell it out to her. He didn't want there to be any misunderstandings. She deserved the truth.

That familiar groove appeared.

'I need you to understand. It isn't you. It's me.'

Now her features darkened, her lips thinning, her shoulders hunching together.

'I know that's a line a lot of men use, but in this case it's the truth.' He reached out to capture a lock of ebony hair. She flinched away from him, stepping back. 'Emily, we can return to Europe and pick up where we leave off here—enjoy each other's company and have fantastic sex—but nothing can ever come of it. We have no future. *I* can't give you a future.'

'How do you know that?' she whispered.

'Because I can't give you the babies you want.'

She wrapped her arms around herself. 'I don't recall us ever discussing children.'

'We didn't need to. I *know* you and I know family is

everything to you.' He remembered the light in her face when she'd been swinging little Ava in the air. If there was a woman made to be a mother, this woman was it. 'I know you want children, and one day you will have them, but I can't be the man to give them to you. I almost destroyed my ex-fiancée over it and I won't destroy you too.'

Emily loosened her arms, a questioning frown appearing.

'Yana and I were together for years,' he said, needing to help her understand. 'She'd always wanted children—we both did—so when we became engaged we thought it be best I get tested. I'd always known I could be sterile but I needed to be sure before we made that final commitment.' He shook his head, remembering how the results had knocked him sideways.

While he had always known he *could* be sterile, he'd never truly believed that he was. He'd come out the other end of treatment physically unscathed, so how could life throw him this at so late a turn?

It was as if fate had turned around and stuck a fork in him for daring to hope he could have a future with a family of his own.

'For two years I watched her suffer and turn into a shell of herself.' His voice had become hoarse. 'I would cringe to hear about any of her friends and family becoming pregnant, knowing it was another knife in her heart. But I thought I should be enough for her, that her yearning for a baby was something she should just forget about for my sake.'

'Couldn't you have adopted?'

'That's what Yana suggested, but I'm afraid adoption is not a route I will go down.'

'Your father adopted you,' she pointed out softly.

'And wasn't I made to know it? Hardly a day went by

when Marat didn't rub my nose in the fact that he shared Andrei's blood and I didn't, that I was the cuckoo in the Plushenko nest. Andrei himself used the fact of Marat being his blood to undermine my point of view about bringing him onto the board at Plushenko's.' He raised his shoulders. 'I can't do that to a child. I won't see another person suffer for their blood not being the same as the family they live with.'

'How ridiculous.'

Whatever reaction he'd expected from Emily, scorn most definitely was not it.

'You don't know what you're talking about,' he refuted tightly.

'Rubbish. You have your mother's blood for a start—'

'Which meant nothing to her when she took Andrei and Marat's side.'

'You put her in an impossible situation. What was she supposed to do? Tell you that your irrationality was justified? I don't care what your father said, I'm certain he never meant it in the way you took it. He worked his fingers to the bone to keep you alive. If that isn't love then I don't know what is. For goodness' sake, he even got his hands on black market copies of *Top Cat* for you to watch when you were too weak to do anything else. Blood doesn't come into it.'

Her words were like tiny barbs being thrown at his skin, all landing straight in his chest. It took all his control to stop his hands from shaking.

He'd always been able to temper his anger but now... now he could feel it slipping.

She'd done this to him. He didn't know how or why but Emily pushed buttons in him that no one else could even find.

'You think because we've made love that you have a right to tell me how I should *feel*, is that it?'

'I never said that. There are thousands—millions, for all I know—of orphaned children in this world begging for a family to love them, and you won't consider taking one of them in and building a family of your own because of Marat's jealous attitude towards you.'

'You do not know what you're talking about.'

'Then explain it to me.'

'I don't have to explain anything to you.' He stared down at her. She gazed right back, her eyes full of hurt, but also full of a powerful anger. 'I've explained this much because after everything we've been through over these past few days I thought I owed you an explanation. I can't give a woman a baby and I will not be party to an adoption. Eventually, resentment rears its head and snap—' he snapped his fingers for emphasis '—the end of the relationship follows along with the mourning for wasted years. I couldn't give Yana the baby she wanted but in my arrogance I thought my love would be enough for her. It wasn't. She turned into a shell of herself and I won't—I can't—do that to you too. I won't watch the light in your eyes die.'

All the anger emanating from Emily's pores dissipated. She tilted her head, shaking it slowly. 'If Yana *had* loved you enough then you really *would* have been enough. Yes, I want children, but if I fell head over heels in love with someone who couldn't have them I would cherish the relationship for what it could give me and not what it couldn't.'

'You mean you would do what you have always done and stifle your desires for someone else's sake,' he said, unable to keep the bitterness from his voice.

'I feel sorry for you,' she surprised him by saying. 'Love isn't a tick-box or a competition. I *know* I need to reclaim my life for myself but I will always be there for the people

I love. I've let my father's depression and the way it affects me take over my life, always feeling I wasn't enough. I need to stop thinking like that and remember the good times with him, because when he's well our relationship is great.

'*That's* what I meant about cherishing a relationship for what it could give me rather than what it could not. And if I loved you, Pascha Virshilas, I wouldn't care about your sterility so long as you loved me back, and so long as I knew you would always be there for me.'

'But that's you all over, isn't it, *milaya moya*? And it's that life and passion you contain within yourself that lets me know I am right about this. I would not wish for all that life to die out. You deserve to have it all.'

'But not with you,' she finished for him softly.

'No. Not with me. I can't give you it all. All I can give you is unfulfilled dreams that will eventually eat into your soul and destroy you.'

'Then I guess there's nothing else for us to say,' she said quietly. Reaching up, she pressed a chaste kiss to his cheek. 'I hope one day you can look in the mirror and see a man who deserves to have it all too.'

CHAPTER THIRTEEN

EMILY HEARD THE front door open.

She took a sip of her lukewarm coffee and pushed her plate of half-eaten chicken pie to one side. She wasn't hungry.

She'd hoped with all her heart that her father getting out of bed was the first step towards recovery. But her return had set him back.

She'd returned to the house late last night, so had waited until the morning to give him the good news about the money and relay everything else Pascha had said. There had been no reaction, not even when she'd told him his job was there for him to go back to if he wanted.

He'd spent the day in bed.

She'd spent the day making phone calls and waiting for James to get back from work. It wasn't as if she had a job to go to. As she'd suspected, Hugo had fired her. The letter had sat on the sideboard waiting for her return. No severance pay. Nothing. She kept waiting for the devastation to hit her but, to her surprise, all she felt was relief.

It felt good to feel something. The only other emotion she felt at that moment wasn't even an emotion. It was numbness. She felt empty, as if she'd been drained of all the things that made her human.

'Hi, sis,' James said, stepping into the kitchen and heading straight to the oven where his dinner was keeping warm. 'Good trip away?'

'It was very…productive.' He didn't know about her job situation. Not yet. He could wait a little longer.

'Right. Well, I've rebooked my trip to Amsterdam and I'll be leaving on Friday.'

'When are you going back home?'

'After I've eaten this.' He winked at her, taking the seat opposite her at the kitchen table. 'I've missed my flat.'

'Funnily enough, I've missed mine too.' Emily waited for him to swallow his first mouthful. 'I've been thinking.'

'Did it hurt?'

For once she didn't laugh at her brother's quip. 'This can't go on. We can't fix Dad on our own—no, *I* can't fix him on *my* own. He needs professional help and he needs it now. I've phoned the doctor to get the ball rolling about getting proper home care for him.'

James eyed her shrewdly. 'What's brought the big change on? I thought you were adamant we didn't need outside involvement.'

'I was wrong. And I was wrong to give up my flat. I've given my tenants their month's notice. I'll be moving back in as soon as they're out. From now on, you and I are going to share responsibility for Dad.'

She didn't wait for a reaction, simply got up and reached for a shelf stacked with her mum's old cookbooks. She pulled one down and lobbed it on the table next to him.

'What's this?' he asked suspiciously.

'That, darling brother, is a sign from your little sister that it's time to grow up and learn to take care of yourself. Oh, and seeing as I cooked dinner, you can do the clearing up.' This time it was Emily's turn to flash a wink before heading out of the kitchen and up the stairs.

When she reached the landing, she took a deep breath.

That had been easier than she'd anticipated. There was definitely something to be said for not giving the other person time to answer back.

She heard the creak of her father's door and turned to find him standing at the threshold in his pyjamas, his eyes watery.

'There's something I need to tell you,' he said. And just like that, her slightly lighter mood plummeted.

Pascha sat in the back of his Lexus gazing absently out of the window.

It had all gone to hell.

Everything.

His driver turned the corner onto the road that housed his London office. A flash of curly black hair made him do a double-take.

Craning his neck for a better look, he soon realised the Monday morning street was so thick with bodies he must have imagined it.

He'd imagined he'd seen her a handful of times that day already. And a dozen the day before, when he hadn't even left his house.

If he was to see her now, in the flesh, he didn't know how he would react.

They pulled up outside his building and he got out, heading inside.

As usual, he was greeted by a bustle of activity. Normally he enjoyed the vibrancy and energy. Today he could do without it.

Today he wanted to be alone.

He didn't know what had propelled him to leave St. Petersburg late on Friday evening and come to London. After his confrontation with Marat, he could have gone anywhere. Why here?

Ignoring all the welcoming although still nervous smiles, he went straight up to his office. As he punched in the code to his office floor, he remembered he still hadn't changed it since Emily had sneaked in.

Cathy, the executive secretary he'd inherited when he'd bought Bamber Cosmetics, was there to greet him. His PA must have warned her to expect him.

'Can I make you a coffee?' she asked once the pleasantries were out of the way.

'No. I don't want any visitors or calls today either.' He swept into his office, closing the door firmly behind him.

The morning dragged.

He'd spent the weekend in his London home doing nothing but going over the events of the preceding week in his mind, which had culminated in his disastrous encounter with Marat.

He rubbed at his eyes with his palms and got to his feet. He needed to find some energy. Regardless of what had happened with Marat, he still had a business to run. More coffee should do the trick.

In his private room he switched the coffee machine on and read an email from Zlatan.

He was about to pour his coffee out when movement on the monitor caught his attention.

He stared. And stared some more.

No. He wasn't seeing things. There really was someone in his office. A pixie with a cascade of curly black hair.

Eyes fixed on the monitor, he took long, deep breaths and swallowed away the enormous lump that had formed in his throat.

Only when his composure was assured did he pour his coffee out and step through the door to her.

'You seem to be making a habit of breaking into my office,' he said, striding over to his desk.

Emily was sat on the visitor's seat. As he passed her he caught a waft of her earthy honey scent. He tightened his grip on his cup, glad to place it on his desk as he took his seat.

Finally he could look at her properly.

What he saw made his heart wrench and his stomach dip.

She looked dreadful— really dreadful. Her skin was pale, her eyes red-raw, her hair even wilder than usual. She wore a deep-red jersey dress and thick black tights, her arms wrapped tightly around her waist as if for warmth or protection.

'I'm sorry for having to break back in,' she said, speaking tentatively.

'Evidently not sorry enough or you wouldn't have pulled the same stunt twice,' he said icily.

She blanched. 'I needed to see you. I didn't want this conversation over the phone. Cathy let me know you'd come in. She said you weren't accepting visitors so I waited until she went on her lunch break before sneaking in.'

'You know Cathy?'

She nodded.

And, just like that, everything fell into place: Cathy was the mole. His own executive secretary had given Emily his schedule and the code for the floor.

And, as all the pieces of the jigsaw slotted together, Emily's face crumpled as she realised what she'd given away.

'Oh, please, please don't punish her. Please. She did it for my family. She's worked here as long as my dad has— years ago, she was his secretary. She was my mum's best friend and used to babysit me and James. Please don't sack her. It's my fault. She didn't want to tell me anything but I used emotional blackmail to get your movements and the code out of her.'

Pascha held up a hand to stop the torrent of words spilling from her lips.

He had too much to think about as it was; his brain was overloaded. 'I will think about Cathy later. Tell me why you're here.'

A fat tear rolled down her cheek. She let it fall all the way to her chin.

He would *not* react to it. He would not react to her.

She reached into her large handbag and pulled out an envelope which she handed to him.

Wordlessly, he opened it. Inside was a cheque made out to him for the sum of a quarter of a million pounds.

'What is this?'

Emily's chin wobbled, her lips trembling, her eyes filling. 'It's the money I blackmailed you into paying my father. His bank account was credited late last week. I couldn't figure how to return it. Pascha, I… My…'

He waited while she tried valiantly to compose herself, hating that he had to fist his hands to stop them reaching out to her.

'You…were right all along,' she finally dragged out, her words stark. 'My father stole the money.'

Emily was still having trouble digesting it. For the past few days she'd thought of little else. She'd been so certain her father was innocent—one-hundred per cent positive. Doubt had never entered her head.

It wasn't just her father's actions she was trying to comprehend, though. The magnitude of what *she'd* done had hit her too.

She'd broken the law. She'd wilfully broken into Pascha's office with the sole purpose of stealing his files…had been prepared to use blackmail to get what she wanted… and for what? Because she'd wanted to fix her father.

Because she wanted him to love her when he was in the darkness as well as the light.

She couldn't fix what was in his head any more than she could fix him if he broke his leg. It was time to accept that.

'I already knew your father had taken the money.'

That shook her. 'You did?'

'It took Zlatan five minutes to learn that the money trail led straight to an account held by Malcolm Richardson.' Something that looked like sympathy flickered in his cold eyes before he cast his gaze back down to the sheaths of paper spread out before him.

Why was he being so cold?

Why wouldn't he look at her?

'He gave the money to the hospice Mum spent her last days in.'

'That doesn't surprise me.'

'How long have you known?'

'Zlatan told me an hour before the beach party.'

'Why didn't you tell me?' she whispered. 'Why did you transfer all that money into his account when you knew he was guilty?'

'Your father is ill. I do not want the money back and I will not be pressing charges.' To compound his point, he picked up the cheque and ripped it into little pieces. 'Keep this money. Use it to pay for full-time nursing care until he's well enough to care for himself.'

'It's too much,' she whispered.

'As far as I'm concerned, this is the end of the subject.' He indicated the door. 'Go home and tell your father he has nothing to fear from me. I wish him nothing but the best.'

What was *wrong* with him?

There was something…unkempt about him. A barely contained anger she hadn't picked up on initially because she'd been too full of the need to purge herself of her guilt.

He picked up an expensive-looking pen and made a mark on a sheet of paper. 'Emily, I have a full schedule.'

'Too full to spend ten minutes with me?'

'Yes. Please leave.' He picked up a folder and opened it.

Legs shaking, she stood.

He really was dismissing her. After everything they'd been through, he was dismissing her as if she were nothing but a lowly employee.

Something inside of her went *ping*, a rush of fury that fired out of her fingers and had her leaning over his desk to wrench the folder from his grasp and toss it in the air.

As it fell to the floor, dozens of pieces of paper fell from it, floating and landing around her.

'What the hell did you do that for?' he snarled, his face contorting.

'I had to do *something* to get your attention. You're acting as if I'm nothing to you, as if I'm some stranger who's parked herself in your office. You won't even look at me!'

'That's because looking at you…' Whatever he was going to say, he cut himself off, punching his desk with a roar.

Shock at his response rendered her mute. All she could do was stare at the man she loved and watch the unprecedented fury flow from him like a torrent.

Something was badly wrong.

'Why are you still here?' He got to his feet. 'I told you to leave.'

'What is *wrong* with you? Did something go wrong with the Plushenko deal?'

It was the mention of the word 'Plushenko' that sent Pascha's fury erupting through his skin.

Because of Emily, he'd finally understood that family meant more than pride.

Because of Emily, he'd gone to his brother with the truth, believing that this time things could be different.

He'd lost it all. Any hope of redemption and forgiveness was gone.

He'd laid everything on the line, revealed that he was the face behind RG Holdings. Revealed his need to make amends for their father's memory. When he'd finished his speech, he'd extended a hand. 'So what do you say?' he'd said. 'Are you prepared to draw a line under the past?'

Marat had stared at his hand before his thin lips had formed into a sneer. He'd pushed his chair back and got to his feet. 'I told you two years ago that I wouldn't sell the business to you. I would rather it went to the dogs than fall into your hands.'

How had he ever allowed himself to think that this time things might be different?

There had been no point in prolonging the meeting. He knew Marat, knew the entrenched look in his eyes. Pascha's reasoning had been disregarded. To try any more would have been akin to trying to reason with a toddler. 'I'm sorry you feel that way. I wish you luck in finding another investor.'

He hadn't reached the door when Marat had pounced, pinning him to the wall. '*You*,' he'd spat. 'It was always about *you*. No money for anything, not even the basics, because it all went on keeping *you* alive, the cuckoo in the nest who didn't belong there.' He'd abruptly let go and stepped back, throwing his hands in the air. 'And look at you now—rich and handsome. All that chemotherapy didn't even stunt your growth. You got everything.' His eyes had glittered with malice. 'But you didn't get Plushenko's. And you never will.'

Pascha had held onto his temper by the skin of his teeth. He was almost a foot taller than his adopted brother and, with around ninety-five per cent more muscle mass, all it would have taken was one punch to floor him and curb his cruel mouth.

Instead, he'd straightened his tie, dusted his arms down and said, 'It was never about Plushenko's. It was about family. Goodbye, Marat.' He'd left the office, striding past the waiting room where the lawyers were holed up, through the foyer and out into the cold St. Petersburg air.

He felt it now, as raw as if he were still in that conference room with his brother.

'The Plushenko deal is dead. It's over.'

Ignoring the ashen pallor of Emily's skin, he kicked his chair back and stormed over to stand before her. 'Plushenko's was built from my father's sweat and my mother's tears and now it's *gone*. Marat's hell-bent on destroying our father's legacy and there's nothing I can do to stop him.'

'You told him the truth?' she asked, her voice a choked whisper.

'Yes, I told him the truth. He threw my offer back in my face.'

Marat hadn't wanted anything to do with the cuckoo in the nest.

Why had he ever been foolish enough to believe otherwise?

'You wonder why I can't bear to look at you? You have *everything*—a family who loves you. You made me believe I could have that too. You gave me hope that Marat would accept me. You made it sound so easy. It was all a lie, a big, damnable lie, and every time I look at your face all I see is what could have been!'

Because of Emily, and that strange alchemy she had spread over him that had re-awoken his desire for a family of his own, everything had blown up in his face.

The path to his mother's forgiveness had been detonated. And that was the worst part about it.

'I'm sorry it didn't work out the way you hoped it would,' Emily said, breathing heavily, her face no longer pale, angry colour staining her cheeks. 'But at least you can look at yourself in the mirror and say that you tried, that you fought for a relationship with Marat.'

'It's destroyed everything. What hope is there for my mother to believe in me now?'

'Oh, get over yourself and stop being so defeatist!' Her fury seemed to make her expand before his eyes. 'As if presenting her with the gift of Plushenko's would magically have made things better between you—it hardly worked when you bought an island in her name, did it? Give her the one thing she hasn't got—her son. *You.* If I can love a stubborn fool like you, then I'm damn sure your mother can as well. She is *not* Marat. If you allow your stupid pride to kill your future with her, you have no one to blame but yourself.'

Leaving him standing there, his head spinning, she turned on her heel, pushed the door open and strode out, her head held high.

She didn't look back.

The miniature castle Pascha's mother called home was a world away from the small, dark house he'd been raised in. No flickering lights, no heaters where the oil level was checked with an anxious look, always quickly disguised if her young son happened to be watching her.

If Plushenko's shares continued to drop and its revenue continued to plummet, this beautiful home, with its bright, spacious rooms and indoor swimming pool, in theory would have to be sold.

Whatever the outcome of this meeting with his mother,

he would ensure this home remained hers. He would buy her a dozen homes if she let him.

He'd arrived unannounced but she hadn't looked surprised to see him at her door. She'd invited him in with hardly a murmur.

Sitting on the sofa in the immaculate living room while she fetched them refreshments, his eye was caught by a photo above the fireplace of his mother and Andrei's wedding day. Everything about them looked cheap, from their wedding clothes to the cut of their hair.

The love shining between them, though, was more valuable than any Plushenko diamond.

He rose as his mother came through the door carrying a tray of coffee and biscuits.

'You're looking well,' he said after she'd taken the seat across from him. There was nothing cheap about his mother these days. Her salt-and-pepper hair had been expertly coloured a pale blonde, her calloused hands smooth from regular manicures.

'Thank you,' she said, with a warmer smile than he'd been expecting. 'You're looking good yourself.'

After a few minutes of small talk while they caught up on each other's lives, she rose to sit beside him. She patted his thigh. 'I know about you trying to buy Plushenko's from Marat.'

He stiffened.

It was the first time his mother had touched him in three years, since slapping him on his face after Andrei's funeral.

And no wonder that she had. In his arrogance, he'd thought she would be happy with the return of her prodigal son, that the promise of an island in her name would be enough to wipe out five years of hurt.

'I also know Marat…declined your offer. But that was to be expected.' She gave a sad smile that didn't reach her eyes. 'That boy always did have a problem with you. He was jealous.'

'Jealous of what?'

'Jealous of Andrei's love for you. Angry that he had to share his father.'

Emily had said the same thing.

She'd also said not to allow his pride—his *stupid* pride—to kill his future with his mother.

It had taken him two long, dark weeks to see how right she was.

Pascha took a deep breath. 'I'm sorry for cutting you and Papa out of my life all those years ago. I'm sorry for changing my surname out of spite. I'm sorry for rejecting all of your and Papa's attempts to reconcile with me, and I'm sorry Papa died thinking I didn't love him.'

'He knew you loved him.' Her voice was sad. 'You were his little shadow. He used to laugh and say if you could fit in his pocket to be carried around then you would. He was so proud that you wanted to be involved in the jewellery business with him. He always said that, without your drive, Plushenko's would have stayed a little firm floating along keeping its head above water.'

She reached out a hand to cup his cheek. 'You're not the only one to have regrets, Pascha. Andrei had them too. He blamed himself for your leaving, for forcing Marat onto the board against your wishes. And I regret spurning you after the funeral—my only excuse is that I was grieving. But I have no excuse for not reaching out to you since.' Her eyes flickered with emotion. 'I think you must have inherited your pride and stubbornness from me. You're my son and I love you. I've always loved you. Andrei loved you too.'

She must have caught something in his eyes, because she continued, 'What he said about Marat being his blood—he didn't mean it to be taken that that made Marat more important than you. He meant that Marat was *as* important—that you were *both* his sons. He couldn't choose between you. He never gave a thought that you were not of his blood—to him you were his son and he loved you as fiercely as if you were.'

Pascha swallowed away the lump that had formed in his throat.

Emily had been right. Again.

Of course she had.

Her words had echoed in his head for the past fortnight, smothering his thoughts until he'd hopped onto his jet and demanded he be taken to St. Petersburg.

Emily understood love. She gave it freely, without conditions...

'Has Marat spoken to you about this?' he asked.

'I rarely see him,' she said with a shrug. 'Since Andrei died he doesn't bother with me. It wasn't just you he didn't want in his life. He didn't want to share Andrei with anyone. With me, he was just more subtle in showing his dislike.'

Pascha sighed and leant his head back. Now he thought about it, he could never remember Marat displaying any affection to her. He was always polite and cordial but never affectionate. Never a son.

And never a brother.

'If Marat didn't tell you, how did you know I tried to buy the company off him?'

This time his mother's smile carried to her eyes. 'I will show you.'

She left the room for a few minutes, returning with a folded up piece of white paper. 'This arrived last week from England. It was sent by courier.' She laughed. 'I think the sender used some kind of Internet translation for her Russian.'

Her?

His heart thundering, Pascha took the letter from his mother's hand and opened it. He knew who the sender was before he even started reading.

Printed out from a computer, he saw what his mother had meant. Emily's sentences were all jumbled, a literal translation from English of what she had tried to say. But her meaning was clear. Her words were heartfelt. Her plea was transparent: for his mother to understand just how much her son loved her and how their estrangement was destroying him.

'This Emily, she must love you very much,' his mother said after he'd read the letter all the way through three times.

He inhaled deeply, trying to hold on to emotions that threatened to smother him more than his thoughts had.

'Does this mean there is a wedding to look forward to?' she asked hopefully.

He shook his head slowly before dropping it forward and cradling it in his hands.

After everything he'd said to her, the blame he'd unfairly heaped on her shoulders, Emily had done *this* for him?

It had been a fortnight since he'd seen her. A whole two weeks without a word.

He'd missed her, badly enough that some nights he couldn't breathe through the pain.

How quickly the world could turn and change everything.

In all his years he'd never met a woman like her. Someone full of life. Someone with such intense loyalty… And an infinite capacity to love, just as Andrei had had…

He'd spent two weeks torturing himself with thoughts about whether or not she really had said she loved him. Her words had been shouted out in anger, to make a point.

Now, for the first time, his heart dared believe…

'I need to go,' he said, gripping his mother's shoulders and kissing her cheeks. 'I love you.'

'I love you too.' She smiled. 'Maybe soon you can take me to this island you named after me?'

'I would like that,' he said.

'And maybe I'll be able to meet this Emily?'

He attempted a smile of his own. He failed. 'I'm going to try my hardest to make that happen.'

CHAPTER FOURTEEN

PASCHA COULDN'T REMEMBER the last time he'd been to a photo shoot. When he'd first started buying fashion brands, he'd been fascinated with every aspect, but the novelty had soon worn off. Photo shoots were the worst. He was more than happy to leave the experts to deal with the day-to-day matters. After all, what did he know about fashion? Regardless, he didn't buy companies to tear them apart. He bought them to make a profit. Some needed restructuring or, in the case of the luxury luggage company he'd bought three years ago, a new marketing strategy. A few simple changes and that particular company had seen a four-thousand per cent increase in turnover—in its first year. Now that company alone had an annual turnover of half a billion dollars.

As he stepped into the vast white room filled with bodies hanging around not doing much at all, a small man with a silly flat cap on his head looked at him. 'You're too late. You were supposed to be here eight hours ago. We got a replacement for you.'

Taken aback, Pascha said, 'You must have me confused with someone else.'

'Aren't you a model?'

'No.'

'Shame. You could make a fortune.' He winked at him.

Too exhausted to react, Pascha said, 'I'm here to see Emily Richardson. I was told she was here.'

'She's through that door,' the small man said, pointing at the far end of the room. 'She's fitting Tiana into the last dress, so keep it quick—some of us want to get home tonight.'

Nodding his thanks, Pascha strolled to the door, aware of jumbled whispers around him. Someone had recognised him.

He opened the door.

'Two minutes,' the figure on the floor said without looking up.

Emily knelt barefoot at the feet of a statuesque model he assumed must be Tiana, doing something— he couldn't see what—to the hemline of the dress she was wearing

'Hello, handsome,' the model said, her eyes glittering.

'I will wait,' he said, ignoring her and parking himself on the nearest uncomfortable chair. On a rational level, he knew the model was beautiful. On a base level, she barely registered.

It was Emily he was here for. Emily, who he could see was a million miles removed from the gothic vamp he had first met, dressed in a pair of silver leggings and a green-and-orange-striped top that fell to her knees. He would wait for her for ever if he had to.

Tiana squealed. 'Ow! Watch what you're doing, will you?'

'Sorry,' Emily said, pressing her thumb to Tiana's ankle where she'd just inadvertently stabbed her with a sewing needle.

Hearing that voice for the first time in two weeks and in such an unexpected place had shaken her with the force of a battering ram.

Too scared to turn around and look at the waiting figure, she forced her concentration on the job in hand. Except her hands were shaking. She could feel his stare fixed upon her. How she didn't stab the model again, she would never know.

Only when she was done and she'd sent Tiana back into the studio for the last shoot did she take a deep breath and turn her head.

She tried to speak, give a greeting of some kind. Her tongue wouldn't move.

She hadn't believed she would ever see him again.

She'd told herself she never *wanted* to see him again, but deep down she'd known it to be a lie. She would never seek him out, though. She was not a dog; she would not beg for scraps. Ironically, it was Pascha who had shown her she was worth more than that.

'How are things, Emily?' he asked, breaking the ice.

She nodded vigorously and forced herself to speak. 'Good. Good. Thanks.'

'I'm pleased to hear it.'

There was something different about him. She couldn't place what it was but it was there all the same. His hair? It didn't look quite as well groomed as it usually did. And he could do with a shave. The only animation on his face was his eyes boring into hers.

Unable to bear the weight of his stare, she began packing her things away, waiting with her lungs only half-working for him to give his reason for being there. There had to be a reason.

Did he know what she'd done?

'Are you enjoying working for Gregorio?'

'It's fabulous,' she said, forcing an injection of enthusiasm into her voice. It really was fabulous—she was loving every minute of it; she could hardly believe she'd landed the job so quickly.

She'd left Pascha's office full of anger and anguish, but also full of resolve.

Pascha had made it perfectly clear on his yacht that they had no future. Their awful confrontation in his office had made her accept it.

She could either allow herself to fall apart—and she knew it would be easy to do that; too easy—or she could pick herself up and carry on. And the best way to carry on was through work.

So she'd gone straight to the House of Alexander and spoken to Hugo, who was already feeling guilty for sacking her. He'd offered her her job back. She'd thought about it for all of two seconds before shaking her head. Working for Hugo, as great as it had been and as much as she'd learned, had stifled her. Instead, she'd asked if he would write her a reference.

The next day, armed with her portfolio and a glowing recommendation, she'd hit the London fashion houses. By the time she'd returned home, her phone was ringing. The House of Gregorio wanted her to come in for 'a chat'. Two days later, she'd started her new job.

Gregorio had a much more collaborative approach to design than Hugo. He wanted to see his designers' ideas whether or not they fitted with his 'visions'.

Work had kept her sane.

She'd tried to push Pascha firmly from her mind. And she thought she'd succeeded.

Seeing him again, though, only went to prove that all she'd been doing was suppressing her emotions.

The constant numbness in her belly had evaporated, jumbled knots tightening in its place.

'How's your father doing?'

'Much better.' At least she could speak coherently. 'The

medication he's on is finally working and we've got him proper home help. It's making all the difference.'

'And is James now pulling his weight?'

She actually smiled, only fleetingly, but a smile all the same. 'I don't give him any choice.'

'I'm pleased to hear it.'

Looking him straight in the eye, she said, 'It's down to you. And for that I thank you.'

'You *thank* me?'

She nodded. 'Our time together...it made me see how much of myself I've supressed over the years, always trying to mould myself into what I think other people need. Now I have the courage to just be me, and if I need help now I ask for it. I know I can't fix everyone on my own. At least, I'm trying...' Her voice lowered as she considered what she'd done just a week ago.

Still on her knees, Emily used her hands to sweep the scraps of thread and material littering the floor around her. All she could concentrate on was breathing, trying with all her might to control the acceleration of her heart.

She'd regretted sending the letter the minute it had left her hand and gone off with the courier.

'I know about the letter you sent to my mother.'

She paused and dipped her head, closing her eyes. 'I'm sorry,' she said hoarsely. 'I don't know what possessed me.'

'I do.'

She jerked to feel his warm hand on her wrist, opened her eyes to find him on his knees beside her.

He put his palm on her cheek. 'You did it because you couldn't *not* do it. You did it because you have so much love flowing in your veins that you can't bear to see someone you love suffer, even if that person isn't deserving of your love.'

The feel of his skin on hers was almost too much to

bear. 'Please tell me I didn't make things worse.' It was the one thing that haunted her.

He shook his head. 'You couldn't have made them worse.'

'I just felt so guilty for suggesting you to speak to Marat—'

'That wasn't your fault,' he cut her off. 'You made a suggestion, that's all, and I'm sorry for ever blaming you. I was hurting and full of guilt and I lashed out at you.'

'But…'

Before she could say another word, he kissed her, a gentle pressure that sucked all the air from her lungs.

'But nothing,' he said, his breath hot on her cheek. '*I* made the choice to speak to Marat, knowing damn well what the outcome might be. The letter you sent to my mother made a difficult situation easier. She was prepared for me to turn up on her doorstep.'

'I should never have interfered.' She turned her face away, tried to break away from him.

Such was his strength that he pulled her down and onto his lap, holding her tightly to him as she tried to move away. 'You're not going anywhere.' His large hands stroked her back with a firm tenderness.

'I swore I was going to stop trying to fix people.'

'But I love that you try and fix them.'

She froze.

'It's how you're wired,' he said gently. 'When you love someone, it's with everything you have. And I understand it now, because I know there is nothing in this world I wouldn't do for you.'

She raised her head to look at him.

'I always thought love was finite, that people were born with a certain amount they could give. I believed Marat when he told me I was the cuckoo in the nest and that our father could never love me like he loved him. You've shown me how wrong I was. The love I have for you binds me more tightly to you than any drop of blood ever could.'

He traced a finger down her cheek. 'I would give my soul for you and I can't ever apologise enough for the way I spoke to you in my office. I swear on everything I have that I will never speak to you like that again.'

He meant it. She could see it in his eyes. 'You were in pain,' she whispered. 'That's why I wrote to your mother—because it hurt me to see it.'

'Yes, I was hurting, but I should never have taken it out on you.' He breathed in deeply, inhaling her scent. 'I was scared. I've spent so many years believing myself to be unworthy of love that I couldn't see past it. That letter you sent to my mother—I can't tell you how that made me feel, knowing you had done that for me. If I could capture that moment I would cherish it for ever.' Now his eyes burned into hers, searching. 'You said on my yacht that if you loved someone you would cherish them for what they could give you and not what they couldn't.'

'I love *you*, Pascha. Sterile or fertile, it makes no difference to me.'

'I know you do. If there's one thing you've taught me, it's that love is infinite. Andrei loved me, truly loved me. And if you and he can love this stubborn fool of a man then I know I can love a vulnerable child who's desperate for a home.'

Pascha couldn't hold himself back any more. He needed to kiss her. Properly. He crashed his lips onto hers, holding her so tightly, kissing her so thoroughly, being so thoroughly kissed in return that all the tightness inside him loosened.

'Please, say you'll marry me? Will you become Emily Plushenko?'

'Of course I will…' That familiar groove formed in her brow. 'Emily *Plushenko*?'

He smiled sadly. 'I kept thinking of the butterfly tattoo in the small of your back and what a personal memorial to your mother it was. It made me think. If I can't restore Andrei's legacy, then I can honour him personally. I've changed my name back to Andrei's. I should never have turned away from it in the first place. But one thing I don't want to change is *you*. I love you for who you are, exactly as you are.'

'And I love you exactly as you are too.'

Suddenly it dawned on him, *really* dawned on him, that this passionate, crazy, loyal woman loved him. She loved *him*. She belonged to him just as he belonged to her. The only thing that bound them together was love.

And as he smothered her mouth in a kiss full of all the emotion pouring out of him, he knew their love would last a lifetime.

EPILOGUE

EMILY STEPPED ONTO the soft white sand holding onto her father's arm, the minuscule grains slipping between her bare toes. In the distance by the lapping waves she could see the archway covered in frangipani where the registrar stood beside an obviously nervous Pascha. She almost burst into laughter to see him in his traditional morning suit but with his own feet bare too.

With her simple yet traditional white wedding dress designed by Gregorio himself blowing in the gentle breeze, she walked towards him. She had no power to contain her beaming smile.

The look in his eyes made the beam grow even stronger.

The entire staff of Aliana Island was standing close by, all dressed in their finest, happily mingling with her family, Pascha's glamorous mother—who took one look at her soon-to-be daughter-in-law and burst into tears—and their few closest friends. Cathy—who Pascha had kept on without even revealing that he knew the truth about her being the mole—had an enormous smile on her face.

The only thing that marred the occasion was the absence of her mother and his father. And Marat. They'd sent him an invitation despite knowing they would get no response. Her loving, determined fiancé would never give up on that relationship. Whether Marat liked it or not, Pascha saw him as his brother; the ties that bound Pascha to him were too strong to be severed. Emily hoped with all her heart that one day Marat would come to accept him. She didn't hold any great hope, but for Pascha's sake she wanted it to happen.

In the meantime, her family had accepted him into the fold as if he'd always been there. He'd even let her brother organise his stag do, something he'd privately admitted he didn't want but had gone along with because he could see how much it meant to James. To his surprise, he'd actually enjoyed it, and now he and James were as thick as thieves, enough that Pascha had asked him to be his best man.

Best of all, they were going to create a family of their own. They'd already started the adoption process and were hopeful that, within a year, their home would be filled with the sound of a squealing child. Not one of them would be bound by blood, but they would all be bound by the one thing that mattered above all else. Love.

* * * * *

MILLS & BOON®

Why shop at millsandboon.co.uk?

Each year, thousands of romance readers find their perfect read at millsandboon.co.uk. That's because we're passionate about bringing you the very best romantic fiction. Here are some of the advantages of shopping at www.millsandboon.co.uk:

* **Get new books first**—you'll be able to buy your favourite books one month before they hit the shops

* **Get exclusive discounts**—you'll also be able to buy our specially created monthly collections, with up to 50% off the RRP

* **Find your favourite authors**—latest news, interviews and new releases for all your favourite authors and series on our website, plus ideas for what to try next

* **Join in**—once you've bought your favourite books, don't forget to register with us to rate, review and join in the discussions

Visit **www.millsandboon.co.uk**
for all this and more today!